EDGE OF REASON

Warrior's Path Book 2

MALCOLM ARCHIBALD

Published 2021 by Next Chapter

Edited by Lorna Read

Cover art by Cover Mint

For Cathy

PRELUDE

THE PLAINS OF ABRAHAM, CANADA, SEPTEMBER 1759

"Come on, Hugh," Tayanita urged over her shoulder. "Before the redcoats come."

MacKim followed, padding between the tall trees with his musket at the trail and his bonnet cocked forward over his forehead. Behind him was the structured security and discipline of the British Army; ahead stretched the unknown hazards of the Canadian wilderness. MacKim knew he was exchanging the constant companionship of Fraser's Highlanders for the smile of a local woman, and he was happy with his choice. He smiled as he watched Tayanita's lithe body weaving in front of him, with her braided black hair bouncing between her shoulder blades. Tayanita was unlike anybody he had met before, a stubborn, loving, adaptable woman with whom he fully intended to spend the remainder of his life.

At that moment, Corporal Hugh MacKim of Fraser's 78th Highlanders was as happy as he had been for the past fifteen years. His troubles lay behind him, and life beckoned with a golden finger.

"I'm coming, Tayanita!"

MacKim did not see who fired the musket. He only heard the report and saw the result as the lead musket ball smashed into Tayanita's forehead. He could do nothing as Tayanita's skull disintegrated, with shreds of bone spraying outwards, together with a film of blood and grey brains.

"Tayanita!" MacKim reached out, just as a second musket fired, and then a third, with the sound echoing hollowly through the trees of Sillery Wood.

Tayanita crumpled as the musketry continued. The balls whirred around MacKim, one burrowing into the ground, and another thudding into the tree beside him. MacKim swore in Gaelic, English and French. Years of experience in this war in North America had made him knowledgeable about wounds. He knew that Tayanita was dead. Nobody could survive the degree of injury the musket-ball had wrought, yet MacKim still attempted to reach her, to pull her away from the so-far invisible enemy.

The voices sounded then; Canadian-accented French mingled with Abenaki. They were all around MacKim, closing in, shouting to encourage each other as they searched for more British or Colonial soldiers. The Canadians would not be successful, for MacKim was alone, struggling to desert from the recently-captured city of Quebec in this contested country of Canada.

Rolling to the shelter of a fallen tree, MacKim readied his musket, searching for a target. He would mourn Tayanita later; his first inclination was for revenge, and his instinct was to retaliate. MacKim knew he was a dead man fighting; he would not escape from the war-party of mixed Canadians and Abenaki in this forest country. At that minute, he did not care; he only wanted to kill at least one of the enemy who had murdered his woman.

Silence descended. MacKim lay still, scanning the trees for any sign of the enemy. He needed only a glimpse of a Canadian or an Indian, and he would fire; the Rangers and Light Infantry had trained him well.

"Please, God, allow me one shot," he pleaded. "One shot before they kill me. One shot to avenge Tayanita."

The foliage remained undisturbed. Not a leaf shifted, not a branch moved. MacKim waited, with his finger on the trigger and his eyes never still, scanning the forest for anything untoward. A whiff of powder-smoke drifted to him, acrid and familiar.

The attack came from his left. Two Abenaki warriors burst out of the trees, painted faces screaming, upraised hands holding gleaming tomahawks. MacKim aimed at the leading warrior, waited until he had a clean shot and pressed the trigger.

There was a spurt of smoke and flame; the Brown Bess musket kicked back into MacKim's shoulder and he grunted. He knew he had hit his mark and, with no time to fix his bayonet, he held the musket like a club, awaiting the onset of the second Abenaki.

"Caintal Davri!" MacKim roared the regimental warcry. The 78th Highlanders were new to the British Army list but had already proved their worth in the savage fighting to gain Quebec. MacKim added, "Tayanita!" as he challenged the charging Abenaki. He had a glimpse of a third man approaching him, a tall, lean Canadian with tattoos disfiguring his face, and then the Abenaki warrior was on him.

Not caring if he lived or died, MacKim swung his musket at the painted warrior, who sidestepped and tried an upward swipe with his tomahawk. MacKim jerked backwards, rammed his musket-butt into the Abenaki's face, felt the satisfying crunch of contact, and gasped as the warrior's tomahawk scored across his ribs. Instinct forced MacKim to lunge forward, pressing his musket into the Abenaki's face, breaking the gristle of the man's nose so blood spurted, and then the Abenaki threw him to the ground and leapt on top. They grappled, each man wounded and bleeding, gasping with effort. Each sought an advantage, with the Abenaki the taller and heavier, but MacKim desperate to avenge Tayanita, uncaring of any injuries the warrior inflicted.

As the Abenaki straddled MacKim and lifted a long knife, MacKim thrust a thumb into the man's eye and pressed hard. He felt momentary resistance, then heard a distinct pop as the warrior's eyeball burst. The Abenaki flinched and reared back, so MacKim threw him off and reached for the hatchet at his belt, only for the tall Canadian to push him back to the ground.

MacKim looked up and tried to swing his hatchet, but the Canadian clamped a massive hand on his wrist, then trapped him with his knees. When he glared down, MacKim saw tattoos on both sides of his face, blue-dyed spirals that extended from his cheekbones to the corners of his mouth. The Canadian smiled, showing perfect teeth.

As the Abenaki rolled in agony beside MacKim, another man appeared. Squat, bald, and broad-shouldered, he hawked and spat on the ground.

"Scotchman," he said, in a flat English accent. He stared at MacKim with no expression in his dead eyes.

MacKim tried to throw off the Canadian and roared as he felt a terrible, tearing pain on the top of his head. He yelled again, aware that the Canadian was scalping him. Shouting in mingled agony and rage, MacKim lunged forward and sank his teeth into the tattooed man's neck.

They remained in that position for a second, with MacKim worrying the Canadian's flesh and the Canadian hauling at MacKim's scalp. Pain gave MacKim extra strength, and he wrestled a hand free and grabbed hold of the Canadian's wrist, grappling with sinewy muscle, feeling the power of the man.

The squat man spoke again, and although MacKim could not understand the accent, he knew it was a warning.

MacKim made a final effort that heaved the Canadian from him, with the man holding a portion of MacKim's scalp in his hand. Blood flowed freely down MacKim's face and from the gash across his chest. He spat out a mouthful of the Canadian's skin and blood, tried to ignore the incredible pain in his head and forced himself to stand. The Abenaki was staggering away with one hand to his beleaguered face as the squat man backed off, watching MacKim and still talking as the Canadian followed, moving with long, loping strides.

The musket shots echoed through the trees, with honest Scottish accents as an accompaniment.

"Hugh!" That was Chisholm's voice as he ran forward with a section of the 78th at his back.

"Over here!" Hugh MacKim lifted a weak hand as pain and loss of blood drained his strength.

"Oh, good Lord help us," Chisholm said. "I've got you, Hugh."

MacKim felt Chisholm's strong arm around him as he collapsed.

I

QUEBEC, AUTUMN 1759

"They killed Tayanita," MacKim muttered, as the dual emotional and physical pain threatened to overcome him.

"I know," Chisholm said, his ravaged face set in sympathy. "Come on, Hugh, let's get you to a surgeon."

"They killed Tayanita."

After those words, MacKim's entire world dissolved in pain. He was unaware of Chisholm and Private Ranald MacDonald carrying him in a blanket to the ruins of Quebec. He was unaware of the fingers pointing to the raw wound across his head, or his blood that dripped onto the ground. He was only vaguely aware of the deep-eyed surgeon who examined him, and barely aware of the brandy an assistant forced down his throat. However, despite the spirit's supposedly numbing effect, MacKim groaned as the surgeon stitched the long gash across his chest.

"Lie still, man," the assistant grumbled, as MacKim writhed under his hands.

MacKim screamed as the surgeon tried to dress the horrendous wound on the top of his head, with the assistant attempting to hold his face still. After that nightmare of agony, there was nothing but pain, until MacKim recognised it as an old, trusted companion. It was there, waiting for him. It would not let him down. The physical pain shielded MacKim's mind from the mental and emotional agony of Tayanita's death, so he clung to the former as a counterbalance for the latter.

MacKim did not know how long he lay in the makeshift hospital. It might have been days or weeks. Time did not matter; only the mingled pains and his feeling of desolation. From time to time, he was aware of other men beside his bed, although he did not know that Chisholm and Private Ranald MacDonald were checking on his progress.

At length, as the Canadian autumn descended towards the long midnight of winter, MacKim's head began to clear. He looked around the long room with its rows of suffering patients.

"Tayanita?" he called weakly.

"You're awake, then," an orderly said. "You were lucky. We thought you was going to die."

"Lucky?" When MacKim tried to sit up, the recently healed wound in his chest protested. He gasped, grunted and fought the pain. His head pounded as if a hundred farriers were making a hundred horseshoes on top of his skull.

"I heard that the savages caught you," the orderly said cheerfully. "They were scalping you when some of your regiment chased them away."

"I remember." MacKim looked down at his chest, where the long, puckered scar was inflamed and red, with prominent stitching where the surgeon had worked. He remembered the tall, tattooed Canadian, the Abenaki and the squat man with the flat English accent.

"Was there anybody else there when the Highlanders rescued me?" MacKim wondered if Tayanita was not dead. Perhaps he was wrong. Maybe he had imagined the bullet smashing through her skull.

The orderly screwed up his face. "Blessed if I know."

"I have to find out," MacKim said, swinging his legs out of bed.

"You'll stay where you are," the orderly said. "Your chest may be healed, but I don't know what you'll do about your head. It was as red-raw as fresh liver last time I saw it."

"My head?" MacKim winced as he touched the bandages that swathed his head. His headache increased.

"The savages took half your scalp," the orderly said, as MacKim slumped back onto his bed. "You lie there, Sawnie, and recover. It's bedlam outside, anyway."

Tayanita. The name ran through MacKim's head, together with an image of the woman with whom he had intended to head west. Now, he was back in the army, a corporal in Fraser's 78th Highlanders. If he were lucky, nobody except Chisholm would realise he had intended to desert. *Lucky*? The Canadians and Abenakis had killed his woman and robbed him of half his scalp. What was lucky about that? MacKim closed his eyes as the tiredness of physical weakness mixed with emotional strain overcame him.

Tomorrow, MacKim promised himself. *I'll try to get up tomorrow. Or maybe the next day.* He closed his eyes as the image of Tayanita returned, with the musket ball smashing through her head. He felt the tears biting at his eyes.

"HAS ANYTHING HAPPENED SINCE I'VE BEEN IN THE hospital?" MacKim asked.

Chisholm mused for a moment before he replied. "No. We've been sitting around on our arses doing nothing, just like you."

"I thought I heard gunfire a few days ago," MacKim struggled to sit up, but the flashes of pain in his head prevented the attempt.

"You did hear gunfire," Chisholm said. "A French flotilla sailed down the river, and our artillery had a go at them."

"Did we sink them?" MacKim asked.

"Not even one," Chisholm said. "I don't think we scored a single hit because they were out of range of our guns. That would be on the 23rd of November, I think." He shook his head. "But never fear, little Corporal MacKim. Not long after, Canada provided a storm that sent three of them onto a sandbank and left them there."

MacKim smiled, then winced at the pain even that simple gesture caused him. "The Navy would love that," he said.

"Oh, the Navy loved it all right," Chisholm said. "One of our frigates virtually denuded herself of men to strip everything from the largest French shipwreck. They were happily plundering when the damned Frenchie blew up. I heard that the French captain threw a match into the powder room, but that might only be a story. Our seamen were all lost, and the Frenchies boarded and captured our frigate, which had only a skeleton crew."

MacKim sighed. "A victory for the French, then," he said.

"A hint of revenge to pay us back for capturing the capital of New France," Chisholm said.

"And a reminder that the French won't give up easily," MacKim said. "Is that all that has happened?"

"No," Chisholm said. "While you've been lying at your ease, we've unloaded tons of stores and dragged them from the Lower Town to the Upper Town."

"I'm glad you do something to earn your eight pence a day," MacKim said. "Anything else?"

"There has been a bit of marching and counter-marching, and a lot of work on the fortifications here." Chisholm grinned. "No doubt you'll be doing your bit once you're up and about."

MacKim sank back. "Suddenly, I feel weak. I might need another few weeks in bed."

"We'll see you soon then, Corporal," MacDonald said, without understanding the joke.

MacKim did not reply. For all his attempted humour, he felt sick at the thought of losing Tayanita. When he closed his eyes, he could see her face smiling at him through her deep brown eyes. And then he saw the musket bullet smash through her head, and a wave of intense hatred replaced his sorrow.

I will kill those men. I will kill that Canadian with the tattooed face, and that renegade with the flat accent and dead eyes. I won't allow Tayanita to go unavenged.

The decision gave MacKim strength. After weeks of waiting to recover, he now forced himself to move, leave his bed and fight. He had a purpose in life once more.

❦

"Reporting for duty, sir!" MacKim saw Lieutenant Gregorson study his head as if he could see the scraped scalp through MacKim's bonnet.

"It's good to have you back, MacKim," Gregorson said. "Have you fully recovered?"

"Nearly, sir," MacKim lied. He did not mention the terrible headaches that plagued him, or the nightmares in which he saw Tayanita slowly falling as pieces of her head sprayed around the ground. Such things, MacKim vowed, he would keep to himself. There were some secrets that a man did not wish to reveal to the world.

"If you are certain." Gregorson continued to study MacKim's bonnet.

"Yes, sir." MacKim did not admit that the hospital had depressed him, with its daily intake of sick and dying soldiers. The army that Wolfe had led to victory was slowly disintegrating with scurvy and other diseases. MacKim was confident he would fare better in the company of active soldiers, rather than in a hospital bed. In the ranks, he would have duties to perform and his comrade's banter to sustain him. In the hospital, all he had were gloomy thoughts and the moans of the sick.

"Report to your quarters then, Corporal," Gregorson said.

"Yes, sir!" MacKim marched away, listening to the rattle of drums and hoarse shouts of a sergeant. He was back in the army, subject to iron discipline, ready to obey orders at an instant's notice. He was a soldier of King George, a mindless killing machine, yet MacKim knew that he did not belong.

Before he entered the house that his company of Fraser's 78th Highlanders had converted into a barracks, MacKim studied the city. The once-proud city of Quebec, the crowning glory of French Canada, was a mess. MacKim could think of no other word to describe it. The British bombardment with shot and shell had ruined nearly all the buildings in the Low Town, leaving hundreds as little more than rubble, and damaging what it had not destroyed. Knowing that winter was bitter-cold in Canada, General Murray had ordered the men to tear down all the wooden fences in the city for firewood, and then start on some of the wooden houses.

"Corporal!" Captain Donald MacDonald caught MacKim before he entered the barracks. "I have a working party collecting firewood for the barracks. Join us."

I'm back, MacKim thought.

"See what we're reduced to?" Chisholm said, as MacKim arrived at his side. "We're common labourers now, not gentlemen soldiers."

MacKim hefted a pile of floorboards on his shoulder and wished his head would stop aching. "It's not why we accepted King Geordie's silver shilling," he said.

"Why *did* we join up?" Chisholm asked the rhetorical question.

"I joined up to avenge my brother's murder," MacKim reminded him, "and because the clan chief told me to." He carried the floorboards through the streets, with Captain MacDonald in front giving directions.

"Clan chiefs have too much power, ordering men to war on a whim."

"It was no whim," MacKim said. "Fraser wanted to impress the government with his loyalty so they'd give him his lands back. We were just the small change he used to buy governmental favour."

"Nice to know how important we are," Chisholm said and led MacKim up a narrow street in the Upper Town, the section of Quebec on the west, furthest from the St Lawrence and closest to the Heights of Abraham. The barracks were in a collection of houses, mostly half-ruined, with roofs and walls damaged by the British bombardment when they besieged Quebec.

"Aye," Chisholm said, as he made space for MacKim in the corner of one of the rooms. "This was somebody's home once. War can be hard on civilians. They fight differently over here in the Americas, without the idea of quarter for the innocent."

Thinking of Tayanita, MacKim nodded and collapsed onto his cot. It was close to the fire, as befitted his rank as a corporal.

"While you were lazing in the hospital," Chisholm said happily, "the army had a splendid time plundering what our artillery left of Quebec."

MacKim looked up from his cot. "Did they leave anything for me?"

"Alas, no." Chisholm shook his head. "General Murray is coming down hard on looters, and everything else."

MacKim placed his kit on the hard cot, checking to ensure everything was in order. He lifted a small square of colourful beadwork and closed his eyes. That beadwork was the last thing Tayanita had given him; she had made it herself and pressed it into his hand.

"So you remember me when I am not here," Tayanita said.

"You'll always be with me," MacKim replied.

Tayanita held his gaze, with her deep brown eyes solemn. "We do not know what the future holds."

MacKim held the beadwork. Tayanita had been correct; nobody knew what the future held. A few weeks ago, MacKim had all of Tayanita; now, he had only her memory and this small, colourful square. MacKim pressed the beadwork against his chest, feeling a surge of emotions from deep sorrow at her loss, to the vicious desire to avenge her.

"You're back then?"

MacKim hurriedly hid the beadwork when Harriette Mackenzie entered the barrack room. He had known Harriette as Corporal Gunn's wife, but when the French killed Gunn, Harriette had married Chisholm. A foul-mouthed, hot-tempered and warm-hearted woman, she greeted MacKim with a smile, flicked the bonnet from his head without a by-your-leave and examined his scarred head.

"I'm back," MacKim confirmed.

Harriette pursed her lips. "What a bloody mess!" she said. "The Indians made a good job of you."

"Thank you," MacKim said. "It wasn't the Indians. It was a Canadian and a renegade Englishman."

Harriette tossed the bonnet back to MacKim. "You're lucky, Hugh. Nobody can see the scar, otherwise you'd be nearly as ugly as Chisholm."

MacKim forced a smile. James Chisholm had been badly wounded during the Fontenoy campaign in the previous war, the War of the Austrian Succession, and had remained in the army rather than returning to normal life. A deep burn covered half his face, twisting his lip into a permanent scowl and narrowing one eye. Chisholm was very aware of his looks and avoided civilians if he could.

"Aye, I married the ugliest man in the army," Harriette said. "Well, when the French or Canadians or the Indians kill James, you're next on my list to marry, Hugh," she blew him a kiss, "as long as you are still alive then. I seem to be attracted to the ugly ones."

"Thank you." MacKim gave an elaborate bow. "I am honoured."

Harriette slapped MacKim's shoulder. "Until then," she said, "I'm Chisholm's, so keep your hands to yourself." She swivelled her hips towards him, temptingly.

"Come on, James. You're off duty, and I want your body. We'll make Hughie jealous." Grabbing hold of Chisholm's hand, Harriette steered him to the ragged blanket that screened off a corner of the room; behind the blanket was the only privacy married other ranks knew.

Holding the square of beadwork, MacKim left the two of them together and stepped out of the barrack-room to look around Quebec.

It was the cold that MacKim noticed most. The hospital had been chilly, but outside, the temperature dropped until every breath became painful, and condensation froze on his chin. Within a few moments, the cold reached MacKim's knees and began to spread upwards.

Stamping his feet, MacKim walked as fast as he could on the icy streets. The devastation was appalling, with fragments of stone buildings thrusting upward like broken teeth in a giant's mouth and piles of rubble littering the lesser-used roadways. Every so often, MacKim came across one of the civilians who the British bombardment had forced from their homes. When the British took possession, they made a bad situation worse by requisitioning the least damaged houses as billets for the men and forcing the citizens out. Some Quebecers moved into friends' houses, and many left Quebec altogether. Ragged, cold and resentful, the people of Quebec avoided MacKim as if he carried a disease.

"I don't blame you at all," MacKim said, as one young boy

retreated into the corner of a building and threw a stone. "I'd do the same if I were you." The missile missed MacKim, to bounce harmlessly from a wall. MacKim remembered the aftermath of the Jacobite Rising in Scotland when the British Army had spread terror across much of the Highlands. Back then, he would have happily stoned anybody in King George's scarlet coat.

"Here." MacKim reached inside his sporran for his last scrap of biscuit. "It's not much, but better than starving." He tossed it to the boy and spoke in French. "It's a biscuit. It's hard as stone so watch your teeth."

The boy looked at MacKim, snatched the biscuit and stood against the wall, cramming the food into his mouth. MacKim favoured him with a wink.

"Feeding the enemy?" a grenadier asked, with a sneer on his face.

"Children are not my enemies," MacKim said.

The grenadier was a head taller than MacKim, with his mitre hat making him taller still. He looked down on MacKim, as if about to say something else, saw the expression in MacKim's eyes, changed his mind and walked away.

MacKim grunted, released his grip on the hilt of his bayonet and realised the boy was still watching him. He mustered a grimace that was nearly a smile and walked away, gasping at the cold.

When MacKim returned to barracks, Chisholm was cleaning his musket. He grunted when he noticed MacKim's discomfort.

"Aye, the cold gets to your essentials, Hugh." He winked at Harriette. "What do you think, Harriette?"

Harriette grinned. "The nuns in the Ursuline Convent will help you there, Hughie."

"Who?" MacKim stood as close to the fire as he could, hoping that frostbite had not set in.

"The good ladies of the convent are not happy with the Highlanders," Harriette said, with a grin. "Every time a Highlander bends forward, half the women of Quebec – and a disturbing number of the men – gawp at what is revealed." Harriette laughed. "The ones that act terribly shocked are the ones who look the most assiduously."

MacKim forced a smile. "That sounds about right."

"Apart from the nuns, the local Canadian women tend to like Highlanders," Harriette said. "General Murray has already banned marriages between the Canadians and us."

MacKim felt the heat gradually return to his body. He could not imagine why any British soldier should marry a Canadian woman after the atrocities during the campaign to capture Quebec.

"The final straw came only the other week in Mountain Street," Chisholm muttered, as he inspected the lock of his musket minutely.

"What happened?" MacKim asked.

Chisholm's grin made his burn-scarred face even more hideous. "Do you remember that sleet storm? Oh, no, you were too busy lying in state with the nurses pampering you like a baby."

"I remember," MacKim said. "The frost froze the blankets to my bed." He waited for a response to his lie.

Chisholm nodded. "As I said, you were lazing in bed when we were carrying out your duties, Corporal MacKim."

"What about Mountain Street?" MacKim asked.

"The frost covered the streets in sheet ice. Men and horses were sliding and slipping and falling all over the place." Chisholm's grin became even broader. "It was quite amusing to see the streets full of men and even women falling on their faces and lying on their backs."

"Major Ward's wife had fun when she took a tumble," Harriette said, laughing. "She was face-down with her skirt up over her waist and half the garrison laughing."

"Forget her," Chisholm said. "That day of the bad ice, General Murray ordered the 78th to mount guard at the Royal Battery in the Lower Town."

Although MacKim had not had time to learn Quebec's geography, the names of Upper Town and Lower Town told their own story. "That's downhill then," he said.

"Aye, hard by the river. We had to descend Mountain Street, which is steep. Jamie Munro lost his footing and fell, with his kilt around his chest." Chisholm could not stop himself laughing. "At least half a dozen nuns were staring in shock." He bit off the end of a twist of tobacco. "It may not have been shock, but the sight certainly made them stare."

MacKim tried to share Chisholm's amusement, but Tayanita's memory interfered.

"Well," Chisholm continued, "I was next in line, and had no intention of ending up in disorder like Jamie Munro, or of providing free amusement to the nuns, so I sat on the ground and slithered down. My kilt slid up, so I was a bare-bum warrior, with the nuns giggling fit to frighten the French, which they are, of course. And ever since then, the nuns have been knitting long woollen hose as if their lives depended on it – or our modesty, perhaps."

"More than your modesty, Chisholm!" Harriette added coarse details that had the two other wives in the room laughing.

Despite Chisholm's attempt at humour, MacKim knew that the garrison of Quebec was suffering terribly with the cold, and the 78th was the worst affected. Men sick with frostbite and scurvy filled the hospital, and the list of dead increased every day. With the ground frozen too hard to dig graves, General Murray piled the corpses outside the city, a macabre wall of the dead, frozen together, a gruesome reminder of man's mortality. Even the men supposedly fit for duty were coughing and sneezing.

"Things could be worse," Harriette said. "Imagine how bad it would be if Wolfe had lost his battle."

MacKim nodded without replying. If the French had won on the Heights of Abraham, he might still have had Tayanita. He pushed the thought away.

As the weather grew colder, desertions increased, and General Murray used ever more extreme measures. Floggings grew more frequent, with sentences of hundreds of lashes, and some men were hanged.

Yet none of that mattered to MacKim as every night, unless he were on sentry duty, he lay in bed clutching Tayanita's beadwork and thinking of the two men he had to kill.

2

"Some of the Quebecers are agents of the French," Lieutenant Gregorson addressed a gathering of the NCOs. "They are encouraging men to desert, or soliciting intelligence from us. Warn your men not to associate with the Jesuit priests or the nuns. If you see a Quebecer walking on the city walls or near our artillery batteries, arrest them."

MacKim nodded. He had every intention of carrying out his orders, although he remembered what it was like in a country occupied by an alien army.

"Remember, men," Gregorson said, "if you see anything that looks suspicious, report it to me. We are holding a hostile city in the midst of a conquered country. The Canadians have no reason to like us, so trust nobody."

The NCOs muttered their agreement as Gregorson dismissed them. Each man knew the sacrifices the British Army had endured to capture the capital of New France and had no intention of throwing their conquest away.

MacKim took his part in the routine patrols around the city, searching the Quebecers' carts as they left the city to ensure the owners were not carrying away provisions, soap, candles or other banned objects. He helped maintain the curfew that Murray imposed and questioned any man who appeared suspicious.

At first, the Quebecers were surprised that this slim Highlander with the haunted eyes spoke French so fluently, but they soon learned to avoid him as one of the more officious of the occupying soldiers.

At night, MacKim clutched Tayanita's beadwork and said nothing. He did not care what anybody thought of him. He did not care that most of the Highlanders walked wide of his presence. Nothing mattered except his increasing hatred of the tall, tattooed Canadian and the squat renegade with dead eyes.

❧

THEY MOVED IN A LONG, SILENT COLUMN, SLIDING ON THE frozen ground and hunch-shouldered against the cold. With their muskets held close to their shivering bodies and layers of whatever clothing they could borrow covering them, the Highlanders looked more like a straggle of poaching gypsies than British soldiers.

"If the Frenchies come tonight," Ranald MacDonald muttered, "we'll be too cold to fight back."

"Maybe the enemy feels the cold as well," Chisholm said.

"Not them." MacDonald shook his head. "These Indians don't feel anything. They're impervious to cold or heat."

As they took up their positions at the Sailor's Battery, overlooking the River St Charles and the dark lands beyond, MacKim stamped his feet to restore his circulation. "I hope the bastards come."

"You're the only one, then," Chisholm said. "The rest of us have had enough fighting and want a quiet life."

Beyond the river, pinpricks of light gleamed through the dark.

"That'll be the French, watching us," MacDonald said. "Like Chisholm, I hope they stay where they are."

"If I were the French commander," MacKim said, remembering the weak state of the garrison, "I would take the opportunity to attack now. They still outnumber us, and they're used to the climate. I hope our Rangers are out there, watching them."

Chisholm grunted. "Most of the Rangers and the Louisbourg Grenadiers have returned to their posts, scattered all over North America. We've got less than a hundred in Quebec."

MacKim forced a smile. "See what happens when I go into hospital? The place falls to pieces."

Chisholm thrust a long pipe into his mouth. "It's worse than you imagine, Hugh. Williams and most of the siege-guns, the heavy artillery, are overwintering in Boston."

"What's Murray thinking of?" MacKim asked. "We're virtually asking the French to come in." He looked over the battlements at the iced St Charles River and the vastness of Canada. "I hope we have some outposts out there."

"Not many," Chisholm said. "We've got a few small detachments, but nothing else, except General Murray is beginning to build some blockhouses on the Plains of Abraham."

"We should have outposts to watch the French," MacKim continued with his theme. "That's where the Rangers should be. They're the best soldiers we have. Without them, the French and Canadians outmatch us in forest warfare,"

Chisholm grunted. "Not now that you're back, corporal." His eyes were never still as he searched through the night. "It's been quiet so far."

"The French general, de Levis, must know how weak the garrison is. How about the Navy?"

Chisholm puffed at his pipe. "They've mostly gone. Admiral Saunders could not remain in the St Lawrence." He walked along the ramparts, huddled against the cold, yet holding his Brown Bess musket like an old friend. "The ice would destroy his ships in days. He's left HMS *Racehorse* and HMS *Porcupine* and a handful of small vessels, but they're out of the river until the spring thaw comes."

MacKim remembered the part the Navy had played in operations during the previous summer's campaign. The Navy had carried the Army across the Atlantic and onto every combined operation from the capture of Louisbourg to Quebec. In MacKim's eyes, Admiral Saunders had been just as much the victor of Quebec as General Wolfe.

"We're cut off, then," MacKim said.

"We are," Chisholm agreed, "until the ice breaks in the spring." He paced the length of their beat and stared over the parapet again. "But with Commodore Lord Colville at Halifax with the 74-gun HMS *Northumberland* and a pretty powerful naval squadron, the French can't come across the Atlantic to reinforce de Levis's army, either."

MacKim stamped his feet again, with the sound echoing in the dark. "We're both under siege, then, with the climate holding us prisoner."

"It's a straight fight between General Murray in Quebec and the Chevalier de Levis in the rest of Canada," Chisholm grunted. "They still outnumber us. They know the terrain better than us and, as you said, without our Rangers, they are our superiors in Forest warfare." He straightened to attention as Captain Donald MacDonald passed, huddled against the cold.

"Triumph!" Captain MacDonald gave the parole – the password – for the night.

"Victory." MacKim gave the countersign as Chisholm hurriedly hid his pipe.

"Anything to report, Corporal?" Captain MacDonald asked.

"No, sir," MacKim said. "We were watching the lights a cross the river and wondering if the French were there."

"They will be." Captain MacDonald passed a quid of tobacco onto Chisholm.

"Your pipe will go out, Chisholm," he said, with a smile. "Keep alert, men, and notify me if anything changes. Keep your muskets handy, boys. Look after Bess, and she'll look after you."

"We will, sir," agreed MacKim.

Captain MacDonald lifted a hand in salute and continued on his rounds.

"He's a good man, Captain MacDonald," Chisholm said. "At the forefront in battle and never lets his men down."

As soon as Captain MacDonald strolled away, the Highlanders resumed their conversation, pretending to be casual while each man scanned the blackness. MacKim counted the pinpricks of firelight, marking their position so he would know if any moved. He listened to the wind blowing across the St Charles River, aware the ice could bear the weight of a man, allowing a French raiding party to cross. With the walls of Quebec high here, the French would have to use scaling ladders, but they might arrive, kill a sentry or two and withdraw, purely to unsettle the defenders.

"Why is the musket called a Brown Bess?" Private MacNicholl asked during a lull in the conversation. "Captain MacDonald told us to look after Bess." He held his musket up. "Helloa, Bess."

"Ah," Chisholm turned against the wind to re-light his long-stemmed pipe, "I know the answer to that."

"Tell us," MacKim said, "but keep your voice down in case the captain returns, and keep alert, all of you."

"It was during the War of the Spanish Succession, so sometime between 1705 and 1712. The army was marching hither and yon, and in every camp, and on every march, a group of very friendly Spanish women turned up."

"Very friendly?" MacNicholl repeated, hoping for salacious details.

"*Very* friendly!" Chisholm lowered his voice. "But you're too young, MacNicholl. A child like you should be learning his ABC, not thinking of women. The friendliest of them all was a brown-haired, buxom girl that the soldiers called Bess. When the army left Spain, they called their muskets Brown Bess in her honour."

"Is that true?" MacNicholl asked, as MacKim scrutinised the lights across the river.

"Probably not," Chisholm said. "The name more likely comes from us pickling the musket barrels to protect them from rust."

"Oh," MacNicholl said. "I prefer your story."

"So do I," Chisholm said.

MacKim raised his head. "Listen! Something's stirring out there."

"I can't hear anything," Chisholm said.

MacKim put a hand on Chisholm's arm. "Keep quiet and listen. Something's moving to the north."

The musketry began a moment later, sporadic at first, then rising to a crescendo, and dying. The muzzle-flares were visible, like a score of bright sparks in the night, momentary, deadly and then gone, leaving deeper darkness in their wake. The scent of powder-smoke drifted in the wind, acrid and sour. A single shot sounded, followed by a hoarse challenge, hollow in the dark.

"Triumph?"

"The Frenchies are attacking one of our outposts," MacKim said.

"Triumph?" The voice sounded again, faint with distance. MacKim thought how lonely the picket would be, out there in the hostile night.

"It sounds like our lads beat them off." Chisholm knocked out the ashes from the bowl of his pipe and stared into the black. "They might try here next." He checked the lock of his musket, ensured the flint was sharp and crouched lower behind the parapet.

MacKim took a deep breath. "Aye, they might." He imagined the tattooed Canadian and the squat renegade mounting the ramparts here and fingered the long bayonet at his hip. *Please, God, grant me the opportunity to avenge Tayanita. I don't care if I die afterwards, I only want to kill her murderers.*

The screaming started a few minutes later, long-drawn-out, rising and falling to an agonised, hopeless bubble.

"That will be the Indians and Canadians torturing a captive."

Chisholm gripped his musket more firmly. "I detest those bastards."

MacKim loosened his bonnet as his scalp began to tingle and burn. He thought of the terror of a man waiting to be tortured by the Indians and spoke in a low, intense tone that held Chisholm's attention. "Since they murdered Tayanita, I want to destroy everything French, and wipe them from the map," he said. "I'd take an adze and draw it from the Gulf of St Lawrence to the Great Lakes and down the Mississippi to New Orleans. I'd remove anything remotely French from the entire continent."

MacKim was aware that Chisholm was watching him as he wiped the spittle from his chin. "I'll destroy every single man," he whispered. "And send the women and children back to France."

Chisholm opened his mouth to speak, and closed it quickly as the screaming began again, even higher-pitched than before, raising the small hairs on the back of MacKim's neck.

"Jesus." Chisholm breathed out hard. "There was nothing like this during the Fontenoy campaign. We fought each other like soldiers, not savages. There is something evil in this continent that makes men act in such a manner."

MacKim checked the flint of his musket, aware the screaming had unsettled him. "I want to kill the French," he said. "I want to kill the French, the Canadians and the Indians."

"Tayanita was an Indian," Chisholm reminded him.

MacKim's glower should have killed Chisholm where he stood. "I know." MacKim turned away, feeling the tears turn to ice on his cheeks. "I know."

3

The head arrived the next morning. An Abenaki warrior ran up to the battlements beside the Ursule Redoubt in the west, threw it over the wall, and ran away.

"Shoot that bugger!" the duty sergeant ordered. With the reports of their muskets flat in the sullen cold, three men fired, but none of the shots came close.

The head rolled on the ground and lay still, staring upward through the hollow pits that had once been eyes, with the nose, ears, scalp and lips cut off.

"Welcome home, Private Dawson," a grenadier sergeant of Bragg's 28th Foot said laconically. "He was as useless in life as he is in death." He pushed the head with his foot, so it rolled away.

Others of his regiment did not treat Dawson's torture and death as lightly, and MacKim felt the anger surge through the garrison. He allowed it to ease over him, augmenting his hatred as he stood outside Fort Louis at the edge of the Upper Town, listening as a section of Bragg's marched past, cursing.

If the French had merely skirmished with the outposts, caused a few casualties and withdrawn, they would have succeeded in their objective in unsettling the garrison. By torturing and murdering prisoners, they created anger and a desire for revenge.

"Murdering bastards," MacKim said as he cleaned his kit that evening. "Dirty, torturing French bastards!"

"Enough, now Hugh," Ranald MacDonald said. "Think of something else." He stepped back as MacKim approached him, bayonet in hand.

"Easy, Hugh!" Chisholm warned, but it was Harriette who stepped in front of MacKim.

"You don't need the blade, Hughie." Harriette spread her arms to protect Ranald MacDonald. "Fight if you must, but murder is a hanging offence."

Reaching across, Chisholm took the bayonet from MacKim's grip. "We know you miss Tayanita, Hugh, but putting a bayonet in Ranald won't bring her back."

MacKim glared at Chisholm and took a deep breath. He thought of his brother, murdered as he lay wounded on Culloden Moor, and of Priscilla, married to another man, and now Tayanita. It seemed that fate stole away everybody that mattered to him.

"Maybe you'd best keep clear of me, Chisholm," he said, retrieving his bayonet and sliding it into the scabbard. "And you too, MacDonald."

"Aye," Chisholm said. "Maybe we'd best, at that."

"I'm not myself at present."

"No," Ranald MacDonald said. "You're not."

MacKim took a deep breath, held the beadwork close to his chest and turned away. He could feel his hatred seething within his head.

THE DRUMS WOKE HIM AS THEY BEAT OUT REVEILLE, THE staccato sound hammering around the city, chasing away sleep and informing the world that another day had dawned.

MacKim groaned, looked around, gave the beadwork a final hug and thrust it inside his knapsack. "I hate these bloody drums."

The army lived by the drums, which regulated every action the soldiers made and marked the passage of every day. At the break of dawn, the drums beat Reveille to drag the men from their beds and advise the night sentries that their lonely vigils were nearing an end. The next call was Troop, which summoned the men to the parade ground for the roll call and officer's inspection. At ten in the evening, or an hour earlier in summer, Tattoo ordered the men to retire to their quarters for the long night ahead.

"I hate these drums," MacKim repeated.

"We all do," Harriette said, dragging the covers from him. "Up you get!" She was smiling, although the shadows in her eyes revealed her concern. "The harder you work, the sooner you'll be back to normal."

Ignoring the near-constant ache in his head, MacKim joined the work parties in the city. Apart from the routine guards on the walls, the men helped repair some of the hundreds of houses the British bombardment had destroyed, making barracks and quarters for the officers and men. They also opened embrasures in the curtain walls and hauled cannon to watch over the Plains of Abraham, the plateau that dominated the western side of the city.

"If de Levis ever tries to recapture Quebec," Chisholm said, "this is the wall he will assault."

MacKim looked over the wall, imagined the French coming and nodded. It was only a few months since the late General Wolfe had won his battle on the Plains of Abraham, and now the British held Quebec, it seemed inevitable that the French would try and recapture the city.

When not toiling on the walls, working parties built stockades to block the avenues in the suburbs and made fascines – bundles of brushwood used to strengthen any earthen redoubt or trench – until the city had a reserve of over four thousand in case of need.

To give the men variety, the officers ordered the men to make creepers – grips that attached to the bottoms of their boots – sleighs, sledges and toboggans.

"We'll be as well prepared for winter as possible," Captain Donald MacDonald said cheerfully. "It takes more than a strong arm and a broadsword to defend a city."

Occasionally, MacKim led a section working outside the city, with Major Patrick MacKellar, the chief engineer and his assistants directing them in chopping trees to make redoubts a few hundred yards from the walls, to keep any raiding French away.

They worked until the drums beat the retreat, and men filed thankfully back to have the roll called, and then Tattoo ordered them back to bed.

The days passed in toil, with the hours of darkness lengthening and men dropping with disease. Despite the garrison's efforts, in the absence of most of the Rangers, French raiding parties controlled the night. As well as skirmishing with the British pickets, they captured the cattle, the garrison's food-on-the-hoof, and brought an air of nervousness to the men.

"These damned Canadians were out last night," Chisholm said. "They stole a score of beef cattle and killed two men."

"It's time we were striking back," MacKim said.

"You tell General Murray that," Chisholm said. "I'm sure he'll listen to your advice."

Harriette looked up from the fire. "If you don't tell the general, Hugh, I will. Somebody has to teach those French to keep their distance."

Perhaps the thought of being confronted by the formidable Harriette spurred General Murray to action, for the next day, he organised two columns of men to extend the borders of British-controlled territory.

He sent the first column, of two hundred men, to St Foy, a small village a few miles to the south-west on the edge of the

Heights of Abraham. MacKim and a section of the light infantry marched with them and immediately began to fortify the village, much to the disgust of the priest in the chapel.

"It's all right," Captain Donald MacDonald told him in fluent French. "If your French friends don't attack us, we won't damage anything."

From St Foy, the British detachment could watch the road the French would have to travel if they marched north from Montreal and warn the Quebec garrison of impending danger.

The Highlanders only remained for a few hours, sufficient to consolidate the position, and then they returned to Quebec, leaving a strong force behind.

"Aye," Chisholm said. "Murray must have listened to you, Harriette. Not only can we watch the French, but we also have a few Canadian parishes under our control now, so we can take the fresh produce to help combat the scurvy." He looked up. "That's our main enemy here, lads and lassies – the climate, salt provisions and disease. We can beat the Frenchies in a fair fight, but if we're starving and diseased, we won't be able to stand, let alone fight."

The main French advanced post was at Jacques-Cartier, upstream from St Foy towards Montreal on the north shore of the river, with a forward position at St Augustin. Levis had most of his regulars in winter quarters between Trois Rivières and Montreal, with his outposts as sentinels to deter any British raids.

Murray's second and larger column of four hundred men marched inland to Lorette and established a strong outpost there, with patrols into the lands beyond. With both armies settling in for the winter and their territories secured, most of the British hoped for a quiet winter.

"We need more Rangers," MacKim said. "De Levis will be pushing his advantage in men and experience, sure as anything."

"We must work with what we have," Chisholm said. "Anyway, we have the Royal Americans and the Light Infantry."

MacKim nodded. "We have, and both are good bodies of men. I hope they can lead us to Montreal."

"How far is Montreal?" Ranald MacDonald asked.

"About one hundred and sixty miles," MacKim said. "As the crow flies."

"How far for an army to march?"

"We'll travel by water," MacKim said. "As will the French, as soon as the St Lawrence is navigable."

With his outposts established, Murray became more aggressive and sent a strong force of seven hundred men, mainly light infantry, to raid the French forward base at St Augustin. When MacKim volunteered to accompany them, Captain Donald MacDonald shook his head.

"I commend your keenness, MacKim," he said solemnly. "If ever the 78th is involved, I'll seek you out." He glanced at MacKim's bonnet. "How is your head healing?"

MacKim started; he had not expected an officer to remember his ordeal. "The skin is growing well, sir, thank you."

"Well done." Captain MacDonald strolled away with his kilt swinging slowly around his legs.

MacKim watched the British return from the raid, marching with a swagger as they brought back French prisoners and a herd of cattle to boost Quebec's food supply. When he saw the French, MacKim had to control his surge of hatred.

"Easy, Hugh." Chisholm held his arm.

"Easy, be buggered!" MacKim shook Chisholm off. "I hate these bastards."

Even with the new supply of fresh food, the garrison suffered. Every morning, sick parade saw another quota of men trail to the overcrowded hospital, victims of the cold, scurvy and dysentery that were prevalent when thousands of men crowded into a semi-ruined city. Every day, the garrison's fighting strength shrank and, despite the British outposts, the French and Canadians prowled closer to Quebec's walls.

"I thought that we defeated the French and control most of

Canada," MacNicholl said, as he hauled another cart of rubble from a ruined house to strengthen the walls and build a covered way to protect the men inside the defences.

"It's only a pity that nobody told the French that." Chisholm pushed the cart, with MacKim at his side. "They think we only won a single battle."

MacKim grunted, saying nothing. He worked with a cold frenzy, piling the stones onto the cart and pulling it over the rough, shell-battered streets as if he alone could rebuild the city and defeat the French.

A private from Amherst's Foot began to sing, with some others of his regiment joining in.

"Our troops they now can plainly see
May Britain guard in Germany;
Hanoverians, Hessians, Prussians,
Are paid t'oppose the French and Russians,
Nor scruple they with truth to say
They're fighting for Americay."

"That song is correct, of course," Chisholm said. "Britain is paying all these foreign armies to keep the French occupied in Europe while we grab their empire of New France in the Americas."

MacNicholl looked at the ruins of Quebec and the rain that teemed down. "Well, Chisholm, the French can have it. I'd prefer to be at home."

The night-time skirmishes increased as the defenders lost a slow drift of casualties at the outposts. However, the occasional success as pickets repelled the harassing Canadians and Indians ensured that morale never collapsed. In common with the others, MacKim followed General Murray's standing orders never to undress at night but to remain ready to repel any attack, with his musket at his side.

"I hope they come tonight," MacKim said every evening as

he loaded his Brown Bess. "I hope the murdering French bastards come tonight." He checked his flint was sharp, tested the edge of his bayonet on his thumb and glared at the wall. He saw Tayanita there, crumpling to the ground with the musket ball destroying her head. "I hope they come tonight."

"We don't hope that," Ranald MacDonald said, edging away from MacKim.

Chisholm passed over his water-bottle. "I've no idea what this is," he said. "Some Quebec woman gave it to me in exchange for a twist of tobacco."

MacKim tasted the contents and coughed. "That's rough," he said. "I'll stick to spruce beer." The authorities sold spruce beer to the Highlanders at two pence three-halfpenny a gallon, but as supplies were running short, the price rose beyond the capabilities of the poorly-paid soldiers.

"You're getting soft since you spent half your life in the hospital bed," Harriette said.

"Give me that." MacKim grabbed the bottle and half emptied it.

"Now he'll sleep, and we'll feel safer," Harriette said as MacKim slumped onto his bed. "The poor bugger's taken Tayanita's loss hard."

"Aye," Chisholm said, "but death is part of a soldier's existence. He should know that by now."

Harriette patted MacKim's shoulder. "I'm not sure that our Hughie's all there. Part of him is away with the fairies, poor lad."

"Maybe, but he befriended me," Chisholm touched his fire-ravaged face, "when nobody else would. He's got a good heart in him."

"Watching his brother tortured affected him worse than I thought," Harriette said. "He needs a good woman to look after him." She glanced at Chisholm. "If you would get yourself decently killed, Chisholm, I'd look after Hughie."

Chisholm laughed. "That might happen, Harriette, but I'm not rushing to die yet."

❧

"WHERE'S MURDO MACLEAN?" MACKIM ASKED, LOOKING around the room.

"He's run," Chisholm said shortly. "He prefers the Frenchies to us."

"Aye." MacKim was not surprised. It was only a few months since he had tried to desert, so he could not criticise. With everybody on short rations, sickness raging, and the cold biting harder every day, the British garrison of Quebec was not happy.

"Come on, Hughie." Harriette touched MacKim's arm. "You've got another parade this morning. Best get your section ready for it."

MacKim took a deep breath as his head cleared. "You're right, Harriette." He struggled to regain control of his emotions. He had not felt so bad since the redcoats murdered his brother after the battle of Culloden. "Sorry, lads," he said. "I'm a bit out-of-sorts just now."

"Aye," Ranald MacDonald said, still watching MacKim. That one word conveyed a hundred meanings.

"There's another flogging this morning," Chisholm said. "That's the third this week."

Flogging was not common in Highland regiments, so MacKim had been shocked to witness his first. Now, after years in the army, he had seen dozens, yet he could never reconcile himself to the ritual torture of British soldiers on the orders of British officers.

"General Murray has detailed the 78th to watch," Chisholm said.

"Why? To discourage us from looting and deserting?" MacKim grimaced. He knew that Murray was also trying to stop the British soldiers from fraternising with the citizens of Quebec. Murray's idea was to remain on good terms with the citizens and local farmers while preventing British soldiers from becoming too friendly with the French-Canadians. The suspicion of spies was endemic, with some officers nearly paranoid in their concern to stop information leaking to the French.

The flogging was routine; the unfortunate man was stripped to the waist and spread-eagled to the halberds while the drummers with the cat-o'-nine-tails prepared to strike. The officer in charge gave the order, the attendant surgeon gave the victim a cursory inspection, and the punishment began.

After the first three strokes, red marks appeared across the back and shoulders of the victim. After the first six, the man's back began to swell, and then the blood started to flow.

After two dozen, the surgeon examined the victim, the drummers cut him down, and everybody marched back to barracks or wherever duty dictated.

When MacKim returned to barracks, feeling humiliated and slightly sick, he saw at once that the room was in disorder. The usually pristine beds were untidy, the clothes strewn across the floor and clothes everywhere.

"What's happened here?"

"Somebody's broken in," Chisholm said at once.

"Harriette!" MacKim shouted. "Did anybody come in here during the parade?"

Harriette shook her head. "I was in the cookhouse, and the sentries were watching the punishment." Harriette looked around the room. "They've made a right mess, whoever they were. Best get it tidied up before the duty officer calls. It's Lieutenant Gregorson today."

"Is anything missing?" MacKim shouted. "Everybody check your kit."

"I've lost a shilling," Private Mackay said a minute later.

"I've lost tuppence!"

The calls came in; small amounts of money that meant a great deal to men who earned only a pittance.

"I've lost my tartan shawl," Ranald MacDonald said. "My sister gave me that for luck when we left Scotland."

MacKim checked his kit. He had no money to lose, but

something infinitely more important was missing. "I've lost Tayanita's beadwork," he said, standing up. He glared around the room, ready to fight anybody for any reason.

"It might turn up yet," Harriette said.

"It might." MacKim tried to hide his despair.

At that moment, MacKim thought that the world could not get any bleaker. He had lost his woman, and now somebody had stolen his last link with her. He slumped on the bed, expressionless, and began to sharpen his bayonet, bringing the sharpening stone along the glittering blade again and again.

He knew he was muttering to himself but did not care. He felt the edge of the blade and continued to sharpen as the shadows lengthened and the drums beat retreat.

4

As the weeks dragged past, General Murray took ever more drastic action to eke out what stores Quebec had. He ordered a survey of the camp followers and discovered nearly five hundred and seventy wives and other women; mouths to be fed yet arms that did not carry a single musket.

Murray cut the women's rations to two-thirds that of the men and ordered them to labour, stacking timber, filling sandbags or tending to the always-increasing number of sick. When the General and Ursuline Hospitals were unable to cope with the number of sick, General Murray created a new army hospital, with the wives as nurses.

"Me, a nurse?" Harriette gave her coarse laugh. "Dear God in heaven, I hope none of you boys come under my care. I've got the nursing skills of a lump of peat."

"That's true," Chisholm said, until Harriette slapped him.

"When do you start in the hospital?" MacKim asked.

"Tomorrow," Harriette said.

As winter strengthened its grip, the ice on the rivers thickened, and the garrison found it hard to locate fresh water, adding to their tribulations. Dysentery spread through the city, and

General Murray tightened the curfew as the sentries caught some citizens sneaking vegetables out of the gates. When two local men broke the curfew, Murray ordered them to be whipped through the streets.

Unlike during a military punishment, Murray did not order the garrison to watch, and Fraser's Highlanders regarded the spectacle with mixed feelings.

"THEY MIGHT HAVE FORGOTTEN ABOUT THE CURFEW," MacRae said, "or had to visit their old, sick mother." MacRae was a dreamy-eyed man from the far north-west of Scotland who had a reputation for being fey.

"Or they might be spies," MacKim said. "Reporting our movements to the French. They knew the rules."

"You're turning into a bitter man, MacKim," Chisholm growled, as Harriette watched through narrow, worried eyes.

Even the most hardened soldier was affected when Murray ordered two women to be flogged through the streets for selling rum to the garrison. The men watched, stony-faced, as the drummers stripped the women to the waist. One by one, the drummers tied the women to the back of a cart, which slowly drove through the streets, stopping at various places for the drummers to lay on the lash.

"This never happened in Europe," Chisholm said out of the corner of his mouth. "We never treated women like this."

MacRae looked away as the carts rumbled past, with the women staggering behind. "I've got three sisters," he mumbled. "If anybody ever touched them, I'd put a knife between their ribs. It's barbaric."

MacKim watched without seeing. In his mind's eye, that was Tayanita tied to the cart; and he felt a surge of hatred for the man wielding the whip.

"Bloody barbarians," he whispered. "Bloody, savage barbarians!" At that moment, he did not know to whom he was referring. He only knew that he hated the world and everybody in it.

FROST GLITTERED IN THE SPACES BETWEEN THE LOGS AS MacKim stared into the dark. Outpost duty in North America was always nerve-shredding, with the possibility that a raiding party of Indians or Canadians lurked only a few yards away. MacKim stood still, listening for any tell-tale sounds, looking for anything that did not belong in the silent black of the Canadian night. Here at St Foy, the British felt vulnerable to attack all the time.

Three yards away, Private Callum MacNicholl checked the flint of his musket, stamped his feet, blew on his frozen fingers and peered over the parapet of mixed earth and timber.

"I think I heard something, Corporal," MacNicholl said.

MacKim silenced him with an imperious movement of his hand. He had heard the sound as well. He was unsure what it was, but it did not belong in the iced Canadian night.

Kneeling on the frozen ground, MacKim thumbed back the hammer of his musket. He strove to control his breathing as he remembered the ambush that killed Tayanita. That sound came again, short and abrupt. MacKim remained still, swivelling his eyes in the direction of the noise.

MacNicholl was breathing harshly now as his nerves took control. MacKim did not know him well but remembered him at the Battle of the Plains of Abraham. On that mad day, MacNicholl had wielded his broadsword like a hero of old, charging at the French army with all the reckless courage expected of a Highland warrior. MacKim did not doubt MacNicholl's nerve, yet he knew that it took a different kind of bravery to hold a night-time outpost against creeping Indians than to charge in the fire of battle.

When MacKim put a steadying hand on MacNicholl's arm,

the soldier started and nearly fired his musket. MacKim put a finger to his lips, frowning. Although the enemy would already know the location of every British outpost, MacKim had no intention of making it easy for them.

The thunder of a French cannon split the silence, making both soldiers duck, although the shot did not fall near them. MacKim saw the reflection of the muzzle flash on the low cloud, and then the French fired again.

"Jesus! When did the Frenchies drag artillery out here?" Ranald MacDonald asked.

"Are they going to attack?" MacNicholl mouthed.

Before MacKim replied, the British artillery retaliated, with the two pieces at the outpost firing a salvo that ripped above MacKim's head to land somewhere on the French side of the frontier.

"What sort of piece is that?" MacNicholl asked.

"General Belford's gun, I think," Chisholm murmured. "A short six-pounder, lighter to drag out here."

Sitting under the arc of artillery was never pleasant, but crouching at night, when the muzzle-flashes starred MacKim's night vision, a shot could fall on him at any time.

"Don't lose your concentration," MacKim snarled. "The artillery might be a cover for Canadian patrols." He tried to concentrate on his duty, watching and listening for the enemy, but it was impossible with the cannon roaring and the shells tearing through the air overhead. One French shot landed short, to crash over the frozen ground, unseen but noisy, fifty yards from MacKim's position.

"This isn't fun," MacNicholl said.

MacKim agreed.

The artillery duel lasted for half an hour, with each shot ruining MacKim's night vision and the noise reverberating through the forest of St Foy. When MacKim looked toward the village, he saw the church spire highlighted against the night, a sign of hope amidst the nightmare of war.

"God must be sleeping this season," Chisholm muttered, echoing MacKim's thoughts.

"Keep alert," MacKim mouthed. "This bombardment is a decoy. The French are planning something."

MacNicholl took a deep breath and coughed as powder-smoke from the artillery drifted onto them.

The musketry started a minute later, far to the left of their outpost. As on the previous occasion, there was a single shot and then a spatter of fire. MacKim heard somebody shout a hoarse challenge, with a voice replying in French.

"Not long now." MacKim fitted his bayonet with a soft click. "Fix your bayonet, Callum. f they come at us, you'll need it, and you won't have much time."

"What makes you think they'll come here?"

"They've fired to our right and probed to our left; now they'll try the centre. That's us. Keep your wits about you."

"Yes, corporal," MacNicholl said.

They came without further warning, a dozen warriors sliding from the dark towards MacKim's outpost. If he had not been expecting them, MacKim would have been killed or captured in the initial few seconds. As it was, he shot the leading man, bayonetted the second as he mounted the breastwork and was in the act of withdrawing his bayonet when the third loomed through the dark.

MacNicholl fired his musket, with the lock only inches from MacKim's ear, nearly deafening him. At that short range, MacNicholl could not miss. The one-ounce lead ball caught the Indian high in the chest, knocking him off his feet. Two more Indians emerged from the dark, tomahawks raised and faces hideously painted.

"God help us!" MacNicholl shouted, putting himself on the on-guard position.

"Murdering bastards," MacKim threw himself over the breastwork, snarling as he lunged at the nearest warrior.

Taken by surprise, the Indian swung his tomahawk a fraction

too late as MacKim slashed his bayonet across the warrior's throat. The man stood, spurting blood but still alive. Without a pause, MacKim continued the sideways swipe of his bayonet towards the remaining warrior, yelling an inarticulate scream of hatred. Warned by the wounding of his companion, the last Indian sidestepped and swung his tomahawk in a circle, underhand. MacKim blocked the haft of the weapon with the butt of his musket, snarling.

"Tayanita!"

"You bloody idiot, Corporal!" MacNicholl had clambered over the breastwork to help. "You'll get us both killed!"

Attacked by two Highlanders, the remaining warrior fled. It was not in his culture to make a heroic last stand or to fight against odds for no reason.

"MacKim!" MacNicholl grabbed MacKim's sleeve. "Get back to the trench!"

Ignoring MacNicholl, MacKim faced the grievously wounded Indian and poised his bayonet. The man crumpled before MacKim could act. He watched the man's dying convulsions, and the rage cleared from his eyes. The enemy had become a man, the ogre of the night a human being, wounded and afraid.

"You're right, MacNicholl," MacKim said and slowly returned to the outpost. He wanted to get his revenge on the men who had killed Tayanita, but chasing Indian warriors into the dark was not the answer.

MacKim reloaded his musket, crouched behind the defences and pondered his future. He and Tayanita had planned to desert the army and head west to find Tayanita's tribe and family. Tayanita's death had shattered all of MacKim's hopes. Now he only wanted revenge.

There were two methods that MacKim could take. Either he could pursue his original plan and desert. Once free of the restrictions of army life, he could try and hunt down Tayanita's murderers, somewhere in the vastness of North America. The second option was to remain in the army.

If he remained in uniform, he was subject to strict discipline and the will of the officers in command. However, MacKim knew the army also provided food and support. Moreover, he knew that Generals Murray and Amherst had to finally defeat the French in Canada to gain security for the British colonies. There would be no significant campaigning in winter, and early spring would bring flooding around the Richelieu River, preventing the British from using that route. The tattooed Canadian and the renegade were with the forces facing Murray in Quebec, so, following that train of thought, MacKim knew that if he remained in the army, he might face the murderers and could legally kill them.

How many men were in the French army? Around 7000? 10,000? More? What were the chances of recognising, let alone meeting, the men who murdered Tayanita? MacKim grunted: what were the chances of even surviving if he deserted and tried to hunt the murderers alone?

None.

In the vast expanses of North America, with the war putting every man's hand against another, MacKim knew that a lone man had little chance of avenging Tayanita.

MacKim pondered his other choices. He could put Tayanita behind him and do his duty as if he had never met her. No. MacKim shook his head. He could not pretend that Tayanita had never existed, and he could not forgive her killers.

The tradition of MacKim's clan was to avenge a murder and the instinct of centuries was too strong to ignore.

"Corporal MacKim!" MacNicholl's voice broke through MacKim's thoughts. "The reinforcements are here."

A section of the 78th trotted to the outpost, with Corporal Mackay in command.

"We heard shooting," Mackay said. "Was there any trouble here?"

"No trouble," MacKim said. "Only a minor probe that we repulsed."

MacNicholl gave a fuller account of the night's events.

"You're a bloody idiot, MacKim," Mackay gave his considered opinion. "You'll get yourself killed if you carry on like that."

MacKim nodded. "That's possible," he said. He did not admit that he did not care.

❧

WHILE OUTPOST DUTY COULD BE DANGEROUS, THERE WAS ONLY work, sweat and more work during the day. With the garrison's insatiable desire for firewood, General Murray sent parties to the L'Île d'Orleans to the east of Quebec and the forest at St Foy to chop down trees.

"Come on, boys." Lieutenant Gregorson was in charge of the detail at the L'Île d'Orleans. "We need sixteen thousand cords of timber for the hospital and quarters, and you lucky men are the chosen fellers."

MacKim was one of the two hundred amateur woodsmen, sawing and hacking at trees until the sweat soaked through his uniform, and he hated the very idea of trees.

"Consider this," Chisholm said. "Every tree we fell is one less for the Canadians to hide behind."

MacKim looked at the forest and shook his head. "Aye, we'll conquer Canada tree by tree."

"But there's an awful lot of trees," MacNicholl said.

Piling the logs onto sledges, the men dragged them towards Quebec, with a small escort of armed guards in case of ambush.

"Tree by tree?" MacNicholl said, straining at the harness that secured him to the sledge. "By the weight of this sleigh, we're pulling half the forest!"

Those were the last words that Callum MacNicholl said. The shots came from the forest a full fifty yards from the tree-fellers, and MacNicholl staggered as two smashed into him. He looked down at his body in astonishment as the blood eased through his tunic. As if reluctant to admit he was dying, he fell slowly, kicked as he lay on the ground, and lay still.

By the time MacNicholl hit the ground, the escort had already retaliated, firing into the trees from where the shots had originated. They moved out in extended order, with two men reloading while the others advanced.

"Callum!" MacKim knelt at MacNicholl's side. "He's dead."

Grabbing his musket from the side of the sledge, MacKim gave orders. "Extended order, boys. Follow me, and we'll catch the raiders."

MacKim's impulse was to lead a charge straight into the trees, but he knew that the enemy would expect that. They would have men waiting in ambush, ready to get behind any British soldier and cut them off.

"Keep in touch with one another," MacKim ordered, "don't allow the enemy to capture you."

The escort was already deep in the trees, calling to each other as they vainly searched for the attackers. MacKim moved more slowly, probing into every thicket and checking behind every tree. He had Chisholm on his immediate left and Ranald MacDonald on his right, both experienced men.

They moved slowly.

"Here," Chisholm pointed to the ground beneath one of the trees. The impression of a human body was outlined on the grass.

"One of them lay here." MacKim pressed a hand to the ground, seeking residual warmth. "He left recently, so he's close by. Tree all, lads, and watch out."

The Highlanders each crouched behind a tree and searched the surrounding woods. They could hear the escort still calling to each other and then a cacophony of sounds, musketry, yells and oaths, with a French voice shouting orders and the terrifying war-whoop of the Indians.

"Keep together," MacKim ordered, heading towards the

noise. He knew his men were behind him, muskets ready as they advanced.

Two of the escort were down, with the other three fighting desperately against a host of Indians.

"Kneel," MacKim ordered quietly. "Pick your man and fire." He knew how inaccurate muskets were, especially when men were excited. A standing man had even less possibility of hitting his target, as it was difficult to hold a heavy musket steady in a standing position. The end of the muzzle would waver, spoiling any possibility of accuracy. A kneeling man, with the barrel balanced on a branch, would be more accurate.

Ranald MacDonald fired first, with the musket's thud reverberating in the trees, and Chisholm and MacKim a second later. One of the Indians fell immediately, and a second spun as a ball slammed into his arm.

"Charge," MacKim said quietly, as he clicked his bayonet into place. He was unsure how many Indians there were, but knew that a determined charge would unsettle them.

MacKim only had a glimpse of the tall Canadian. Enough to know the Canadian was in charge of the raiding party and to see the swirling tattoos that covered the man's face.

"*You!*"

As he leapt forward, MacKim felt the madness surge over him. He heard the crack of a musket and felt the wind of a ball passing close, and then he was among the enemy. The next few moments were blurred. He knew warriors were opposing him and British soldiers, Highlanders and Amherst's Foot, fighting at his side, but all he wanted to do was kill and be killed. He stabbed and hacked, swore and grunted, smashed his musket butt onto a human head and thrust a bayonet into somebody's stomach, screaming his hatred.

"Corporal! Hugh!"

MacKim felt somebody pulling at his shoulder. He turned around, snarling, and raised his bayonet.

"Hugh!" Chisholm parried the bayonet thrust.

The madness cleared from MacKim's eyes. "Jesus, James, I might have killed you." He looked around. Four Indians lay on the ground, one with numerous bayonet wounds, and two British soldiers. The others were looking at him, and there was no sign of the tattooed Canadian. MacKim wiped the blood and sweat from his face. "I think we'd better get back to work."

"I think we'd better," Chisholm agreed.

"Pick up our dead," MacKim ordered, "and we'll get back."

The wood lay as they had left it, with the firewood on the sledge and MacNicholl's body still in its harness. The only thing missing was MacNicholl's head.

5

"They took his head," MacRae mumbled as they returned to Quebec. "The savages took MacNicholl's head."

"We know," MacKim snapped. He wondered if he should have left a guard on the wood while they chased away the Indians. No, he told himself. If he left a single man, the Indians would have killed him, while leaving more than one would have weakened the counter-attack.

The memory of that tattooed Canadian haunted MacKim as he gave the parole – the password – to enter the city. That was the man who had murdered Tayanita.

"Mister," the small voice broke through MacKim's thoughts. "Mister Corporal." The small boy was there, hovering out of reach, unsure whether to plead for food or flee for safety.

About to chase him away, MacKim swore and reached for any fragments of biscuit he had retained. He found a corner and tossed it to the boy. "Here," he said.

MacRae grunted. "That lad will probably grow up to hate us, Corporal," he said. "In ten years, he'll be ghosting through the forest, hunting British soldiers."

"Maybe," MacKim said. "But in ten years, we'll likely be dead or back in Scotland."

"No," MacRae shook his head. "In ten years, we'll still be here, still fighting the French in this God-forsaken land."

MacKim looked around Quebec's ruins, with a platoon of red-coated British soldiers marching to their station on the walls as a group of civilians watched. He shook his head.

"I hope you are wrong," MacKim said. "I hope we capture Montreal and end this campaign next year."

"Even if we do," Chisholm said, "what will it matter? The government will hand Canada back to France in exchange for some border fortress in Picardy, and we'll have to reconquer the place in the next war or the one after that. New France is only a pawn in the European chess game."

MacKim saw MacNicholl's headless body lolling on the back of the sledge and shook his head. "What are we doing here, James? Why are we here?"

"We're doing our duty, Hugh," Chisholm replied. "And trying to survive."

❧

AS THE GARRISON FROZE AND SUFFERED FROM SCURVY, THE French became bolder, skirmishing right up to the outposts, interrupting the tree-felling and occasionally firing at the sentries.

"We'll have to do something about the Frenchies." Chisholm put a length of shattered timber on the barrack room fire and stepped back as a ribbon of sparks dashed up the flue. "They wiped out a party of Otway's Foot last night."

"I heard the shooting," MacKim agreed, trying to steal some of the fire's heat. He had not realised how cold he was.

Chisholm puffed out foul-smelling smoke from his pipe. "Aye, shooting and butchery, once more."

"I know about butchery," MacKim said.

"You do," Chisholm agreed. He was quiet for a few moments.

"So do the French. They didn't leave a single survivor. They killed every man and took away their heads."

MacKim looked up. "Why did they do that?"

"I have no idea," Chisholm said. He puffed more smoke into the already-smoky room. "I've never heard the like before."

"The old-time Celts used to cut off people's heads," MacKim said. "They put them around their houses or decorated their horses with them."

"Maybe these French are doing that, too," Chisholm said. "If they were French. More likely to be Canadian or Indian."

"Probably," MacKim said. "Things are grim when the French turn to head-hunting."

Chisholm lay on the nearest bed and took hold of the stem of his pipe. "Maybe we'd best tell General Murray to do something about it."

"That's Harriette's job," MacKim said. "She's good at giving people orders."

Harriette lifted her skirt and sat on the edge of MacKim's bed, toasting her legs at the fire. "I'll see what I can do," she said, puffing at a stubby clay pipe. She winked at MacKim. "I might put the general on my list. Once Chisholm is dead, and the French kill you, Hugh, I'll get Jimmy Murray to warm my bed."

MacKim nodded. "I hope General Jim will enjoy sharing a room with a dozen soldiers."

"Oh, no," Harriette said. "We'll be in a four-poster bed in the Governor's mansion, with servants running after us and all the dainty food in the world." As she looked around the Spartan quarters, Harriette's face fell, and MacKim knew she was contemplating the differences in lifestyle between the officers and the other ranks.

"I wish I could have a little of that," she said.

MacKim looked into the fire, knowing Harriette was wasting her time. A son of Lord Elibank, General Murray came from the upper strata of society, a position to which Harriette, or any of the other ranks in the army, could never aspire.

A log glowed red and collapsed in a welter of sparks and smoke. Momentarily, MacKim remembered the peat fires of his home and shook away the memory. Nostalgia was unhealthy; he might return to Scotland some time, and he might not. He grunted; was it any worse being at the beck and call of military drums than obeying the whim of a clan chief?

"What are you thinking, Hugh?" Harriette put a brawny arm around MacKim's shoulders.

MacKim shifted away. "I'm thinking that it's time I did my rounds before the duty officer arrives," he said. The past was gone, and the future could take care of itself.

MURRAY SEEMED DETERMINED NOT TO SIT QUIETLY AND ALLOW the French to control the lands around his city. He sent two hundred men, a mixture of grenadiers and light infantry, across the St Lawrence river, to overawe the Canadian settlements. Travelling along the south shore of the river, the British disarmed as many of the Canadians as possible and made them swear an oath of allegiance to King George. They returned without seeing an openly hostile Frenchmen or firing a shot.

"A lot of nonsense, of course." Chisholm gave his opinion as they sat in the barrack-room after another day of labouring. "A forced oath is no oath, and as soon as we turn our backs, the Canadians will resume their allegiance to France."

"Yes," MacKim agreed, "but we do have access to some fresh produce which might keep down the scurvy."

Harriette turned her back on the fire, lifted her skirt and bent forward. "That's better," she said. "I have to warm myself properly in this place. You're mistaken, though, Hugh. There will be little fresh produce at this time of year."

"They might have vegetables in storage." MacRae was watching Harriette, with his eyes busy on her legs. "I heard the

French had been moving, too. They've reinforced their outposts at Pointe-Aux-Trembles, St Augustin and Le Calvaire."

Chisholm became aware of the direction of MacRae's eyes. Without saying a word, he flicked down Harriette's skirt and sat her on the bed. His glare warned MacRae to look elsewhere.

"Have you heard the news?" MacRae turned his attention away from Harriette. He was always first with a new rumour. Sometimes they were accurate, but more often only wild guesses. MacKim had learned to listen with a large pinch of salt.

"What news?" Harriette was always willing to listen to gossip. She curled her legs beneath her and perched on MacKim's cot, eyes bright.

"General Murray is concerned about losing so many men on outpost duty." MacRae spoke as if imparting a secret, with his voice hushed and his eyes wide. He looked around the crowded room as the Highlanders gathered to hear him. "He's going to organise a mobile picket to patrol outside the defences and catch the Frenchies before they attack our outposts."

MacKim stared into the fire. "How's he going to do that? We've only a handful of Rangers in the garrison. Half our men would march out in full regimentals and roar out a challenge, and the other half is dying with scurvy."

"I'm sure I don't know." MacRae sounded downcast. "I'm only repeating what I've heard."

"The general will have to recruit from the lights," Chisholm said.

"Aye, as long as he takes away the scarlet uniforms," MacKim agreed. "We may as well wave the Colours and sound the drums."

"The Royal Americans may be the best." Chisholm ignored MacKim's cynicism. "Monckton's Royal Americans are the next thing to Rangers that we have."

Within a day, MacRae's words were proved correct. Rumours spread around the garrison that Murray was considering creating what he called a "flying picket" and interviewed the officers to see who was most suitable as a leader.

"There are three men in line for the position," MacRae informed the crowded barrack room. "One is a man named Captain Robin Lindsay who I don't know, another a New Hampshire lieutenant named Kennedy and the third, our very own Captain Donald MacDonald."

"I've heard of Kennedy," MacKim said. "I don't know this Lindsay fellow." He checked the lock of his musket, eased back the hammer and added a touch of oil. "I hope Captain MacDonald gets the nod; he's one of the best."

"I hope not," Chisholm said. "The regiment can't afford to lose him."

MacKim snapped shut the hammer of his musket. "Aye, James; there is that."

A day later, Murray appointed Captain Robin Lindsay to command the flying picket, and he looked for volunteers from every regiment in the garrison.

MacKim studied the poster that a grumbling private had nailed to the wall. It read:

British Soldiers! For some time now, the French and their Canadian and Indian allies have menaced our garrison in Quebec. Captain Lindsay of Monckton's Foot, an experienced officer, well respected by his peers and loved by his men, is raising a flying picket of chosen men to combat this French menace.

Captain Lindsay is seeking Volunteers experienced in forest warfare to face the French and stop them in their tracks. Only the best men will be selected, men of proven skill and courage able to carry a sack of meal a mile without stopping, fire three shots a minute, and hit a target at fifty paces.

If you think you are suitable, take this bill to Captain Lindsay at his quarters in Fort Louis.

GOD SAVE THE KING!

MacKim considered for less than a minute before tearing down the bill and carrying it to Fort Louis beside the old Governor-General's residence.

Lindsay was a hard-faced man with a scar across his chin. He turned sharp blue eyes on MacKim the moment he entered his room in the fort.

"Another Highlander!" Lindsay looked MacKim up and down as if bored. "You're a bit diminutive but you look the part. Have you any experience of forest warfare except on picket duty?"

"Yes, sir," MacKim said. "I was trained by the Rangers and skirmished around Quebec with the lights."

"Is that so?" Lindsay looked slightly more interested. "Have you ever fought the Indians face-to-face?"

In answer, MacKim removed his bonnet and displayed his partially scalped head. "Yes, sir," he said.

Lindsay's eyes narrowed slightly. "You survived, I see."

"Yes, sir," MacKim said.

"Not many do that." Lindsay examined MacKim's head for a few moments. "You want some revenge."

"I do, sir," MacKim agreed.

Lindsay selected fifty men from the three hundred who volunteered. Most were colonials and Germans from Monckton's 60th Royal Americans, with a smattering of British soldiers and a couple of Rangers. Lindsay paraded them on the open ground of the Plains of Abraham, with the artillery of the city covering them and the blockhouses in front manned and ready for a French attack.

The men stood, some shivering in the cold rain, others with furs over their uniforms. As a veteran, MacKim retained his corporal's stripes and commanded a section of ten men.

"Keep at attention," MacKim said, "until Captain Lindsay orders otherwise." He stood five paces in front of his men, watching Sergeant Speakman on his left side.

"I'd like to train you in the woods," Lindsay said, walking the length of the treble line. "But that's not possible just now. Instead, I'll test your musketry."

MacKim had been through it all before, the musketry drills, the advice to walk quietly, the open formation with each man watching out for the enemy. He reminded the men how to walk in single file and not reuse the same route in case of ambush, and taught the novices in the use of snowshoes and how to fire from cover.

"Don't think you are escaping from routine duties," MacKim warned. "Life is tough in the wilderness."

MacKim did not know from where Lindsay found the uniforms, but within a week, each man of Lindsay's Rangers, as the garrison termed them, wore a mottled green-and-white uniform to make him less visible against the snow. While most of the men looked at their new attire with some distaste, for British soldiers wore proud scarlet, others approved.

"Now the Frenchies won't see us in the forest," a youngster named Ramsay said.

"That's the idea," MacKim agreed.

"All right, men," Lindsay addressed his Rangers after ten days of intermittent training. "We are beginning operations tonight." He gave a rare smile. "As you know, the French have been active against our outposts across the St Charles River and at St Foy. We are going to cross the St Charles at low water tonight and wait for them."

MacKim nodded.

"I want every man to ensure his musket is cleaned and oiled, with thirty-six cartridges, a sharp flint and two spare flints." Lindsay tapped the sword at his belt. "Some of you may carry a secondary weapon, a hatchet, pistol or whatever." He stopped opposite MacKim. "I thoroughly approve of that. Anything that kills a Frenchman or Canadian will help win this war."

Some of the men laughed at that. MacKim found nothing amusing about war; to him, killing the enemy was now a sacred duty.

"Now, nobody knows about this operation except us," Lindsay said, "so we will catch the Frenchies by surprise." His grin was pure devilment. "If we hit them hard enough, we might put them off raiding for weeks."

MacKim touched the hatchet at his belt and the pistol he wore under his tunic. He knew that such heavy items slowed him down when travelling in the forest, but also that if he needed a secondary weapon, he would need it urgently.

Lindsay's Rangers moved off, crossing the St Charles River by the low-water passage beside the King's Magazine and easing into the woods on the opposite side.

The atmosphere altered as soon as the forest closed around them. MacKim could almost taste the tension, with the trees standing like half-seen pillars pointing to the dark bowl of the sky and the snow-covered ground reflecting the light of the moon.

"Single file," Lindsay hissed, "and follow me."

Darkness and the claustrophobic forest magnified every sound so that the fall of snow from a tree sounded like an avalanche and a man's muttered curse like a sergeant's parade-ground roar.

They passed one British outpost, where a dozen grenadiers stared nervously at them, before settling back down to a fraught night. Five minutes later, Lindsay pointed to a slight dip in the ground, with a ring of trees all around.

"I scouted out this place," he said. "We can lie here unseen and listen for the French to come."

Lindsay's Rangers lay down on the snow, with their muskets pointing outwards. MacKim settled into a hollow beside the trunk of a tree, with an arc of vision that gave him a clear field of fire in front.

"Shall I post pickets, sir?" MacKim suggested.

Lindsay pondered for a moment before shaking his head. "No, MacKim. I prefer to keep the men together."

"As you wish, sir." He caught Sergeant Speakman's eye, raised his eyebrow and said nothing. A corporal did not argue with a captain.

The Rangers waited, watching the dark trees and listening to the wind in the branches. Speakman lifted his head and frowned, but MacKim had already sensed the movement. He thumbed back the hammer of his musket as the Canadians and Indians came from all sides, silent as ghosts in the snow.

More prepared than his colleagues, MacKim barked a warning.

"Here they come, lads!"

He fired first, with others following as the Canadians and Indians swept upon them. MacKim shot the leading attacker and, with no time to fix his bayonet, used the musket as a club, swinging it at the next man who loomed from the dark. He heard a prolonged scream from behind him and a succession of gasps and oaths.

"Defend yourselves!" Lindsay shouted a belated warning as the remaining Rangers fired a ragged volley and resorted to butts, boots and bayonets. A hideous painted face reared up before MacKim, and he slammed the butt of his musket against it, yelling, then kicked up into the warrior's groin.

"Aye, would you, you bastard!" MacKim roared, as strong hands grasped his musket, trying to wrestle it from his grasp.

"Fight them!" Lindsay shouted, firing a pistol.

MacKim's adversary pushed him backwards. Half a head taller than MacKim, the man was an Abenaki, with his face painted half-red, half-green and his mouth open in a gape. MacKim swore, released the musket, drew his hatchet and swung underhand, cursing again when the blade became tangled in the Indian's thick clothing.

Somebody fired a musket beside MacKim's ear, nearly deafening him, and the Abenaki yelled a war-cry, dropping MacKim's musket to draw a long scalping knife. Without thought, MacKim brought his head sharply forward, breaking the bridge of the Abenaki's nose and sending the warrior reeling backwards.

As the Abenaki staggered, MacKim chopped at him with his hatchet, hacking at his neck. The Abenaki fell, and MacKim had an instant to look around him. Lindsay was struggling with a Canadian, while half a dozen of the Rangers were down, dead or wounded. The attackers were a mixture of Canadians and Indians, with a couple of what MacKim thought were French regular soldiers.

"Withdraw!" Lindsay ordered. "Get back to Quebec!"

"Come on, lads!" MacKim sidestepped a rush by a Canadian, hacked at the man with his hatchet and stooped to lift his musket. "Rally on me!" He knew that if the Rangers merely scattered, the Indians and Canadians would hunt them down and kill them.

After the first furious rush, the Rangers began to regroup, with some men fighting back and a few panicking. Two fled into the forest as Lindsay backed away, feverishly reloading his pistol.

"They're all around us!" MacKim saw furtive figures moving in the dark. "Keep together! Fix your bayonets, lads, and stand back to back! Where's Sergeant Speakman?"

"I'm in charge here, Corporal!" Lindsay shouted. "Get back to Quebec as fast as you can!"

The Canadians and Indians fired a volley, hitting another two Rangers, and then attacked again, hatchets and knives plunging as they howled from the trees. MacKim slotted in his bayonet, hooked his hatchet onto his belt and snarled at the first of the attackers.

"Come on, then!"

The Indian avoided the bayonet and looked for an easier victim as two other Rangers joined MacKim, standing in a triangle with bayonets pointing outwards. MacKim heard their ragged breaths and realised they were as nervous as he was.

"Move away slowly," MacKim said, taking charge. He raised his voice. "To me, Rangers!" Step by step, MacKim edged towards the river, parrying any attempt to attack and keeping his small group together.

Two more Rangers joined them, and then another three, with MacKim holding them together as they retreated step-by-step with the Indians and Canadians holding back.

"Halt," MacKim ordered. He saw many of his men were frightened, some with wide, panicking eyes, others shaking so hard they could not think straight. He raised his voice to a parade-ground roar, seeking to break through their fear.

"Has anybody got a loaded musket?"

"No, Corporal." The reply came amidst a bevy of shaking heads. One man edged away until MacKim grabbed his shoulder and hauled him back.

"Stay with us, Ramsay! Now, lads, prime and load!" MacKim ordered, as if the men were all Johnny Raws rather than veteran soldiers. He knew they were so severely shaken, he'd have to talk them through every movement.

The men brought the muskets to the priming position, moving automatically to the words of command.

"Take your cartridge!" MacKim shouted, hoping the Canadians did not attack again while his men were in the process of loading. The men drew a cartridge from the cartridge box they all wore. The box held thirty-six rounds and hung above the right buttock, which it rapped with every step. Most Rangers ripped the paper; some bit it through, staining their lips with black powder. One man dropped his cartridge, glanced at MacKim, apologised and fumbled for another.

When all the men were ready, MacKim gave the next order.

"Prime!"

He led by example, pulling the hammer of the musket to half cock, then poured a few grains of black powder into the priming pan. He closed the frizzen – an L-shaped piece of steel that covered the pan – so the priming powder was safe from spillage or damp snow.

"Lower!" The men lowered the musket butt onto the ground and poured the remainder of the black powder from the cartridge down the long barrel. They added the ball and then the wadding to keep the ball in place.

MacKim saw the Canadians and Indians gathering, silent in the dark, but their teeth gleaming and war-paint visible. He had no time to spare, but could not rush the procedure until his men had collected their nerves.

"Draw your ramrods!"

The men removed the ramrods from their positions beneath the musket barrel and tapped down the wadding and ball. Most men took two strokes; the more nervous used three. Only when they were sure the wadding was secure did the men return the ramrods to the channel beneath the barrel. Ramsay left the ramrod protruding from the muzzle.

"You," MacKim said. "Ramsay!"

"Yes, sir," Ramsay answered.

"I'm a corporal, not a sir. Well, Ramsay, take care of your ramrod!"

Ramsay realised what he had done, recovered the ramrod and waited for the next order.

"Present!" MacKim ordered, and every man brought his musket to his shoulder and pulled the hammer fully back.

"Now walk back towards Quebec," MacKim said. "Keep your musket in the present position!"

Stumbling over half-seen roots and fallen boughs, MacKim's men moved slowly, with the Canadians and Indians always present but never attacking again. Twice a lone Canadian fired at them, and MacKim had to restrain his men from firing back.

"Once we fire," he said, "they will charge before we can reload. They're trying to tempt us to weaken ourselves."

Step by step, yard by yard, MacKim guided his men through the forest to the side of the river. Holding the heavy muskets at the present was a strain on the muscles, and the muzzles began to waver and droop until MacKim snarled at them to keep the muskets steady.

"It might save your lives, dammit!"

"The river's higher!" Ramsay exclaimed. "We can't cross!"

MacKim made a rapid decision as he saw the mixture of ice and slush that marked the bank. "Then we'll remain here until the water goes down," he said. "Form a half circle with the river at our backs. You," he pointed to a man, "what's your name?"

"Butler, Corporal." Butler had a colonial accent. Massachusetts, MacKim guessed. "Watch the river in case an Indian tries to sneak up behind us."

They lay in the hard-packed snow while the night eased away. The men jumped at every sound and started at every unexpected shadow as MacKim knelt behind the fallen trunk of a tree, peering into the dark. By four in the morning, the river had fallen, exposing the low water passage.

"One at a time, boys," MacKim said. "Don't trust your weight on the ice and keep a space between each man. Ramsay, you cross first; remember to identify yourself to the first sentry in case he thinks you're a Frenchie. The parole is 'George', and the countersign is 'Rex'."

"Yes, sir," Ramsay said.

"Have you got that?" MacKim pressed. "Tell me." He did not want nervous sentries to fire at them because Ramsay mistook the parole.

"The parole is 'George', and the countersign is 'Rex'," Ramsay repeated.

"Right, off you go." MacKim watched Ramsay stumble into the dark; he heard the hoarse exchange of passwords and then sent a laconic, unsmiling man of Bragg's across.

"You're next."

MacKim remained on the opposite side of the St Charles River until the last man was over, and then he crossed, keeping his face towards the silent enemy. He knew they were there and expected a parting shot or even a rush of warriors. Instead, he arrived at the Quebec side without an incident.

"To me, lads." MacKim gathered together the men who had followed him. "Let's say farewell to the Canadians."

"Are they still there?" Butler asked.

"They're there," MacKim said. "We can't see them in the half-light, and they can't see us, but they're there. Line the parapet, lads." He waited until his men obeyed. "Now you're all loaded and ready, so I'm only going to give one order."

"What's that, corporal?" Ramsay asked.

"This one," MacKim said. "Fire!"

The volley was disjointed as it shattered the silence, but MacKim hoped it had some effect on the invisible enemy. He knew he felt better about the night, having allowed his muskets to have the last word in the abortive mission. Yet he also knew he was no further forward in avenging Tayanita.

6

"How many survived the ambush?" General Murray looked worried as he gathered the Rangers together.

"We lost eight men, sir," Lindsay said. "I brought most back, and one of the corporals came last with a few stragglers."

MacKim felt the men's eyes on him but knew it was pointless to argue. In any disagreement between an officer and a captain, the officer's word would always carry more weight. To disagree was to invite the triangle, or worse. Other ranks must learn and know their place.

"Well done, Lindsay." Murray looked careworn as he struggled to cope with scurvy and the cold in a garrison slowly disintegrating. "What happened?"

"I think somebody told the French what was happening, sir. They knew exactly where we were."

"A spy?" Murray asked.

"I fear so, sir."

"One of these damned civilians, no doubt," Murray said. "I have given strict orders to the men not to fraternise, yet still they do."

"Indeed, sir," Lindsay agreed. "The Highlanders are the

worst. Some of them are Catholic, you see, and I've even heard they have spoken to the local priest."

Murray grunted. "Roman Catholics are not allowed to join the British Army, Lindsay. They are not to be trusted for that very reason. If you hear of any in the ranks, you must inform me at once."

"Yes, sir," Lindsay glanced at the battered remnants of his Rangers. "You don't think it was one of our men, do you?"

"I don't know what to think, Lieutenant." Murray ran a jaundiced eye across the Rangers, pausing momentarily at each Highlander and then stomped away.

THE RANGERS RETURNED TO THEIR QUARTERS TO LICK THEIR wounds, with some of the men watching MacKim as he cleaned his musket.

"Lindsay doesn't trust the Highlanders," Butler said.

MacKim ran a cloth along his musket barrel. "I know. Many people remember the Jacobite Risings and think we're going to revolt again."

"Are you?" Butler asked.

MacKim examined the interior of the barrel for fouling. "Most of the lads had no choice last time," he said. "The clan chief ordered them out."

"Could they not refuse?" Butler asked.

MacKim pondered for a minute. "It's tradition," he said. "It's the old way; it's a bit like us fighting King George's quarrels." He put the musket down. "Besides, if anybody refused to follow the chief, he'd have ordered their houses burned and their families evicted."

"Ah," Butler said. "I thought the Highlanders all loved their clan chiefs."

"Some are better than others," MacKim said, checking his flints.

"You led us well, Corporal MacKim," Ramsay said. "Better than the lieutenant did."

MacKim looked up. "I've fought the Canadians before," he said. "I know how they operate. Lieutenant Lindsay will do better next time."

"You should be an officer," Ramsay said.

MacKim nearly laughed at the idea. "I'm not even a good corporal, let alone an officer. You know that only the upper classes can be officers."

Ramsay copied MacKim in cleaning his musket. "Yes, Corporal, but that's only in the British Army. Not all the Rangers' officers are upper class."

MacKim thought for a minute before he replied. "They're mostly colonials," he said. "They're not British Army."

"What are they then, Corporal?" Parnell was one of the colonials, a lean, sparse man with a long jaw. "If they're not British Army, then what are they?"

MacKim considered for a long moment. "I am not sure, Parnell," he said, meeting the colonial's belligerent eye. "I can't see them standing in line at Minden or Fontenoy."

"The Rangers are not that kind of soldier," Parnell said.

"No," MacKim said. "You're right. They're not that kind of soldier, and the officers are not that kind of officer." He placed his musket beside his bed and began work on his bayonet. "I'm not sure how I would describe them. They're suited for this part of the world, that's for certain."

For a moment, MacKim was back in his childhood when the Jacobite Highlanders charged across the rain-sodden Drummossie Muir against the massed musketry and cannon of King George's redcoat soldiers. He knew the Rangers could not and would not fight in that manner.

"Colonial Army?" Parnell persisted.

MacKim shook his head. "I've been watching the Rangers and the colonials, both in New France and the British colonies. They are different from us, from the people from old France and old Britain." He gave a twisted grin. "They are not so willing to accept the word of an officer, even a titled officer. I could not see the colonials joining the army en-masse, say, merely because the clan chief gives an order."

"Is that a bad thing?" Parnell remained belligerent.

MacKim began to sharpen his bayonet. "No," he said. "No. Nobody should have to join the army, or the navy, because somebody else wants them to." He met Parnell's deep brown eyes. "Things are different out here."

Parnell nodded in reply. He seemed mollified by MacKim's answers.

"The Frenchies knew we were coming and where we would be," Ramsay said. "They probably have spies everywhere."

MacKim nodded. "Probably."

As the rumours of spies spread, the soldiers viewed every civilian with suspicion. Murray had already banned all fraternising between other ranks and Quebecers, although MacKim knew that keeping British soldiers from women was an impossibility. Drink and women, in that order, were the twin vices of the British Army, with looting a long way third.

"I heard it was a woman," Parnell said. "A woman told the French where we would be."

"How did she know?" MacKim asked. "Did she follow Captain Lindsay across the river, past the sentinels, and return without being seen?"

"I don't know," Butler said.

"I doubt a woman spied on the captain," MacKim said. "More likely, a Canadian watched him scout."

"Never mind the rumours," Parnell said. "Did you hear the news?"

"Not until you educate us," Butler said.

"After that disaster with Lindsay, General Murray is going to expand the Rangers. He thought the captain did well to extricate us from the ambush."

MacKim felt men looking at him, waiting for a response. He said nothing but lay on his bunk, staring at the ceiling.

"Lindsay is looking for more volunteers to make his Rangers fifty strong, with Lieutenant Kennedy as second-in-command and two sergeants. What do you think of that, Corporal?"

MacKim sat up. "That's up to the general," he said.

"More men for Lindsay to kill," Butler said.

"It wasn't Lindsay's fault," Ramsay said. "It was the spy who told the Frenchies."

MacKim ignored the comments. "Kennedy's a good man. I remember him before we captured Quebec."

Parnell smiled. "I knew Lieutenant Kennedy as a boy," he said. "We grew up in the same New Hampshire town."

"I didn't know you came from New Hampshire," MacKim said.

"Londonderry born and bred," Parnell boasted.

"What's it like?" MacKim asked.

Parnell thought for a while before replying. "Home," he said at last. "It's home. A small village where people look after each other."

MacKim wondered if he would ever see his home again. Or if he even had a home now.

Every day, MacKim saved a scrap of his ration bread for the little boy, and often he scrounged what he could from the cook-house. The boy waited for him a few yards from the barrack door, cupped his hands as MacKim tossed him the biscuit, and scampered away without a word of thanks.

"Ungrateful little bugger," MacKim said without rancour and then noticed the woman watching from a distance. She stood at the doorway of a ruined house, watching MacKim through narrowed eyes until the boy ran up to her. The woman put her arm around the boy's shoulders and both slipped inside the house.

"You could have the manners to thank me," MacKim said and sighed. "You probably hate us for destroying your home, and I can't blame you for that."

The next day, the Rangers began training, with the new men forming up beside the originals, both sets eyeing each other. Lindsay led them onto the Heights of Abraham, outside the city walls, but it was Kennedy who added to their training in the patches of forest at Sillery Woods.

A tall, slender man with a long face and a jaw that seemed permanently half-shaven, Kennedy's eyes moved from man to man.

"The enemy got the better of us last time," he said in his slow drawl. "That won't happen again." His gaze rested on MacKim. "I heard you got some of the men out, Corporal."

"Yes, sir," MacKim said.

Kennedy nodded, his eyes assessing. "We'll try to ensure you're not put in such a situation again."

For two days, Kennedy trained the Rangers in scouting, ensuring every man was familiar with the basics. He had them on sentry duty singly and in pairs, showed them what to watch for and taught them how to listen for sounds that did not belong.

"Work in pairs," Kennedy said, "with each man covering his colleague. We won't ever be caught out again."

Every day, the temperature seemed to drop another couple of degrees, until first the St Charles River froze and then the St Lawrence itself.

"And now things could get interesting," Kennedy said. "The French can cross the frozen river on foot; our outer defences no longer exist."

They sat as close to the fire as they could, some sneezing and coughing, most showing the first signs of scurvy as they struggled to find warmth from the pitiful flames.

"Lindsay is taking us out on another flying picket," Butler said quietly, staring into the fire.

"I wonder how many will come back this time." Parnell hugged his cloak over his shoulders.

MacKim stirred the fire with his bayonet, hoping to provoke more life. "We're playing the Frenchies' game," he said. "If there are spies in Quebec, we should use them against the French."

"How do we do that?" Ramsay asked.

"Give them false information," MacKim said. "Tell them we're going north, when we're heading south, or that we're leaving at ten at night when we leave at eight. Ambush the ambushers."

"That wouldn't work," Butler sneered.

MacKim shrugged. "Maybe; maybe not." He forgot his suggestion as the conversation drifted onto women and then what everyone planned to do after the war was over.

"I'll go back to New Hampshire," Butler said. "I'll maybe get fifty acres and carve out a farm." He sighed. "If this war ends the French menace, I might even head west and see what's out there."

"I don't know," Ramsay said. "I was only a boy when I joined the army. I don't have a trade or anything. I might try to get a labouring job here in the colonies or back home. How about you, Corporal?"

MacKim looked at him. With the death of Tayanita, his dreams had shattered. Now, he forced himself to look at a future when the army no longer needed him and provided for his basic needs. "I have no idea," he said. He could not think of a time when there was no killing; when life consisted of more than creeping around a cold forest or huddling in a ruined building. In MacKim's eyes, every man was suffering from scurvy or frostbite, and every Frenchman and Indian was an enemy. "This war will never end," he said. "It's already dragged on for five years, with no prospect of peace. The enemy will send men from Old France, and if we defeat one Indian nation, there are hundreds more. There is an entire continent of Indians."

"Well, you're a cheery cove," Butler said.

MacKim looked away and began to sharpen his hatchet. He knew it was already sharp enough to shave with, but it occupied his hands, if not his mind. He could not imagine his life. Would he return to Scotland? Only a few months ago, he had dreams of walking into his native glen with Tayanita by his side, greeting his mother and settling down to growing oats and raising cattle on the lower slopes. Now, Scotland seemed too far away, and visions of peace an impossible dream.

All MacKim saw was a future of killing until, inevitably, some Frenchman, Canadian or Indian killed him.

"And that will be the end of a sore song," he muttered to himself. "A bitter life ended in bloodshed and nobody the loser." He knew he was on the edge of reason, with madness hovering at the fringes of his mind, for sane men did not think as he did.

"I don't care," he said. "I don't care at all."

And that, he knew, was one of the most telling signs.

"Madness or death; both are the same, and I'd rather be dead than locked in bedlam." He looked around at the room full of sick men and then thought of the shattered city under siege. "Great God in heaven," he said, "we are already in a worse bedlam than any hospital, for what insanity inspired men to fight and kill each other to place a flag in a foreign land?" He looked up as a drummer beat for assembly. "Right, boys," MacKim said. "Here we go again."

When MacKim returned to the barrack-room that night, the small boy was waiting for him. Still wordless, he pressed a small leather bottle in MacKim's hand and scampered away.

"Thank you," MacKim called out and tasted the contents. "Spruce beer," he said and shared it with the men in the room. At a time when scurvy was increasingly prevalent, spruce beer helped alleviate the symptoms. "I'll be looking for more bread from you boys," MacKim said as he finished the bottle.

"ARE YOU CORPORAL MACKIM?" THE SOLDIER WAS OLD beyond his years, with sunken eyes and a mouthful of loose teeth.

"I am," MacKim admitted.

"Lieutenant Kennedy wants you," the man said. MacKim did not know him.

"Why?" MacKim asked.

"He didn't tell me," the soldier said. "Officers aren't in the habit of telling me what they plan."

"Where is he?"

"Fort Louis."

The army used Fort Louis as their headquarters in Quebec, with officers' quarters scattered inside the walls. A smart grenadier of Bragg's Regiment pointed the way, and MacKim presented himself at Kennedy's tiny room.

Lieutenant Kennedy greeted MacKim with a smile and invited him to sit down.

"I'd rather stand, sir," MacKim said. No officer had invited him to sit down before.

"As you wish." Kennedy stood with his back to the fire, smoking a long pipe. "Some of the men told me about the dozen men you saved after the late ambush," he said.

"It was only ten men, sir," MacKim said.

Kennedy smiled again. "Only ten, I stand corrected. Only ten lives saved; only ten souls that can be rescued for redemption."

MacKim said nothing. Other ranks did not volunteer information unless asked and only spoke in response to a direct question.

"That was good work, Corporal."

"Thank you, sir," MacKim said.

"Private Parnell tells me that you had some ideas about defeating the French."

Was that a statement? Or a question? MacKim was not sure. He remained silent, standing at rigid attention as he surveyed Kennedy's quarters. The room was tiny, if luxurious compared to the stark barracks of the other ranks. It boasted a cot-bed and straw mattress, a small, bright fire, and a simple table with two chairs.

"Tell me your ideas, Corporal."

That was a direct order, allowing MacKim to respond.

"If the enemy has spies in Quebec, sir, I thought we could give out false information."

"Tell me more, MacKim. I am listening." Kennedy sat on one of the chairs, stretching out his legs. "Sit down, man. I'm not one of your hidebound British officers!"

MacKim hesitated, unsure how to act before such an eccentric officer.

"Sit down, man – that's an order!"

"Yes, sir." MacKim sat at attention.

"Now, tell me how you plan to spread your information, MacKim, and any other ideas you may have."

MacKim hesitated again. The life of a private soldier was constrained and disciplined, with any thought limited and actively discouraged. Now, an officer was asking him to use his brain, which seemed to have atrophied from neglect. MacKim stared at Kennedy for a good thirty seconds before he began to talk.

"I thought we might let out some information, sir. Tell the world that we are going to patrol one area when we're actually going to another."

"Would that help?" Kennedy asked.

"It would keep the enemy away from us, sir. They would be preparing an ambush at an empty place."

Once MacKim started, it seemed that years of repression ebbed away, and the ideas flowed as his brain began to function.

"We could do better than that, sir. We could maybe prepare an ambush for the French. We could tell them we will be in a certain spot at, say, eight at night, but we can go at six and wait. When the French arrive to ambush our flying picket, we'll already be there, waiting for them."

"Ambush the ambushers, eh?" Kennedy sucked at his pipe, blowing blue tobacco smoke into the room. "I rather favour that idea. But the French, or the spies, might see us coming. Have you any other thoughts, MacKim?"

MacKim stared into the fire for a minute. "Yes, sir. Maybe. Carry manikins with us, somehow, Go out fifty strong and leave, say, ten men in ambush, but make it look like we come back with the same numbers. Each man can carry part of a manikin, a dummy, in his pack, make them up in the forest and come back supporting them, arms around their shoulders or something."

Kennedy grunted. "That may work. I like the dummy idea, but not like that."

"No, sir," MacKim said, growing in confidence as Kennedy did not mock his ideas. "We could do the opposite. Carry the dummies, as I said, but leave them in a position, like a forward picket. When the Canadians ambush them, we could have a real picket hiding a few yards away and then ambush the ambushers."

Kennedy nodded slowly, then pointed the stem of his pipe at MacKim. "That picket would have to be small, and they'd be vulnerable to Indian attack."

"Yes, sir," MacKim said.

"We'd need to call for volunteers," Kennedy said, adding tobacco to the bowl of his pipe. "Who would want such a dangerous post?"

MacKim shrugged. "I'd go, sir."

"I rather thought you would, MacKim." Kennedy eyed him for a long thirty seconds. "I heard some strange rumours about you, MacKim."

"Did you, sir?"

"I did. Just barrack-room gossip, of course." Kennedy puffed out more smoke. "Something about an Indian woman. Is there any truth in the rumours?"

MacKim lifted his chin higher. "I haven't heard the rumours, sir, so I can't say."

"Quite so, Corporal. Quite so." Kennedy puffed at his pipe again. "What was her name?"

"Tayanita, sir."

Kennedy nodded. "The rumours say the French killed her."

"Do they, sir?"

"They do. The rumours also say that you care more about revenge than you do about your life."

Again, MacKim thought silence was the best reply.

"The rumours claim that you charge into numbers of the enemy and fight like a Norse Berserker, hoping for death. Is that true?"

MacKim pondered for a moment. He knew it was true; he lived on a delicate balance between reason and insanity, and any incident could topple him over the edge. "I don't hope for death, sir."

"I am glad to hear it, MacKim. I have no place for an NCO with no concept of caution."

MacKim nodded. "Yes, sir."

"My NCOs have to look after the men," Kennedy said. "Corporals with a death wish cannot do that."

"I understand, sir."

"Good," Kennedy said. "You and I will wait in ambush, Corporal. I have a little surprise for our opponents." Kennedy's smile was as wicked as anything MacKim had ever seen. "Now, let's see about spreading some rumours."

7

As winter increased its bite, the cold grew more severe. Men relieving sentries found them frozen to death, while others reported to the hospitals with severe frostbite in fingers and toes. Some exhausted soldiers contemplated suicide to escape constant suffering.

"We're heading over the St Charles again," MacKim thundered, as he and Ramsay passed a group of civilians.

"When?" Ramsay asked.

"In three days," MacKim said.

They walked on, with MacKim wondering if he was too obvious. He knew that others of Lindsay's Rangers were spreading the same information, each man putting in more details for the spies to report so the French spy-masters could place the pieces together and come up with another ambush.

"I'll buy some of that spruce beer," MacKim said to the seller.

"Can you afford it?" The gaunt-faced woman looked MacKim up and down. "Most of you private soldiers have no money."

"I have enough," MacKim said, "unless you've put the price up."

"It's threepence a gallon," the woman said.

"It was less last time."

"Are you buying or complaining?" the woman asked. "The officers don't complain about the price."

MacKim glanced at Ramsay. "What do you think?"

Ramsay shook his head. "No, Corporal. We won't get to drink all of it before we cross the St Charles, and then somebody will sneak into our quarters and steal it anyway."

The woman shook her head. "When are you crossing the St Charles?"

MacKim glanced around as if searching for a French spy. "Thursday afternoon," he said. "We're going to leave a picket there to surprise the French."

"You're brave men going out there when the Indians are around," the woman said. "But the price is still threepence."

Shaking his head, MacKim walked away, with Ramsay unhappy at his side. "You shouldn't have told her about the picket," he said. "It's meant to be a secret."

"That's the idea," MacKim said. The ale seller was the first person who had shown any interest in the forthcoming expedition. He resolved to watch for her in future.

The small boy was waiting at the barrack-room door with the now expected bottle of spruce beer in his hand. He looked disappointed when he noticed what MacKim was carrying, grabbed his bread and ran. The woman was waiting for him at the street corner. When MacKim shouted "Thank you," she gave a shy half-smile before hurrying the boy away.

"One day, that woman is going to speak to me," MacKim said.

Ramsay nodded. "Yes, Corporal. I wonder if she's the spy?"

MacKim shook his head. "A spy would ask questions, or at least listen. That woman never comes close." Yet he watched her retreating back, unconsciously noting the sway of her hips. "Maybe one day she'll speak," he repeated.

The reconstituted Lindsay's Rangers set out from Quebec on Thursday afternoon. They left shortly after two, fifty men marching single-file across the thick ice, with their snowshoes sounding hollow and their reflections clear on the frozen water.

"Winter's strengthening its grip," Parnell said. "The worst is yet to come."

The forest opposite was dull green, glinting where the light caught the snow.

"Keep five paces apart," Lindsay reminded them, as MacKim watched Kennedy and the new men, wondering how they would cope with conditions across the river. Once again, he stepped into the woods, with his snowshoes padding on the surface. Since their last abortive expedition, General Murray had established a strong fortification immediately beside the passage, with a timber palisade and a section of grenadiers.

"Victory," Sergeant Speakman gave the parole.

"Britannia," came the laconic countersign as a burly grenadier eyed them up. "Where are you boys off to?"

"We're patrolling for the Canadians," Butler replied.

The grenadier gave a gap-toothed grin. "Best of British to you, Rangers. If you don't come back, the Indians will return your heads."

"Aye, no doubt," MacKim said.

The first few hundred yards were easy, with the path well-trodden, and then they passed the outlying pickets and marched on. Once again, MacKim felt the trees close around him, with every bush or shadow hiding a possible enemy. Lindsay's Rangers moved more quietly than a British line regiment, but with more noise than the more experienced Rangers with whom MacKim had served on the previous campaign. Given time, they would improve, but that depended on luck as much as anything else. MacKim knew the Indians would hear them, if any were present.

After an hour, Lindsay called a halt. "This is as far as we go, boys," he said. "We'll establish our base here and send out fighting patrols to search for the enemy."

"We'll post pickets as well," Kennedy growled.

Using their training, the Rangers created a defensive perimeter with logs and hastily dug trenches, while Kennedy posted four pairs of men on picket. Half the men manned the barricades, with Lindsay remaining in charge of the base camp while Kennedy took out patrols in all directions.

"Sergeant Speakman, Corporal MacKim; you are with me," Kennedy said. "The better we know this terrain, the easier it will be to defeat the French."

Ramsay started as some animal dislodged snow from an upper branch, the sound like the thunder of drums through the silent forest.

"We're not the first here." MacKim pointed to the ground, where the distinctive marks of snowshoes showed where men had walked.

Kennedy knelt beside the tracks. "Indians and Canadians," he said and looked up with a twisted grin. "I think."

"Are they here now?" Ramsay looked around nervously.

"I hope not," Kennedy said. "It defeats the purpose of the picket if they see us."

The patrol was uneventful if a strain on stretched nerves, and they returned as the light began to fade.

"We've dug you a nice little nest twenty yards in front," Lindsay said.

"Thank you, sir." Kennedy glanced over the work. The Rangers had created a narrow trench behind a fallen tree and piled snow around as natural camouflage. Even from ten yards away, Lindsay's nest was hard to see.

"Now we have the hard part," Kennedy said cheerfully. "MacKim, you and I remain here, with privates Parnell and Ramsay, both volunteers. The rest will return to Quebec once they have emptied the contents of their pouches."

Mystified, the men handed over what they had carried from

Quebec until a strange pile lay in front of Kennedy. As they worked, MacKim checked the surroundings, touring the pickets to ensure no prowling Indians watched them. The forest remained silent, save for the occasional animal sound and a distant bird.

"You'd best get away, sir," Kennedy said to Lindsay, who was looking nervous. "MacKim and I know what to do here."

"That would be best," Lindsay said. "We're only a burden."

When Lindsay led the Rangers away, MacKim suddenly felt vulnerable.

"Come on, Corporal, we have work to do."

"You lads, keep a sharp watch," MacKim ordered, and Ramsay and Parnell took stations fifteen yards on either flank.

MacKim and Kennedy created four dummies from the pieces of wood and cloth the Rangers had carried. Once the figures were vaguely human, MacKim covered each in a scarlet uniform, complete with the mitred hat of a grenadier, and Kennedy placed ten pounds of gunpowder in a pouch inside the tunic of each dummy.

"There now." Kennedy glanced at the sky. "The last of the daylight is disappearing, boys. Time we got ourselves ready."

Carrying the dummies to the strongpoint that Lindsay had created, Kennedy and MacKim placed each one in a position of defence, with worn-out muskets as weapons.

"Nearly there," Kennedy said. Using a powder-horn, he laid three thin trails of black powder back to the position he had chosen for his small party to spend the night, merging them at one point close to him. "Let's hope the Frenchies don't see that."

"They won't see it in the dark," MacKim said.

"We're going to have a cold night," Kennedy observed, as the four Rangers prepared to wait. They had created a small dug-out, necessarily shallow because of the frozen ground, with fallen trees as protection and branches pulled on top as camouflage. Each man faced a different direction, with the tension brittle in the air. MacKim thought he saw Tayanita standing in the shadow of a bush, blinked, and the vision had vanished.

The light faded and died. A wind grew, whistling through the branches, masking sounds so that the men started at the drip of falling snow and the creak of a tree. Ramsay shifted uneasily until MacKim placed a hand on his shoulder, calming him down.

MacKim found his mind wandering, so he forced himself to concentrate on the world around him, peering into the darkness.

Am I going mad? Has the death of my brother and Tayanita brought me to insanity? I might be a lunatic, for no sane man would volunteer to sit out here inviting an attack by Abenakis and Canadians. Can I regain my sanity? Do I want to? For a sane man would be a poor soldier, never taking any risks, cowering behind cover whenever the fighting started. I thought I saw Tayanita in the trees; it was only a shadow, and the war playing on my nerves.

The bark of a cannon sounded through the dark, with the shot miles from the Rangers' position.

"Sit tight," Kennedy whispered.

The cannon had woken MacKim from his reverie, so he heard the sound. It was faint, but he recognised the scuff of a snowshoe on the ground.

"They're close," he whispered, wishing he could communicate without making a noise.

MacKim saw the forms sliding across the snow, alternatively appearing and disappearing among the trees. He was unsure of the number, guessed at a dozen and tapped his foot against Kennedy's leg.

The lieutenant nodded to signify that he had also seen the enemy.

One Canadian stopped ten yards from where MacKim crouched. For a moment, MacKim saw his face, marked with spiral tattoos, and the scalps that adorned the belt around his waist.

That's the man who murdered Tayanita!

MacKim felt the hatred grip him and nearly rose to attack.

He wondered if his scalp was there, alongside the fine blonde hair that had undoubtedly belonged to a child, perhaps the daughter of a settler. The Canadian moved on, silent in his snowshoes. With his musket in his hands and a knife thrust under his belt, he looked like the predator he was. The squat renegade was next, moving in a half-crouch as he slithered across the snow.

MacKim breathed again. He could feel Ramsay trembling at his back, sensed Parnell's tension, and eased his cold finger onto the trigger of his musket. His hands felt so numb that he wondered if he could press the trigger when the time came. The Canadian nodded towards the false position, lifting a hand to show four fingers, and the raiders moved forward, one man touching a low branch, so a shower of snow descended. Instantly, the whole force froze into inaction, deadly statues in the night.

Kennedy tapped his foot against MacKim's, who passed the signal on to Ramsay. MacKim felt the tension mount further, waiting for Kennedy to make his move. The lieutenant did not rush, but waited until the raiders clustered close to the false position. Hiding his tinder box behind the fallen tree, Kennedy scraped a spark and ignited the trail of powder. Immediately he did so, the raiders heard the sound and saw the flare of powder. Two turned towards the British, eyes gleaming in the powder-light.

"Fire," Kennedy said laconically, although MacKim sensed his tension.

MacKim was ready, with his finger on the trigger and his musket already cocked and aimed at the Canadian. The pan flashed, then the musket roared with a jet of red flame and white smoke from the muzzle. Parnell was a fraction slower, and then Ramsay, with Kennedy last of all. MacKim did not see the results of their ambush, for the raiders scattered, with some leaping into the false position and others running into the forest.

"Keep firing," Kennedy ordered. "Make them believe there are a dozen of us here. Yell your heads off, Rangers!"

MacKim obeyed, loading and firing as fast as possible, with

the movements mechanical after countless hours of parade-ground drills. He heard Parnell muttering quiet curses as he worked alongside him, with Ramsay whimpering slightly as if he fought his fear.

"Shout!" Kennedy repeated his order. "Grenadiers! At the dogs, Grenadiers!"

"Keep it up, lads," MacKim encouraged. "We're paying them back for the last ambush."

The powder trails fizzled and sparked across the snow. Although two died, the third reached its destination, and the ten pounds of black powder within the dummy's tunic exploded. The flare extended to the remaining mannequins, and their powder also blew up with a tremendous roar and a flash so bright, it dazed MacKim and his companions in the concealed position.

"Keep firing!" Kennedy ordered, as the bank of powder smoke rolled over them. "Don't aim, as you won't see anything, just load and fire."

"Come on, you French dogs!" Ramsay shouted. "We're the Rangers! Kennedy's death-dealing Rangers!"

"Lindsay's Rangers," Kennedy corrected.

Loading and firing, the four Rangers blazed into the woods until their night vision returned, and then Kennedy ordered them to cease fire.

"Load, boys," Kennedy said, "but sit tight for a moment. Wait here until I see what's happened." He slithered over the parapet and disappeared into the night.

"Did we beat them?" Ramsay asked. "Have they gone?"

"We don't know yet," MacKim said. "Keep quiet and keep alert." He examined the surrounding forest, taking one section at a time and moving on to the next. He felt the residual heat from the barrel of his musket and loaded automatically, while somewhere in the dark, men were moaning in pain.

"Somebody's coming!" Parnell whispered, fixing his bayonet.

MacKim heard the soft slide of feet on the snow. He took a deep breath and readied his musket.

"Here!" Parnell cocked his musket and brought it smartly to his shoulder. "I see him!"

"Victory," MacKim half-whispered the parole.

"Britannia," Kennedy replied.

"Wait!" MacKim pushed Parnell's barrel down. "That's the lieutenant!"

"There's two of them," Parnell hissed.

MacKim raised his musket and rested his finger on the trigger. "Ramsay! Guard our backs! Parnell, get ready, but don't fire until we see who it is!"

The figures loomed up, vague shapes of darkness against the lesser dark of the night.

"Easy, lads," Kennedy said. "I've got us a prisoner. Time to go."

When MacKim saw the wounded Abenaki, he closed his eyes. He had a vision of Tayanita dying and had to fight the desire to ram his bayonet into the Indian up to the hilt.

"MacKim!" Kennedy urged. "Take the rear."

"Sir!"

"I've scouted around," Kennedy said. "I saw four dead men, or bits of men, and blood trails that indicate that others were injured. Then I found this beauty lying on the ground. He tried to gut me."

MacKim grunted, knowing that Kennedy was relating only part of the story. He could imagine the bloody struggle in the dark, the lithe colonial and the muscular Abenaki warrior, until Kennedy got the better of the encounter and disabled his adversary.

The Abenaki was injured, barely conscious as Kennedy half-carried, half forced him between the trees. They moved quickly, while listening for a return of the enemy, each man except Kennedy checking their surroundings, stopping to look behind them, listening for every alien sound. Twice MacKim dropped to his knees to look behind him, and each time he saw nothing but the trees, looming in the dark.

"How far?" Ramsay asked.

"About half a mile yet," MacKim said. "Keep quiet."

Twice, MacKim heard the soft pad of snowshoes, only to realise it was only the slither of snow falling from a branch, and once a spatter of musketry had them diving for cover.

"It's not near us," MacKim said, hoping the French were not attacking the outpost guarding the causeway.

They moved on, step by step, with the night gradually fading until Kennedy hissed them to a halt.

"The grenadiers' strongpoint is ahead. Wait here. MacKim, guard the prisoner."

The Abenaki lay on the snow, more dead than alive as his blood seeped away. MacKim stood over him, fighting the temptation to use his bayonet.

"Are you all right, Corporal?" Ramsay asked. "You look queer-like."

"I'm all right," MacKim said. "Keep alert. The enemy is as likely to be here as anywhere else."

Kennedy returned within ten minutes. "I had to warn the grenadiers that we were coming," he said. "They're a bit nervous and might have fired on sight."

MacKim nodded and lifted the Abenaki. Over the river, the battlements of Quebec looked like home. He had a last look at the forest, hoping to see Tayanita among the trees, but she was not there. He was alone once more, save for his madness.

8

"Bring him in here," General Murray said, as Kennedy, Parnell, and MacKim dragged in the prisoner. Captain Lindsay already stood beside Murray, gently sipping at a glass of claret.

Even after the surgeons had patched him up, the Abenaki was a sorry sight. Weak from loss of blood, and with a bandage over his chest and left arm, he drew himself to an impressive height and glared at the British.

"Well, my fine fellow," Murray said. "It seems that the fortunes of war have not favoured you." He waited for Kennedy to translate as MacKim and Parnell stood at attention, bayonetted muskets ready if the prisoner tried to escape or attack the general.

The warrior said nothing, staring at Murray in an open challenge.

"With your permission, sir, may I speak to him?"

"Please do, Lieutenant." Murray adjusted his wig slightly as he contemplated the Mohawk.

Kennedy spoke to the prisoner, quietly at first and then with more violence. "I am telling him that the French are defeated, sir."

"Indeed." Murray stood with his back to the fire. "Translate exactly for us, please, Kennedy. I'd like to hear what you are saying, word for word."

"Yes, sir," Kennedy said and hesitated. "They think differently from us, sir. Some of the language may not make sense."

"Word for word, Lieutenant, if you please."

"Yes, sir." Kennedy glanced at Lindsay, who nodded and repeated, "Word for word, Lindsay."

"As you wish, sir," Kennedy said, "I told him that the British were formerly women and now have been altered into men. I said we were as thick all over the country as the trees in the woods."

MacKim watched Murray as Kennedy spoke. The general seemed slightly amused by the lieutenant's words but without any show of dissent.

"Continue, Kennedy." Murray sipped at a glass of French claret.

"I told the Abenaki fellow that the British have taken the Ohio, Niagara, Ticonderoga, and Louisbourg and now lately taken Quebec." Kennedy stopped to draw breath as the prisoner looked curiously at the maps on the wall. "I said that the British would soon eat the remainder of the French in Canada and all the Indians that adhered to them."

"Cannibals, by George," Murray murmured. "I didn't know we had descended so far."

"I meant we would defeat them, sir." Kennedy sounded miserable, as if talking to the general was a greater ordeal than facing Canadians and Indians in the winter-cold woods.

"I gathered that, Lieutenant," Murray said and stopped as the Abenaki began to speak, with his words rolling sonorously around the room.

When the prisoner finished, he lifted his chin in pride and spat directly into the fire.

"What did the rude fellow say, Kennedy?" Murray asked. "Word for word."

Kennedy took a deep breath. "He said, 'You are all deceived. The British cannot eat up the French; the British king's mouth is too little, his jaws too weak, and his teeth not sharp enough. Our father Onontio – that's the Governor of Canada, sir – has told us, and we believe him, that the British, like a thief, have stolen Louisbourg and Quebec from the Great King while his back was turned, and he was looking another way."

"Interesting concept, by God," Murray said. "Continue, Kennedy."

"Yes, sir. The prisoner said that now the Great King has turned his face and sees what the British have done, he is going into their country with a thousand great canoes. He said the Great King's warriors would take the little British king and pinch him till he makes him cry out and give back what he has stolen, as he did ten summers ago, and this your eyes will soon see."

Murray raised his eyebrows. "Well now, could you translate that, Kennedy?"

Kennedy pondered for a moment. "I think the Indians believe that the French will come back to Canada in strength, sir, and try to remove us."

"I see." Murray poured more claret into his glass and topped up Lindsay's. "I've little time for the French or for anything that comes out of France. Ask the fellow if the French have any intention of attacking us in Quebec, Kennedy. Don't bother to translate your words for me."

"Yes, sir." Kennedy spoke to the prisoner again. "He said that the French are fighting for their great king and will soon bring the big guns to batter the walls of the city and eat up all the British here."

"Big guns?" Murray looked concerned. "Which big guns, Kennedy? Does he mean a siege train? Ask him what artillery are the French bringing?"

Kennedy tried again, but the Abenaki clammed up and said no more.

"It's no good, sir. Either he doesn't know any more, or he's not willing to tell us anything."

Murray nodded. "I see."

"I could get him to talk, sir," Kennedy suggested.

"You mean we should torture the fellow?" Murray shook his head. "No, Lieutenant. We'll leave the headhunting, scalping and burning to the Canadians and savages. We are British soldiers and don't resort to such tactics. Lock him in the guardroom for the present."

"Yes, sir," Kennedy said.

"You did well, Lindsay, capturing this man and deceiving the French," Murray said.

"Thank you, sir." Lindsay gave a short bow. "I thought if we spread false intelligence, we could lure the French into an ambush. Give them a taste of their own medicine."

"Quite a novel idea," Murray said and lowered his voice, "although it does prove there are spies within the city. We'll have to improve our security, Lieutenant, and watch what we say in front of the civilians."

MacKim heard no more as he escorted the prisoner outside General Murray's quarters in Fort Louis and into the city.

MacKim saw the woman as he returned to barracks from the guardroom. His mind was busy with Lindsay's words, as the captain claimed the credit for ideas that had originated elsewhere. The woman turned a corner as MacKim approached, but he glimpsed the colourful shawl she wore over her head.

That's Ranald's shawl! That's the shawl that Ranald's sister gave him when he left Inverness.

"Here, you!" MacKim shouted and hurried after the woman. "Come back here!"

The women glanced over her shoulder, lifted her skirt higher and ran, sliding on the frozen slush that covered the ground.

MacKim followed, coming closer with every stride until the woman turned up a narrow alley. Only a few steps behind, MacKim grabbed at the shawl and held tight, bringing the woman to a halt, uncaring that he gripped her hair beneath the material.

"All right, you," MacKim growled. "That shawl is not yours. You stole it from the 78th's barracks."

The woman twisted and tried to back away, her eyes wide in a pinched, hungry face. Shaking her head violently, she replied in French, speaking so rapidly that MacKim had to order her to slow down.

"What did you say?" He felt no sympathy for the woman.

"I didn't steal the shawl." The woman was young and might have been pretty if hardship and hunger had not etched deep lines on her face.

"Then where did you get it?" MacKim shook her roughly.

"I bartered for it." The woman tried to break away, but MacKim's grip was too powerful.

"Where?"

"Over there. I'll take you if you let go."

"Take me." MacKim relaxed his grip, and the woman tried again to escape, as he had anticipated. Grabbing her a second time, MacKim held her arm tightly. "Take me," he repeated, hearing the hard edge in his voice. "Take me, or by God, I'll hand you over to an officer!"

"No!" The woman paled and turned away. She led MacKim to what had once been a beautiful house set within extensive grounds. Now it was a shell, with shattered walls thrusting to the uncaring sky and piles of broken masonry cowering under a covering of snow. The number of footprints around the front door told their own story.

"In there," the woman said.

"Come with me." MacKim pushed the woman ahead of him. If she were leading him into a trap, she would take the first ball.

The building's interior was as stark as the exterior, except for the small crowd of people gathered around a central fire. They looked around when MacKim entered, and some backed away.

"What's happening here?" MacKim shouted, threatening the group with his musket. "Selling stolen property is against the law!"

The half dozen women and two men stared at him, with three pinch-faced children standing as near to the fire as they dared without actually sitting in the flames. MacKim looked around what had once been a splendid room. "Who here stole from the 78th?" He held up the tartan shawl with his anger growing. "Who stole this?"

The crowd stared at him and began speaking in French, so rapidly that MacKim could not understand a single word.

"You!" MacKim pointed to a woman who stood in the centre of the crowd. "I know you! You sold me a gallon of spruce beer. Tell me who robbed the barracks of the 78th, the Highlanders."

The beer seller started, shook her head and spoke in a torrent of French. Realising that MacKim was alone, the two male civilians began to recover their courage and moved towards him.

"Take one more step, and I'll spit both of you," MacKim snarled, meaning every word.

"Bread!" The little boy ran into the room and pointed to MacKim. "Bread," he said again as his mother followed.

"What's happening here?" The boy's mother pulled back her son and held him close.

"I'm looking for a thief," MacKim said, glad to calm things down now his initial anger was diminishing.

The mother frowned. "Onc of the British soldiers who looted our houses, perhaps? Or the British generals who wish to steal our entire country?" She was handsome rather than beautiful, with strong features around a sharp nose and clear eyes.

"The thief I seek stole this shawl from a friend of mine." MacKim could not acknowledge the justice of the woman's remarks.

"You have your friend's shawl back," the woman said. "You should be happy. I have a dozen British grenadiers living in the house they stole from me."

MacKim lowered his musket, knowing he would not use it against people who scrabbled to survive. "I'm looking for a piece of beadwork," he said. "It's not large or valuable, but it means a lot to me."

"Why?" The woman turned her clear eyes onto him with a gaze as penetrating as any MacKim had experienced.

"A woman gave it to me," he said.

"A woman?" The clear eyes nearly smiled as they assessed him.

"If you find it, let me know." MacKim found himself uncomfortable under the woman's scrutiny. He gave a little bow. "And thank you for the spruce beer."

"It keeps the scurvy at bay," the woman said. "As army bread fights starvation, Corporal MacKim."

"You know my name?"

"Hugo asked who you were," the woman said. "Corporal MacKim sounds better than the Bread Highlander."

"Hugo is your son," MacKim said. By now, he had forgotten why he had entered the house and ignored the crowd around the fire.

"I know," the woman agreed solemnly.

"He's a fine boy," MacKim said. "I was wondering what his mother calls herself."

The woman backed away as if afraid where the conversation might lead. "She calls herself Madame Claudette Leclerc."

MacKim bowed again clumsily. "Madame Leclerc," he said. Attempting to be polite after years in a barrack-room was not easy.

"Mama." Hugo was looking up at his mother, evidently desperate to speak, but she hushed him with a shake of her head.

"Come along, Hugo," Mrs Leclerc said. "It is time we were gone."

"But Mama," Hugo said. "We always stay here longer, and the Bread Highlander is here."

"Come along." Mrs Leclerc hustled him out of the door, leaving MacKim feeling isolated in a room full of Canadian civilians.

"Pardon me," MacKim said and backed away. If he was no closer to finding the barrack-room thief, at least he had Ranald's shawl, and he had seen the Canadian woman's face and learned her name.

9

The sound of musketry echoed from the low clouds, muted by distance.

"Something's happening." MacKim peered over the parapet of the Diamond Battery at the very corner of Quebec's defences. Only the distant stars penetrated the intense dark.

"Somewhere," Butler said. "Not in our parish, though. That was well upstream."

"I thought we had conquered this country," Ramsay complained. "Don't the French know that we beat them?"

"Maybe they haven't learned yet," Parnell said. "Maybe we have to teach them all over again."

MacKim nodded. "Lieutenant Kennedy is the man for that," he said.

It was two days before the news filtered through that the Royal Navy had sent a small bomb-ketch upriver with ammunition and stores for the Quebec garrison. The bomb-ketch had become iced in, and the French had attacked. Although the crew tried to defend themselves, the French overwhelmed them, killed or captured the crew and looted the vessel.

The news depressed the already suffering garrison as they

shivered on duty and attempted to fend off scurvy and frostbite at night.

"This isn't war anymore," Butler said. "It's organised theft and murder. We destroy and loot their homes, and they do the same to us. We're not soldiers, we are brigands, and we'll continue until there is nothing left in Canada but a wasteland."

"They took the cannon and powder barrels from the bomb-ketch," Parnell said. "I heard that the French are short of powder."

"That's as well for us," MacKim said. "Otherwise, they would be bombarding us as we did them last summer."

The men were quiet as they remembered the British cannonade of Quebec that had reduced much of the city to rubble and destroyed the homes of most of the inhabitants. Nobody wished to be on the receiving end of such a bombardment.

"Thank God the French don't have a siege train here," Ramsay said.

"Not yet, anyway," Parnell grunted.

General Murray had the same fears, for he called Lindsay to his quarters and, later that day, Lindsay called together his Rangers.

"Well, men," Lindsay said as they gathered around him, a half-circle of strained faces under the rough cover of a repaired house. "We have been on two operations so far. On the first, we fought off a French ambush and brought most of the men back safely to Quebec. On the second, we ambushed the French, caused them some casualties and brought back a prisoner."

The Rangers listened without comment. MacKim glanced at Kennedy, who kept his face expressionless.

"Now General Murray has given us another task, the most difficult yet, but I know I can rely on you to follow my leadership and bring more success and lustre to the name of Lindsay's Rangers."

If Lindsay expected wild cheering, he would have been disappointed, for the men stood as they were, listening without comment.

"As you know, the French captured a bomb-ketch downriver from here," Lindsay said, "and stole the guns and ammunition. We don't know what they intend to do with either, so General Murray has given us the task of finding them and blowing up the gunpowder." He gave a wry smile. "The French are short of powder, so without it, the guns are just so much scrap metal."

"When do we leave, sir?" Sergeant Speakman asked.

"An hour before dawn tomorrow," Lindsay replied. "First, we will go to the site of the piracy, and then we will follow the trail the French must have left."

"They'll have a few days' start on us, sir," Speakman said.

"Yes." Lindsay replied so quickly that MacKim wondered if the sergeant's questions and the captain's answers were rehearsed to prevent anybody else talking. "But they'll be carrying gunpowder and dragging cannon. They will move slowly, and we move fast." He smiled at the men. "Remember, lads, we're Lindsay's Rangers, the best of the best, and we'll find glory out there."

"Here we go again." Parnell checked his flints and added a final spot of oil to the lock of his musket.

"Remember, we're Lindsay's Rangers," Butler said and spat on the ground. "That's for you, Captain glorious Lindsay."

MacKim raised his voice. "That's enough of that, Butler." Although he agreed with Butler's sentiments, he could not allow seditious talk in the ranks. "Everybody ensure they have all their kit, eighty cartridges, spare flints, bread and a full water bottle."

The Rangers checked, some automatically, others with care. MacKim nodded to Ramsay, the youngest and most nervous man there.

"All right, Ramsay?"

"Yes, Corporal."

"Right, lads. Look after each other."

With Captain Lindsay marching at their head and Lieutenant Kennedy at the rear, the Rangers, fifty strong, marched out of Quebec in the quiet of pre-dawn. Each man carried his musket and any other weapon he deemed fit, with eighty cartridges, a blanket and sufficient provisions for four days in the forest. After that, they would have to fend for themselves or steal from whatever farmhouses they chanced to come across.

As they left the city, MacKim looked behind him. Quebec's streets were deserted, with no civilians and only a few soldiers as they changed the guard. The flagpole on the citadel was bare, with no flag to prove ownership over the once-proud capital of New France.

For a second, MacKim saw Tayanita walking beside Captain Lindsay, then he blinked, and the vision was gone.

I am going mad, he told himself.

Crossing the St Lawrence on the ice, they headed downriver, travelling in easy stages over land that was theoretically under British control, yet where the inhabitants could change their allegiance as soon as the fortunes of war turned.

The bomb-ketch lay on her side in the iced river, with her two masts at an acute angle. MacKim could see the ugly stains on her deck and the scars left by gunfire. A litter of debris led from the stricken vessel into the scrubby woodland.

"That's a sad sight," Ramsay said. "I don't like to see a ship like that."

"The Frenchies left us an easy trail to follow." MacKim indicated the ground, where the passage of hundreds of feet and a dozen guns was evident. "The French must have brought sledges to carry the guns."

"They were well prepared," Parnell said. "We all thought Pikestaff had flattened them last year." He shook his head. "Nothing like. The Chevalier de Levis is a tough fighter."

"There's the trail." Lindsay spoke loudly. "Lieutenant

Kennedy, you take the van with ten men. I will follow with the main body."

"Yes, sir," Kennedy said and quickly picked ten men, with MacKim as the NCO. They moved ahead rapidly, following the broad trail the French had left as they pushed into the forest. Twice they passed farms, one vacated in the late fighting for Quebec, and the second inhabited.

"*Qui est là?*" ("Who is there?") The challenge showed the farmer was wary and alert.

"*Un ami*!" MacKim replied after Kennedy hesitated.

"I didn't know you spoke French," Kennedy said.

"Yes, sir," MacKim said.

"*Qui êtes-vous?*" ("Who are you?") the farmer asked. "*Nous sommes nombreux, tous armés! Restez à l'écart*!" ("There are many of us, all armed! Keep clear!")

"We're British soldiers," MacKim called, "passing by. We mean you no harm." He translated the farmer's words to Kennedy, adding, "The farmer's scared."

"So would I be, with Frenchies, Indians and British redcoats rampaging around," Kennedy said drily.

They moved past the farm, with Kennedy sending Ramsay back to keep Lindsay informed about the nervous farmer. Dogs barked from a small hamlet, where the church steeple pointed hopefully in a quest for peace, as they moved on. The daylight strengthened and the trail was clear as a highway before them. The sledge marks were deep in the snow, proving the vehicles were heavily laden.

"How many French do you think there are?" Ramsay asked.

"Sufficient to overpower the crew of a bomb-ketch and drag the guns away," MacKim answered. "I'd say a hundred or more." He gestured to the footprints at the side of the main trail. "A mixture of Canadians and Indians in snowshoes and regular soldiers in boots."

Kennedy gestured MacKim to his side. "If I were the French

commander," he said, "I'd know the British would send a force after me. Don't you agree?"

"Yes, sir," MacKim said.

"If you were the French commander, MacKim, what would you do?"

MacKim was not used to an officer asking his advice. Low-ranking soldiers in the British Army were not encouraged to think; their job was to obey orders immediately and without question. "I'd lay a false trail if I could," MacKim said, "and I'd leave an ambush or two for the British."

Kennedy nodded. "We think alike, MacKim. Keep your eyes open."

"I could scout in front, sir." MacKim knew that by making a suggestion, he was leaving himself open to a stinging rebuke or a charge of insolence.

"Be careful, MacKim," Kennedy replied, accepting the offer. "Take somebody with you. Two pairs of eyes are better than one."

"Yes, sir," MacKim pondered for a moment before selecting Parnell. He did not particularly like the man, but knew he was as good a backwoodsman as any in the company.

"Are you trying to get me killed?" Parnell glowered at MacKim as they moved in front of the forward party.

"I'm trying to save us all from the French," MacKim said.

Even twenty paces ahead of Kennedy, the atmosphere felt more menacing. The trees seemed hostile, as if they sheltered a hundred predatory eyes and fifty Abenakis were waiting to pounce on them at every twist of the path.

"Look," Parnell nodded ahead. "The trail splits here."

Parnell was correct. They had entered an area of thin forest, with fewer trees and where the ground undulated in a series of small ridges. The French force had divided into two, with one set of sledge-and-footprints heading south and west and the other continuing doggedly west.

"Clever buggers, the French," MacKim said. He knelt to

examine the trail. "If I were the French, I'd leave an ambush here to shoot at us as we decide which trail to follow."

"Jesus save us," Parnell blasphemed, staring around him. "They'll be watching us now."

"Aye," MacKim said, "keep your voice low. The French will want more than a couple of scouts. They'll wait until we call up the main body and then attack. That's what I would do."

"What will we do?" Parnell half-cocked his musket. MacKim saw a sheen of perspiration appear on his face, despite the cold.

"I'll wait here," MacKim said. "You report back to Kennedy; tell him what we've found and that there's a possible ambush."

Parnell moved at once, leaving MacKim alone. He moved back slowly until he found a defensive site behind a tree, knelt and waited for Kennedy to appear. He saw a deer nose through the forest, stepping daintily. It stopped on the larger of the French trails, sniffed at the air and continued, stepping wide of MacKim's position.

That deer is not afraid, MacKim told himself. *Maybe I am wrong. Perhaps there is no ambush.*

"Have you seen any French?" Kennedy slipped beside MacKim, peering into the trees.

"Not a whisper," MacKim said. "Only a deer."

Kennedy nodded, breathing hard. "It's unlikely a deer would pass close to an ambush site, even an Indian one."

"I could scout ahead, sir," MacKim suggested.

Kennedy looked along both trails, then produced a small telescope from his pack and studied the trees. "No. If the French have placed an ambush, they'll let you pass unmolested. I don't think they're here. We follow the left-hand path."

"Yes, sir." MacKim agreed with Kennedy's choice. The ruts were deeper on the left path, so the sledges held heavy objects, such as cannon.

"Butler, Ramsay," Kennedy said. "Go and inform Captain Lindsay that we're taking the left-hand fork."

The two men left at once, running back along the track.

Moving cautiously, MacKim and Parnell returned to the front of the column, examining every copse and every dense patch of woodland as they led Kennedy's forward party.

By nightfall, they had travelled fifteen miles without sight of a Frenchman, and they camped for the night on a wooded knoll. Lindsay sent out pairs of sentries in all directions as they settled for the night.

"MacKim," Kennedy said quietly. "You are unlike any British soldier I've ever met."

MacKim nodded. "I am what I am, sir," he said. "I am what life has made me."

"You're Scottish," Kennedy said.

"Yes, sir."

Kennedy produced a pipe, stuffed tobacco into the bowl, drew on it until the tobacco glowed red and offered it to MacKim.

"Thank you, sir, but I don't indulge." *I won't smoke again until I kill that Canadian.*

"Very wise," Kennedy said. "It's a filthy habit." He puffed contentedly for a minute. "So what brought you into the army, MacKim?"

"Simon Fraser of Lovat was raising the regiment, sir, so I joined."

"Ah." Kennedy blew out a ribbon of blue smoke. "Loyalty is a noble thing, MacKim."

"Yes, sir," MacKim agreed.

Kennedy was silent for a few moments. "Did he repay your loyalty, this Fraser of Lovat? Your chief, isn't he?"

MacKim contemplated his immediate past. "I am not sure what his position is now, sir, and I am not sure if he repaid anything. He is the colonel of my regiment, the 78th Foot."

Kennedy smiled around the stem of his pipe. "The world changes, doesn't it? Old certainties end, ancient loyalties fade, and a new world dawns every morning."

"Yes, sir." MacKim was unsure what Kennedy meant. Life in

the ranks had not prepared him for thought. For the past few years, survival and revenge had dominated his life; philosophical musings were alien to him.

"What do you plan to do after the war, MacKim?"

"I don't know, sir," MacKim said. "Sometimes I think the war will last forever, with fighting and killing and then more fighting."

"It feels like that, doesn't it?" Kennedy said. "We thought the French would capitulate after the fall of Quebec, but instead, they rallied and besieged us within our conquest. It seems as if they're determined to hold onto New France. The Chevalier de Levis is as good a soldier as we'll ever meet."

"The French are tough men, sir," MacKim said.

Kennedy's face darkened. "Well, by God, we won't allow them to retain Canada." He removed the pipe from his mouth and added more tobacco, tamping it down with a furious thumb. "You haven't lived on the frontier when the Indians are on the warpath, MacKim. Until you do, you won't know what true savagery is. They torture, murder, scalp and kill without any concept of mercy, and those they enslave are the most unfortunate of all."

MacKim glanced at Kennedy, aware the lieutenant had dropped his mask to allow the real man to emerge. "Who did you lose, sir?"

Kennedy's eyes were dark with suffering when he looked at MacKim. "My mother, back in '48, and my father three days later. My wife in '58 and my daughter."

MacKim drew in his breath. "That's bad, sir."

"It's bad," Kennedy said. "On the frontier, we live with the constant fear of savages raiding us, and when the French wars start, the danger increases." He puffed at his pipe with his eyes far away. "Kings and princes and politicians think they are so clever when they start their wars and move their little flags from one place to another. They claim this border fortress and that piece of territory, without any idea what it's like on the ground, on the bitter frontier."

"Where in New Hampshire are you from, sir?"

"Originally Londonderry, although we moved to the back-country when I was young," Kennedy said. "It's the most beautiful land in the world, MacKim, and there is so much potential there. We don't have clan chiefs, lords or belted earls telling us what to do. Each man is his own master, and we can carve out our lives from the wilderness."

"Except for the French and the Indians," MacKim said.

"Yes," Kennedy said. "The Abenaki, the Ottowas and the French. Three nations I would grind into powder."

MacKim nodded. "Yes, sir." He did not share his experiences. Tayanita's death was too raw and the murder of his brother too distant.

Kennedy finished his pipe, tapped out the ashes and glanced at MacKim. "You don't talk much, do you, Corporal? You'd be a good man to tell a secret to and know it was safe."

"I've not a great deal to say, sir. I'm only a soldier."

Kennedy smiled. "Are you indeed?" He rose. "Best check the pickets, Corporal, and settle in for the night. We have Frenchmen to catch tomorrow."

❧

RISING BEFORE DAWN, THEY MOVED OFF, MARCHING QUICKLY as they followed the trail. Once again, the French split up, this time with both tracks showing deeply laden sledges.

"They're being very clever," Kennedy said as he examined the tracks. "Either both groups have cannon with them, or they're trying to fool us. Scout around and see what you can find."

Leaving six men in a defensive perimeter, Kennedy led the remaining four in circuits, each time expanding the radius to take in a larger area of ground.

"Sir," Butler said. "Drag marks."

Something had flattened the snow in a series of deep, ragged grooves, each one three feet or so wide.

"What's happened here, I wonder?" Kennedy pondered.

"Tree trunks." MacKim pointed to fragments of bark and loose twigs at the side. "The French have hauled fallen trees onto sledges to weigh them down."

"Clever people, the French," Kennedy said. "I wonder who is in command of this little expedition." He examined the tracks. "More importantly, I wonder which trail has the cannon and which is false?"

"They both look the same," Parnell said. "I'd say they're about twelve hours ahead of us."

Kennedy nodded. "Twelve hours hauling a heavy load. I'll wager a fast-moving man could catch them in two hours, with luck." He looked up. "I want two volunteers, one to follow each trail. Run ahead, ignore everything until you discover which French convoy carries cannon and which has firewood."

MacKim was on his feet. "I'll go, sir," he said.

A man named Van Dyke also stood. "And me, sir."

"Well done. MacKim, take the left trail, Van Dyke, take the right. Don't get caught and don't get involved in a fight. I want intelligence, not casualties."

MacKim nodded as Van Dyke tapped his musket.

"I'll have Captain Lindsay wait here until one of you returns," Kennedy said.

"Yes, sir," MacKim said and set off at a fast trot. He hoped that the French had not set an ambush on the trail, but if so, it would be closer to their convoy, so the ambushers would not lose touch with the main body. That meant he had at least an hour's travelling before he needed to worry.

As he hurried, slowed by his snowshoes, MacKim sensed somebody was in front of him. He saw nobody but knew that Tayanita was there, keeping him company.

I haven't forgotten you, he promised. *I'll even the score.*

The trail was easy to follow, yet as he moved, MacKim

looked ahead and left and right. A lone British scout would be an easy target, possibly too tempting for an Indian or Canadian to ignore. After an hour, MacKim slowed down and knelt to inspect the ground. The grooves left by the sledge were pronounced, with the edges still sharp, well defined and obviously recent.

You're not far ahead now, MacKim said to himself. *If I were the French commander, I'd place my ambush soon. Well, you won't get the chance to kill me, my friend.*

Leaving the track, MacKim slid into the trees and moved in a wide circle. If the French were in ambush, they'd be on one side of the main track, ready to fire a volley and then charge as the British were in disarray. MacKim moved two hundred yards into the woods and then headed roughly in the direction of the trail, stopping to check his surroundings. The terrain was rugged, with a series of wooded gulleys filled with soft snow, so even with snowshoes, MacKim sunk ankle-deep, slowing him down.

After five more minutes, he stopped. Voices drifted towards him, speaking French and Abenaki. He heard somebody laugh, then a curse, and he moved on, slower, sliding from tree to tree and watching all around in case the French had scouting parties on the flanks. The ground rose to a hillock, crowned with tall trees. For a moment, MacKim was tempted to climb up, but the position was so prominent that he knew the French would have placed a picket on top.

Avoiding the hillock, MacKim slid on, found a sheltered spot beneath a tree and waited for the French to pass. Five minutes later, he saw them, two laden sledges and a dozen men, all moving around and tramping hard on the ground.

They're making themselves appear to be a larger force, MacKim realised. Both sledges only held tree trunks. *This is the decoy convoy, and Van Dyke is following the real one.*

With no reason to remain, MacKim made his way back. He remembered one of Major Robert Rogers' cardinal rules never to return by the same route and forced himself on a long but possibly safer detour in an even larger circle. He moved quickly, aware that the French would be unlikely to place an ambush on a decoy.

Tayanita was back with him, invisible, yet MacKim sensed her presence. He blinked to remove her, shook his head and swore.

You're not there, Tayanita. I know you're not there, and I am imagining things. The image remained until MacKim smelled her hair and felt the touch of her hand.

Oh, dear God in heaven, don't allow the madness to overcome me.

10

"Sir." MacKim came to attention as Lindsay stepped towards him.

"Well, MacKim?"

"That's the decoy convoy, sir. There are two sledges carrying logs and less than twenty men."

"I thought as much," Lindsay said. "We've wasted enough time here kicking our heels." He raised his voice. "On your feet, men, and follow the Frenchies."

"Tricky devil, whoever commands these French," Kennedy said. "Come on, boys, we're in the van again!"

The column moved on, faster now, knowing they had lost time while checking out the divide in the trail.

"Has Van Dyke come back yet?" MacKim looked over the ranks, identifying each man.

"Not yet," Parnell said.

"Shall I run ahead and find him, sir?" MacKim asked Kennedy.

"No." Kennedy shook his head. "You've done enough for one day. He'll return by and by, and he'll be pleased to see us. Double, lads!"

The advance guard speeded up, marching as fast as possible

with snowshoes on their feet. It was nearly dark before they found Van Dyke.

"There's something on the trail ahead," a Connecticut man named Waite reported.

"What sort of something?" Kennedy asked.

"I am not sure, sir. It's in the middle of the track."

"Easy, boys, spread out," Kennedy ordered. "Tree all until I have a look."

"Tree all" was one of Major Robert Rogers' orders that every man was to find cover among the trees. MacKim settled down in the shelter of a fir, checked his flint was sharp and cocked his musket. He watched as Kennedy scouted ahead, moving slowly and looking on both sides in case of an ambush.

"Oh, dear God," Kennedy said. "It's Van Dyke."

The French, or their Indian allies, had captured Van Dyke, tortured and killed him. They had placed his head, minus the scalp, eyes and nose, on a stake in the middle of the path.

"The French bastards!" Waite gripped his musket until his knuckles gleamed white.

"Bloody savages!" Ramsay said.

"Come on." Butler half rose, shaking with anger. "Let's get at them!"

"Easy, boys," Kennedy calmed them down. "The French want us to get angry and charge ahead. They're trying to unsettle us. Remember your training, move fast and watch for ambushes."

"What about Dykie? We can't leave him like that," Butler said truculently.

"No." Kennedy nodded. "We'll bury him here."

MacKim was not sure if Kennedy had made the correct choice. He understood that the men's morale would suffer if the Rangers failed to bury Van Dyke's remains, but the advance lost precious time, allowing the French to creep closer to their destination. The Rangers clustered close to the grave, where the NCOs interred Van Dyke's head with all the solemnity they could muster while two men stood watch in case of ambush.

Kennedy murmured a few words over the grave, and then the advance continued, with the Rangers angry, hoping to meet the French to gain their revenge.

"Stay alert," Kennedy warned. He glanced at MacKim. "Get in front, Corporal. You know what to look for."

MacKim nodded and moved forward. He was tired after the long day, but also more experienced in this type of warfare than many of his companions. He searched for the signs, keeping his musket ready, padding slowly over the snow.

The silence alerted him. Even in the deep snow of winter, there should be sounds; the flutter of a distant bird, the brush of snow as a deer passed by, the rustle of a small animal. The absence of sound indicated that something was wrong.

MacKim sank to a crouch and moved off the trail, searching his surroundings. He could nearly feel the predatory eyes on him as his heart-rate increased and cold sweat trickled down his spine. He knew the French, or Canadians and Indians were waiting, although he could see nothing.

I don't mind dying, but not tied to an Indian torture stake as they burn me slowly to death. I can withdraw now and report to Kennedy that I think there is an ambush, or I can carry on and see what's ahead, knowing the Indians are between me and any support.

No. I was wrong last time; I must make sure.

Lifting his musket, MacKim shouted, "I see you!" and fired, with the report of the shot hideously loud in the silent forest. He began to load at once, trying to ignore everything around him as he ripped open the cartridge, poured the priming powder in the pan and then tipped the remainder down the barrel. He was vaguely aware of the chorus of yells from all around and was ramming down the ball when the warriors erupted from the trees.

"Well, at least you can't scalp me!" MacKim said, lifting the musket to his shoulder. "Come on, you savages! I've got a ball for the first and a bayonet for the next!" Strangely, he felt no fear. If he lived, he lived, and if he died, then his death did not matter.

MacKim fired, with the powder-smoke momentarily blinding him as a gust of wind blew it into his eyes. He looked away, blinking, and reached for his bayonet. Years of training ensured he clicked it in place and stood on guard, ready to kill.

"Tayanita!"

The volley came from behind him, with the shots hammering into the warriors, downing two of them.

"I thought you were in trouble." Kennedy appeared at MacKim's side, with a pistol in each hand and a faint smile on his face. "I thought I'd find your head at the end of a stake."

"You would have if you'd been two minutes later," MacKim said. "Thank you, sir."

"Thank me when we're disposed of these fellows," Kennedy said, firing one pistol and then the other.

"Yes, sir." MacKim reloaded and aimed at a brawny warrior with a yellow-painted face.

As the Rangers formed a circle around their lieutenant, with half firing and the others loading, the attackers melted away. MacKim glanced at the tall Canadian with a tattooed face who looked directly at him before vanishing into the gloom.

"That's him." MacKim jabbed his bayonet in the Canadian's direction. "That's the leader; I'll wager my soul on it!"

"Load, boys," Kennedy ordered. "How the devil do you know that, MacKim?"

"I saw him when the French ambushed our first operation," MacKim said and paused as a memory came to him. He remembered Tayanita falling, with her blood spraying over the ground and forming a pink film in the air. He remembered lying prone with somebody straddling him, sawing at his scalp.

"Are you all right, Corporal?" Kennedy asked.

"Yes, sir," MacKim said. "I saw him before that as well. That's the man who scalped me."

Kennedy stared at MacKim for what seemed a long minute. "Are you sure, Corporal?"

"Yes, sir," MacKim said. "I'm sure. That's the man who scalped me and who led the party who murdered Tayanita."

"Maybe the least said about that episode, the better," Kennedy said, "I'm aware of the rumours."

"Yes, sir," MacKim said, with his mind full of the tattooed Canadian. "I want to kill him, sir."

"I'll bet you do, Corporal," Kennedy said. "I bet you do." He raised his voice. "Come on, lads, let's push on."

"I'll be with you in a moment, sir," Parnell said, kneeling beside a man he had killed. As MacKim watched, Parnell drew a circle on the man's head with his knife and ripped off the scalp. "A trophy," he said, tucking the bloody scalp beneath his belt.

None of the Rangers commented. In this savage frontier war, the normal rules did not apply, and men did what they thought appropriate.

Kennedy sent men to check the surrounding trees, broke the Indians' muskets and ordered the Rangers to move on. They advanced in extended formation, each man protecting his neighbour and examining the trees as they passed.

"The ruts are sharper, sir," Parnell observed five minutes later. "They're fresh."

"We're catching them," Kennedy agreed. "We'll meet their rearguard soon. Parnell, Waite, go out on the left flank and see what you can see. Butler and Ramsay, take the right. Go wide." He glanced at the small area of sky he could see between the trees. "It will be dark soon, so be careful."

"Yes, sir." The Rangers moved out, long-striding into the trees. With the example of Van Dyke fresh in their minds, they did not need the reminder to be careful.

"Form a defensive perimeter," Kennedy ordered, indicating a slight rise at the side of the trail. The Rangers dug themselves in, ate a third of whatever rations they had left and prepared for a long night.

She was back again. Tayanita stood outside the defensive

perimeter, watching MacKim with a quizzical smile on her face. She shook her head, sending her long black hair across her face.

"What are you trying to say, Tayanita?" MacKim asked. "I don't understand. I know you're trying to tell me something."

"What was that, Corporal?" Kennedy asked.

MacKim realised he had spoken his thoughts. "Nothing, sir. I was just thinking out loud."

Kennedy raised his eyebrows and looked away as MacKim wondered again if he was tipping over from sanity to madness.

Parnell returned first, out of breath and agitated. "The French are two miles ahead, sir," he said. "They're in a strong encampment at the banks of the St Lawrence, with artillery redoubts and about three hundred men."

"So many!" Kennedy looked over his handful of tired, hungry Rangers. "I didn't think there would be half that number. How many are Canadians?"

"I'd say a hundred and fifty are French regulars, sir, with the remainder Indians and Canadians."

Kennedy sucked at a gap between his front teeth. "Get some rest, lads. We'll move off at two in the morning and hit them before they're ready. Did you find any ambushes?"

"Nary a one, sir. And here's Ramsay now."

"Sir!" Ramsay and Butler threw simultaneous salutes, with Butler speaking. "The Frenchies have a strong picket a mile down the path on the right-hand side. I saw about twenty men, mostly Abenakis, with some Canadians as well."

"Thank you, gentlemen," Kennedy said. "We'll avoid that route."

Lindsay arrived then with the remainder of the Rangers and listened as Kennedy explained his plan, before nodding assent.

Sergeant Speakman shook his head. "Three hundred is a lot of French, sir, and we're less than fifty strong, even if Captain Lindsay agrees."

"I'm aware of our numbers, Sergeant." Lindsay had an edge

to his voice. "Lieutenant Kennedy and I have discussed the plan, and we will pursue it tomorrow. Now, grab some sleep."

MacKim found he could sleep. While others lay awake, he rolled up in his blanket in the snow, trusted the sentries and allowed his mind to drift. He wondered why he felt more at peace while on campaign than in barracks, tried to push his incipient insanity from his mind and woke when Sergeant Speakman shook him.

"Come on, MacKim, it's time to go."

"How can you sleep when the Indians are all around?" Parnell asked, with his eyes like hollow pits in his unshaven face.

MacKim shook his head. "How can't you sleep, Parnell? Lying awake only makes you tired and less able to fight." He munched on army-issue bread, as hard as granite and cold as snow.

"You're crazy-mad, MacKim." Parnell turned away.

"So I've been told." MacKim tried to sound nonchalant, although the accusation augmented his already troubled mind. Had he already tipped over the edge of reason? He shook away the thought and tried to concentrate on the day ahead. He checked the lock of his musket, ensured his flint was sharp and cartridge box easy to open, tested the edge of his bayonet and hatchet and said a prayer.

"Oh Lord, I may too busy this day to remember you, but please do not forget me. If this is my last day, please make my death quick, and allow me to meet the man who murdered Tayanita before I go."

"Do you think the Lord will listen to the likes of you?" Butler asked.

"The Lord listens to everybody, saints and sinners alike," Ramsay told him solemnly.

MacKim saw Kennedy in the background, with his mouth twisted in a cynical sneer.

The Rangers stumbled into the night, with Parnell showing the way and MacKim one of the flank guards. In the dark, every tree assumed the shape of a lurking Indian, and every soft fall of snow sounded like the feet of a Canadian rifleman. Without the broad track to follow, walking was more difficult, slowing them down, testing their patience and stamina.

"Two miles? It seems more like twenty," Ramsay complained, until Speakman shushed him into silence.

"Here!" Parnell lifted a hand, and the Rangers stopped, each man readying his musket in case of an ambush.

The noises drifted over to MacKim; the sound of men's voices, the soft slither of sledges on snow and a scraping sound he could not identify.

"Down!" Lindsay ordered and crawled forward with a telescope. He ascended a small ridge that afforded him a view ahead, extended his telescope and lay still. The Rangers waited, with the tension mounting.

Lindsay returned, looking agitated. "They're crossing the river," he said quietly. "The French are taking the guns and stores across the ice. They've stolen a march on us."

Kennedy nodded. "Hit them now," he said. "Hit them as they cross. They don't know how many of us there are."

MacKim listened. The thoughts of a private soldier would not be welcome as the officers deliberated tactics.

"The longer we wait here, the more French will cross," Kennedy urged. "Hit them now. The French don't know we're only fifty strong. If we make a lot of noise, cheer and yell like an entire battalion, we can unsettle them."

Lindsay bit his lip, a man burdened by responsibility. He looked around the expectant Rangers, then raised his head to listen as the noise from the French increased.

"Move forward slowly." Lindsay seemed to agonise over the order.

"Come on, boys, you heard the captain. Remember Van Dyke," Kennedy said.

The Rangers eased forward, some nervously, others keen to fight. MacKim encouraged his section, winked at a scared-looking Ramsay and stepped in front. He was as prepared as he could ever be.

Parnell led the Rangers to the top of a low, wooded ridge, from where they looked down on the French position. Fortunately, the French had illuminated the area with a circle of torches, which cast flickering, if smoky, light over the scene.

"How the devil can we damage that?" Lindsay said.

The French had constructed a rudimentary fort at the end of the track, with timber barricades and log-and-earth redoubts for artillery. One cannon stood in place, with a group of bored-looking artillerymen huddled beside a fire. Two sentinels stood beside the open gate, one smoking a pipe and the other pulling his greatcoat closer to him against the biting cold. Beside the fort, scores of men were busily hauling a dozen sledges loaded with artillery and stores. The river broadened here, with an island halfway across, well wooded.

"We're out of musket range, sir," Kennedy said. "We'll have to move closer."

Lindsay nodded. "We can't do anything from up here."

The Rangers crossed the summit ridge, crawling to avoid being seen for, even at night, the Indian allies of the French had sharp eyes. With Lindsay and Kennedy in the lead, they descended the far side of the slope, closer to the fort.

"There are too many of them," Lindsay said. "We'll have to report their numbers to General Murray."

"It will take us two days to reach Quebec," Kennedy reminded him. "By that time, the French will be long gone, and we'll have lost an opportunity."

"No, Lieutenant," Lindsay said. "We can't fight these odds."

MacKim felt the tension between the two officers. The senior officer's decision would have ended the discussion in any regular British regiment, but the Rangers were more free-thinking. Kennedy glared at Lindsay for ten seconds and then raised his voice in a wild shout. "Come on, men! Follow me!" Standing up, he ran towards the fort.

"Stand firm!" Lindsay ordered, but MacKim and the Rangers of the forward party were already pounding down the slope behind Kennedy. Without a preliminary volley or any other warning, the sudden rush took the defenders by surprise.

"Into the fort!" Kennedy ordered and ran straight for the open gate.

Too late, the sentries looked up at the explosion of men charging towards them. One shouted a challenge and lowered the musket from his shoulder while the second tried to pull the gate shut on his own.

Kennedy rammed the butt of his musket into the face of the first sentry, while Parnell clubbed the second and then ran into the fort. The majority of the Rangers followed, in a long ribbon of determined men. MacKim heard Lindsay shout a futile order.

"Stand, Rangers!" Lindsay roared.

The French inside the fort gobbled in astonishment as the Rangers appeared. MacKim knocked an unarmed regular to the ground and looked around for the tattooed Canadian. Kennedy shot one man, then ran up the basic ladder to the timber walkway within the palisade.

"Come on, boys!" Kennedy shouted, pushing a startled sentry over the other side and grabbing his musket. "Sergeant Speakman! Round up the French in the fort. MacKim, close the gate!"

MacKim ran to the gate and pushed it shut, calling over Ramsay to help him drop the reinforcing bar into its sockets. He hoped the tattooed man was trapped inside.

Over thirty of the Rangers had occupied the fort, and most were already at the palisade. They fired their muskets at the Frenchmen toiling to cross the iced river towards the island. Some of the French fled, sliding and slipping on the ice; others fired back, and two officers approached, shouting that they were French and the occupants of the fort were making a mistake.

MacKim translated the words for Kennedy's benefit.

"A mistake? What mistake?" Kennedy said. "Don't they know we're British Rangers?"

"The flag!" Speakman shouted. "We're flying the wrong flag!"

MacKim glanced upward, where the French flag hung limply from the flagpole. Even out here in the wilderness, where scalping and torture were accepted methods of war, it was a cardinal crime to fight under a false flag. MacKim dashed to the flagpole and hauled the French colours down. The flag made a neat pile around his feet and, for one betraying moment, he wondered how Tayanita would have liked the silk and what she would have done with the material.

"Get up on the parapet, MacKim," Speakman yelled. "Every musket helps!"

MacKim ran to the parapet, where the Rangers were firing and loading as fast as they could. The French on the ice had recovered, with some forming a firing line and others shoving and hauling the sledges.

"Target the leading sledge," Kennedy said.

The Rangers responded with an aimed volley. As the sledge was beyond the extreme range of the Brown Bess, most balls fell short, although a few chipped the ice and ricocheted around the sledge. Not a single Frenchman fell as they redoubled their efforts and slid the sledge over the rough ice.

"They're too far away, sir," Parnell said. "We should have a rifle with us."

"Try again," Kennedy said as the French pushed on, but every shot in the next volley fell short.

"After all our struggles to get here!" Kennedy sounded like a man in despair. "Try the second sledge."

The second sledge was about a hundred yards out, which was still beyond accurate musket range. Of the Rangers' shots, only two came close, and now the French had pushed their firing line closer, with their musketry knocking chips from the parapet and buzzing around the Rangers' heads.

"We're doing nothing here," Kennedy swore, loading his musket.

"Sir," MacKim said. "What about the cannon?"

"The what?"

"The cannon, sir. It has a longer range than our muskets." MacKim indicated the French cannon that stood, abandoned and forlorn, with its muzzle pointing inland.

"Can you fire the damned thing?"

"No, sir, but the French artillerymen can, and I am sure we could persuade them to help us."

Kennedy glanced towards the French, who were struggling to push the sledges over the frozen river, easing further away from the Rangers' muskets by the minute. "Try it!" He raised his voice. "Sergeant Speakman! Bring the prisoners out and have them haul the cannon to the battlements facing the river."

At first reluctant to help, the French proved more willing when Sergeant Speakman said he would personally scalp anybody who refused his orders. MacKim translated with zest, adding a few refinements of his own.

"You would not," one suave artilleryman said.

"He would." MacKim took off his hat and showed his head. "The sergeant scalped me when I was late on parade."

After that, the prisoners dragged across the artillery, glancing at Speakman as if he were some sort of monster. The sergeant added to his image by growling and kicking anybody, Ranger or Frenchman, who looked like they were shirking work.

"We won't get the cannon on the battlements," MacKim said. "We'll have to knock a hole in the wall."

"How?" Speakman asked. "We've no picks."

"Use the cannon," MacKim said.

Again, the French were reluctant to help until Speakman found a length of rope and began to thrash them. With that encouragement, the artillerymen loaded and fired into the wall of the fort. It took three attempts for the light gun to make an impression, and then Speakman had the French load the cannon and roll it forward. On the second attempt, the muzzle protruded from the splintered hole they had made.

"Let's hope the Frenchies are still in range," MacKim muttered, "after all the artillerymen's kind efforts to help us."

The French were nearly halfway to the island now, with a strong rearguard waiting if the Rangers tried to attack.

"They still don't know how few we are," MacKim said.

"Fire at the leading sledge," Speakman ordered the prisoners.

The French artillerymen shook their heads. The suave man spoke to MacKim. "You can torture us or kill us, but we will not fire on our men."

"Very well," Kennedy descended from the battlements. "Sergeant, put all these men in the guardhouse if you can find one, except him." The lieutenant pointed to the suave Frenchman.

"Oh, there's a guardhouse, sir. Depend on the French for building a jail," Speakman said.

As Speakman hustled the bulk of the prisoners away, Kennedy drew the knife from his belt, grabbed the suave Frenchman and held the blade to his throat.

"Now show us how to fire this cannon, monsieur, or I'll slit you from ear to ear."

Visibly shaking and deprived of his colleagues' support, the Frenchman obliged, with MacKim translating for Kennedy's benefit. It took a full fifteen minutes for the cannon to be loaded and ready, and by then, the French convoy was more than two thirds across the river.

"We'll never get them at this range," Kennedy complained.

"Perhaps not, sir," MacKim said. "Shall I fire?"

"Yes, fire."

When MacKim applied the quick match to the touchhole, the cannon roared and jerked back.

"Jesus!" MacKim jumped away smartly to avoid being injured. The first shot was a hundred yards left and far short, crashing into the ice, bouncing and rolling. The second veered right, and the third soared past the French sledges.

"Now, lower the elevation." MacKim had grasped the basics of firing the cannon. As Speakman forced the prisoner to carry cannonballs to the gun, MacKim loaded with care. Ignoring Kennedy's urging for more speed, he selected the roundest of the cannonballs to increase accuracy and rolled it into the muzzle of the gun.

"All right," MacKim said, "let's see if this is any better." He poured powder into the touch-hole, stepped back and applied the match. The powder fizzed and smoked, and a second later, the gun roared. The ball soared out faster than the eye could follow, hovered in the air and then fell.

"Short again," Kennedy said and swore. "Load the thing again, and stand aside."

MacKim sponged out the muzzle to remove any lingering powder remnants and loaded with powder and ball again. This time, Kennedy adjusted the aim, sighted along the barrel, revised again and took hold of the match.

The French had redoubled their efforts, moving across the ice with more speed as the cannonballs skidded around them.

"Pray for a hit," Kennedy said, "before the French are out of range."

The cannon barked again, with shot rising to its apex and falling again. MacKim saw the ball as a faint black line against the grey sky, and then the shot plunged onto the ice ten yards short of the central sledge.

"Nearly, sir," MacKim said.

"Load the damned thing again!" Kennedy snarled.

As MacKim bent to the work, Kennedy blasphemed again. "Would you look at that, MacKim?"

Perhaps the last ball had landed on a weak spot on the ice, or maybe the repeated bombardment, added to the sledges' weight, had caused some damage, for a crack appeared on the frozen surface. As MacKim and Kennedy watched, the split in the ice lengthened and deepened, travelling towards the French as they frantically tried to move towards the far bank of the river.

"The Lord has answered our prayers," Kennedy said, as the

crack reached the closest of the sledges, which slid sideways into the water despite the efforts of the French to save it.

As the crack widened, subsidiary faults appeared until the sledge convoy moved along a surface of rapidly splintering ice.

"Those poor men," MacKim said, as his professed hatred of all things French shrank. "They must be terrified."

"So was my wife when the Abenaki tortured her to death," Kennedy said. "And the French sent them." His face was flint-hard as, one-by-one, the sledges disappeared under the ice. Most of the men scrambled towards the far bank, where the island waited invitingly.

"Your tattooed Canadian and English renegade led the Abenaki." Kennedy spoke so softly that only MacKim could hear him. "Load," he ordered. "Load that damned cannon, MacKim."

"Yes, sir." MacKim's moment of weakness had passed. He loaded the cannon and stood back as Kennedy adjusted the rudimentary sights.

"Fire," Kennedy said quietly. "Blow the bastards to Kingdom Come and beyond."

MacKim nodded and applied the match. Once again, the cannon roared, with the white smoke jetting out around the muzzle flare and the ball hurtling towards the distant French.

The ball landed ten yards in front of the largest group, sending splinters of ice flying, then bounced and rolled among the men, knocking one soldier off his feet.

Kennedy watched through his telescope. "He's dead," he said laconically.

MacKim loaded again. "Ready, sir."

"Is that your man, MacKim?" Kennedy handed over his telescope. "The fellow standing at the river's edge, ushering his men onto the island. Is that the man who led the last raiding party?"

MacKim focussed the telescope with some difficulty. "Yes, sir." The Canadian seemed so close that MacKim could nearly reach out and touch him. Tall and broad, he glared across the river. Even at this distance, MacKim could sense the Canadian's frustration at having brought his convoy so far, only to lose it while crossing the river.

"Aim at him," Kennedy ordered. "He's the French leader. Kill him."

MacKim remembered Chisholm telling him a story about the battle of Fontenoy, when the British gunners had the enemy commander in their sights and asked the Duke of Cumberland for permission to fire.

"Why, no, sir," the British general said. "That is scarcely honourable. Generals have more important things to do than shoot at each other. For shame, sir, act like a gentleman."

It seemed that the idea of honour and gentlemen did not apply out here in the North American wilderness.

"It's already loaded, sir," MacKim said. "With your permission, I'd like to aim."

"Sorry, MacKim, that's my prerogative. I only wish I had the renegade in my sights."

The Canadian was on the shore, encouraging his men, helping some from the freezing water, pulling at the laggards and shouting orders that MacKim could not hear.

Kennedy peered over the cannon's sights, ordered MacKim to adjust the angle of the barrel, swore, and stepped back. "Fire," he said softly.

MacKim applied the match and stepped back smartly. The cannon roared again, with white smoke obscuring their vision and the shot soaring past the Canadian to vanish somewhere in the trees at his back.

"Reload," Kennedy ordered. "I've not finished with them yet."

MacKim reloaded, toiling with sponge, rammer and ball until the cannon was ready. By that time, all the surviving French had reached the island, and the Canadian stood alone on the shore. When he shouted an order, a French officer handed him a telescope, and he studied Kennedy and MacKim, so all three men stared at each other across a frozen channel of the St Lawrence River.

"Stand aside," Kennedy said and altered the angle of the cannon. "Give me the match." He took a last look at the Canadian, applied the match and waved his hand in a vain attempt to clear away the choking powder smoke. When the smoke eased, the Canadian still stood where he was, watching through his telescope. He lifted a hand in farewell and slid into the trees.

"We'll never catch him now," Kennedy said.

"No, sir," MacKim agreed. He thought he sensed Tayanita beside him, watching with disapproval in her eyes.

"Here's the captain, sir," Speakman warned.

"Thank you, Sergeant," Kennedy said. "Now we'll see if he can charge us with mutiny and disobeying an order in the face of the enemy."

11

"What the devil are you doing, Kennedy?" Lindsay had arrived with the remainder of the Rangers. "I gave you a direct order not to attack the fort."

"Sir!" Kennedy said. "You must be mistaken, sir. I am sure you said to take the fort."

MacKim stepped back, remaining at attention. It was not a corporal's place to interfere when two officers disagreed.

"I distinctly ordered you to halt, Lieutenant," Lindsay said.

"My apologies, sir. The cold must have affected my hearing. May I offer my congratulations on achieving your objective, sir? By capturing the fort, as I believed you ordered, we managed to fire on the column of French and tip their cannon and stores into the river."

MacKim saw Lindsay's expression alter as he digested this information. "I see. Give me your spyglass, Lieutenant."

Lindsay focussed the telescope on the island, now bereft of any sign of life, and then scanned the ice, on which a few items of stores lay. "I can't see any bodies."

"Some of the French drowned, sir," Kennedy said.

"Only some?"

"Most escaped." Kennedy hesitated for a moment. "We estimate there were about three hundred French, sir, including Canadians and Indians. We could cross the river and pursue them if you wish."

MacKim saw Lindsay's face pale when he heard the number of Frenchmen.

"No," Lindsay said at last. "Our orders were to damage the convoy, and we've done that. I think it best that we report to General Murray."

"As you wish, sir," Kennedy said. "We have some French artillerymen as prisoners."

"They might give valuable intelligence," Lindsay said. "We've done very well, and now we'll head back to Quebec."

❦

THE RANGERS MARCHED WITH A SWAGGER AS THEY PASSED through the gate at Quebec's St Louis Bastion. Each man knew they had achieved something few other British units could even try. Claudette Leclerc was standing amongst the crowd of onlookers. She looked up, caught MacKim's eye and lifted a hand in acknowledgement.

"That woman's waving to you," Sergeant Speakman said.

MacKim nodded. "She probably thinks I am somebody else," he said.

"That must be it," Speakman agreed. "Why would any woman want to wave to an ugly dog like you?"

"That's what I thought, too," MacKim found he had straightened his shoulders. "Especially when there is such a handsome sergeant as you." He gave Speakman a twisted smile. "Are you sure she was not waving to you?"

Speakman mused for a second, turned to look over his shoulder and smiled. "Do you know, MacKim, I think you might be right."

They marched on, with Captain Lindsay immediately entering Fort Louis to report to General Murray and Lieutenant Kennedy ensuring the men returned to barracks.

"Eat and sleep, boys," Kennedy said. "Back to routine tomorrow." He leaned against the door, with his uniform as tattered and faded as any of his men. "I have no idea what the official account of our mission will be, but I'd say we did well."

MacKim glanced over the room. It was as tidy as when they left, except for his bed. "Somebody's been in here," he said. "Check your belongings, Rangers."

In common with any British infantry unit, the Rangers had few possessions, and what they owned, they tended to carry with them. However, the men looked for the odds-and-ends they had secreted around the room.

"Nothing missing, Corporal," Parnell reported. "You must be mistaken."

"No," MacKim said as he lifted his thin straw mattress. "Somebody has undoubtedly been here." The square of beadwork lay on the unyielding boards of the bed, a splash of colour against the dull brown. MacKim lifted it with suddenly trembling hands, remembering Tayanita's eyes as she handed it to him, remembering her smile and scent.

"Are you all right, Corporal?" Ramsay asked.

"Yes." MacKim tried to hide his pleasure. Either Claudette Leclerc or her little son had been in the barracks, for nobody else would have returned this precious object. Holding the beadwork in his hand, he lay on his side and closed his eyes.

❧

"I HEAR THAT GENERAL MURRAY IS VERY PLEASED WITH Captain Lindsay," Butler said, when they returned from guard duty the following day. "He wrote a glowing report of Lindsay's successes, ready to send to William Pitt in London, once the frost lifts."

"How about Kennedy?" MacKim asked. "Did Captain Lindsay mention the part Kennedy played?"

"I don't know," Butler said. "I was talking to the general's clerk, and Murray seems to believe that Lindsay is another Major Roberts."

"God save us all," Waite said. "Lieutenant Kennedy may be, but Lindsay?" He shook his head in disbelief.

"Did the clerk say anything else?" MacKim asked.

Butler nodded. "These French artillerymen we brought as prisoners were so pleased that we didn't leave them for the Indians that they were happy to talk."

"What did they say?"

Butler shook his head. "That's all I heard. The clerk thinks he's above mere soldiers such as us."

Lieutenant Kennedy was more forthcoming when he called his Rangers together a few days later.

"The French are building floating gun batteries somewhere between here and Montreal," he said, looking at the circle of hungry, tired faces. "They know that the Royal Navy will sail up to Quebec as soon as the ice releases its grip, and they want to challenge them."

MacKim nodded. He remembered the French floating fire ships down the St Lawrence during the previous year's campaign. The battles on the river were an extension of the great naval encounters at sea, with fleet actions deciding the fate of colonies as much as any actions on land.

"General Murray wants us to find and destroy the building yard and capture or kill the boat builders," Kennedy said.

The Rangers looked at each other and said nothing. They had barely been back a week, and most were still recovering from their endeavours.

"This will be our longest and most vital mission yet," Kennedy said. "The French artillerymen have given us a rough idea where the yard is, but it's sure to be well guarded, so I only want volunteers."

"How many Rangers do you want, sir?" Speakman asked.

"We're hoping for a hundred, with as many of you lads as wish to come, plus others from the garrison, mainly from the Royal Americans."

The Rangers glanced at each other; they had grown used to each other's company and knew that an influx of new blood would alter the dynamics of the unit.

"Will you be in charge, sir?" MacKim asked the question he knew others were thinking.

"Captain Lindsay will again be in command," Kennedy said. "I will be second in command, with Sergeant Speakman and, he glanced at MacKim, "newly promoted Sergeant MacKim next."

MacKim shook his head as half the Rangers turned to look at him. "I don't wish to be a sergeant, sir."

"You already are, Sergeant. Captain Lindsay confirmed my recommendation this morning. Congratulations, and please begin your duties immediately."

"Yes, sir," MacKim said, as men pounded his back and shoulders. He had no desire for the extra responsibilities of a sergeant. He just wished to be left alone with his thoughts and his search for revenge. His hand sought the square of Tayanita's beadwork.

"I also want you to learn to fire the long rifle, Sergeant," Kennedy said. "Our frontiersmen use it, but the British Army does not. Some of the Royal Americans have them as hunting pieces, and I have requisitioned four for the Rangers."

"Yes, sir," MacKim said.

Kennedy continued. "You'll remember how our muskets were out of range when the French crossed the St Lawrence. This time, we will have a few weapons that can carry further."

"I have no doubt they'll prove useful, sir," MacKim said.

"Good. Have Sergeant Speakman instruct you in your new duties, MacKim, and then get used to the new rifles. Oh, and congratulations again."

"Thank you, sir," MacKim said.

MacKim had seen some of the civilian backwoodsmen carrying very long firearms but had never had the opportunity to see the rifles in action. Now, Jack Dickert, a blond-haired man who had joined the Rangers from the Royal Americans, brought one to him.

"My father made this one, Sergeant," Dickert said, with the German of his ancestors still apparent through his Colonial twang.

The first thing MacKim noticed was the extreme length of the weapon, at nearly seventy inches long, yet it was beautifully balanced and weighed only ten pounds. As the Brown Bess weighed a fraction more and was over fifty-eight inches long, the Long Rifle was light for its length.

"How was it made?" MacKim held the piece, sighting along the barrel.

Dickert gave a slow smile. "We start with a flat bar of soft iron," he said, holding his arms wide to demonstrate the length, "and forge it by hand into a gun barrel."

MacKim nodded, appreciating the labour involved in this initial process.

"We have to bore it through and create the rifling, because it's the rifling that makes the ball spin and increases the accuracy."

"What sort of tools do you use?"

"Hand tools," Dickert said proudly. "Everything is done by hand."

MacKim nodded again. "It's a work of art," he said.

Dickert continued, smiling. "Then we carve a maple wood stock from the forest and fit it onto the barrel."

MacKim lifted the rifle. "Where do you buy the locks? The nearest town?"

Dickert shook his head. "We make our own on the anvil." His smile broadened. "We are pleased with the result."

"It's a masterpiece," MacKim agreed, "light and graceful. How much powder does it use?"

"Less than the Brown Bess," Dickert said, "and it fires a smaller ball with more accuracy up to two hundred yards."

MacKim checked the piece was not loaded and then squinted down the barrel to see the rifling. "It will take longer to load," he said.

"That's the drawback," Dickert agreed. "That and the length of the barrel." He gave a slow smile. "But it's a hunting rifle; hunters don't load in haste. A Brown Bess will take maybe twenty seconds to load. This one," he screwed up his face in his effort to think, "maybe forty to forty-five seconds."

"Twice as long, then, with twice the range."

"Yes, Sergeant, and three times the accuracy," Dickert said.

"Could you show me how to fire it?" MacKim asked.

"With pleasure." Dickert seemed genuinely pleased at the thought of teaching, so that evening, MacKim listened as Dickert explained how to aim and fire the long rifle. After two hours, MacKim thought he had mastered the basics.

"It's very accurate," he said.

"A good man can shoot the eye out of a pigeon at two hundred paces," Dickert said.

"A few of these, in the hands of skilled marksmen, could turn the tide in any battle," MacKim said. "Why, a marksman could target the enemy's commander and principal officers and leave them leaderless."

Dickert gave his characteristic slow smile. "That's right, Sergeant. Maybe the British Army could have whole regiments of riflemen someday."

"Maybe they will at that," MacKim said. "We did that with fusiliers and grenadiers, so why not with riflemen? We could shoot the enemy to pieces even before he gets his muskets in range."

As the days wore on and the officers made their plans for the proposed raid on the French shipbuilding yard, recruits and hopeful recruits dribbled into the Rangers' ranks. Kennedy or Lindsay rejected most right away, for the various regiments were attempting to pass their incorrigible characters onto the Rangers, where discipline was notoriously lax. Eventually, the officers accepted less than thirty men, all with experience of forest fighting.

While the officers made their decisions, MacKim sought out Claudette in the ruined building where the homeless Quebecers congregated. He held up the square of beadwork. "Thank you," he said.

Claudette looked up from her place beside the fire. "I did not make that," she said.

"No, but you found it for me."

When Claudette smiled, MacKim could see the beauty beneath the hardship lines. "Hugo found it, not me."

"Please thank him for me." MacKim handed over a larger-than-usual share of army bread with a hunk of hard cheese. "It's not much, but it's from the heart."

Claudette accepted the bread and cheese with a small hand. "Thank you, Sergeant MacKim," she said and returned her attention to the fire.

"GOOD GOD, THEY'VE MADE HIM A SERGEANT!" CHISHOLM'S voice sounded around the Ranger's barrack room.

"So they have," Ranald MacDonald said. "They can't know him very well."

MacKim looked up from the duty roster on which he was working. "What the devil are you reprobates doing here? Don't you know this is the Rangers' barracks? Real soldiers, not parade ground pretty-boys."

Chisholm grinned. "Real soldiers? Ha! You've never seen a

real battle, Hughie! That affair on the Plains of Abraham was hardly even a skirmish. Now, if you had been at Fontenoy like me... "

"If I had been at Fontenoy," MacKim interrupted, "I'd talk everybody to death about it, just like you do." He held out his hand. "Have you lads joined the Rangers?"

"Only for this one expedition," Chisholm said. "Married life is all very well for a while, but it is very restricting."

Ranald MacDonald looked around the room. "Harriette told him that somebody had to look after you," he said. "She's got her eye on you for her husband number three, remember. Or is it number four?"

MacKim shook both their hands. "She'll have a long wait," he said. "Chisholm is indestructible. Anybody that can survive Fontenoy deserves to live forever. Why did you come, Ranald?"

"I heard the food and accommodation was better," he said. "Although the NCOs are said to be right bastards."

"Aye, that bit's correct." MacKim stepped back. "It's good to see you both, although you might regret your decision. We're destined for a perilous operation."

Chisholm shrugged. "We can die out in the forest or perish of cold and scurvy behind the city walls. What difference does it make? We're all going to die out here in New France, anyway."

Ramsay looked up. "No, we're not. Lieutenant Kennedy leads us, Chisholm, and he is a good man."

"Kennedy? I thought that we were Lindsay's Rangers."

MacKim nodded. "Aye, we are, but as Ramsay said, Kennedy's a good man. He knows the ways of the forest as well as any Canadian or Indian."

MacDonald stamped his boots on the floor. "Well then, we'll see what must be done. When are we leaving?"

"Not until we train up you green men, God help us," MacKim said.

While Kennedy and Sergeant Speakman trained the new

Rangers in forest fighting, MacKim found the best four shots and asked them to volunteer to carry the long rifles.

"You mean as well as our muskets?" Parnell asked.

"No, instead of," MacKim said.

Parnell nodded. "All right then." He was one of the four chosen, along with Dickert, Waite and Duncan MacRae.

"You four are different from the others," MacKim told them. "You are the best shots in the company, so possibly the best in the garrison."

The four men looked at him without speaking. All had been in the army long enough not to trust a sergeant's praise.

"You will not take part in any mad bayonet charge, nor endanger your lives unless expressly ordered to," MacKim said. "You are the marksmen; you will fire at picked targets that our muskets cannot reach and care for your rifles as if they were your wives. Dickert will teach you how to do that. Now, go and practise shooting."

The marksmen glanced at each other, pleased that they had chosen an easier life than their companions.

"I will inspect your rifles from time to time," MacKim brought them back down to earth, "and if I find even a speck of rust or dirt, you'll wish the Indians had got you."

The riflemen looked at him, unsure if he was joking or not. MacKim allowed them to wonder as he sought Lieutenant Kennedy.

"When do we leave, sir?" MacKim asked.

"Friday night," Kennedy said. "It's a full moon, and we'll leave as soon as it rises. The French artillerymen have kindly drawn us a map. I have a copy, and Captain Lindsay has another."

"Yes, sir," MacKim said.

"If anything happens to us, you and Sergeant Speakman will fall heir to the maps. Once we have destroyed the boatyard, we will head back to Quebec, for I suspect the Frenchies will be hard on our tails." Kennedy smiled. "We hoped for a hundred men; we have seventy-five volunteers. In my mind, seventy-five volunteers are better than five hundred pressed men."

"Yes, sir," MacKim agreed.

MacKim paid Claudette a final visit, fully aware he may never see her again.

"So, you Rangers are off again," Claudette said.

"We are." MacKim was no longer surprised that a Canadian civilian knew the army's supposedly secret movements.

"Come back safe, MacKim," Claudette said.

"Stay safe, Madame Leclerc." MacKim gave another stiff bow.

When he turned at the doorway, Claudette was still watching him, with Hugo at her side.

Quebec was tense that night as if the city knew that its trials were not yet over. MacKim ensured his men had eighty cartridges apiece, with their water bottles full of water, not rum, and a supply of bread. Three men had already dropped out, as the ever-prevalent scurvy prevented them from marching any distance at all.

"Well, Hugh," Chisholm was sharpening his flints, "what's to do?"

"Just the war, James," MacKim said. "It's all that matters now."

"A sergeant, eh? It's a long step from the Johnny Raw you were when I first met you."

MacKim shrugged, a habit he had acquired since mixing with the inhabitants of New France. "Aye; Louisbourg seems a very long time ago. We were all Johnny Raws to the colonial way of warfare."

"Once we've captured Montreal," Chisholm said, "the Frenchies will give up, this bloody campaign will be over, and all our colonies in the Americas will have peace from the Canadian and Indian raids. We'll have brought them security, Hugh, and we can go home."

"Home?" MacKim thought of the glen where he had grown up and the mother he had left only a few years ago. Only a few years, yet it seemed like a lifetime, and MacKim knew he was a different man to the raw young soldier who had landed in New France in 1758. "I don't know, James. Where is your home?"

"Here, in the army." Chisholm touched his face, so ravaged by fire that civilians turned away from him. "The army doesn't care how I look, as long as I can march and shoot. No civilian would employ me. You can go home though, Hugh, back to Scotland. A wig will disguise your head, and nobody will see the scar on your chest. Your wounds are hidden."

MacKim nodded. "Aye, my wounds are hidden." *Nobody knows how deep they are,* he thought. *Nobody knows how hard I have to hold on to prevent my sanity from slipping away. Unless it has already done* so.

"You have your wife," MacKim said. "Harriette will support you. You could open a tavern somewhere; Inverness maybe, or Edinburgh, maybe even London. Nobody will care about your scars as long as you sell good ale."

Chisholm smiled. "If only that were true, Hugh. Harriette belongs in the army as much as I do, perhaps more. She was born in the ranks and knows nothing about civilian life."

MacKim nodded. After his years in uniform, he understood the attractions as well as the dangers of military life. The Army gave men food and usually shelter, with companionship and a sense of belonging. In civilian life, there were no guarantees; life was work or starve, and work for the unskilled, men or women, was poorly paid, with accommodation worse. For many, army life provided a sanctuary from the desperate poverty of the streets.

"Are you ready, boys?" Kennedy asked softly.

MacKim nodded. "My lads are ready, sir."

"Then let's go and find the French," Kennedy said.

The Rangers filed out of Quebec onto the Plains of Abraham, where General Wolfe had fought his epic battle the previous autumn. With the moon high and full, they had no difficulty finding their route and marched across the undulating plain, with Lindsay at their head and Kennedy halfway down the column. MacKim provided the rearguard with a handful of veterans.

"May God be with us, boys," MacKim said.

"God and good marksmanship." Dickert tapped the lock of his rifle.

The Rangers moved fast, using the light to cover as much ground as possible before the moonlight faded.

"We know the dispositions of the French outposts," Kennedy explained at their first stop, "so we'll get around them without difficulty." He grinned. "We're the predators," he said. "We're the point of King George's sword, the hard-hitting dogs of war."

"Yes, sir," MacKim said, watching the shadows on the plains as clouds flitted across the moon. He preferred a still night, for shadows disrupted the lie of the land and fooled men into seeing things that were not there.

"We're crossing the St Lawrence on the ice," Kennedy reminded, "and moving down the opposite side of the river, where the French will never expect to see us."

They halted at the St Lawrence, checking along the banks in case of a waiting Canadian or Indian picket. To MacKim, the flat ice plain invited danger, for a column of men in the open was easily seen.

"Kennedy," Lindsay ordered. "You take the van. Sergeant Speakman and I will take the centre and MacKim the rear."

"Sir," Kennedy said. He organised the dozen men of the van, gave them quiet orders and stepped onto the iced river.

MacKim watched as Kennedy's party eased over the ice, muskets held ready, green uniforms like dark shadows, snowshoes making them ungainly. They seemed to take an age, and then they were in the trees, forming a bridgehead to protect the remainder.

Lindsay gave Kennedy five minutes before he led the main body of fifty men, including MacKim's marksmen, onto the ice. When they were halfway, a cloud eased across the moon, and then the shooting began.

❧ 12 ❧

The musketry shattered the silence, a hundred muskets firing at once with the muzzle flares destroying the night and the clouds of powder-smoke acrid and white.

"Scatter!" Lindsay shouted as men began to fall. "Fire back on my word!"

"Stand!" MacKim ordered his men. He could tell by the muzzle-flares that the French were all on the south side of the river. His men were all on the frozen river, exposed and vulnerable. "Extended order, boys. Move forward slowly and be prepared to support Captain Lindsay."

The main body of Rangers was confused. Some tried to fire back, others ran to the nearest shore, and some stood still, waiting for coherent orders. Kennedy's men began to fire, the disciplined volleys a sign that the lieutenant had them in hand.

"We must help them," Ramsay nearly pleaded.

"Wait," MacKim ordered. "Move forward slowly and wait until the captain gives definite orders."

The French continued to fire, with Rangers dropping and firing. MacKim could not see Lindsay in the confusion and swore softly.

"Captain Lindsay!" he called, sending his voice across the river. "Any orders, Captain?"

The firing continued.

"Sergeant Speakman!" MacKim roared, without response.

"The sergeant's dead!" an anonymous voice replied.

"Right, lads," MacKim ordered. "We're going across to support the van. Keep in extended order, fire at the muzzle flashes when we get in range and ensure you don't hit our men. Lieutenant Kennedy will be hard-pressed."

Taking a deep breath, MacKim led his men across the ice. Although he knew he was still well out of range, he felt exposed, as if every Frenchman and Indian in Canada was aiming his musket directly at him. He moved in a half-crouch, with the bewildered survivors of the main body joining him as he came closer to the south shore. "Across the river, boys. We'll support the lieutenant."

Thankful for somebody to give orders, the Rangers followed.

"Has anybody seen Captain Lindsay?" MacKim asked.

Nobody had.

"Extended order and don't fire until we're in range," MacKim reminded.

After their initial volleys, the French remained silent until MacKim's men neared the opposite shore, and then they opened up. Only one Ranger fell, with the darkness now a protective cloak.

"Fire!" MacKim ordered. "And then move before you load. Don't allow the French to target you by your muzzle flare."

The rearguard ran forward, stopping to fire, moving again, loading and running as best they could on the ice. As the Rangers crossed, MacKim gathered the survivors of the vanguard. He found Sergeant Speakman lying dead with a ball in his chest.

"Is that you, MacKim?" Kennedy asked.

"Yes, sir. I lost one man in the crossing. I'm not sure of the main body's casualties." MacKim said.

"Did you see Captain Lindsay?" Kennedy could not hide his anxiety.

"No, sir," MacKim shook his head.

"Right; we must assume the French hit him." Kennedy looked around his position, where the Rangers crouched or stood behind trees, exchanging fire with the French. "Let's drive these French fellows away before we do anything else. Find out how many men we have."

MacKim did a quick roll call and found forty-eight fit men at the bridgehead, some shocked and three without muskets.

"Forty-five armed men, sir," MacKim reported.

"Sergeant Speakman?"

"Dead, sir."

"Very well. We're not waiting here," Kennedy said. "We'll go for the throat and scatter the Frenchies." He grinned, white teeth in a drawn face. "They won't expect that. Your rearguard will guard the rear and keep up."

"Yes, sir," MacKim saw his four riflemen among the defenders, loading with care and aiming before they fired.

"Adopt a diamond formation," Kennedy ordered, "with no scouts. We keep together this time and don't leave any man behind. I won't give the savages a present."

With Kennedy in the lead, the Rangers moved forward, shooting at anything that might be French, Canadian or Indian. Within twenty minutes, MacKim realised that there was little resistance, with nobody responding to his men's firing.

"The French have gone," he reported.

"I agree," Kennedy said. "Call the roll."

They halted beside a small village, where the inhabitants peered anxiously at them from the doors of their houses, and the priest held his Bible as if to ward off evil spirits.

"It's all right, Father," Kennedy called in English. "We're not here to hurt anybody."

MacKim translated the lieutenant's words and then called

the roll, including some stragglers who arrived, gasping and afraid.

"We have fifty-eight men," he reported. "We've lost Captain Lindsay, Sergeant Speakman and twelve soldiers."

"So many! That's a grievous loss," Kennedy said. "Did you see who led the French?"

MacKim shook his head. "I only saw the flash of muskets and shadowy figures among the trees," he said.

"I saw that Canadian fellow," Kennedy told him, "the man with the tattoos. I only had a glimpse of him, but he was clear as day in the musket-flares."

MacKim controlled his surge of anger. "We seem to have a private war with that man."

"We do." Kennedy had an edge to his voice. "He ambushes us, we ambush him. He won that round."

"He won't win the war," MacKim promised.

"Set a defensive perimeter, Sergeant," Kennedy said, "and we'll decide what to do. Should we continue with the attack on the boatyard? Or withdraw?"

"You're the ranking officer, sir. The decision is yours."

With pickets set out to watch for the French, Kennedy sat alone for a quarter of an hour, drawing plans in the snow with a stick. Eventually, he scuffed his foot across his work and called for MacKim.

"Sergeant, find our wounded and take them back to Quebec with the dead. Then we will continue. I'll not allow that Canadian fellow to dictate our movements."

"Yes, sir."

It was mid-morning before the Rangers located and carried their casualties across the St Lawrence to Quebec. "Did anybody find Captain Lindsay's body?" Kennedy asked.

"Not a sign of it, sir," MacKim reported.

"We can only hope the French captured him rather than the Indians," Kennedy said. "Most of the French are gentlemen and know how to treat a prisoner properly."

"Yes, sir," MacKim agreed.

"The unfortunate thing is that the French will also have the map, showing our objective," Kennedy said. "They will expect us."

"Yes, sir, unless they figure that we may abort the mission," MacKim said. "We could spread misinformation again."

"To whom?" Kennedy asked.

MacKim indicated the village. "I know these Canadians have taken an oath of allegiance to King George, sir, but I doubt they feel much loyalty to a nation who spent much of last year burning their crops and killing their men."

Kennedy nodded. "You're a cunning man, MacKim."

"Thank you, sir."

"We'll fabricate a story that we've changed our plans. Now we are going to raid the French at Jacques Cartier. That's quite plausible and should keep them guessing." Kennedy smiled again. "We'll hold a meeting in the village. The men will be confused, but that can't be helped."

"I doubt many villagers will speak English," MacKim warned. "We'll have to emphasise 'Jacques Cartier' a few times to drive the message home."

The church was central to the village, with a small civic square in which the Rangers gathered. Some nursed minor wounds, a few smoked pipes or chewed tobacco and one or two eyed the watching villagers through suspicious eyes. After the French ambush that cost so many men, they were subdued. Chisholm caught MacKim's eye and winked, with MacDonald testing the lock of his musket. MacRae was staring up at the sky, with his mouth moving as he intoned a Gaelic prayer. Dickert made slight alterations to his trigger, concentrating too hard on his rifle to notice Butler stealthily remove some bread from his pack.

"You can put that back, Butler," MacKim said.

"I was just seeing if I could do it, Sergeant." Butler replaced Dickert's bread.

Kennedy mounted the steps of the church to give his speech, talking loudly to impress the villagers.

The Rangers listened as Kennedy announced a change in their plans, telling them they would raid the French at Jacques Cartier instead. When Butler muttered a quiet complaint, MacKim reinforced the lieutenant's message with a snarled reprimand.

"Jacques Cartier it is, Butler, whether you like it or not." He hoped that the priest was taking notes.

As Kennedy got the Rangers ready to march on, MacKim bought some extra supplies from the villagers.

"Now we march," Kennedy said. "You have the rearguard, MacKim."

With scouts in front and on the flanks, the diminished troop of Rangers moved on. They were familiar with this section of the journey, so they knew where the enemy might place ambushes. They made good time that day and rested for the night, with pickets out and a slight wind in the trees.

When Kennedy saw the Rangers safely camped, he told the Rangers he held to the original plan.

"Just as bloody well," Butler said.

"Let's hope they believe our story," MacKim said.

Kennedy sighed. "That's war, MacKim. We must play the cards fate deals us and hope for the best."

There was no sign of enemy activity in the next two days, as the Rangers made slow progress. Whenever they reached a village, Kennedy encouraged the men to mention Jacques Cartier, paid for vegetables to supplement their hard bread and moved on, always wary of ambushes.

"We're nearly there." Kennedy called MacKim over in the shelter of a bush. He unfolded the map and laid it on the snow. "The boatyard is two miles away, where this little creek meets the St Lawrence River."

"We can expect a more prolific French presence now," MacKim said.

"Who are our best backwoodsmen?" Kennedy asked.

"Parnell and Butler," MacKim replied at once.

"Send them forward," Kennedy said. "Tell them to deal with any French sentries quietly, and hide the bodies."

The Rangers heard the instructions impassively and shifted ahead, with the rest of the men following until they came within sight of the St Lawrence.

"Halt, and spread out." Kennedy stopped in the fringes of a dense copse and extended his telescope. He grunted, shifted his stance slightly and nodded.

The boatbuilding yard was more extensive than MacKim had expected, with the workforce busily constructing large barges for floating gun batteries. The sound of hammering carried to the Rangers.

"If the French float these things down the St Lawrence," Kennedy observed, "the Royal Navy can say goodbye to its chances of reinforcing us." He passed his telescope over the MacKim. "How many can you see, Sergeant?"

MacKim took the telescope. "Ten, sir. No, twelve, and maybe more being built further back."

"Twelve is what I reckon," Kennedy said. "With another twelve a-building." He retrieved the telescope and examined the yard. "I can't see many defences."

"Nor could I, sir," MacKim said. "But I did see several boats being built as well."

"Boats?" Kennedy swept the telescope around. "Yes, you are right. I see them now: long, open boats, galleys suitable for carrying infantry when the ice lifts. That's their plan then, Sergeant. They're going to come downriver in the spring and have a regular siege of Quebec. The floating batteries will prevent our ships from bringing reinforcements, and the French will assault the city."

"They won't find General Murray willing to surrender," MacKim said.

"No, the general will fight," Kennedy agreed, "but you've seen the state of the garrison. They're riddled with scurvy and frostbite. I doubt one man in three is fit to stand, let alone resist a French attack."

MacKim nodded; he remembered the hospital, with the number of sick men increasing daily and the piles of frozen corpses awaiting burial. "Well, sir, we'll have to do our best here. We might delay the attack until the Navy comes upriver."

Kennedy pulled the Rangers further back, making his base in a small farmhouse. The Canadian inhabitants sat in a sullen group in the furthest corner of the largest of the four rooms as the Rangers took over their home.

"It's all right," MacKim reassured them. "We won't kill, torture or scalp you." He tried to smile. "We're British soldiers, not savages." For a moment, he remembered the actions of the British redcoats in the Jacobite campaign, torturing, looting and hanging civilians with impunity. "You're safe," he said, as much to convince himself as the Canadians.

"Now..." Kennedy spread out the map on the kitchen table, weighing down the corners with heavy items of crockery. "We know where the shipyard is and how to get to it. We do not know the disposition of the sentries and guards. I do not believe the handful of men we saw are all they have."

"I can take a patrol towards them, sir," MacKim said. "That Canadian fellow is bound to have sent his Indians ahead to warn them of our intentions. They can travel through the woods as fast as we can march on a road."

"Probably faster," Kennedy said. "Yes, take a small patrol out, but for the love of God, don't get caught."

"I'll try not to, sir," MacKim promised. When he looked to his left, Tayanita stood there, nearly as solid in death as she had been in life.

13

"Tayanita!" MacKim said, reaching out, only to grasp at air. Tayanita had vanished.

"Are you all right, Sergeant?" Kennedy asked.

"Yes, sir," MacKim said. "Parnell, Waites, Chisholm and Butler; you're with me." All four men were veterans, and three had grown up in the North American backcountry and had vast experience in forest warfare.

"We're not going to fight," MacKim said. "We're only looking at the French dispositions."

Chisholm touched his burned face, a sure sign he was thinking. "The Canadians may think otherwise."

MacKim grunted. "That's why we have Parnell and Waites here," he said. "They can out-fight and out-manoeuvre any Canadian."

Chisholm nodded. "I hope so, Sergeant."

Waiting until dark, MacKim eased them forward, moving very slowly and frequently stopping to listen for the enemy's movements.

Parnell touched MacKim's arm and nodded ahead. MacKim saw the slight blurring of movement, the too-regular shape and then the full figure of a man leaning against a tree with a musket in his hands.

MacKim waited, for the French would not post a lone sentry, and within five minutes, he saw two more men, one behind a timber barricade with only his head showing and the other crouching behind a tree.

MacKim led his men fifty yards back. "That outpost must be part of the outer ring of the French defences," he said. "I want to penetrate it and see what else they have."

The Rangers looked at him, with Chisholm shaking his head. "They'll catch us, Sergeant."

"They would catch four of us," MacKim said. "I'm going alone. "If I'm not back in two hours, make your way to the lieutenant and tell him what we've discovered."

"I'm better out there than you are, Sergeant," Parnell said.

"Follow my orders, Parnell," MacKim snapped.

"Be careful, Hugh." Chisholm touched his shoulder. "Harriette will not like it if you get killed."

"Look after this." MacKim handed over his musket and slid away. He knew that fast movement would only attract the enemy's attention, so he slowly crawled forward, keeping a good fifty yards from the French sentries. There was another outpost a bare twenty yards to MacKim's left, with three Canadians sitting on the timber barrier, staring into the dark.

MacKim crawled past with the blood drumming in his ears, paused as one of the Canadians shifted his stance, and moved on, listening for the sound of voices. Sure enough, the inner defence line was more relaxed, with young French regulars in white uniforms leaning on their muskets and talking quietly to each other. MacKim listened for a moment and smiled as he realised the French soldiers' conversation was no different from British soldiers. They were discussing what they would like to do to their sergeant and how they missed the women in Montreal.

MacKim slid past to see the shipyard gates in front, securely barred and with another clutch of sentries. Moving around the perimeter, MacKim saw two patrols of six men, with an NCO in charge of each. He returned by a different route and nearly crawled into an artillery position, where half a dozen men slept behind a battery of two light field pieces.

"They're making sure," MacKim reported to Kennedy. "One outer ring of outposts seventy yards apart manned by Canadians and Indians, and an inner ring with French regulars, plus artillery. There are also guards at the gate and at least two mobile patrols of seven men."

"They're expecting us," Kennedy said and leaned back in the kitchen chair. "Our decoy attempts didn't work, so I'll have to ponder this for a moment before I decide what to do."

MacKim felt the tension of the night's patrol overcoming him, and he lay down in the front room of the house, which the Rangers had taken over as their own. The warmth from the fire soon encouraged him to sleep. He saw Tayanita walking in front of him, her shoulders and hips gently swaying, her braided hair bouncing off her back.

"Sergeant! MacKim!" The voice was urgent in his ear.

"Chisholm?" MacKim opened his eyes.

"We're moving." Chisholm looked down on him. "You've been out for eight solid hours, Hugh."

"What's happening?" MacKim tried to ease the sleep from his eyes.

"We're on the move, Sergeant." Kennedy appeared behind Chisholm. "We're removing the outer ring of French defences, then capturing the artillery battery, as we did at the fort in the last expedition."

MacKim hauled himself up, automatically checked his musket, and then his men. The square of beadwork was within his shirt, comforting against his chest. Munching on a hard biscuit, MacKim stumbled into the dark, feeling the snow crunch under his snowshoes. No sooner had the last Ranger left the farmhouse than the woman emerged, shouting.

"*Les Britanniques sont là*!" ("The British are here!")

"Shut that damned woman up!" Kennedy said, as the woman repeated the phrase, with her voice high and loud in the night.

"Sir." Parnell ran back, grabbed the woman and clapped his hand over her mouth. "Shut your bloody mouth," he snarled, "or I'll slit your gizzard!"

At his words, the children of the farm emerged, adding their shrill voices.

"Shut up!" Parnell struggled with the woman, before swearing and throwing her to the ground and kicking her. "The bitch bit me," he said.

"Tie them up and gag them," Kennedy ordered and watched as the Rangers obeyed his orders. "And let's hope nobody heard them."

"They made more noise than a parcel of Boston whores!" Waite said, as he wrapped a cord around the legs of the oldest son of the house.

Shaken and unsettled, the Rangers strode away from the farm with MacKim cursing himself for not thinking to tie and gag the family before they left.

They covered the distance to the outer circle of French outposts in rapid time, to see the Canadians alert, with a mixed patrol of Canadians and Indians scouting in front of their positions.

Kennedy glanced at MacKim and Parnell, then nodded to the five-man French patrol. MacKim understood, passed his musket to MacDonald and tapped Parnell, Waite and Chisholm on the arm. As the French came clear, Kennedy moved first, with the Rangers only seconds behind.

Kennedy smashed his hatchet on the victim's head, cleaving the skull clean in two and killing his man instantly. MacKim thrust his knife into the side of an Indian's neck, then pulled it sharply to the side, tearing out the man's throat, so he collapsed with little more than a gurgle of blood. Parnell was equally efficient, thrusting his knife into a Canadian's heart and twisting, while Chisholm plunged a bayonet into his man. Only Waite's Canadian realised what was happening. When he saw the Rangers lunging from the night, he gave a single shout of warning and tried to level his musket.

Waite knocked the musket to the ground before the Canadian could fire and leapt on the man, stabbing with his knife, but the Canadian was powerfully built and threw the lighter Ranger off before turning to run.

"Stop him!" Kennedy hissed.

MacKim threw his hatchet, which spun in the air, so the blunt side cracked on the Canadian's head. The man staggered without falling, but he was clumsy in his snowshoes, and Parnell caught him within ten strides. MacKim was only half a second behind as the Canadian looked over his shoulder, opened his mouth in a scream and died as Parnell stabbed him in the throat.

"That was messy," MacKim said, cleaning his knife on the Canadian's tunic.

"It was," Kennedy agreed, then stooped to the man he had killed and scalped him with a neat, circular movement of his wrist and stood, holding the bloody trophy in his hand. "What's sauce for the goose," he said, as if challenging MacKim to object.

MacKim touched his head, which was still tender months after the French had scalped him. "Aye," he said. "Let's hope that Canadian's cry didn't further alert the French."

"Too late to hope that," Chisholm said, as the French sentries shouted out, one to another, across the whole outer line of defences.

"There's no point in pretence now, boys." Kennedy seemed quite relieved. "Straight down their throats now! Charge!"

MacKim recognised the pattern, retrieved his musket and followed Kennedy at once, with the remainder of the Rangers following in a crazy dash across the snow, yelling like maniacs. The nearest French outpost met them with a spatter of musketry, and then the Rangers arrived, hacking with bayonets and axes until two of the French were dead, and the third fled for his life.

"That's the way, boys!" Kennedy shouted,. "Don't stop now!"

The French had expected a creeping assault rather than a charge. The guards at the outposts shouted challenges and fired wildly into the dark, not knowing how many Rangers there were.

Rather than remove the entire outer ring as he had planned, Kennedy punched a hole and led the Rangers forward. He dashed through the dark towards the inner defences, which were hesitant to fire for fear of hitting the outer defenders.

"Keep on, boys," MacKim shouted. "Yell like devils!" MacKim knew that no soldiers, however brave and skilled, could remain unperturbed when an unknown number of screaming Rangers descended on them in the middle of the night.

The French remained behind their defences, gripping their muskets and shouting challenges, more to reassure themselves than to seek information. As Kennedy's men lunged from the dark, the French fired a single panicked volley and were struggling to reload when the Rangers fell on the nearest post.

Of the five defenders, one dropped his musket and turned to run, and the others remained to fight, which was brave but suicidal. The Rangers massacred them in seconds and stood for a second, panting and glaring around them.

"What now?" MacKim asked, breathing hard. He saw the torches flaring around the boat-building yard as the defenders prepared to fight.

Kennedy made an instant decision. "Now we mop them up. The French don't know how many we are, so we take the inner posts while they're in confusion." Even in the dark, MacKim saw the gleam of his teeth as he grinned. "I want these cannon you saw, Sergeant."

As the Rangers gathered around him, Kennedy divided them into two groups. "MacKim, take twenty men and head that way," Kennedy pointed in the direction of the artillery post. "I'll take the rest and move left. Take the outposts from the rear and keep moving. The faster we move, the less time the French will have to prepare. Go!"

MacKim looked at his men; they were panting, wild-eyed after their mad charge, and still eager for the assault. Chisholm touched his bayonet suggestively.

"Extended order, lads, so we're less of a target," MacKim said. "Fix your bayonets, and hit hard and fast. Follow me!"

With speed essential, MacKim took few precautions, although the French were awake and more alert by the minute. The men from the outer ring were shouting challenges and firing into nothing, which further unsettled the French in the inner defences.

"They don't realise we're behind them," MacKim said. "Come on, boys!"

MacKim fell on the next redoubt with bayonet, boot and hatchet in a murderous killing spree, with no thought for quarter. One of the youngest French regulars screamed in terror as the green-coated Rangers suddenly appeared. Parnell killed him with a bayonet thrust to the stomach and ripped the triangular blade upwards.

"Keep going," MacKim shouted, as his men paused to gather breath. "Don't give them time to recover!"

Chisholm looked around, nodded and moved on, with the Rangers surging behind MacKim. The French at the next post did not wait for the attack but fired a single ragged volley and fled, with the echo of the young soldier's scream in their minds. Their panic was infectious, as the next redoubt emptied of men without even a show of resistance.

MacKim raised his voice to increase the French confusion. "*Courez, les Britanniques sont derrière nous. Les Rangers sont là!*" MacKim shouted. ("Run, the British are behind us! The Rangers are here!")

The artillerymen, more intelligent or better trained, showed more fight, trying to pull their cannon in MacKim's direction as the Rangers surged up.

"Extended order!" MacKim roared. "Don't give them a target! Keep moving!"

The Rangers spread out, some men stumbling in the dark, others surging forward as they surrounded the artillery redoubt. One of the guns fired, blasting case shot that ripped through the dark, killing one man outright, and then the Rangers were amongst the gunners. It was a mad melee of bayonets and hatchets, rifle butts and knives, with men reduced to a killing frenzy with no pretence at civilisation. MacKim knew the images would return at night, the open-mouthed screams of the wounded, the spurting blood, the splintered bones and tumbling intestines.

There was no glory in war, only horror, murder, suffering and butchery.

"Don't let them spike the guns!" MacKim shouted, as the artillerymen frantically tried to render their cannon useless by driving a nail into the touchhole. MacKim bayonetted one artilleryman and swung his musket like a club at a second, while his Rangers swept into the redoubt around him. Only one of the French survived, to scramble clear of the redoubt and run to the rear, sobbing in fear.

By that time, the entire French outer ring had collapsed as the defenders realised the Rangers were behind them. The Canadians and Indians deserted their posts and fled, while the French regulars retired in some order, with wide eyes and flailing legs. Some of the Rangers shot at them as they passed; others merely jeered.

"Sergeant MacKim!" Kennedy's voice boomed through the fading dark. "Have you taken the guns?"

"Yes, sir!" MacKim shouted.

The French retreat was in full flow, with Canadians, Indians and regulars running to the gates of the shipbuilding yard in a mob of frightened men.

"Follow the French!" Kennedy ordered. "Push them back!"

The sentinels at the gates stared at the dozens of retreating men, unsure what to do. MacKim understood their dilemma. Their orders would be to keep the gates locked and guard them, but their humanity would urge them to allow the terrified refugees to enter and escape the unknown number of Rangers.

"Push on!" Kennedy shouted from the flank. "Don't stop!"

MacKim saw Kennedy's men running forward, herding the panicking French before them as the guards at the gate hesitated.

In the half-light, MacKim knew the French would not calculate the British numbers. They would only know that their defences had crumbled and would see two masses of Rangers pouring towards the gate, one from each flank. The guards might panic and leave the gates shut, abandoning their unfortunate men outside. However, they might open up, allow the refugees access, and in doing so, make life easier for Kennedy's men.

Roaring, yelling and trying to act as if they were much more numerous than they were, the Rangers pushed at the retreating French, who clamoured for the guards to open the gates.

"Form a line and fire at them," Kennedy ordered. "Go for speed more than accuracy."

MacKim nodded; rapid firing would help disguise the Rangers' lack of numbers.

A few of the more scrupulous Rangers protested, for although they would happily shoot down an active enemy, killing a defeated mass of men seemed more like murder.

"Fire," Kennedy ordered softly. "If the French build floating gun platforms, they can stop the Royal Navy and recapture Quebec. If they hold Quebec, they can retake New Canada and launch their savages against our settlements all along the Ohio Valley and deep into our colonies. We need to capture this shipbuilding yard."

The logic was brutal but unmistakable. The Rangers took station behind trees or wherever there was cover and began to shoot at the panicked, broken mass of French, Indians and Canadians.

"Fire, boys," MacKim said. He noticed the original Rangers and colonials, the men who had experienced the assaults of the

Canadians and Indians, had fewer scruples about shooting the French. The British regulars, although hardened by war, were more concerned. “Riflemen,” MacKim addressed his marksmen, “target the officers; prevent the French from rallying.” He hoped to see the tall, tattooed Canadian there as he lifted his Brown Bess.

The marksmen were loading and firing, commenting on the men they shot down with their accurate long rifles, while the musket-men made poor practice, firing fast and wild.

Huddled against the gate, some of the French began to scream, others begged for quarter, while most hammered to be allowed inside. At length, the guards moved to the wooden beams that held the gates shut. The second they removed the bars, the crowd rushed forward, knocking back the guards in their panic.

“Now!” Kennedy rushed forward, with the Rangers following at once. The success or failure of the mission depended on the next few moments.

14

MacKim knew this was the moment of truth, for as soon as the defenders realised how few Rangers there were, they would rally and repel them by sheer numbers. Kennedy had to rely on confusion and momentum to keep the French unbalanced, for panicking men cannot reason.

Stepping over a writhing regular, MacKim chased after the fleeing French and into the shipbuilding yard. His section followed, cheering like madmen as they spread out.

The officer in command of the yard had not wasted his time. A company of French regulars formed up in two lines, their white uniforms gleaming, their tricorn hats all at an identical angle, and their muskets aligned in perfect symmetry.

"Jesus!" Waite blasphemed, as the French officer rapped a command and every musket lowered to aim at MacKim's oncoming Rangers.

"Down!" MacKim ordered. "Everybody lie down!" He had a memory from his youth, a recollection that the old Scottish Highlanders used to throw themselves down when the redcoats fired a volley, then jump up and attack with the sword. If it worked with British regulars, it would work with the equally precisely-trained French.

The Rangers under MacKim's command obeyed at once, with a few of Kennedy's wing also dropping to the ground. Others continued to advance when the French officer barked the order to fire.

Eighty French muskets fired, with muzzles flaring and spurting smoke. Four of the scattered Rangers fell, and then MacKim was on his feet, roaring an old Gaelic battle cry as he charged. He knew his Rangers were following; knew they were also shouting and yelling, wielding their muskets and hatchets, but he could neither see nor hear them. In his mind, he was a Highland warrior, charging with his broadsword in his hand. He was Angus Og MacDonald at Bannockburn; he was Somerled fighting the Norse; he was the legendary Ossian, and then he was wee Hughie MacKim fighting to avenge Tayanita.

"Tayanita!" he roared as he crashed into the French lines. Struggling to reload, the white-coated infantrymen staggered under the Rangers' charge.

MacKim had a momentary glance of a startled French face as he ran at him, bayonet poised, and then the French line broke in sudden panic. Chisholm had informed him that few troops stood up to a bayonet charge, and there were very few occasions when masses of infantry fought bayonet-to-bayonet. The Rangers' success proved the truth of Chisholm's words as the French fled from less than half their number of Rangers.

"We've got them beat!" Kennedy exulted, firing a pistol at the retreating French regulars. "MacKim, keep the Frenchies on the run with your men. I'll fire the boats."

"Yes, sir!" MacKim had no idea how he and his twenty men could chase an entire company of French regulars, plus however many Indians and Canadians might appear.

"Keep them moving," MacKim shouted. He stopped behind a stack of cut timber, reloaded and fired into the retreating mob of white-coated French. "Marksmen! To me!"

Parnell, MacRae, Waite and Dickert joined him, all panting, wild-eyed with the activity. They slumped behind the timber-stack, each man holding his long rifle with infinite care.

"Look for French officers and NCOs," MacKim ordered. "Without leaders, the French won't rally. As soon as you see an officer or NCO, shoot them."

"Yes, Sergeant." MacRae calmed himself down with a deep breath. He took up position behind the pile of logs as the other marksmen found their own niches. "I can see an officer," he said, cocked his rifle and took careful aim.

"Be careful not to shoot any of our men," MacKim warned and ran forward as the remainder of his men followed the French, loading and firing as fast as they could.

One middle-aged French officer appeared, shouting to his men. MacKim saw a dozen infantry pause and gather around him until a shot rang out. It was different from the report of the Brown Bess, sharper, and MacKim knew without looking that it was MacRae's long rifle. The French officer looked at the spreading red stain on his coat, and then a second rifle shot sounded; the officer jerked back and crumpled to the ground.

At the sight of their officer down, the French soldiers scattered again, with only a young corporal attempting to rally them. When one of MacKim's riflemen shot the corporal, MacKim led a charge, and the French broke and fled without firing a shot.

"We're winning," Ranald MacDonald said, stopping in the shelter of a warehouse wall as he reloaded.

"We are, as long as the Frenchies don't realise how few we are," MacKim said. He smelled smoke from behind him, glanced over his shoulder and saw one of the gun platforms ablaze, with the smoke coiling upwards.

"Lieutenant Kennedy's got started." Chisholm sounded laconic.

"Thank God. We can't stay here much longer," MacKim said. "It won't be long before the French officers gather their men."

Chisholm knelt, fired and reloaded. "Somebody's shouting orders already," he said.

The voices were hoarse, half-heard above the irregular musketry and the crackle of flames as Kennedy's party worked on the gun-platforms.

Despite the marksmen's work, the French were again rallying, with officers and NCOs gathering small groups in the shelter of various buildings. They began to return the Rangers' fire, at first in single shots, then in irregular volleys, as the officers collected more men.

A musket ball hummed past MacKim; another burrowed into the snow beside his right foot, forcing him to jump away.

"We can't advance any further." MacKim withdrew to the shelter of some cut timber. "Find some cover, lads, and keep the French away until the Lieutenant has the gun-platforms ablaze."

Although the volume of smoke had increased, showing Kennedy was setting more of the gun-platforms on fire, the French resistance was stiffening. MacKim knew that his handful of Rangers could not daunt such doughty fighters as the Canadians and Indians for long. Already, the French were pushing at the flanks, creeping forward inch by inch.

"Hold them!" MacKim shouted. He crouched behind the stack, fired at a group of Canadians, and was frantically loading when he saw an Indian crawling over the top of the logs. Dropping his musket, MacKim drew his pistol, fired, saw the Indian grab hold of his leg, and tucked his pistol away. He was faster loading a musket than a pistol. Something thudded against the corner of the stack, scattering wood splinters past MacKim's face.

"They're on the left flank, Sergeant!" Chisholm shouted, firing and loading like a man possessed.

"Keep them back!"

"They're outflanking us!" Chisholm warned.

MacKim swore, glanced behind him to see the progress of Kennedy's arsonists, and nodded. Most of the gun-platforms were ablaze, with smoke coiling aloft and spreading across the shipyard.

"Pull back!" MacKim pointed to the log-stack where his marksmen were holding out. "Form a stronghold at that stack!"

The Rangers pulled back, each man covering the next until they reformed behind and beside the log stack. Seeing their enemy retreat, the French advanced, opening a heavy musketry on the logs so that chips of wood flew through the air.

The French officers were shouting orders, their voices hoarse but the meaning clear as the French pushed forward.

"It's getting hot, Sergeant!" MacDonald said, taking a snap-shot and then ducking behind the logs to reload. "And I don't mean because of the flames."

"We'll hold them as long as we can," MacKim said, "and give the lieutenant time to destroy as much as possible." He coughed in the smoke. "And let's hope we can get out before we're burned as well."

"Got me another one," Dickert said. "A sergeant that time." He reloaded with care, whisking his ramrod up and down the long barrel of his rifle. "I like to shoot sergeants; they are such harassing people."

MacKim nodded. "I'll be harassing you if you don't stop talking and get on with the firing."

Dickert gave a low laugh. "Yes, Sergeant. That's four so far, MacRae. How many for you?"

"Three stone-dead," MacRae said. "One possible."

"Sergeant," Ranger Hackett was nearly black with soot and smoke as he approached MacKim, "Lieutenant Kennedy says it's time to get out!"

"Thank you, Hackett," MacKim said. "Pray to inform the lieutenant that we'll be back directly." He raised his voice. "Right, boys, we've done our duty here. Move out in pairs, each covering the other." MacKim was surprised how easily authority came to him. He did not consider himself a natural soldier; he did not wish to be in the army, but years of campaigning had taught him the difference between a good and a bad NCO.

"I'll cover you, Sergeant." Chisholm aimed, fired and reloaded as calmly as if he were on the parade ground in Quebec.

"Come on, lads," MacKim said, watching the progress of his men and ensuring the marksmen left first so their longer-range rifles could cover the rest.

As soon as the Rangers began to withdraw, the French increased their firing, pushing forward on each flank.

MacKim shot at a Canadian on his left, saw his ball spread splinters from a pile of logs and reloaded. In front, a detachment of French regulars was forming in open order, preparing to advance.

"Time to go, boys," MacKim said. "There's only five of us remaining here, too few to hold them." He ducked as a ball whined past his head.

Chisholm loaded and glanced at Ranald MacDonald, who nodded. "We're ready, sir."

"Go!" MacKim ordered and fired at the regulars in front. Without waiting to see if his ball took effect, he lowered his head and followed his Rangers, running fast and jinking to spoil the enemy's aim. He knew that the French muskets were every bit as inaccurate as the British, but it was possible that one or more of the enemy owned a rifle and would love to shoot a sergeant. Dickert's words echoed in MacKim's head: "I like to shoot sergeants; they are such harassing people." No doubt, the French and Canadians shared Dickert's opinion.

"Sergeant!" Chisholm skidded towards a stack of barrels and made room for MacKim. "In here!"

MacKim rolled behind the barrels, with little spouts of snow and dirt showing where French musket-balls were landing behind him. He glanced over his shoulder to see flames leaping skyward while thick, acrid smoke concealed the gate to the yard. For a moment he saw Tayanita, shaking her head as if to warn him of something, but he pushed the image away.

"Where's the lieutenant?"

"I don't know!" Chisholm had to shout above the increasing crackle of the flames and sound of musketry.

MacKim nodded and loaded his musket, glancing around to check on his men. Miraculously, only one was missing, despite the volume of fire coming from the French. "Where's Hackett?"

"Dead, Sergeant," Parnell said. "Shot clean through the heart."

"At least it was quick. Right, lads," MacKim shouted. "Each man fire another round and reload. When we're all ready, we're heading for the gate, somewhere in the smoke."

One by one, the Rangers acknowledged with a lift of their hand or a word. Their eyes were huge in smoke-blackened, sweat-streaked faces.

"Seek a target and fire," MacKim ordered and watched as the Rangers fired. Veterans all, the Rangers did not rush but found their targets, aimed and squeezed the trigger, with each shot a flat crack amidst the bedlam of battle. After they fired, the men loaded, working with speed yet no haste, not dropping a grain of powder and ramming home the ball with methodical efficiency.

These are good men, MacKim thought; *they are as good as any soldiers in the world.*

"Two at a time," MacKim said. "Run for the gate. Chisholm, you and MacDonald first. Move!"

He watched each pair disappear in the smoke, wondered briefly if he would see them again, and then named the next couple. The men moved on his order, with nobody questioning his authority.

These men trust me, MacKim thought.

"Parnell and Dickert, you're last! Go!"

"How about you, Sergeant?" Dickert asked.

"Go!" MacKim shouted again.

With the last of the Rangers gone, MacKim knew he could do no more. He was alone, the most forward British soldier in New France. For one betraying moment, he considered standing up to give the French a clear shot so he could join Tayanita, but shook the idea away. No, he would not allow that tattooed Canadian the satisfaction of victory, the pleasure of another death.

Was that tattooed man in the yard somewhere, with his dead-eyed renegade companion? Or had he escaped to Jacques Cartier, or even Montreal? MacKim pushed the thought away. It hardly mattered now.

The smoke was thicker than ever, with the crackle of burning timber so loud that MacKim could barely hear the hoarse shouts of men, although the hammer of musketry was plain. At that stage, only the muzzle-flashes revealed the musket men's position, and MacKim could only guess who was firing, Canadians or regulars.

Taking a deep breath, MacKim peered into the smoke, hefted his musket and ran, jinking again, clumsy in his snowshoes. No sooner had he left his sanctuary than he saw two Canadians crawl over the top of the barrels.

"Thank you, Lord," MacKim said as he fled into the smoke, gasped as a ball ploughed into the ground a yard to his left and searched frantically for cover.

"Over here!" Chisholm shouted, and MacKim dashed towards his voice.

"Welcome back, Hugh." Chisholm lay prone behind a length of dressed timber. "I thought the Frenchies had got you. Harriette would be so disappointed. She would have to choose a new replacement when I get killed."

"They nearly did," MacKim said, slumping beside Chisholm. "Where are the others?" He peered into the smoke, blinking his eyes at the sting.

"They're all behind us." Chisholm sounded nonchalant. "Ranald and MacRae are over there," he indicated his right, "and the others scattered to the left. Are you ready for the next hop? The French are getting bolder as we retreat."

"Ready," MacKim said and shouted. "On my word, Rangers; all the way to the gate. Ready?"

The acknowledgements came in amidst a splutter of coughing.

"Go!" MacKim said and held his musket ready to fire. He heard the Rangers moving, their feet sliding on the snow, some slipping, others crisp. One man swore in a low monotone – that would be Butler, MacKim thought, and another prayed openly – that was Ramsay. *My men*, MacKim thought. *I am responsible for them all. How could I possible contemplate allowing the French to kill me when I have such men at my side?*

"Move, you useless bastards!" MacKim roared. "Stop dawdling!"

He counted to ten, slowly, allowing his men time to escape, watching all the time for the French. When he saw movement in the smoke, he aimed and fired, fully aware that his chances of hitting anything were remote and reloaded.

"Sergeant!" That was Chisholm's voice. "Come on!"

Rising at once, MacKim had only taken three steps when he felt something like a hammer crash into his right foot. He knew at once that he had been hit, although there was no pain, only the sensation of shock. He lay on the ground, momentarily stunned.

"MacKim!" That was Chisholm again. "Hugh!"

"I'm all right!" MacKim scrabbled for the musket that lay beside him. "Get to safety!" He held the weapon close, determined to blow his brains out rather than allow the Indians to torture him. He laughed out loud, thinking *at least they can't scalp me; that's been done already,* heard the hysteria in his voice and took a deep breath.

Where am I?

I am near the gate of the boatbuilding yard.

Where is the enemy?

All around, waiting to kill me.

Where are my men?

They are hidden in the smoke, waiting to save me.

Can I walk?

I don't know.

Then find out, Sergeant MacKim! Don't just lie here.

MacKim tested his leg. It was still intact, if numb. He had no feeling below the knee, but one glance assured him that everything was in place. His foot was there, with no blood, and the musket ball had only shattered his snowshoe.

Dear God! I'm not wounded at all. The French ball hit my snowshoe, that's all.

"I'm coming for you, Hugh," Chisholm shouted. "Cover us, Ranald!"

"I'm all right," MacKim said and tried to rise, but his right leg was too numb to take his weight, and he staggered to one side. Chisholm grinned at him, making his scarred face even uglier.

"I can see you're all right," Chisholm said. "Lean on me, Sergeant. Imagine what Harriette would say if I left her favourite prospective husband for the Indians!" He laughed, supporting MacKim on his broad shoulders. "I could always bring back your head, although I think it's another part of you she wants."

"Stop talking nonsense, James," MacKim said. "You'll shock the French."

Rangers loomed from the smoke, some looking concerned, others aiming and firing at Frenchmen that MacKim could not see.

"Get back to the gate, boys," MacKim said. "Don't wait for me."

"Sergeant," Kennedy had a musket in his hands and a thin trail of blood down the side of his face, "are you badly hurt?"

"No, sir," MacKim said. "I'll be all right in a few minutes. A ball hit my snowshoe and numbed my leg."

"Can you carry on?"

"Yes, sir, as soon as I get feeling back in my leg."

The Rangers formed a diamond shape as they withdrew through the gate, with the fire throwing up huge flames and providing a providential smoke screen.

"Follow me, boys!" Kennedy sounded almost light-hearted as he led them through the abandoned French outposts.

The first bullet took them by surprise, and the irregular volley felled two men.

"They're waiting for us!" Butler shouted. "We're trapped!"

15

"Form a circle," Kennedy responded quickly. "Each man face outward."

MacKim looked around. With the French within the shipyard reorganised and seeking revenge and an enemy force of unknown size outside, the Rangers were indeed trapped. Until Lieutenant Kennedy could analyse the situation, the Rangers could do little except sit tight and fend off any attackers.

"Can anybody see who's out there?" Kennedy asked.

"I see Indians and Canadians," Waite said. "No French regulars."

"Sergeant MacKim," Kennedy said. "Take over the rearguard. We're going to move away from the shipyard."

"Sir," MacKim acknowledged. "Form a half-circle, boys, turning every five steps to face the shipyard. We'll keep any French counter-attack away."

"All ten of us, Sergeant?" Butler asked.

"All ten of us." MacKim ignored the sarcasm.

The Rangers checked their muskets and stepped forward, towards the new enemy force, with MacKim's men at the rear. Encouraged, the French within the shipyard formed a column and marched out with a tall officer and a drummer at their head.

The drums tapped sonorously, showing the regulars had recovered their discipline and were as dangerous as ever.

"Dickert," MacKim said. "Can you shoot that officer?"

"Not while I'm moving, Sergeant," Dickert replied.

"Don't try, then." MacKim did not wish to stop their momentum or leave a man alone when there were Indians and Canadians around.

"I can try, Sergeant." MacRae was always keen to prove himself better than Dickert.

"Save your ammunition, MacRae. We'll likely need it before long."

MacKim watched the French column march closer as other men began to fight the fire. He dragged his injured leg, hoping he did not have to move fast.

"There they are," Kennedy said, as the second French force emerged in a semi-circle around the Rangers. "We're surrounded; head for the artillery." Despite the tension in his voice, he sounded calm, as though leading a small force of Rangers against unknown numbers of the enemy was just part of his day's work.

The artillery redoubt was strongly-built, with three cannon pointing at different angles and logs and fascines in place as protection against musketry. The Rangers settled around the redoubt, each man finding a secure billet as French musket balls zipped and hummed around them. One ball struck the barrel of a cannon with a musical ping, then ricocheted high in the air.

"Our job is to watch for the French coming from the shipyard," MacKim reminded them. "Marksmen, the same rules apply. If you see an officer or an NCO, shoot him."

"Is that any officer or NCO, sir?" MacRae asked.

MacKim shook his head, recognising Highland humour. "No, MacRae; only if they are the enemy."

"Yes, sir."

The Rangers were firing without haste, only shooting when they had a definite target.

"What time is it?" Butler asked.

MacKim glanced at the sky, surprised to see that the sun was well past its zenith. "About two," he said.

"The French will keep us pinned down until dark," Parnell said, "and then they'll send in the Canadians with the Indians."

"No, they won't," Kennedy said. "We're moving out at sunset. We'll push right through the middle of them."

MacKim nodded, hoping that his foot was up to an advance. The numbness was wearing off, and his lower leg and foot was beginning to ache abominably. He tested his foot by pressing it against the ground and winced at the subsequent pain.

Dickert fired and gave a little chuckle. "Got him, Sergeant."

MacKim saw the tall French officer was down, kicking in the snow with blood spreading from a wound in his stomach. "Good man, Dickert; keep it up."

The French column had halted, with the drummer still busy as the men began to reform into a triple line, each soldier a uniform distance from his neighbour.

"These lads think they're at Fontenoy," Chisholm said. "When they come closer, they'll halt, and each line will fire a volley."

MacRae grunted and fired. "That lad won't," he said. "That's one ranting sergeant who'll never see la belle France again." He reloaded without haste, glancing over at Dickert. "How your score, Dicky?"

"Better than yours, MacRae!"

"You marksmen keep shooting," MacKim said, testing his foot again.

"What's happening there?" a Ranger asked, and MacKim looked over his shoulder, where a knot of Canadians and Indians were busy on a knoll, three hundred yards away and well out of effective musket range.

"Watch your front," MacKim growled. "The Frenchies might be trying to divert our attention."

Parnell squeezed his trigger. "That's another Frenchie less to murder our families," he said with satisfaction.

The French regulars appeared through the smoke, advancing in three lines, with bayonets extended and tricorn hats in a regular line. MacKim glanced at their precision compared to the ragged Rangers and grinned; he knew that a smart appearance did not signify a more efficient soldier in the wilderness.

"Here they come, boys," MacKim said. "Marksmen, pick some off. The rest of us will wait until they're in range." He checked his ammunition, aware he had fired off several cartridges, and there was no possibility of another supply until they returned to Quebec. "Don't waste your shots."

"That's the captain!" Parnell shouted and swore. "Oh, Jesus, Lord! Look what they're doing to him!"

MacKim gritted his teeth. He could only imagine what the Indians were doing to Captain Lindsay. "Don't look round, boys! Our duty is to repel the French from the boatyard. Let Lieutenant Kennedy deal with the front."

The first scream sounded then, a high-pitched, strangled sound that lifted the small hairs on the back of MacKim's neck. "Look to your front!" he ordered. The French were good soldiers, he knew and would take advantage if the Rangers were distracted.

The French were a hundred and fifty yards away, still with the smoke from the shipyard partly obscuring them. Their white uniforms were pretty under the late winter sun, their breeches twinkling as they advanced, and the occasional shaft of sunlight reflecting from the long line of bayonets. There was martial beauty in the French advance and terrible danger. Two drummers now marched in front with their drums' regular rhythm as a backdrop to the incessant spatter of musketry. One drummer threw his sticks in the air, caught them adroitly and marched on without upsetting the beat of his drum.

"Riflemen, target the NCOs; musket men, hold your fire," MacKim ordered. "Face your front! We can't affect what's behind us!"

Captain Lindsay was screaming again, the sound unnerving

all of the Rangers. Disregarding MacKim's orders, Butler and Ramsay turned to look over their shoulders to see what was happening.

"Dear Lord," Ramsay said and began to pray. "Our Father, who art in heaven, hallowed be thy name..."

"Right, boys." MacKim tried to close his ears and mind to Lindsay's suffering. "Present!"

The Rangers muskets raised, a short line of browned barrels, pointing towards the advancing French.

"Fire!"

Ten muskets fired as one, with white smoke jetting. MacKim did not need to give the order to load; the Rangers were ahead of him, as the riflemen fired at their own speed. Four of the Frenchmen had fallen, one lay still while the others writhed, kicking at the snow; the remainder closed ranks and walked on, seemingly leisurely, towards MacKim and his Rangers.

"Sergeant!" Kennedy appeared at MacKim's side, his eyes frantic. "Give me two of your riflemen; the best two."

"Dickert and MacRae, you heard the lieutenant!"

When the two riflemen left, MacKim was left with a weakened defence line, and the French infantry marched on, remorseless behind the rap of the drums.

"Present and fire," MacKim ordered, knowing his orders were unnecessary.

The closer the French came, the more accurate the Rangers' fire, until the casualty rate increased and the French line wavered.

"They're running!" Ranald MacDonald shouted, stepping out from cover. "Chase them back, boys!"

Some of the Rangers stood, fixing their bayonets preparatory for a charge until MacKim ordered them to get back down.

"Get back down! We're staying together," he said. "Keep firing!"

The French attack had failed; the regulars ran back, leaving a scatter of men, dead and dying, on the ground. MacKim spared them a moment's sympathy; he knew that a wound from a soft lead bullet was almost invariably fatal. The luckiest died at once; others could survive for hours or days in terrible agony. There was nothing remotely glorious about lying wounded on a battlefield.

When the French regulars were out of musket range and half-hidden by the smoke, MacKim checked what was happening with Captain Lindsay. He turned around slowly, dreading what he would see.

The Indians had tied Captain Lindsay to a stake with a fire a few yards away. The flames licked across the naked captain, slowly roasting him alive.

"Savages," Parnell said. "Brute beast savages."

"Beasts would not do such a thing," MacKim said. "Only men sink to such depths." He heard the crack of a rifle and looked up expectantly, but the range was too long even for Dickert's marksmanship.

"I'm aiming at the Indians, Sergeant," Dickert said.

"We could try a sally, sir," MacKim suggested. "I could take half a dozen men across to free the captain."

Kennedy shook his head. "That's what they want, MacKim. Look," he handed over the telescope.

MacKim examined the area, deliberately avoiding Lindsay's suffering. He saw a strong force of Indians hiding in the trees at the foot of the hillock.

"I see them, sir," he said. "But we can't just leave the captain to be burned alive."

"No, we can't." Kennedy flinched as the flames licked across Lindsay again, setting his hair alight.

After the repulse of the regulars, the French in the boatyard seemed content to sit tight and fire the occasional hopeful shot while the Indians kept the torture fire bright.

"Sir," MacKim said. "We have the cannon. We've used artillery before."

"The French spiked them," Kennedy reminded shortly.

"Permission to check, sir? Our advance was fairly fast, so the gunners might not have done the job properly."

The first two guns of the battery were spiked, with a barbed steel spike driven into the touch-hole, making the cannon impossible to fire – but when MacKim checked the third, he found the gunner had only half-inserted a wooden plug in the touch-hole. "We can use this one," he bellowed, ducking as a bullet pinged off the barrel, leaving a streak of blue lead on the steel.

"How long will it take to clear?" Kennedy ran towards him, keeping his head down for fear of French balls.

MacKim examined the touch hole. "I don't know." Using his bayonet, he tried to extract the plug, swearing when the wood split and only splinters came out.

"Hurry up, MacKim!" Kennedy urged as Lindsay's screams increased.

MacKim dug his bayonet's triangular point in deeper and levered the plug out, a fraction at a time. The enemy seemed to be aware of what he was doing, as musket shots clattered against the cannon.

"Marksmen!" MacKim shouted. "Try and keep these French busy, can you?"

The plug split again, with MacKim easing most out, while a sizeable segment remained in the touch hole. MacKim swore, thrusting the point of his bayonet as deep into the hole as he could.

"Come on, MacKim!" Kennedy said.

"That isn't helping, sir." MacKim felt sweat running down his back.

"Here! Permit me!" Kennedy pushed MacKim out of the way and thrust his hunting knife into the touch hole, swearing when he realised that the blade was far too broad.

"You're better with the bayonet, sir." MacKim returned to his work. "It's got a narrower blade." He flinched as a ball tugged at his coat, nearly knocking him off his feet.

"There's only a fragment left in the touch-hole," Kennedy said. "Leave it! The powder should burn it off."

MacKim was about to disagree but clamped shut his mouth. Sergeants did not argue with commissioned officers. "Yes, sir."

"Aim the blasted gun at these Indians waiting in ambush, Sergeant," Kennedy ordered. "If we can scatter them, we can rescue the captain."

MacKim nodded. It was fortunate that, in their precipitate retreat, the French artillerymen had abandoned their equipment. MacKim lifted a wooden handspike from the ground and traversed the gun, finding that it moved with surprising ease. He sighted along the barrel, realised it was too low and turned the elevating wheel. After three turns, he sighted again, with the barrel in line with the trees where the Indians waited.

By that time, the enemy's fire had slackened, with the accurate shooting of MacKim's four marksmen effective against the musketry.

"Where's the charge bags?" MacKim looked around frantically. "There should be charge bags here."

"What's this?" Kennedy opened a box and threw across a small, thick-paper bag of powder.

"That must be it." MacKim pricked the bag and poured the fine powder into the touch-hole. "We're probably doing this in the wrong order."

"Just load the bloody thing," Kennedy said, as Lindsay's screams rose to a new height.

"Yes, sir!" MacKim stuffed a serge bag of powder into the barrel, rammed it down with the rammer, rolled a round iron shot on top of the powder and rammed that home as well.

"That's us ready, sir," MacKim said.

"I'll fire it; where's the portfire?"

"Jesus!" MacKim blasphemed as he looked around him. "It's gone out!"

The portfire, a length of quick-match attached to a wooden handle, lay on its side, as cold as the surrounding snow.

"Tinder-box!" MacKim yelled, reaching into his knapsack. "I need a tinder-box!"

Kennedy was faster, scratching a spark that he applied to the edge of the quick match. He needed three attempts before the match took fire, and Kennedy shielded the sputtering end with the palm of his hand.

"Fire the cannon!" MacKim shouted, momentarily forgetting the difference in their respective ranks.

Kennedy nodded. "Stand back from the carriage!" He applied the match, waited for a second as the powder in the touch-hole fizzed and smoked, and swore as the fragment of wood in the hole leapt out, burning fiercely, and the cannon roared and jumped back.

MacKim watched the fall of shot as the cannonball soared to the apex of its flight, then crashed down, well past their target. "Too high!"

"Try again! Adjust the angle!" Kennedy shouted as they pushed the cannon back to its position. The French had placed handy wooden tracks for the carriage-wheels, which eased the procedure considerably.

MacKim bent to the elevating wheel, turned it a notch and loaded again. He was so busy with the cannon that he did not realise the musketry had increased and then died away completely, leaving only Lindsay's moans as a backdrop.

"Fire," Kennedy said softly and applied the match.

Again the cannon roared, and this time the ball ploughed through the woodland where the Indians waited.

"Better," Kennedy approved. He looked up as the Rangers began to fire again. "Here come the French; you carry on, and I'll see about sending the Frenchies back." He raised his voice. "Rangers! I want a volunteer to help Sergeant MacKim with the cannon. That'll be you, Chisholm."

Chisholm hurried over. "What are you doing, Hughie, man?"

"Trying to fire a bloody cannon!" MacKim said.

"Don't fire solid shot if you're aiming at a scattered target,"

Chisholm advised. "Try shells. They'll explode in the trees and cause more damage."

"Shells?" MacKim stared at him. "Where the devil can I find shells?"

Chisholm opened the solid boxes in the redoubt, one at a time. "Artillerymen are always better organised than we are. Here! Here are your shells, and here are the fuses."

MacKim nodded. "You'd better be accurate when you cut the fuses, Chisholm, or you'll blow us all to Kingdom Come."

Chisholm raised his right eyebrow; his left was missing, burned away. "I thought that's what you wanted, Hugh? You are seeking death, remember?"

"Get on with it." MacKim readied the cannon as Chisholm measured and cut the fuse.

"Now you can pray, Hugh," Chisholm said, carefully pushing the shell into the cannon's barrel.

"I am," MacKim said.

"Stand well back." Chisholm applied the match and stepped smartly away.

The glowing fuse made it easier for MacKim to watch the shell's progress, but the first attempt exploded before it was halfway to its intended destination.

"Try again," MacKim said. "We'll have to be careful we don't hit the captain."

"He'll find death a mercy." Chisholm was already measuring the next fuse.

The second veered left and landed among the trees, and not until the third shot did they find the target.

"Dear God!" MacKim watched in awe as the shell exploded. Splinters of wood, broken branches and fragments of men rose in the air to descend into the smoke and fury on the ground.

"Now!" Kennedy had not been idle as MacKim worked the gun. The second the third shell exploded, he led a dozen men forward in a crazy dash towards Lindsay. The other Rangers fired and reloaded and fired again in an effort to keep the French from countering Kennedy's attack.

MacKim wielded the sponge like a man demented as he and Chisholm did the work of five men, loading and aiming the cannon. By the time they were ready, Kennedy's party had reached the torture pole. Shocked by the shell, the Indians had fled without resistance as the Rangers scattered the fire and cut down Captain Lindsay. When one wounded Indian emerged from the trees, two of the Rangers shot him at close range, then finished him with their hatchets.

MacKim waited until Kennedy's men were clear of the hillock. "Fire!" he said, and Chisholm pressed in the quick match.

The cannon jerked back, nearly running over MacKim's foot, and he watched the shell arc and explode only a few yards from the previous attempt. This time there were no pieces of men, only fragments of trees.

Kennedy's party hurried into the Rangers' position, exchanging fire with the French and carrying Lindsay with them.

"Put him down gently," Kennedy ordered.

The Rangers obeyed, placing the blackened, bleeding Lindsay on a blanket. MacKim glanced over without moving. His duty was with the cannon.

"Load again," he ordered, adjusting the aim to where he imagined the bulk of the enemy were.

"The French regulars are gathering in the shipyard," Chisholm warned. "Can we swivel the gun around that far?"

"We can try," MacKim said. He saw the French regulars forming up in column, with the drummers at their head. "These boys don't give up, do they?"

"He's dead," Kennedy announced. "Captain Lindsay is dead."

MacKim nodded. After being subjected to torture, Lindsay was probably glad to escape to death. "Push the cannon, Chisholm." He raised his voice. "MacDonald, Ramsay, Butler! Lend a hand here!"

The extra muscle power succeeded in traversing the cannon until its muzzle pointed in the opposite direction, towards the still-smouldering shipyard. The French regulars were on the march, with officers in front and sergeants on the flank. The drummers tapped their drums, swaggering as if they had never faced a repulse in their lives.

"Brave men," Chisholm said.

"Aye, but unimaginative," Butler said. "If a frontal attack did not succeed half an hour ago, why should it work now?"

"Load with shell again." MacKim ignored the conversation. "You three, MacDonald, Butler and Ramsay, take positions facing the yard. If you see any French, shoot them."

The French were leaving the yard, with the agile drummer throwing his sticks in the air and an officer drawing his sword.

"Ready, Chisholm?"

"Ready, Sergeant." Chisholm poised the quick match.

"Fire!"

Chisholm applied the match, the cannon roared, and the shell screamed away, far above the waiting French, to explode inside the yard. The French officer watched its passage without flinching.

"Lower the barrel," MacKim said, hiding his disappointment as the regulars continued their slow advance.

"Sergeant – Hugh." Chisholm took hold of MacKim's sleeve. "Look!"

Flames rose where the shell had exploded, increasing at a tremendous rate, and as MacKim watched, something exploded.

"The tar barrels, I think," Chisholm said. "The barrels we sheltered under."

"Tar doesn't explode," MacKim said. "That was gunpowder."

"A mixture, then," Chisholm said, then stared at MacKim. "We took shelter under barrels of powder!"

"Somebody's looking after us." MacKim remembered his momentary image of Tayanita. "Thank you."

"For what?" Chisholm said, confused.

As they watched, the fire spread, with burning tar reaching out towards the infantry. As the fire licked towards them, the French altered their slow advance into a rapid march and then a trot.

"They're running away from the fire, not charging towards us," Chisholm said.

"Shoot them anyway," MacKim ordered. "Load the cannon."

"Sergeant!" Kennedy appeared at MacKim's side, looking elated despite the caked blood on the side of his face. "The enemy is in disarray, their shipyard is in flames, the shelling unsettled the Indians, and we've rescued the captain's body. I'm going to lead an attack and scatter the enemy."

"Yes, sir." MacKim nodded. He hoped his throbbing foot and leg would stand the strain of movement.

"Load, boys," Kennedy said quietly. "We're going to break out and head for home."

The Rangers nodded agreement. They did not need Kennedy to tell them the operation was perilous.

Everybody started as Chisholm fired the cannon. "Sorry, Frenchies," he said.

The shell exploded a few yards in front of the regulars, felling half a dozen of them and scattering the remainder.

"These boys won't be a threat for a while," MacKim said.

Kennedy nodded to the cannon.

"Can you fire a couple more shells at the French in front, Sergeant?"

"If the lads help me swing the gun around," MacKim said, and willing hands moved the cannon to its original position. By now, Chisholm and MacKim were expert at loading, and within five minutes had the first shell in the air, with the glowing fuse plainly visible against the gathering dark. MacKim followed with the second, and the instant it exploded, he laid a fuse to the remainder of the shells and joined the Rangers.

"There will be a huge explosion there in five minutes, sir," MacKim said. "We'd better not linger."

"What about the captain's body?" Parnell asked.

"We haven't time to bury it," Kennedy said. "At least he died among friends and not among gloating Indians."

Formed in a rough diamond, the Rangers moved out, shooting at everything that moved. MacKim limped along with them, stopped to remove a snowshoe from a dead Frenchman and hurried on. "Keep going," Kennedy urged. "We'll leave our dead behind and carry the wounded with us."

After a day of violent endeavour, even the Rangers were fatigued, yet nobody complained as they pushed through the enemy, with muskets firing and men shouting. MacKim had sufficient trouble keeping pace with the others to fire and was grateful for Chisholm's occasional helpful hand on his arm.

"The French will follow us," Ramsay said.

"That's for sure," Waite agreed.

"Save your breath," MacKim said, staggered on his weak leg and recovered. "We've a long way to go."

The night eased on them, moonless and quiet save for the men's harsh breathing and the swish of snowshoes.

"The snow is softer," Parnell said. "I think the spring melt is coming."

It was more difficult to walk through soft snow than hard, so the Rangers slowed down. MacKim did not know how many miles they covered that night, only that it was a nightmare of trudging, with the rearguard watching behind them for pursuing Indians and Canadians and the men gasping for breath. He fought the pain in his foot and strove to keep up, hiding his fatigue.

"When did we last eat?" Waite asked.

"Yesterday, I think," Butler said. "If we don't get back to Quebec soon, I'll be eating you."

"I'm tough stuff," Waite said. "Better with Ramsay or MacDonald; they're young and tender."

It was three in the morning before Kennedy called a halt, with the Rangers collapsing on the ground.

"Does anybody have any food left?" Kennedy asked.

Nobody volunteered. The men looked at one another with hope gradually fading.

"Take an hour's break," Kennedy said, "and then we'll move on. The French will soon recover and send their Indians and Canadians after us."

MacKim leaned against a tree. As well as his injured foot, his chest wound was stinging, and his scalp pounding. He closed his eyes and felt for Tayanita's beadwork. He could hear her voice in her ear.

"I know you're dead," MacKim whispered. "Are you watching me from beyond the grave?"

When he opened his eyes, Tayanita stood beside him, her eyes sad. MacKim smiled up at her, then reached out.

Tayanita shook her head and stepped away.

"Don't go yet," MacKim said.

"What was that, Sergeant?" Chisholm asked.

MacKim jerked awake. "I must have been dreaming," he said. The rough Rangers surrounded him, men unafraid of man, God or devils. They would not understand if he told them.

"I hope it was a good dream." Chisholm's scarred face creased in a hideous grin. "We're setting off again."

Tayanita was gone. There was only the forest around them and the leaden sky above, with the ever-present threat of French and Indians.

16

"Was she in your dream?" MacRae asked, when MacKim struggled to his feet and tentatively tested his injured foot.

"Who?" MacKim asked.

"The Indian woman," MacRae said, with his dreamy eyes fixed on MacKim. "The one who sometimes walks at your side."

"I don't know what you mean," MacKim said, but MacRae's words shook him. MacRae had a reputation for being fey, but MacKim had not expected such a solid example of the man's abilities.

MacRae gave a quiet smile. "Maybe I'm seeing what's not there," he said. "I do that sometime."

MacKim gave what he hoped was a sceptical grunt and limped to the head of his section.

"Parnell, MacDonald, you're the scouts. Look for ambushes. The rest, follow me." He was back in the war again, with Tayanita pushed to the back of his mind.

Am I going mad? Has the loss of Tayanita pushed me over the edge? Oh, God, I don't wish to end my life chained in some bedlam, with people paying to see me perform.

Parnell saw the lights first, flickering like fireflies through the trees. "Over there, sir," he said. "It might be the French."

Kennedy slid behind a tree and focussed his telescope. "Maybe," he said, "but I think it's a small village."

"Food." Butler looked up hopefully. "A village will have food, sir."

Kennedy nodded. "What do you think, Sergeant? The men are hungry, but the French might have a garrison in the village, while any delay will give the pursuers time to catch up."

MacKim did not hesitate. "The men will move faster once they've eaten, sir, and any garrison will be small. I think it's worth the risk."

"Is your foot still bothering you, Sergeant?"

"It's not bad, sir."

"It's not good either, I think," Kennedy said. "Parnell and I will inspect the village. If we're not back in half an hour, take the men home, MacKim."

"Yes, sir," MacKim said. He knew it was the right decision; Kennedy could move faster than he could.

MacKim watched as Kennedy and Parnell eased forward towards the light. "Form a defensive circle, men," he ordered, "and keep alert." He poked at Ramsay, who had his eyes closed. "This is no time to sleep, Ramsay."

"I'm tired, Sergeant."

"Aye, we're all tired, but you'll be dead if the Indians catch you."

Concentrate on the war; I am not mad, and I do not see Tayanita. A man cannot see the dead.

MacKim thought that MacRae was watching him. "What the devil are you doing, MacRae?"

"Looking for the enemy, Sergeant," MacRae answered at once.

That was too quick an answer. MacRae is watching me; he thinks I am insane.

A faint wind stirred the branches above, shaking loose snow onto them, punctuated with the slow drip of water.

"Parnell was right," Chisholm said. "The snow is melting."

"That means the ice will melt, too." MacKim forced his mind back to the war. "If the ice melts, the French in Montreal will be able to attack downriver. It will be a race between the French at Montreal and the Royal Navy from Halifax. Who will be first to reach Quebec?"

"If it's the Chevalier de Levis and the French," Chisholm said, "we'll be in trouble. Most of Quebec's garrison is sick with scurvy; they can hardly stand, let alone fight."

"Let's hope the Navy reaches us first, then," MacKim said.

"Somebody's coming." MacRae slid his rifle forward.

"It's a small village," Kennedy emerged from the gloom, "with no garrison. Come on, boys, but be careful; the Canadians are sure to be armed, and they know how to use their weapons. Treat them gently."

Kennedy posted MacKim with ten men as a guard, facing outwards and led the remainder of the Rangers into the village. MacKim heard the startled cries of the villagers as the Rangers descended on them, the frantic barking of dogs and the Rangers' gruff voices. He tensed, expecting gunfire, but there was none. Half an hour later, the Rangers returned, each man carrying bread, sides of bacon or some other item of foodstuff.

"Here you are, lads!" Kennedy shared his bounty with MacKim and the sentinels. "We can eat on the march, for the further away we are from here, the safer."

"The villagers are bound to alert the French," Parnell said.

MacKim nodded. "Then the faster we march, the better." He set the example by striding on, grimacing every time his left foot hit the ground.

It was two hours before Kennedy allowed them to halt, with dawn lightening the sky and the thaw increasing by the hour.

"Two hours, boys," Kennedy said.

Somebody lit a fire, while most Rangers threw themselves

down and curled up to sleep in the snow. MacKim detailed four unhappy men to mount guard and woke to find his foot throbbing worse than before.

Kennedy looked up from cleaning his musket. “There’s no sign of pursuit, Sergeant, so I’m going to chance a fire. It will cheer the boys up.”

They sat around the campfire with the flames casting weird shapes in the branches while the aroma of wood smoke was pleasant in the night.

“What are you going to do when all this is over?” Kennedy chewed on a leg of roast chicken.

MacKim considered for a moment. He remembered Chisholm asking him something similar, months and a lifetime ago. “I don’t know,” he said. “I can’t see an end to it. I can’t see me returning to civilian life again, worrying about crops, the cattle’s welfare and how the peat is drying. What are you going to do?”

“I’m going to London,” Kennedy said. “I’ve heard that it’s the greatest city in the world, with everything a man could ever want. I’ve never been to a big city, so I want to see the biggest.” He stirred the fire with a stick, watching the embers brighten and sparks jump. “I will visit a theatre in Covent Garden and see the players; I’ll visit a hundred taverns; I’ll see the ships on the river and cross London Bridge and stare at the Thames. I might even look at the king, the man we’ve fought for all these years.”

MacKim looked up as something moved beyond the ring of firelight, then relaxed as he realised it was only a deer. “I’ve never been to London,” he said. “I’ve never been to England. We sailed directly from Scotland to the Americas and I’ve been in Canada, and in some of the New England colonies, ever since. I’ve never considered visiting London.”

“It is the capital,” Kennedy said.

“Aye, I suppose it is,” MacKim agreed. “I’m no great lover of cities, though.” He was silent for a few moments, listening to the crackle of the fire and the sounds of the forest. “I suppose it would be something to tell my grandchildren, if ever I have such creatures."

"It would at that," Kennedy said. "They say the River Thames in London is packed with shipping, three, maybe four times as much as Boston or New York."

"I've never seen New York," MacKim said. "I was in Boston though, a season or two ago."

"What's Edinburgh like? Scotland's capital?"

"I've never been so far south in Scotland," MacKim admitted. "I've travelled far more in the Americas than in Scotland."

Kennedy laughed. "That's a soldier's life for you," he said. He grew serious again. "This war could go either way. If the French use the thaw," he pointed to the dripping trees, "to come downriver, they could recapture Quebec and start the entire procedure all over again. The last I heard, General Amherst was at Crown Point, and with a long journey if he hoped to capture Montreal. If the French prevent his advance and recapture Quebec, where will the British gather another army or another Wolfe?"

MacKim did not answer for a while. "Perhaps we are destined to repeat the same campaign, marching and fighting through these endless forests as a punishment for something we did in this life or another."

"That is a very morbid thought," Kennedy said. "I prefer to hold onto my idea of visiting London." He looked across the fire, suddenly hesitant. "Perhaps you could join me, MacKim."

"Me?" MacKim could not hide his surprise.

"You; we are comrades in arms, you and I. We've seen the worst that man can do to one another; Captain Lindsay was an example of that. When this hellish war is over, I'd like to explore the good." Kennedy looked pensive. "I am sure man is better than merely fighting, torturing and killing. I want to see the creative arts; I want to see fine buildings, paintings, plays and theatrical performances, palaces and castles and kings."

MacKim stared into the fire, comparing Kennedy's dreams

with the reality of sitting in the middle of a dripping forest with predatory Indians and Canadians eager to kill them. "I can't believe that such a world exists," he said.

Kennedy gave a slow smile. "It must, somewhere," he said. "Otherwise, what is the reason for all this slaughter and suffering? What's war for if not to build a better world? I don't believe it's only a game for kings to control another border fortress or piece of territory. There must be a bigger reason, an advance of civilisation, and I aim to see it before I die." He looked across to MacKim. "Well? Will you join me?"

MacKim thought of a theatre; he had never seen a theatre. He thought of architecture that was not designed to fend off artillery and houses that were not built in fear of an Indian attack. "I think I'd like that," he said. He tried to imagine sleeping without the expectation of a night alarm, of walking without carrying a musket, of not checking behind him every time he turned a corner or starting at every unexpected footstep. "I have something to finish off here, first."

Kennedy stirred the fire with a stick. "So have I," he said softly and looked up. "That Canadian with the heavily tattooed face?"

"Aye, that's the man. He killed my woman, or he led the men who did, and he took my scalp."

Kennedy nodded. "He led the men who burned my home and killed my wife and daughters."

MacKim pulled his bayonet free and began to sharpen it. "Once we've finished with him, we'll go to London together and visit a theatre in Covent Garden."

"Once we've finished with him," Kennedy repeated.

Only MacKim saw Tayanita at the periphery of the firelight, and only MacKim saw the frown on her face.

17

The ice on the St Lawrence River was breaking as Kennedy led his Rangers towards Quebec. They marched in a rough formation, with scouts in front, to the rear and on both flanks. They were unshaven and ragged, with torn and patched uniforms or no uniforms at all. Most had snowshoes tied together with pieces of rags, but all carried bright and oiled weapons and walked with the assured swagger of veterans. They were soldiers who knew their worth, soldiers who had fought greater numbers of French and Canadians in their own territory and defeated them. The Rangers were men who had faced and conquered fear; neither God nor the devil, and nothing in between, could scare them now. The French might kill them, but would never defeat them.

Some of the garrison watched the Rangers return, with officers shaking their heads at their shabby appearance and the men counting the gaps in the ranks.

Hugo stood in the small crowd that watched the Rangers march in, and he waved when he saw MacKim, then dashed away.

"He's looking for a biscuit," Ranald MacDonald said.

MacKim nodded. "That must be it." He limped on, ignoring

the onlookers as he unconsciously scanned the garrison, seeing four sentinels where there should be six, gaunt faces with the hollow cheeks of scurvy, and an increasing pile of corpses outside the walls.

"Captain Lindsay!" an officious major snapped. "Where's Captain Lindsay?"

"He's dead, sir," Kennedy said. "I'm Lieutenant Kennedy, officer commanding this unit."

"Well, Lieutenant Kennedy," the major snapped. "General Murray would like to see you at your earliest convenience." The major looked Kennedy up and down. "But for God's sake, man, get yourself cleaned up first. You can't talk to a general looking like some tramp."

Kennedy gave his slow smile and turned to MacKim. "Get the men fed and watered, Sergeant. I will report to General Murray immediately." He raised his voice to ensure the major heard him. "I am sure he's seen a fighting soldier before."

Without washing or changing, Kennedy marched to Murray's headquarters in Fort Louis, leaving the major incandescent with rage.

"You impudent rogue!" the major choked, as MacKim watched, hiding his amusement.

"Come on, lads," MacKim said. "Let's get ourselves settled back in."

MacKim called the roll, wrote down the men present and arranged food for everybody before feeding himself. The Rangers ate hungrily as Harriette led a delegation of wives looking anxiously for their men.

"I see you, Chisholm, you ugly bugger!" Harriette pushed through the Rangers. "I thought you'd have the decency to get yourself killed so I could marry Corporal MacKim."

"Sergeant MacKim now," Chisholm said.

"All the more reason to marry him," Harriette said, standing back to look at Chisholm. "God, but you're ugly."

"I'm glad to see you, too," Chisholm said.

"Look at you," Harriette said, shaking her head, "all skin and bone and only the dirt holding you together. What did you get up to out there?"

"Just fighting and marching," Chisholm said. "The same as always."

"I don't like that uniform." Harriette shook her head as she slipped her hand inside Chisholm's. "I think a man looks more handsome in scarlet. Not you, of course. You won't look handsome in anything except a mask."

MacKim walked away, leaving them to their banter. He felt all the energy draining from him as soon as he stepped inside the barrack room. He only wanted to lie on his bed and sleep. When he removed his snowshoes and boots, his left foot was swollen and bruised, but not as bad as he had feared. It would mend in time. MacKim lay on the bed and allowed his weariness to overcome him.

"Well," Harriette said, as soon as Chisholm slumped at her side. "You men missed all the fun."

"What happened?" Chisholm asked.

"You must know that de Levis hoped to carry Quebec before the navy came, so he's been preparing an assault."

"We know that," MacKim responded to Harriette's words. He sat up, knowing he'd get no peace until the wives had passed on all their news. "That's what we've been trying to prevent out there."

Harriette settled herself beside the Rangers' fire, lifting her skirt as was her habit, so her legs were bare below the knees.

"Mungo Campbell told me that the Frenchies spent months making tackets – that's snowshoes to you – for all their men and building scaling ladders for mounting our walls."

"Aye," Chisholm said. "We burnt a load of them."

"Did you?" Harriette was too intent on her story to pay attention to her husband. "Mungo said that the Frenchies even exercised themselves in mounting and scaling the ladders so they would be expert when they came here."

"I wonder who told Campbell all these things," MacKim said.

"Some whore from the streets, no doubt," Harriette said.

"Ah." MacKim nodded. "Evidently, she is an expert in military matters."

"The French were to attack in the middle of February," Harriette ignored MacKim's words, "and although they tried to keep things secret, our spies found out and informed General Jim."

"You people had all the excitement when we were wandering around in the snow," MacKim said.

"We did," Harriette said. "The French sent a company to Point Levy and made a redoubt there, then gathered all the local Canadians together. Despite General Jim's efforts on the south shore of the St Lawrence, the French got the Canadians to reaffirm their allegiance to France."

"Poor Canadians," Chisholm said. "They must wonder what's happening; one day French, then British and then French again."

MacKim said nothing.

"The French marched companies of grenadiers to reinforce their outposts at St Augustine and Calvaire, and we all expected to hear their drums and see the French flag on the Heights of Abraham," Harriette continued. "We knew they were gathering provisions from the Canadians, so General Murray sent over the lights and a company or so of our grenadiers and pitched the Frenchies right out of Point Levy. We only captured a dozen of the rogues, but we got all their stores." Harriette laughed. "We should encourage them to establish posts more often, so we capture their foodstuffs. Anyway, we built a couple of redoubts, so now we're comfortably nestled on the south side of the river, around St Joseph's Church."

"That's not right," MacRae said. "We shouldn't use a church for military purposes."

"It's all right," Harriette assured him. "It's a Roman Catholic church, not a proper Christian one."

"I'm Roman Catholic," MacRae said.

"I wouldn't shout that out," MacKim advised. The British Army did not allow Roman Catholics to join the army, although some were in the Highlanders' ranks.

A few days later, the situation took a more serious turn when the French returned in force to reclaim Point Levy.

MacKim and the Rangers were not included in the subsequent action as the drums summoned three British battalions to march across the still-frozen St Lawrence.

MacKim stood on the ramparts, watching the haggard soldiers heft their muskets and slide over the ice.

"Better them than us," Chisholm said.

"Aye," MacKim agreed, "half these lads can hardly stand, let alone fight. God help us if the French launch a major assault."

"What's the plan, Sergeant?"

MacKim fiddled with Tayanita's beadwork. "I hear our lads hope to cut off the French that are besieging St Joseph's church."

"Maybe MacRae was right; we shouldn't base soldiers in a church." Chisholm touched his ravaged face. "May God go with you, boys."

God must have been listening to Chisholm, for with the three weak British battalions advancing from the rear and the light infantry attacking from the front, the French decided their position was untenable. Rather than fight, they retreated, leaving the British in control. Having chased the French away, the British strengthened the redoubts while the French established themselves at St Michael, well downstream.

THE SKIRMISHING CONTINUED AS SPRING SET IN AND BOTH sides sought an advantage. Everybody knew that de ` had to attempt to reconquer Quebec before the Royal Navy forced a passage up the St Lawrence, and small parties of men fought desperately to advance their nation's position.

The French next attempted to attack the woodcutters at St

Foy woods, and the Rangers skirmished with them, driving them away in a vicious encounter among the trees, while Murray sent the Light Infantry to fortify Cape Rouge.

"Things are getting hot," Kennedy said, puffing at his pipe as they stood on the battlements, looking across the Plains of Abraham. "It won't be long now before the real fighting starts." He gave a mirthless grin. "I wonder if we'll meet our tattooed friend again?"

MacKim gripped his musket. "I imagine so, sir," he said. "We seem destined to cross each other's path."

"Good." Kennedy nodded. "Next time we meet, I will kill him."

MacKim said nothing. He reached inside his tunic and touched Tayanita's beadwork.

On the 2nd March, General Murray sent Captain Cameron of Fraser's Highlanders to take command of the British outpost at Lorette.

"You know why that is, of course," Chisholm said.

"Yes," MacKim replied. "The general has analysed the intelligence the Rangers brought him, and he knows the French are preparing for an attack as soon as the frost weakens further." He looked up from checking the flints of his musket. "Captain Cameron speaks fluent French – I think he served in the French Army for a while after the '45 Rising – so he can listen to the enemy's conversations and interrogate any prisoners the patrols bring in."

"Things are moving fast," Dickert said. "The Chevalier de Levis knows General Amherst will move against him in the thaw, so he wants to get us out of the way first."

"War is like chess." Chisholm reverted to his favourite analogy. "Strategy and tactics, move and countermove, with the generals using regiments as pawns, while soldiers like us matter less than the dust on the board."

On the 18th March, with a slight thaw in the offing, General Murray pre-empted any French advance with a raid on the

French forward post at Calvaire. MacKim saw Captain Donald MacDonald lead five hundred of Fraser's Highlanders, all the fit men and many who were weak and reeling with scurvy, out of Quebec and along the road. They moved purposefully and silently, without the pipes to encourage them.

"I wish I were going with them," MacKim said.

"Aye, we feel left out when the lads go into battle without us," Chisholm said. "Once this siege is over, I'll transfer back to Fraser's."

"Don't you like us anymore?" Ramsay asked.

"I like the Rangers fine," Chisholm said, "but Fraser's is my home."

"Chisholm's wife is in Fraser's," MacKim explained quietly. "Waiting for him. She visits from time to time, but she's a Highlander at heart."

Ramsay laughed. "I doubt she'll be waiting for long. She'll be playing the two-backed beast with half the Highlanders in creation!"

"You foul bastard!" Chisholm roared, leaping on Ramsay with his bayonet in his hand.

MacKim pulled Chisholm off Ramsay, prising the bayonet from Chisholm's fist. "It's not a good idea to kill each other," MacKim said. "And Ramsay will apologise after he runs around Quebec's walls twice, backwards." He hardened his voice. "Move, Ramsay!"

At the expression in MacKim's eyes, Ramsay fled.

Captain Donald MacDonald led his men back the next day, with a much-changed atmosphere. The Highlanders were laughing, some wearing captured French clothing and carrying French equipment. Although some of the men were bloodstained, none appeared to be injured.

"They look happy," MacRae said.

"They should. They penetrated the French lines and brought back over sixty prisoners without the loss of a single man."

MacKim nodded. "Captain MacDonald led an elegant operation."

Harriette nodded. "I heard the boys were ruthless, killing any Frenchmen who resisted and chasing them like deer to catch prisoners."

MacKim said nothing as he stroked Tayanita's beadwork. He knew that Highlanders could be as merciless as any other soldiers, yet it felt strange to think of men he knew as laughing companions hounding down the fleeing enemy. He wondered if the French viewed the Highlanders and Rangers much as the British did the Indians and Canadians – savages beyond the pale of civilised warfare.

Harriette looked into the fire. "James says war is like chess, with the generals making moves and counter-moves."

"I've heard him say that," MacKim agreed.

Harriette touched MacKim's arm. "The generals don't think of the effect their little games have on us, do they? They don't think of the wives watching their men march away, wondering if they'll ever return, or if they'll come back without an arm or a leg."

"I don't suppose they do," MacKim said.

"Well, listen here, Hugh. I've seen two of my men die in war, and I don't want to see a third, ugly though he is. As soon as this war ends, I'll take James out of the army. We'll settle in the Americas, I think. We can get land here that we'd never get in Scotland."

MacKim held his beadwork tightly. "James is nervous of his scarred face," he said. "He thinks civilians wouldn't accept him."

"Well then," Harriette leaned closer to MacKim, "if the civilians don't accept my James, they'll have me to deal with, and I don't take prisoners."

MacKim replaced the beadwork inside his tunic. "You're a good woman, Harriette, and a man needs a good woman. You look after James."

"I will," Harriette said. "And I was sorry when you lost that woman of yours. You'll find another, Hugh when the time is right."

"Aye, maybe," MacKim said. He stared into the fire. Tayanita's face stared out at him, with her eyes dark and her mouth tight with disapproval.

I don't want another woman. I want Tayanita.

18

"What's that?" Parnell pointed at something in the river.

"It's a chunk of ice," Butler said.

MacKim nodded. Since the thaw had begun, the St Lawrence had been a mixture of fast-flowing water, sheets of ice, large icebergs and smaller pieces that the current had swept past them. General Murray had ordered patrols along the riverbank to watch for any French waterborne raiding.

"There's something on the ice," Parnell said.

They all peered into the river, although, with the sun reflecting from the ice, the glare made distinguishing anything next to impossible.

"It's an animal of some sort," Butler said.

"Animal be damned," MacKim said. "It's waving at us. Animals don't wave."

"It's a man," Parnell said. "No, damn it all, it's just a boy."

For a moment, the Rangers watched as the ice floe travelled down the river, turning this way and that, colliding with other pieces of ice, spinning and then straightening up.

"That poor lad hasn't got a hope," Parnell said. "The current will take him all the way to the sea, but he'll die of the cold long before."

MacKim nodded. The boy looked about ten. He raised both hands in a gesture of supplication as he came closer, and then a trick of the current swept him further into the centre of the river.

"We can't let him die," MacKim said. He became aware of a group of Quebec civilians watching, with Claudette in the middle.

"Why not?" Butler spat a stream of tobacco juice into the river. "He's come from upstream, so he'll be either French or Canadian. Either would cut your throat or lift your hair in an instant."

Claudette stepped closer, grabbed MacKim's tunic and pointed to the child. "Please," she said.

"I can't let him drown," MacKim said. He eyed the river. A ridge of ice extended from the shore about two hundred yards into the water, where the edge splintered. "If I can get out there," he said. "I might be able to reach the lad."

"More likely, you'll fall in and drown yourself," Butler said.

"That's a possibility," MacKim said. He handed over his musket, removed his bayonet and pistol and gave them to Parnell. "Look after these for me."

"You're a fool, Sergeant," Parnell said.

"Aye, no doubt."

MacKim inched onto the ice. It was thick at the shore and bore his weight without difficulty and, his confidence mounting, MacKim slid further out. The water rushed past him, greeny-blue, with the occasional small piece of ice clattering against the ridge on which he walked. When one large floe hit the shelf, the edge splintered, making MacKim shudder. He had no desire to end up like the boy, cascading downriver on a fragment of ice.

The boy was thirty yards away, watching MacKim through huge eyes, with a frozen branch blocking the downward passage of his floe. MacKim knew it was only a short reprieve, for the force of the current would soon propel the ice on again. MacKim calculated that the floe would pass within a few feet of the edge of his ice ridge, so he might be able to save the boy. If not, MacKim told himself, the boy had to depend on the mercy of God, for he was not inclined to jump into the freezing river.

The ice under MacKim's feet was bending, and much thinner than it had been next to the shore. He could see the river flowing beneath him, while every collision with ice floes caused it to shudder and broke small pieces off the edge.

"Dear God, is a soldier's life not dangerous enough without attempting such a foolhardy stunt?" MacKim asked himself. "I must be the most stupid man alive."

The edge of the ridge was six feet away, slowly disappearing under the force of the current and the collision with floating ice. Even a casual glance assured MacKim that the ice would not bear his weight. That meant the boy would pass at least ten feet from him, which was too far to stretch.

What the devil do I do now?

MacKim glanced at the shore, where quite a crowd had gathered to watch. He saw Lieutenant Kennedy there, urging him on, and Claudette, watching with narrow, calculating eyes as she held Hugo close to her.

"Your jacket!" Kennedy had to shout above the roar of the river and the constant clinking of ice. "Use your jacket!"

MacKim stared for a moment. The boy's ice floe had detached itself from the branch and was coming downriver, well out of reach. The boy reached out a despairing hand, crying for help.

"Oh, Jesus, help me!" MacKim said. He dragged off his jacket, held it by one sleeve and threw it towards the boy, leaning as far over the river as he could to gain more distance.

"Take hold of the coat!" MacKim yelled, then repeated the words in French. "*Attrapez le manteau!*"

The boy looked at him, understanding but clearly too cold or too afraid to move. His ice floe was small, barely large enough to hold him, and when he moved, pieces fell off.

MacKim tried a second time, withdrawing the coat, inching closer, so he stood dangerously close to the fragmenting edge of the ice-ridge and threw again. "Take hold of the coat, and I'll pull you in!"

The boy tried to speak but failed. He reached out for the coat, missed, made a desperate attempt to remain on the ice floe, which tipped sideways, and he slid into the water.

"Oh, Lord, save us!" For a moment, MacKim watched the boy struggle in the current, and then he stepped in, gasping at the shock of nearly-freezing water. The boy gave him a look of terror and sank beneath the surface.

"I'm coming!"

MacKim took three strokes, grabbed hold of the boy by the hair and hauled him up. A small ice floe rammed MacKim on the shoulder and spun away, tossing on the current.

"Stay alive!" MacKim ordered, gasping, and looked for the ice ridge. The current had already carried them twenty yards downstream, with some of the onlookers keeping pace with them, their voices sounding hollow and very far away. MacKim saw Chisholm on the riverbank, his mouth open as he shouted advice.

The boy was still, not even struggling as MacKim struck out for the shore, feeling his strength drain as he sunk deeper in the water.

"Hold on, lad," MacKim said, "hold on."

The current increased as MacKim neared the shore, with the boy's weight slowing him down. "Get your head above water," MacKim said. "Don't die on me. Breathe, damn you!" The sound of the river was deafening, a roaring of water and clinking of ice. MacKim knew he might survive if he released the boy. *Nobody would know; nobody would blame you,* he told himself. *You've done your best.*

No! No, I won't let go.

With that determination, MacKim pushed harder, kicking with his legs, swimming with one arm as he tried to hold the boy's head above water.

The contact stunned MacKim, so he opened his mouth to yell and swallowed bitterly cold water. For an instant, he could not work out what had happened and then realised the current had rammed him against another shelf of ice. Each twist of the river created a point of ice that stretched from the shore into the water. MacKim reached out, feeling his hand slide over the surface, but held on.

"Are you still with me?"

The boy was only semi-conscious, his mouth opening and closing and incoherent sounds emerging.

"Stay alive!" MacKim ordered.

The ice shelf was thickest at the shore side and collapsing further out. MacKim managed to haul the boy to the side of the ice. He knew it would not hold his weight and remained in the water, feeling the numbness creep up his legs. "Try to climb up," he said.

The boy stared at him, too dazed and cold to respond.

"I'll help you," MacKim said and pushed at the boy with all his remaining strength.

"I've got him." Kennedy ran along the ice, slipping twice, and took hold of the boy. "Now, get out of the water, Sergeant!"

Other men were there, Parnell and Butler, with Chisholm looking anxious as he knelt on the ice and extended a hand. Some civilians were behind them, with Claudette watching, grave-faced.

Once released from the boy's weight, MacKim felt an overwhelming desire to let go, to allow the river to take him, to escape from all his worries. It would be so easy to die here.

"Come out of that!" Chisholm's brawny hands grabbed MacKim by the shoulders and hauled. "Typical bloody sergeant, playing in the water rather than watching for the French."

MacKim lay face down on the ice, spewing water that

seemed to burn his throat and lungs. He saw Kennedy pass the boy over to Claudette, and then strong hands were lifting him.

"We'll have to get them heated up!" Kennedy said. "Take them to that farmhouse there."

MacKim tried to walk, staggered and nearly fell until Chisholm and Ramsay grabbed him. "Come on, Sergeant! No lying down on the job."

The inhabitants of the farmhouse must have watched the drama, for they opened their door without demur, and the soldiers and civilians poured in. The sudden warmth was welcome, and MacKim did not resist as a dozen hands stripped him of his sodden clothing and sat him beside the fire. Claudette watched from the corner of her eyes and then concentrated on the boy.

Somebody brought a couple of towels, and vigorous hands rubbed warmth into MacKim and the boy, while Chisholm managed to find a bottle and forced brandy into MacKim's mouth. He swallowed, choked, coughed, and swallowed some more.

"You saved his life," the woman said in French.

MacKim nodded, still shivering and with brandy tricking over his chin.

"You could have let him drown and saved yourself."

"I nearly did," MacKim said.

Claudette looked at him. "Maybe, but you didn't." Her eyes drifted down MacKim's body, lingering at the evident wound on his head and the scar across his chest. "You've been in the wars, I see."

"Yes," MacKim said. He realised he was sitting near-naked in the presence of a woman and hastened to cover himself up. Claudette gave a little smile without further comment.

"I wonder where the lad came from," Chisholm said.

"He's French," MacKim said. "He didn't understand me until I spoke in French. He must have fallen in the river upstream."

"I'll speak to him when he recovers," Kennedy said. "Or

rather, you will, MacKim. You seem to be adept at the French language."

MacKim nodded. "I speak French, sir." The warmth and the brandy had revived him, but in his ears, he still heard the savage roar of the river and clinking of ice. "We'd best make sure the lad's all right. We don't know how long he was in the water."

"I'll take care of him." Claudette held the boy close as if to protect him from the rough soldiers who had saved his life. "I'll bring him to you when he's fit to talk." She looked at MacKim with a faint smile on her face. "You did a good job, Sergeant Hugh MacKim."

"Thank you." MacKim saw his square of beadwork lying on top of his uniform and picked it up as Claudette knelt to speak to the boy he had rescued.

19

It was three hours before Claudette brought the boy to Kennedy. She spoke in French, with MacKim translating.

"Look after him, Lieutenant, he's had quite an ordeal," she said. "He was on that ice floe for two days, I think, all the time thinking he was going to die."

The boy stood at the woman's side. He was thin, evidently nervous, but his eyes roved around Kennedy's tiny room, taking everything in. He gave MacKim a shy smile.

"Do you have a name, boy?" MacKim asked sternly. The only boys he had met were the regimental drummer-boys in Fraser's Highlanders, cocky, cheeky youths who gave the privates as much trouble as they could.

"Louis, monsieur," the boy replied. He had a squat, ugly face beneath bright eyes.

"This is the man who saved your life, Louis," the woman said quietly.

"Thank you, monsieur." The boy gave a small bow. He looked none the worse for his ordeal on the ice. MacKim had feared frostbite and other horrors.

"You're a tough little soul, aren't you?"

The boy said nothing.

"Right, my lad," Kennedy said. "I want to know where you came from and how you came to be floating past Quebec on an ice floe."

Louis waited until MacKim had translated before he spoke. He seemed quite willing to tell his tale.

"Louis says he was in a party of French soldiers," MacKim said. "They were crossing the ice with stores and a train of battering cannon and mortars when the ice broke, and most fell into the river."

Kennedy glanced at MacKim as they remembered their attack on the French crossing the ice.

"When was this?" Kennedy asked.

"Three days ago, I think, monsieur," Louis replied.

"And where were you headed with the cannon?" Kennedy asked.

"We were going to join the main army, monsieur," Louis said.

Kennedy nodded. "Where was the main army headed, Louis?"

"To Quebec, monsieur," Louis said. "We are going to recapture the town for France." He lifted his chin, frightened but defiant in the presence of his country's enemies.

"I think he is telling the truth," Kennedy said. "A couple of mortars floated past this morning, also on ice floes." He gave a small smile. "General Murray added them to the city's defences."

"I heard the rumours," MacKim said.

When Kennedy passed Louis's information onto higher authority, General Murray sent two spies towards Montreal to see if the loss of their artillery train had deterred the French from attacking Quebec. In the meantime, the General ordered his officers to ensure the city's defences were in order.

"You've got the General all upset, rescuing that boy," Chisholm said as Quebec buzzed with activity. "He's waking up all the outposts."

"So I heard," MacKim agreed. "The next time I see a Frenchman floating past on an ice floe, I'll look the other way."

As Murray ordered the officers in Quebec to ensure their men were fit to fight, the officers commanding the British outposts at St Foy and Lorette sent out strong patrols. The patrols returned with disturbing information.

"The French are becoming more active," Kennedy informed his Rangers. "Pierre de Vaudreuil, one of their commanders, has issued an amnesty for all French deserters who return to the ranks and is recruiting Canadians as fast as he can."

"They're coming, then," Chisholm said, chewing on the stem of his pipe.

"I reckon so," Kennedy said. "I don't know much about Vaudreuil, but we all know the Chevalier de Levis is a redoubtable soldier."

"So are Kennedy's Rangers," Ramsay said.

Kennedy gave his usual small smile, which vanished as he looked directly at MacKim. "De Levis will be on his way the moment the ice melts sufficiently to float his ships. He must get here before the Royal Navy."

"Yes, sir," MacKim said.

"General Murray is preparing the city for a siege," Kennedy continued. "I heard that he plans to order out all the French and Canadian citizens as from tomorrow." His gaze did not stray from MacKim's face. "If any of you men have a sweetheart among the Canadians, I suggest you say your farewells to them today."

THE MOB GATHERED OUTSIDE FORT LOUIS, SHOUTING AND gesticulating. Mostly women, they were shaking their fists, with some holding brooms or other household objects and a few throwing stones at the sentries at the gate.

"What's all the fuss about?" Kennedy asked.

"The women don't want to leave their homes," MacKim said. He stepped aside as a stone landed on the ground at his side and skidded past. "They say the British are breaking the terms of Quebec's surrender last year."

Kennedy grunted. "Do they, now? Would they prefer to be inside the city when the French siege guns open up?"

"They'd prefer us to go away," MacKim said.

"I'd prefer the French not to send their Indians to attack us." Kennedy was not in the best of tempers.

As the crowd surged forward, the sentries blocked their entry to the fort.

"Come on, MacKim," Kennedy said. "We're doing no good here. You go and find your woman."

"Yes, sir." MacKim knew his strange friendship with Claudette was an open secret. In a confined space such as Quebec, the soldiers knew each other's business and barrack-room gossip filled in any gaps with wild speculation.

Claudette was in the shattered house with half a dozen Quebecers around her, all discussing Murray's decision to expel them from the city.

"Claudette!" MacKim called out.

She came to him at once, ignoring the others. MacKim handed her a larger bag of bread than usual. "The boys were generous," he said.

"Thank you." Claudette accepted the bread.

They stood for a moment in awkward silence. "Do you have somewhere to go?" MacKim asked at last. "Do you have friends outside Quebec?"

Claudette shook her head. "No. The British killed my husband last year, and I only have a brother."

"Can he look after you?"

"He's fighting the British," Claudette said simply.

MacKim nodded. "Where will you go?" He lowered his voice as a wild idea occurred to him. "Maybe you can pose as my wife, come into the Rangers' barracks."

When Claudette smiled, her face changed shape. "The soldiers' wives would hate me," she said.

MacKim tried again. "Not if you say you're my wife,"

"No." Claudette shook her head. "I know Quebec better than any British general. "Hugo and I will survive until the French retake the city."

"And if they don't retake it?"

Claudette shrugged. "Then, we will still survive." She gave him a little push. "Thank you, Sergeant MacKim, but I think you should return to your Rangers now."

"I'm trying to help, damn it!" MacKim said.

"I know, and it is very sweet of you." Claudette stepped back. "Goodbye, Sergeant MacKim."

"TRAINING TIME!" KENNEDY SAID TO THE RANGERS. "NO more running around the forests for us. We're part of the garrison now, so we'll be manning the walls like the redcoats."

The Rangers groaned. "We're not line infantry," Butler said. "We're best suited to fighting outside the walls, not standing erect as targets for the French artillery!"

"Well, Butler," Kennedy said. "After our efforts and the French dropping their siege guns in the St Lawrence, I doubt they'll have much artillery left."

"Yes, sir," Butler said.

"All the same, we'll train like the redcoats and get ready to repel the Frenchies when they assault the walls."

The next few days were hectic, as all the fit men in the entire garrison practised manning the walls, marching from one wall to another in case of a French assault, and prepared for anything the French could throw at them.

Murray had the walls strengthened wherever he could, with ammunition distributed in salient points and the gunners trained in loading, aiming and firing.

"Did you hear the rumours?" Butler asked. "The Frenchies

are waiting on reinforcements – regulars, thousands of Indians and all the Canadians they can muster."

MacKim grunted. "Is that so? And where are these French regulars coming from? They can't come from Old France without passing us, and I haven't noticed a French fleet sailing up the St Lawrence. Or did I miss it?"

"I don't know where they're coming from," Butler said.

"Maybe the French general is going to manufacture them from the trees," MacKim continued, "or they'll march up from New Orleans." He shook his head, having made his point.

"There are Indians and Canadians," Butler said.

"Aye, that's true enough," MacKim allowed.

MacDonald looked up from oiling his musket. "I heard that there are two French armies, both marching to join up and attack Quebec."

"The attack on Quebec could be genuine," Chisholm said. "We'll be in the same position this year as the French were last."

"I hope they don't have a Wolfe to lead them," Ramsay said. "Say what you like about old Pikestaff, but he knew how to win a battle."

MacKim said nothing to that. He wondered how Quebec's garrison, vastly understrength and riddled with scurvy, could stand a prolonged siege, let alone an open battle with the French.

"It all depends on the Navy," Chisholm said. "If they get through to us with supplies and reinforcements, the French can whistle for Quebec, but if the French get here first..." he shook his head, "I doubt we can stand for long."

As the garrison rang with rumours and speculation, the thaw continued, with the navigable channel in the St Lawrence widening by the day.

"Royal Navy or French Army." Chisholm stood on the battlements beside MacKim, stuffing a foul-smelling mixture into the bowl of his pipe as he stared at the river. "Which will come first?" He produced a penny from his pocket. "I'll toss, Hugh. Heads it's the Frenchies, and tails it's the Navy."

MacKim nodded. "Go on then, James."

Chisholm balanced the dark copper coin on his thumb, winked at MacKim and flicked it upwards. The penny spiralled in the air, spinning end-over-end before it landed on the battlement wall with a loud clatter. Chisholm covered it with a large hand.

"Well, Hugh?"

"Tails," MacKim said. "I have every faith in the Navy."

Chisholm smiled and moved his hand. The head of King George stared sideways on the coin.

"Best of three?" MacKim asked.

"The decision has been made," Chisholm said. "The Gods of Fate have entered my last penny and decided our fate. The Chevalier de Levis will arrive to besiege us. Now, what happens all depends on the weather and General Murray."

MacKim became aware of the woman standing in the shelter of a building, watching them.

"Good day, madam." He spoke in French, unsure of his reception. "Can we help you?"

Claudette stepped forward, placed a small package on the ground between Chisholm and MacKim and quickly moved away.

"For you," she said. "For the sake of Louis."

"Louis?" MacKim repeated. "What the devil has Louis to do with anything?"

Claudette gave a quick smile, lifted her skirt and withdrew as silently as she had arrived.

When MacKim opened the packet, he found it contained a small bottle and some vegetables.

"I thought it might be brandy," Chisholm said, lifting the bottle. He took a swig and coughed. "It's not. It's only spruce beer. Who is Louis, by the way?"

"Spruce beer fights scurvy," MacKim said. "And Louis is the young French boy we rescued."

Chisholm took another swallow. "Maybe if you rescue a man next time, we'll get brandy."

"Maybe we will." MacKim rescued the bottle from Chisholm's hand. "And *you* can jump into the river to do the rescuing."

❧

WITH THE THREAT OF A FRENCH ATTACK INCREASING BY THE day, General Murray continued to strengthen the defences.

"Where are these lads off to?" MacRae asked, as the light infantry marched out of the gates.

"Cape Rouge," MacKim said. "A few miles upriver from St Foy."

MacRae grunted as he made minute adjustments to his long rifle and sighted along the barrel. "Hell mend them, then," he said.

The light infantry marched out at their accustomed fast pace, muskets on their shoulders and boots hammering on the hard ground. A Quebec winter had thinned their ranks, so less than half the usual number were present, and not one wore a uniform that would pass muster in Hyde Park. Yet, for all their tatterdemalion appearance, they marched like soldiers and carried their muskets with professional familiarity.

"Hell or de Levis," MacKim said, watching the lights march past. "The general has ordered them to build a redoubt at Cape Rouge to prevent the French from landing."

"Here we go again," Chisholm said. "We're back to a game of chess with the French, with the infantry as the pawns. They make a move, we make a counter move, and eventually, the two armies will face each other, and Saint Barbara and the muskets will decide the outcome."

"Saint Barbara?" MacRae repeated suspiciously. "What's a Roman Catholic saint got to do with anything?"

"Saint Barbara is the patron saint of gunners," Chisholm explained. "So by saying Saint Barbara, I am suggesting that the artillery is important."

"Oh." MacRae glared at Chisholm. "Why not just say what you mean?"

Chisholm winked at MacKim. "I'll do that next time, MacRae."

"The lights will prevent the French from landing close to our post of St Foy," MacKim said, "and watch for the French approaching Quebec."

"This flank is the weakest." Chisholm perched on the wall which they guarded. "It's where Pikestaff landed to attack, and it's where the French will land."

Beyond the wall, the undulating Plains of Abraham stretched before them, the scene of Wolfe's victory the previous autumn and the weakest point of Quebec's defences.

"If I were General Murray," Butler said, "I'd dig us in on the Plains of Abraham. I'd have trenches and gun redoubts ready to blast the French from behind prepared positions."

"I'm sure the general would value your opinion," MacKim said gravely. "The next time he talks to me, I'll say what you suggest."

Butler looked up. "Would you, Sergeant?"

"I will," MacKim said solemnly. "However, there is one detail you may have overlooked."

"What's that, Sergeant?"

"The frost," MacKim said. "I know that the river is rapidly defrosting, but the ground is not. If we tried to dig, we'd break our spades."

A rattle of drums sounded from within the city, and Chisholm glanced behind him. "Something's up," he said, pointing inside the town. "The officers are hopping around like blue-ersed fleas."

"We'll know soon enough," MacKim said, "and no doubt we'll be at the sharp end of whatever it is."

Lieutenant Kennedy, now acting in command of Lindsay's Rangers, arrived within the hour.

"Get the men ready, MacKim," he said tersely. "The French are on the move, and that means we are, too."

"What's happened, sir?" MacKim asked.

"The French have come downriver from Montreal," Kennedy said. "We had spies waiting to watch them, but their ships outpaced the spies. They landed at Pointe-aux-Trembles – that is, St Augustin – yesterday, and they're marching towards Lorette."

"Lorette?" MacKim lifted his head. "We've got an outpost at Lorette. Captain Cameron of the 78th commands there."

"Not for much longer. Lorette can stand a raid but not a full-blown attack by the main French army."

"How many men, sir?"

Kennedy shook his head. "I don't know for sure, MacKim. I heard there were between ten and eleven thousand, with about five hundred Indians."

MacKim grunted. "I doubt we can muster three and a half thousand fit men in Quebec." He glanced at his Rangers, who were suddenly all standing at their posts.

"De Levis has acted as soon as his ships could float," Kennedy said.

"If the French take Lorette," MacKim mused, "they can either capture our posts at St Foy and Cape Rouge, or cut us off from them."

Kennedy eyed him shrewdly. "That's probably de Levis's plan, Sergeant. That's what General Murray believes, anyway, so he is leading a detachment of the garrison out to counter them."

"At least the Frenchies are about twenty miles further upriver than our light infantry post. That gives us time," MacKim said. "General Murray knows what he's doing."

Kennedy nodded. "I hope so," he said. "It will take a Marlborough to defeat twelve thousand healthy men, with three thousand sick, and defend a city into the bargain." He stiffened as a young ensign with old eyes panted towards him.

"Lieutenant Kennedy," the ensign said, "General Murray's compliments, sir, and would you do him the honour of attending in his headquarters at your earliest convenience."

"That was a pretty speech, young 'un," Kennedy said. "I'll come directly. Sergeant MacKim, please ensure the Rangers are ready to leave."

"Yes, sir," MacKim said. He thought he saw Tayanita standing on the battlements, but when he looked closer, she was gone.

20

Murray led out a sizeable portion of the Quebec garrison the next day, 27th April 1760. Kennedy's Rangers were in the van, trotting in front of the battered scarlet army, watching for ambushes and checking the route as they moved upriver. Behind the Rangers were the grenadiers, with Amherst's regiment and some artillery, bouncing on the uneven road and sliding on patches of ice. MacKim could hear the hacking coughs of the redcoats and saw them stumbling from weakness as they marched.

"The grenadiers look formidable from a distance," Chisholm said, "but it's all a sham. They should all be in their sick beds, not marching to fight a battle."

"Half the garrison should be in their sick beds," MacKim agreed, "and the other half are worse."

When they reached the light infantry positions at the Caprouge River, the British destroyed the bridges to slow the French advance.

MacKim watched the axemen at work, hacking at the timbers. "All we do is destroy," he said.

"If you want to build things, become an engineer," Chisholm said.

With the bridges down, the British collected the light infantry and marched back to Sillery Wood and the Boulon, on the north bank of the St Lawrence.

"The French can land here," Kennedy said, "and cut off our outposts."

The British sited their artillery and positioned the infantry, fully aware they were not strong enough to defeat a determined landing.

"We can only slow them down," Chisholm said, with a twisted grin.

"Follow me, Rangers," Kennedy ordered. "We're the van, the point of General Murray's sword."

MacKim looked ahead. The Rangers took up position at a gap between two ridges, a natural pass through which the French army must march if it hoped to separate the British outposts from Quebec's garrison.

Murray had stationed his small force with the artillery commanding the pass, so the French would have to advance in column through a murderous crossfire before reaching the muskets of the infantry. They might force their way through, but only at the expense of terrible losses that would be hard to replace without reinforcements from Old France.

"Jim's not a bad general," Chisholm said, as he glanced over the British positions. "We can give the French a bloody nose if they come this way."

MacKim nodded and touched the beadwork under his tunic. He took a deep breath, looked around his men to ensure they were ready and breathed out slowly.

"Here they come, boys." Kennedy was perched on a rock with his bonnet at a jaunty angle on his head, and a red feather thrust up at the side as if challenging the French. "Let them see you. This is not a time to hide and fire. This is a time to let them see how unafraid we are."

"Who's unafraid?" Waite asked. He was leaning against a

tree, smoking a short pipe as if nothing the French could do would interest him.

"I'm not afraid," Ramsay said.

MacKim said nothing as he watched a troop of Canadian cavalry trot forward to reconnoitre the British position. Cavalry was so unusual in this campaign that he had to check to ensure they were the enemy.

MacRae and Parnell readied their long rifles. "No," Kennedy said, "let them past. We want them to see how well defended the defile is. We don't want to fight them, merely to scare them away." Kennedy lifted his hand. "Stand up, Rangers. Let the enemy see you, and then disappear again."

As the Canadian cavalry entered the pass, the Rangers stood, one by one, presented their muskets at the enemy and sank back into cover. The cavalry extended their formation as well as they could in the confined space, with the flank riders loosening their weapons, drawing pistols and holding their carbines.

"We have them rattled," Kennedy said. "Now change positions without the enemy observing you, and show yourselves again."

MacKim grunted as he understood Kennedy's tactics. The lieutenant was pretending there were twice as many Rangers. He ducked into cover, slid away behind the scattered trees and showed himself again, standing proud on the skyline so the Canadians could count him. The others did the same, some understanding, and others only obeying what they believed to be absurd orders.

"Don't fire," Kennedy ordered, as Parnell lined up his rifle. "If we fire, they will either retaliate or withdraw, and the General wants them to see his defences."

"We could kill them all," Dickert said.

"We could," Kennedy agreed, "and then who would report our positions to the Chevalier de Levis?"

The cavalry penetrated the pass, only stopping when they

saw the infantry lined up in formation at the far side and the artillery waiting to catch any advancing troops in a crossfire.

When the Canadian commander gave a sharp order, the cavalry wheeled around as smartly as regulars and trotted in disciplined formation out of the defile. Only when they were at extreme range did Kennedy allow the Rangers to fire.

"Hasten their retreat, boys," Kennedy ordered, and the eager Rangers fired. Two of the Canadians fell, and one horse screamed and kicked.

"We could have got them all," Dickert said.

"I think you'll have plenty of opportunities to fight later," Kennedy told him softly. "Come on, boys." He led them to the southern end of the pass, allowing the French to see him.

The French army was forming up for the advance; regulars in their white uniforms, Canadians who looked so much like the British Colonials it was hard to tell them apart, and the Indians who preferred French rule to British.

Kennedy studied the enemy through his telescope. "Some of those regulars look clumsy," he said. "What do you think, Sergeant?"

MacKim focussed the telescope. "They stand like Johnny Raws," he said. "I think de Levis has stuck a uniform on every Canadian he could find."

Kennedy smiled. "That's what I think, too," he said. "I wonder how long they'll stand when Bragg's or Amherst's veterans fire a few volleys at them?"

"They have artillery as well," MacKim said, indicating the two French artillery pieces in the centre of the column.

"If they march in that close formation," Dickert nearly licked his lips in anticipation, "we'll cut them to pieces."

"If they march into the pass," Kennedy said, "tree all and fire when they come within range." He pointed to the Canadians and Indians who trotted ahead of the main French force. "These boys will be the most dangerous for us. I'll take most of the

Rangers and hold them back, Sergeant, while you thin the main column with your riflemen."

MacKim nodded. He searched the Canadians for the tall man with the tattooed face, but the distance was too great to make out individual features. There were many tall men among the Canadians.

The cavalry trotted past the most forward French forces, and the leader reported to a small group of officers in the centre of the column.

"That must be de Levis," MacKim said. "Riflemen, see if you can pick him off."

Dickert shook his head. "The range is far too long, Sergeant. Our ball would not carry a quarter of the distance."

MacKim nodded. "A pity. Killing their commander would dishearten the French even before the battle started."

"There won't be a battle today," Kennedy said. "Look."

De Levis listened to the Canadian commander and issued orders. The bulk of the French turned around and withdrew.

"They're not coming," Dickert said, with disappointment in his voice. "They're not going to force the pass."

"Very sensible of them," Kennedy said. "Chisholm: present my compliments to General Murray and tell him what's happening." He studied the French through his telescope. "Tell him that de Levis and the main body of French have declined battle, but they have sent their Indians and some Canadians forward, no doubt to harass our rear."

As Chisholm hurried back with the message, the Indians and Canadians entered the pass.

"Now it's time for the fighting, boys." Kennedy could not hide his satisfaction. "Feel free to shoot any of the enemy you like, and the more, the better."

As Kennedy's Rangers engaged the most forward elements of the French, General Murray sent a company of lights to reinforce Kennedy's Rangers. After that, he began his withdrawal to

Quebec, picking up the British forward detachments from St Foy and Lorette en-route.

MacKim knew Murray's strategy, but his own world had shrunk to a series of encounters with the Indians and Canadians as the Rangers and light infantry protected the British rear. MacKim fired whenever he saw a target, fighting automatically without any rancour. He knew the enemy's calibre and took no chances, remaining in cover with as much skill as any colonial backwoodsman. The Canadians and Indians flitted among the trees, firing and ducking away in much the same manner as the Rangers.

"They're not pressing too hard," Dickert said, aiming carefully and firing. "That's one less, anyway."

MacKim agreed. "No, they're only occupying our attention. I don't think they're keen on forcing us back. De Levis must know he far outnumbers us; he's looking for a battle where he can smash us, rather than killing a few men in skirmishes."

"Fire and withdraw, boys," Kennedy reminded. "Don't let them pull us forward into their traps."

The rearguard followed Kennedy's orders, firing and retreating, keeping the French at bay without exposing themselves unnecessarily as the British withdrew back to Quebec. Once they cleared the woods, the Canadians and Indians became more cautious, and the Rangers moved slowly.

"This isn't chess," Chisholm said. "This is some child's game. De Levis is harbouring his men."

"He's got something planned for tomorrow," MacKim said. "Why doesn't he use his artillery? He could fire on Murray's column."

"Maybe he's short of ammunition," Chisholm said. "Some Rangers destroyed his power-store, remember?"

As Murray marched from Lorette to St Foy, emptying the outposts of men and occasionally stopping to form up and challenge the French, de Levis kept his distance. The Canadian and

Indian skirmishers took the brunt of the fighting without inflicting many casualties.

"Murray is performing well," Kennedy said, leaning against a tree to reload his musket. "I doubt we've lost more than a handful of men, yet he's relieved the outposts and faced off the French."

MacKim nodded. "Aye; De Levis has done well, too, sir. He's captured our outposts with minimal loss and forced us back to our main defences. I'd call this day a drawn encounter between the generals."

"Here they come again," MacRae warned and fired a moment later. The Rangers and lights withdrew step by step, until they reached the British redoubts outside Quebec when the Indians and Canadian attacks petered out.

"They've given up," Ramsay said, leaning on his musket.

"Or they've chased us back to Quebec." MacKim peered into the distance. The evening light was fading, with the Canadian skirmishers only a faint smudge in the distance. "Both sides can claim this day as a victory."

Kennedy stepped on top of a rock and extended his telescope. "Tomorrow will be the testing day," he prophesied. "I can't see de Levis giving up now, and Murray is too proud a man simply to wait behind Quebec's walls."

"What do you think will happen?" MacKim asked.

"We'll see tomorrow," Kennedy said, "but whatever it is, they outnumber us by at least three to one, and half our men are sick with scurvy. I can't see the outcome as anything but gloomy."

MacKim loaded his musket. "There will be a battle tomorrow, then," he said.

I might be with you again tomorrow night, Tayanita. Wait for me.

Tayanita was already there, standing seven paces away with her arms at her side and her braided hair hanging below her left shoulder.

I'm coming, Tayanita.

21

Claudette touched MacKim's sleeve as he entered the Rangers' barracks. "You're back," she said softly.

"I'm back," MacKim agreed.

"And all your men."

"They're not my men. I'm only a sergeant."

"I know your rank," Claudette said.

"Should you not be hiding?" MacKim hissed. "You know the general's orders about Canadian civilians!"

"There will be a battle tomorrow." Claudette ignored MacKim's words. Her eyes were shielded as if she did not wish MacKim to read her thoughts or her emotions.

"I believe so." MacKim nodded. He slumped onto his cot with Claudette a few steps behind.

"Your General Murray is preparing for a battle."

MacKim nodded again. "The French will attack the same wall we came for last year, and General Murray will take out the garrison to defend the city, as Montcalm did."

Claudette sat on the cot at MacKim's feet with her legs folded under her. She touched his leg. "You might get killed."

"That's part of the soldier's bargain."

Claudette waited for a moment, but MacKim had no more to say. "Try not to get killed," she said.

"I'll try," MacKim said.

Claudette removed his bonnet and looked at the broad scar on MacKim's head. "Somebody scalped you. I saw the mark when you rescued Louis."

"A Canadian did that," MacKim said. "With an Indian and an English renegade."

"Not many men survive being scalped." Claudette touched MacKim's scalp with hard but gentle fingers. She bent closer to inspect the wound. "Does it hurt?"

"It did at the time," MacKim said. "I still get headaches, but not so often." He did not mention the nightmares, when he woke up bathed in a cold sweat and the Canadian's tattooed face close to his while the renegade watched. Nor did he mention the recurring image of Tayanita, who walked beside him through the forests.

"I've never met a scalped man before," Claudette said, bending to have a closer view.

"I was fortunate," MacKim said and, for some reason, added, "They murdered my woman."

Claudette's fingers hesitated for a second, and then she continued with her massage. "The woman Tayanita," she said.

"How do you know that?" MacKim struggled to sit up until Claudette pressed him back down.

"I made it my business to find out," she said. "I know you were trying to desert with the woman."

MacKim took a deep breath. "You seem to know a lot about me."

"I do, Sergeant Hugh MacKim of the 78th Fraser's Highlanders and Kennedy's Rangers." Her fingers eased from his scar to his face, closing his eyes. "Sleep, Sergeant MacKim. You will need all your strength tomorrow if there is a battle."

MacKim did not object, although he found it pleasant to lie there with Claudette massaging his head.

"Your men respect you," Claudette said, with her accent not quite French, yet very pleasing. "And some fear you."

"Fear me?" MacKim opened his eyes.

"They think you have a streak of madness in you." Claudette did not look at MacKim's face. "As if you wished to kill everybody, or have them kill you."

"They may be right," MacKim said. "Who told you that?"

"The Highlander with dreams in his eyes."

"MacRae." That was about an accurate a description of MacRae as MacKim had ever heard.

"Your MacRae could be a poet or a sage," Claudette said. "Or a killer, but he reads men from the inside."

MacKim sat up. "Where are you living now, Madame Leclerc?"

"Safe in Quebec." Claudette looked around when somebody came into the room, saw it was Harriette and continued. "The man you seek is dangerous."

"He is." MacKim knew that Harriette was pretending not to listen but noting every word. "Do you know him?"

"HIS NAME IS LUCAS DE LANGDON," THE WOMAN SAID AT LAST. "That is the name of the Canadian who killed your woman. He wears her scalp on his belt, and yours beside it."

MacKim heard her words as if from far away, yet they still penetrated his exhaustion. "How do you know that?" He saw Tayanita at the opposite side of the bed, fingering her braided hair.

"Because he's my brother," the woman said.

MacKim was silent for a moment as he digested the information. "Are you sure?"

"I am sure," Claudette said, now holding MacKim's eye.

"Dear God in heaven," MacKim said. "How long have you known we are enemies?"

Claudette smiled for the first time since MacKim had known

her. "There are few secrets in New France," she said. "What your General whispers to his secretary, the birds in the trees sing to the *voyageurs* in Lake Ontario before the secretary's ink is dry."

"I can believe that," MacKim said.

"Lucas and I are half-brothers," Claudette said. "He is a Metis, half-Canadian, half-Ottowa." She smiled again, looking suddenly shy as she dropped her hair across her face. "Such a lot of halves for a full man."

"Are you close?" MacKim asked.

Claudette did not reply at once. "We are blood," she said, "but not close." She looked away. "He is a dangerous man, MacKim."

MacKim nodded. "He is the best man I have met in the forest. But Lieutenant Kennedy is also good." He closed his mouth, hoping he had not said too much.

"Sleep, Sergeant MacKim," Claudette said.

When MacKim closed his eyes, he was aware of Tayanita's scent and the beadwork in his left hand. Yet, he still felt Claudette's touch lingering on the scar left by Lucas de Langdon's scalping knife.

22

That night, de Levis advanced the main French army towards Quebec. They occupied the former British outpost of St Foy, and their Canadians and Indians pushed further forward across the Plains of Abraham. With the British scouts withdrawing before them, the Canadians halted when they were only a couple of hundred yards from Ursule Redoubt, at Quebec's outer defence line.

"Long rifle shot," Kennedy mused as he saw the advanced French positions dim in the spring morning. "Could you reach them, Dickert?"

"Yes, sir." Dickert balanced his rifle on the parapet and sighted on the closest of the Canadians. "I could blow his head off if you give the word."

Far behind the scouts, more French were filing up, with the regulars in white uniforms further back and the Canadians and Indians in less disciplined units. Flags floated above each French regular regiment, the colours of glory, the rallying marks if they were hard-pressed, and the symbols of honour in victory. To the men of each regiment, their flag was as important as life, the physical embodiment of the regimental soul; they would die to defend their colours.

As MacKim peered across the undulating plain, he heard the drums, faint in the distance, tapping the men to battle. He knew that, if he survived to old age, he would never forget the sound of military drums. The drums were the heartbeat of any army. Now the French were issuing their challenge as their drums announced their return to the Plains of Abraham. The future of Quebec and possibly of Canada depended on how General Murray responded to de Levis's invitation.

Kennedy studied the French through his telescope. "I can't tell the number," he said, "But I estimate about eight to ten thousand." He took a deep breath. "Their van is creeping closer," he said. "Dangerous men, these Frenchies."

"I see the van," Dickert said. "May I fire, sir?"

"What? Oh, yes, fire away," Kennedy had not finished speaking before Dickert squeezed the trigger, with the other Rangers marksmen taking the lieutenant's words as an order and also firing. The nearest Canadian crumpled at once, and others fired back, although MacKim could not see the fall of their shots.

"They're firing short," MacRae said with satisfaction.

"Keep it up, Rangers." Kennedy did not need to tell his marksmen to keep under cover and not waste ammunition. The Rangers were all well-trained, experienced soldiers.

As Kennedy's marksmen and the Canadians continued their long-range duel, General Murray called the light infantry and Volunteers together by beat of drum. The General sounded, followed by the Assembly. Major Dalling commanded the lights, while Captain Huzzen was in overall command of the Rangers. MacKim only knew Huzzen by reputation, as Kennedy's Rangers were a distinct body, separate from the official company in Quebec.

The Volunteers came from various regiments and even some civilians, with the active Captain Donald MacDonald of the Highlanders in command. They filed out of the gate with the drums rattling, once-scarlet uniforms now faded and patched, but muskets clean and oiled and the men moving with the casual confidence of veterans, although many reeled with scurvy, or coughed and sneezed with colds and influenza.

The lights formed up in extended lines and moved forward, taking advantage of every scrap of cover as they advanced against the boldest of the French skirmishers.

"Stop firing, boys," Kennedy said, as the Rangers lined the parapets to watch the progress of the light infantry. "You might hit our men."

As the lights advanced, the French skirmishers withdrew, some still firing but offering only minimal resistance. When they were out of sight, the drums recalled most of the lights, with a thin line remaining to watch for further French advances. The main French army, having issued its challenge, withdrew, leaving the ground nearly empty, dappled by the morning sun as if waiting for the blood sacrifice of battle.

"First blood to us," Kennedy murmured. "They'll be calling for the Rangers soon, boys, so get yourselves ready. Forty rounds of ammunition, bayonets and hatchets and whatever other weapons you might need." He glanced over the Plains and screwed up his face. "No need for snowshoes now, so we'll move faster and lighter."

As Kennedy predicted, General Murray had the drums rolling soon after, with every regiment forming up with weapons and entrenching tools. MacKim looked for the 78th. He knew the scurvy had hit them hard, yet hundreds of men answered the tap of the drum. Most looked like walking skeletons, pale and haggard, staggering with weakness yet still willing to fight, still forming up behind the colours.

Chisholm shook his head. "I heard that there were nearly six hundred of Fraser's in hospital yesterday, with scurvy and frost-bite. Now, most are in the ranks, refusing the surgeon's orders so they can fight."

MacKim felt a surge of pride; although he was a Ranger, fighting with men he trusted and respected, his heart was still

Highland, and the skirl of the pipes stirred his blood like no other sound on earth.

"God bless you, men of Fraser's Highlanders," he murmured.

Chisholm nodded. "Aye, maybe we should be with the lads, Hugh."

"Maybe we should, at that," MacKim agreed. The urge to follow the pipes was strong, and he inched closer.

"No." Kennedy shook his head in emphatic denial. "I need you here; you are Rangers now."

With the city drained of civilians, there was no crowd to cheer the army into battle. Instead, there was a worried collection of soldiers' wives, a few camp followers and some soldiers too injured to fight. MacKim allowed his eyes to drift across the anxious faces, searching for Claudette, although with no expectation of seeing her.

At nine o'clock, Quebec's gates opened, and Murray's three-thousand-strong army marched out. Murray was in front, with drums beating and each regiment with its colours flying overhead. MacKim watched the men, gaunt with hunger, staggering with scurvy, huge-eyed with fatigue and deprivation, and wondered that they could march, let alone hope to fight a well-fed, much larger French army.

"Come on, lads," MacKim said. "We're not alone now. We have the entire British army to back us up."

"Or slow us down," Butler said. "Parade-ground soldiers!"

Colonel Simon Fraser of the 78th commanded the left-wing, with three regiments under him – Lascelles 47th, Kennedy's 43rd and his own Highlanders. On the right, Colonel Burton had Amherst's 15th, Anstruther's 58th, Webb's 48th Foot and the second battalion of the 60th, the Royal Americans. In reserve, stamping their feet and watching with intense interest, were Otway's 35th Regiment and the third battalion of the Royal Americans.

MacKim was surprised that a few civilians gathered outside

the walls. He was unsure if they were local farmers or the evicted Quebecers.

"Ghouls," Chisholm gave his opinion. "They're the same sort of people who would enjoy a hanging."

"Perhaps." MacKim wondered what the spectators were thinking, and if they hoped the de Levis's army would kill all these intrusive British who had destroyed their town. Claudette stepped slightly forward from the crowd, held MacKim's eyes for a moment and waved, without lifting her hand above the level of her hips. At her side, Hugo was more demonstrative, waving both hands in the air.

MacKim stiffened to attention in reply and lifted his left hand. He tried to smile, although he guessed the gesture was probably more like a death's-head grimace.

"Right, boys." Kennedy had not noticed the by-play between MacKim and Claudette. "Shoot straight, and don't let the Frenchies shoot you! We're on the left flank, so follow me and keep your powder dry."

The Rangers stepped out, jaunty in their battered uniforms, each man sure of himself, individuals compared to the homogeneous conformity of the line regiments that made up the fighting core of the army. The pipes of the 78th Highlanders screamed their challenge to the Canadian sky, notwithstanding the weak state of the men in the ranks. Behind the pipes, the drums roared out their messages, encouraging the army forward to face the French in open battle once more. Twenty pieces of artillery rattled with the British, splashing through the still snowy ground or sliding on the hard-packed ice.

Murray's men were on the march, the battered survivors of scurvy, starvation and the frost. In front stood Britain's main rival for colonial supremacy, King Louis XV's soldiers, the Bourbon's white-uniformed cutting edge.

"The guns are finding it hard going," Chisholm said. "Saint Barbara won't be at her best today."

MacKim nodded. The artillery drivers were forcing forward

their wagons, with the gunners having to help push the cannon across the ground, easing the guns through deep, slushy dips.

MacKim was relieved when Murray called a halt, and the army took up its position on a ridge, inviting the French to advance towards them. The colours floated above each regiment, the silk flapping in a slight breeze, and only a close observer could see that the gaudy scarlet of the uniforms disguised sick men.

"That's the way," Chisholm said, "let them come to us. We've not sufficient fit men to advance against superior numbers."

The Rangers stood along the left flank of the army, with Kennedy sending scouts to watch ahead.

"Sir," Butler threw a casual salute, "the French are a mile ahead of us. Their van is waiting on a series of small hills at Sillery Wood entrance."

"Good man, Butler. I'll have a look. Look after the men, MacKim." Kennedy ran ahead, musket in one hand and telescope in the other. He returned within five minutes. "MacKim: run over to the general. Tell him that the French van is in front of Sillery Wood, and the main body is on the St Foy road."

"Sir." MacKim saluted and ran back to the main body.

General Murray sat on his horse with his face troubled. He nodded when MacKim passed on his message. "Thank you, Sergeant," Murray said and shouted a string of orders to the officers that surrounded him.

"Gentlemen, we'll never have a better chance to attack. The French have not yet formed up. Take your positions and advance. If the Lord is with us, we'll end the French threat to Quebec on the Heights of Abraham."

"Oh, not a good idea, General," Chisholm said, as the drums tapped the advance. "We're leaving a strong position to attack a larger enemy under a good commander."

"We're only pawns, remember, James? We're not paid to think," MacKim said, as the Rangers trotted forward on the flank.

Chisholm grunted. "You're using my words, Sergeant."

"I have to when they're right." MacKim was aware of the drums tapping behind him and the high wail of the pipes. In front, he could see the French skirmishers waiting, with an irregular popping of musketry where men fired. It all seemed so unreal, so unwarlike, this jousting for the future of a continent. He leapt to avoid a deep, snow-filled hole, slid on a patch of ice and listened to the soft pad of the Rangers' feet over the snowy ground.

Kennedy was in front, jinking from side to side in case any French marksman was aiming at him. "With me, Rangers!"

The British advanced with eight battalions in the first line and two in reserve. Murray believed the main French threat would come from the right, so he placed the light infantry and two companies of grenadiers, the pick of the army, on that side. On the left were Captain Donald MacDonald's Volunteers, the Rangers and a hundred assorted men.

"Let's hope the French don't notice how weak our flank is," Chisholm said. "The Volunteers might be keen, but that group," he jerked his thumb towards the assorted company, "they don't know each other. I doubt they'd stand a single volley."

As the British advanced, the main French body moved into the wood, where they formed up with their grenadiers on the left, tall hats prominent and white uniforms glinting in the morning sun. As with the British, the French standard-bearers were in the front-centre of each regiment, with the spring sunshine catching the colours.

"Battles are such pretty things," MacKim said, "except for the actual fighting. Brightly uniformed men marching in unison as the drums beat rhythms and horses prance." He shook his head. "We do love to glorify the business of ritual killing, don't we?"

Ramsay looked at him strangely. "Yes, Sergeant," he said.

"Sir! Lieutenant Kennedy!" A young ensign approached the

Rangers, his face shining with enthusiasm. He looked from one man to another, searching for the officer.

"Yes, ensign?" Kennedy said. "I'm Kennedy."

"General Murray sends his best respects, sir," the ensign stumbled over the words he had memorised, "and could you try to find the French order of battle and send a report to him, sir, as soon as is convenient."

Kennedy nodded. "Pray to convey my respect to General Murray," Kennedy said, "and inform him that I shall do my utmost to fulfil his orders." He put a hand on the ensign's shoulder. "Now repeat my words, ensign, so I know you have them correct."

The ensign nodded and repeated the words before Kennedy allowed him to run back.

"Right, MacKim. You and I will go forward," he indicated a small rise, "and see how the enemy looks, while trying not to get ourselves killed."

Leaving the Rangers to fend for themselves, Kennedy and MacKim trotted forward and ascended the rise, from where they could see most of the French army. Kennedy extended his telescope and scanned the disciplined ranks. "Memorise this, MacKim."

"Yes, sir."

"I'd say there were ten battalions of regulars, although I'd guess de Levis has filled the ranks by recruiting locally."

"Ten regular battalions," MacKim repeated.

"I can see the colours of the Queen's Regiment," Kennedy said, "maybe five hundred men." He shifted his telescope slightly. "Bayard's, another five hundred and Guinenne's Regiment, about the same number. Languedoc, and then Lafarre's regiment, then Roufillion, all with around five hundred men."

"Yes, sir." MacKim scribbled down the names.

"We're not finished yet, MacKim. Two battalions of Berry's regiment and two of marines, again with around five hundred men in each battalion."

"That's about four and a half thousand regulars, sir," MacKim said.

"About that," Kennedy agreed. "I'd estimate around five to six thousand Canadians as well, and a couple of hundred Indians. I am not sure of the nation, but they are either Iroquois or Ottowas."

"About eleven thousand men, sir," MacKim calculated.

"Against our three thousand invalids," Kennedy said.

MacKim nodded to the left and cocked his musket. "The Canadians have noticed us, sir." A group of Canadians were approaching the rise, moving at speed.

"I see them," Kennedy said. "Here's the French order of battle. I'd say eight or nine companies of Grenadiers in the van, with a couple of companies of volunteers, judging by their mixed uniforms, and the Indians."

MacKim repeated the words.

"I think seven, maybe eight battalions of regulars in the main body, drawn up in four distinct columns, with Canadians between each column, and three, make that four, corps of Canadians on each flank. Maybe two regular battalions also on each flank." Kennedy snapped shut his telescope. "Now, we'd better get out of here; these Canadians are getting dangerously close."

"Yes, sir," MacKim levelled his musket. "How about the reserves, sir? Has de Levis not got a reserve?"

Kennedy glanced at MacKim. "You're a devil for details, aren't you, Sergeant? Details and danger." He opened the telescope again. "Yes, a couple of thousand Canadians in the rear. And now, come on, MacKim."

"Yes, sir." MacKim uncocked his musket and withdrew in some haste as the nearest of the Canadians began to fire. One ball kicked up snow ten yards to the right, while the rest fell far short.

A few moments later, MacKim looked along the length of the British line, with the regiments marching resolutely in the European fashion, looking for a traditional set-piece battle rather than the North American war of skirmishing and firing from cover. He knew he was witnessing history.

Murray gave an order, and the Lights advanced at speed, waiting until they were in musket shot and firing volleys at the French grenadiers. Rather than defend their windmill strongpoint, the French retreated in some haste.

"They're good at running away," Butler said.

"The day is still young," Chisholm said. "I remember them at Fontenoy."

Murray's drums hammered a command, and Kennedy lifted his head. "That's us, boys! We've to attack the French right-wing. Follow me!"

The Rangers gave a hoarse cheer and ran forward, with Captain MacDonald's Volunteers keeping pace and the mixed company slightly behind. The French right held for a few moments, with both sides exchanging musketry, and then the Rangers and Volunteers pushed them back.

The French had occupied two of the incomplete redoubts that Murray had built to defend Quebec, throwing themselves down with muskets ready to repel the British. They opened fire before the Rangers came in range, wasting ammunition and alerting the British to their presence.

"The Frenchies are in our redoubts," Kennedy shouted. "Come on, boys!"

He led the way, with his Rangers at his heels and the Volunteers close behind. As the French in the redoubt reloaded, the Rangers took them from the flank, but Fraser's Highlanders drew most blood. The Highlanders drew their claymores and launched a screaming charge, like warriors from a previous age rather than professional eighteenth-century soldiers. Faced with scores of sword-wielding Highlanders, the French fired a single volley, abandoned the redoubt and fled, with the Highlanders pursuing them until the officers called them back.

"They're retreating," Parnell shouted, as the French retreated at speed, with only a few firing a parting shot.

"We've got them on the run," Kennedy shouted. "Keep pushing, Rangers!"

MacKim glanced along the British line. On the opposite flank, the lights were equally successful, pushing back the French grenadiers and advancing with elan, if in some disorder. In the centre, the French van had not even remained to fire but withdrew as soon as the British front line drew within musket range.

"We're hammering them," Ramsay exulted, kneeling to fire at a running Indian.

"Push on!" Kennedy said, as the British thrust through the wood and out the other side, where the main French force waited. After their initial difficulties, the artillery had advanced to the front of the army.

"Drop your entrenching tools, men." The order came from Murray and passed down the ranks. "We'll catch the French while they are still forming up."

While the British had pushed past the French van, the Chevalier de Levis had not been idle. He had withdrawn the main body of his army and formed them in strong columns. As the British emerged from the wood, de Levis sent one of his columns to support the retreating grenadiers.

"The Chevalier de Levis knows his stuff." Kennedy slowed down the Rangers advance. "Don't advance too far, boys. The French will counter soon."

MacKim nodded. The British force looked impressive as it marched with drums tapping and the colours flying in the breeze, but as the battle wore on, even the most unobservant witness could see the appearance was hollow. Oh, they would fight, he knew, but sick men had neither the strength nor the stamina to sustain a hard battle.

The French column advanced at a speed few British columns would match, came to an area of rising ground, and altered direction to take the lights and the remainder of the British right-wing in the flank. It was a classic manoeuvre, perfected in the parade ground over a hundred attempts, with the French infantry moving like a machine and the British struggling to march through the slushy snow of the St Charles Valley. The British lights halted, then turned and withdrew in disorder, with their scattered men moving across the British right-wing. The British advance faltered as fleeing lights obscured their view.

"The Chevalier has moved his knight," Chisholm murmured. "How will our General Murray respond, I wonder?"

"We have other things to think about," MacKim said. "The Chevalier has moved both his knights."

While one column threatened the British right flank, a second marched toward the left and abruptly wheeled to attack the Rangers in flank.

"De Levis has used his numbers well," Chisholm said. "He's advanced in a semi-circle, threatening both our flanks."

"Meet them," Kennedy shouted. "Move forward and harass them with musketry; try and break down their formation."

The Rangers responded, running forward to find cover and firing at the advancing French. However, tactics that were successful in the forest against limited numbers of men were less useful against a large column. The French advanced at speed, ignoring their casualties, and in such force that they threatened to overwhelm the Rangers and Volunteers.

On the right, the British artillery poured shot after shot into the French ranks, bowling men over and sending bodies, hats, and pieces of men spiralling into the air. A haze of French blood rose, covering the regulars as they advanced. Ignoring their casualties, the French column closed ranks and marched on, with their bayonets glittering in the morning sun. In front of the column, the drummers marched, tapping out the advance as the officers drew their swords. One French drummer seemed devoid of fear, tossing his drumsticks in the air and ignoring the cannonballs that ripped past his head.

"Force them back!" Kennedy shouted, firing and loading beside his men. MacKim shot a running Canadian, rolled into a fold of ground to reload, swore as a ball splintered against a stone near his face, and worked his ramrod furiously.

"Wait for me, Tayanita!" He shouted. "It won't be long now!"

Murray had seen the danger and ordered his thin second line, his only reserve to support the hard-pressed flanks. The third battalion of Royal Americans marched stolidly to support the British left, with Otway's Foot advancing in support of the wavering right.

"It's all he could do," Chisholm said calmly, as the supporting British troops marched to the aid of the Rangers. Even combined, the two forces faced a far larger number of French and withdrew, step by step, firing all the time. Powder smoke lay thick on the Plains of Abraham, acrid, choking and white.

The gunners sought to pull back their guns, but the men were knee-deep in slushy snow, and the guns and gun-limbers up to their axles. As the artillery fire slackened, the infantry saw how heavily the French outnumbered them and how expertly de Levis had outmanoeuvred Murray. Months of sickness took their toll, and British soldiers began to stumble away from the firing.

"Now what?" MacKim shouted. He saw a Ranger rise to fire, just as the French column halted, fired a volley, reloaded and continued their inexorable advance. A scattering of French bodies lay behind them, but now scarlet-coated men also lay on the ground and, more worrying, many British soldiers were looking over their shoulders to the walls of Quebec.

"This isn't like Fontenoy," Chisholm said, as he fired at the oncoming French column. "Our boys have lost heart."

MacKim saw a French ball hit Colonel Fraser. The colonel jerked aside as the shot struck him on the right breast.

"That's the colonel gone," Chisholm said.

"No," MacRae shook his head. "He's all right."

Kennedy focussed his telescope. "The shot hit the metal star of his cartouche box, I think," he said. "Colonel Fraser is still standing."

"Good." MacKim nodded. He did not particularly like the

colonel but recognised him as a good soldier that the army would miss.

The French continued their advance, firing and marching, pushing the weakened and now disintegrating British line back towards Quebec. MacKim heard the rattle of French drums and saw the swaggering drummers, with the agile man in advance of the French infantry, throwing his drumsticks in the air and catching them.

"We've met before, my friend" MacKim said, "in the shipyard. I am glad you survived."

The French drummer threw the drumsticks, turned a full circle, caught the sticks and marched on.

"Cheeky little bugger," MacRae said, aiming his rifle.

"Let him live." MacKim pushed the rifle barrel down. "Concentrate on the officers and NCOs."

As the French advanced, the British line cracked, with man after man retreating. The soldiers who had defeated Montcalm's army on the same ground the previous year were now running. Soldiers who had endured the rigours of the siege, and the fear of dark pickets with Indians prowling, forgot to be brave as de Levis led his French troops forward.

MacKim swore. He knew the British had lost the battle. If Murray decided to stand and slug it out toe to toe, he might lose his entire army, and that would give de Levis virtually open access to Quebec. Murray's three thousand ragged men constituted the only British army presently in Canada, and the General was responsible not only for the men, but also for Quebec, the capital city and lynchpin of New France. If Murray lost his army, the British would lose Canada; they would have to regain it from a triumphant France with sky-high morale.

Nobody was surprised when the British drums beat the Retreat.

"It's logical," Chisholm said. "In this game of chess, Murray is looking for a stalemate until the Royal Navy comes with reinforcements."

"And if the French navy comes instead?" MacRae shot a running French officer, but there were more officers to take his place and many more Frenchmen.

"Checkmate," Chisholm said. "The French have regained Quebec."

Once the retreat sounded, Murray's army withdrew in some haste. Men who had been valiant a few moments previously, suddenly decided that their life was worth saving and much more important than glory for the regimental colour.

"Is this a rout?" Ranald MacDonald asked, as the artillery abandoned their cannon in the snow. They moved towards Quebec at speed, whipping their horses to overtake the infantry. MacKim saw one gun-limber overturned in a deep rut; the axle-tree snapped and both wheels at an acute angle.

"If it's not, it's the closest I've seen to one," Chisholm said. "We didn't act like this at Fontenoy." He yelled and fell forward, holding his neck. "Jesus! I've been hit!"

"Chisholm!" MacKim bent to him, suddenly anxious. Chisholm had befriended him when he joined Fraser's as a young recruit in 1757, and they had survived battles and hardships ever since. "James!"

Chisholm lay for a moment, groaning, then gently put a hand on the back of his neck and swore. "Look at that!" he said and produced a musket ball. "It struck in the queue of my hair." He jiggled the hot, now misshapen lead ball in his hand. "I've never heard the like of that before."

"You're a lucky man, James." MacKim nearly laughed, recognised the onset of hysteria and took a deep breath. "I'll wager Harriette keeps the ball as a souvenir."

"She'd like that." Chisholm continued to rub his neck.

"Keep moving, boys, the French are gaining on us," Kennedy ordered, kneeling to fire. "Support each other; no running, and don't leave any of our wounded on the field. I'm not having any of my men scalped."

The Rangers pulled back, firing and moving as Murray's army

withdrew to Quebec. When MacKim passed the British artillery, he was tempted to spike the touch holes to render them inoperable by the French.

"Can't we save the guns?" MacKim yelled, as French musket balls thudded into the frozen earth at his feet.

"No time!" Kennedy shouted. "Look at them!"

The artillerymen had abandoned the guns in their mad scramble to escape. Some lay on their side in snowdrifts; others were bogged axle-deep in ditches full of slushy or frozen snow.

"We're gifting the French our artillery," MacKim grumbled, "after all our trouble in destroying their artillery train."

"Come on, Sergeant!" Kennedy fired and reloaded, swearing as a ball hummed past his head. "We've got to get back to Quebec!"

The French line was advancing, with Canadians and Indians in front and the regulars marching steadily, shoving aside any feeble British attempt to hold them. The French colours flapped in the breeze, King Louis reclaiming the land his countrymen had hacked out of the forest over the past two hundred years.

"Bloody Frenchies!" Ramsay was nearly sobbing as he loaded, aimed and fired. "Bloody, bloody, French!"

Foremost among the Canadians was a tall man, leading from the front and bawling orders to his men. A few yards behind, the squat renegade marched with the French, firing at the British troops.

"You again," MacKim said. Without thought, he knelt and aimed, feeling the hatred course through him. "Lucas de bloody Langdon."

"MacKim!" Kennedy grated. "You can't fight them all on your own! Come on!"

"He's over there!" MacKim knew his words made no sense as he squeezed the trigger. The musket roared, but MacKim knew he had missed as soon as the ball left the muzzle. He swore and began to reload.

"What? Who's over there?" Kennedy peered into the low

bank of powder smoke, flapping a hand in front of his eyes to clear a passage. "Dear Lord, it's him." Despite his words to MacKim, Kennedy knelt at his side, cocked his musket and fired in the same movement.

Lucas de Langdon came on, with his burly friend at his side and Indians advancing fast behind him.

"Missed!" MacKim said and reloaded, swearing.

"What the devil are you two playing at?" Chisholm was no respecter of rank in the middle of a battle. "The French have outflanked us! If we don't get out of here, they'll cut us off and hand us to the Indians as playthings."

As the red madness cleared from MacKim's mind, he saw that Chisholm was correct. Most of the retreating British were crowding around the gates of Quebec, with the French line extended on either side and advancing at speed.

"You'll keep," MacKim growled to Lucas de Langdon, grabbed Kennedy by the shoulder and ran back to Quebec, with Chisholm and half a dozen Rangers around them. Once he had begun to run, MacKim found it hard to stop and forced himself to slow down.

"I'm damned if I'll let the French see my back," he said.

He knew it was not the French he meant, but Lucas de Langdon.

The Rangers were one of the last units to file into Quebec, with the garrison artillery firing aimed shots to keep the pursuing French at bay. MacKim turned at the gate. Lucas de Langdon stood a bare two hundred yards away, with his musket balanced over his shoulder and his companion at his side. As he saw MacKim turn, he raised his left hand and pointed, and then the artillery fired a salvo, and white smoke gushed between them.

When the smoke cleared, de Langdon was gone, and the French infantry stood in a long, disciplined line along the Heights of Abraham with their commanders in the centre, masters of the battlefield.

23

Claudette stood inside the walls, watching the British army return, shoulders slumped in defeat. She ran her eyes over the battered, shocked men until she found MacKim, and then she nodded to him, only once, and slipped back inside the crowd. MacKim watched her without understanding. His mind was busy with Lucas de Langdon, and his heart was sick with the pain of defeat.

"Seventy-eighth!" Colonel Fraser roared. "You're soldiers, not sorners! Straighten those shoulders! March in!"

The process of returning pride to the men had begun, although it would be some days before the army recovered sufficiently to be called a fighting force.

"How many did we lose, sir?" MacKim asked as he slumped against the barrack-room wall. The taste of defeat was bitter in his mouth.

"I'm not sure," Kennedy said. "I heard we lost over three hundred men, killed or captured, and around seven hundred wounded. I don't know if the figures are accurate."

MacKim whistled. "That's about a third of the men engaged. How about the French?"

Kennedy shook his head. "I am even less sure of their figures,

MacKim. There is a wild story that they lost about two and a half thousand men, but that's improbable. We did break their van, so their losses were not negligible."

MacKim stood up. "And the French captured all our field artillery, too. That was a major victory for the Chevalier de Levis."

Kennedy nodded in agreement. "It was," he said. "The Chevalier is proving himself a redoubtable warrior. He knows we have three armies. We have Murray's in Quebec and have two more under Amherst and Brigadier-General William Haviland readying to advance upon Montreal." He shrugged. "Perhaps they are already marching now that the frost is lifting. De Levis may outnumber us here in Quebec, but once Amherst arrives, we will far outnumber him."

MacKim nodded, with the depression of defeat weighing heavily upon him. "Amherst is a long way from Canada; he has to fight his way up the Ohio."

Kennedy nodded. "Amherst will advance by way of Lake Ontario, Brigadier Haviland by Lake Champlain and the Richelieu River from the south." He sighed. "However, we can't think of Amherst now," he said. "Our fight is with de Levis here, and our hope is that the Navy comes to relieve us before the French assault the town." His grin lacked its usual sparkle. "It's all about survival now, Sergeant."

MacKim nodded. "Maybe it always was."

Kennedy stuffed tobacco into the bowl of his pipe. "With our garrison weakened, and half of them mere scarecrows with scurvy and hunger, the French should be able to pour over the walls at the first assault." He began to puff smoke. "We can thank ourselves that you and I destroyed many of the French munitions, and they lost cannon in the ice. That might slow them down a bit."

"It all depends on the Navy," MacKim said.

Kennedy grinned. "The Navy and General Murray. I can't see

him tamely surrendering anyway. He might not be the best general in the world, but he's too stubborn to give up."

An hour later, a wounded grenadier limped up to the walls, pleading for help. Unnerved by the recent defeat, the sentries refused to open the gates until Captain Donald MacDonald arrived.

"Let that fellow in!" MacDonald snapped, "or by God, I'll send you to the halberds!"

With MacDonald standing at their back, sword in hand, the sentries opened the gate, closing it when the wounded man staggered in.

"Savages," the grenadier said. "Bloody wicked savages."

Captain MacDonald caught him as he fell. "What's happened, private?"

"The French have let their savages loose," the grenadier gasped. "They're scalping our dead and most of the wounded." The soldier was about thirty-five, but hardship and hunger had added years to his face. "I saw them slit a wounded corporal's throat and scalp him as he died."

The news soon spread to the garrison, adding to their discontent as, within the walls, the British soldiers had lost all discipline. They roamed the streets, searching for alcohol, ignoring the roars of the NCOs, breaking into houses to see what they could steal.

Chisholm stood at the barrack door, smoking his pipe. "This riot," he said, "is what comes of recruiting an army from the lowest level of society." He pointed with the stem of his pipe. "You'll notice there are no Highlanders amongst that rabble. We have pride in ourselves and our regiment."

"Aye, and if we act like savages," Ranald MacDonald said, "our families back home would be ashamed."

MacRae was polishing his rifle. "The time is coming when there will be few Highlanders left," he said. "We will fight and die in foreign lands while an alien race takes possession of the Gaeltacht – Highland Scotland."

"More fool us," Chisholm said.

MacKim interrupted before MacRae could turn his fey insight on him. "Well, lads, we'd better get to work. I want the barracks cleaned up, and a guard on the door in case any of that rubbish tries to rob us." He nodded to the drunkards who had once been British soldiers.

As the day wore on and the officers attempted to restore order in the demoralised British ranks, more walking wounded arrived, and more stories filtered in from the battle. There was Lieutenant McGregor of Fraser's who fell on the left flank. The French bayonetted him twice, and he lay wounded on the slushy ground until a party of Indians crept on him. One Indian grabbed his hair, preparatory to scalping the lieutenant, who shouted out to a nearby French officer. Fortunately, the Frenchman intervened and saved McGregor's hair and his life.

"Did you hear about the sergeant from Braggs?" Harriette was happy to spread gossip. "He was an Irishman, and the Frenchies shot him in the chest."

"French soldiers do that sort of thing," Chisholm said.

"Be quiet, Chisholm. I am talking," Harriette said. "So the sergeant lay on the field next to an English Volunteer with a severe leg wound, and half a dozen savage Indians came to torture and scalp the Englishman." She glanced at Chisholm, expecting him to interrupt, and then continued. "Well, the sergeant wasn't having any of that, was he? No, so, wounded as he was, he lifted his halberd, killed two of the savages and then a third, and fetched a French patrol to care for the Englishman."

"Good lad, that sergeant," Chisholm said.

"Even better," Harriette said. "The Canadians swore revenge on the Irishman, so de Levis had him handed back to us, and he's in hospital here." She gave a small nod to show her approval.

"Aye, there's some good in the French, still," Chisholm said.

"Did you hear about the chaplain, though?" Harriette continued. "Our very own man of God and humanity."

MacKim shook his head. "No, but I am sure you'll tell us."

"During the battle, when the French were chasing you lot all over the place, the chaplain proved his bravery by dashing to the front to rescue wounded officers," Harriette said. "Only officers. He didn't think ordinary soldiers were worth saving."

Chisholm puffed smoke into the room. "Aye, even in battle, there's a divide between the officers and the men, the rich and the poor."

MacKim raised his eyebrows and said nothing. To comment on such practices may be sedition, but he stored the information at the back of his mind.

❧

As discipline collapsed in Quebec, Murray resorted to savage methods, with the hangman busy. Blaming alcohol for the soldier's excesses, the general ordered his officers to destroy all private supplies of anything alcoholic. Patrols scoured the streets, dragging drunken redcoats into the cells while drummers prepared their cats-of-nine-tails.

Harriette tossed the musket ball from hand to hand. She examined the back of Chisholm's head. "Not a dent," she said. "I always thought you soldier-boys were only vain with your queues and powdered hair, but I see the sense in them now. Your queue stopped the French ball dead." She winked at MacKim. "Sorry, Hughie; you'll have to wait a bit longer before you share my bed."

MacKim shook his head. "I can't wait forever, you know, Harriette. If the French can't dispose of Chisholm, you'll have to do it yourself."

Harriette slapped Chisholm's shoulder. "I might keep him a little longer, Hugh." She wiggled her hips at him. "You'll have to control your natural lust for me."

MacRae looked over from the furthest corner of the room. "He still has the woman," he said. "She's not left him yet."

Nobody replied. MacKim looked away, holding his beadwork.

That night, the British garrison heard the click and thud of picks in the night and knew the French had begun to dig trenches opposite the walls of Quebec. The siege proper had begun.

Murray sent a patrol of the Royal Americans out to see what was happening, but de Levis countered with a strong force of Canadians. After a sharp skirmish, the Royal Americans returned with some casualties and the intelligence that the French had started the first parallel.

"The first parallel?" Ramsay asked. "What does that mean?"

"It means de Levis has determined on a regular siege," Chisholm explained. "He knows that the wall facing the Heights of Abraham is the weakest, as the Heights dominate the defences, so he'll attack from there."

"First parallel?" Ramsay repeated.

"There is a science about besieging a town," Chisholm explained. "I saw a few such sieges during the last war when I took part in the battle of Fontenoy."

"Sieges?" MacKim kept Chisholm on track.

"Yes." Chisholm tore himself away from his reminiscing to educate his less experienced colleagues. "The French have to isolate us first to ensure that no relieving force comes to our aid. In European warfare, that is vital, but less so here, with only one possible route for a relieving army." He pointed to the St Lawrence. "If our relief doesn't come by water, then it doesn't come at all."

"That's why the French were building the floating batteries we destroyed," MacKim said. "To keep the Royal Navy at bay."

"That's right," Chisholm said. "But notwithstanding that, de Levis will construct lines of trenches and embrasures to keep us in and any relieving force out."

"Isolating Quebec." Harriette showed a quick grasp of the situation.

"Exactly so," Chisholm said. "In Europe, he'd build them all around the town, but here, he'll concentrate on the wall facing the Heights of Abraham. That's our weakest section. He'll have some of his men making fascines, maybe six feet tall."

"What's a fascine?" Ramsay asked.

"A fascine is a bundle of sticks that will reinforce the trench wall and are virtually impervious to musketry."

"That means a musket ball can't go through them," Harriette said helpfully.

"I know what it means! I'm not stupid," Ramsay snapped.

"While some men make fascines, the engineers will survey the land and construct hollow gabions, which are like fascines but about eight foot tall and stronger. Simultaneously, de Levis will have most of his infantry and as many unskilled labourers as he can muster building lines of contravellion, which are positions facing Quebec, beyond the range of our cannon. They'll be quite simple, merely a ditch and a parapet, with maybe the odd redoubt or redan pointing towards us to catch us in a crossfire if we attempt an assault."

Ramsay nodded, listening to every word.

"The lines of contravallation will isolate the besieged town – us – from any possible relieving force. Then de Levis might build lines of circumvallation facing outward to repel any help. In our case, he'll just position his ships in the St Lawrence."

"Then we'll be trapped," Ramsay said. "The nearest British garrison is at Louisbourg, hundreds of miles away."

"And de Levis is aware of that," Chisholm said. "With a willing workforce, these lines could take anything between three and nine days to complete. As the engineers and men work, de Levis and his senior commanders will survey our walls looking for weak spots – or maybe not, as he already knows where to attack."

"That's a bugger," Ramsay said.

"Yes," Chisholm agreed. "I could not have phrased it better."

"What then?" Harriette was busy darning socks, for the regimental wives had to make themselves useful.

Chisholm thought for a moment. "Then de Levis will create

an order of attack, telling each unit its duties. He will organise pickets and guards to prevent us from making any sorties, with a grand guard in the no-man's-land between our walls and his trenches. To augment that, he'll have a trench guard, ready behind the lines. If our general sends out a party to destroy the siege trenches, the French trench guard will be on standby to rush out and repel us." Chisholm smiled. "It's all like a game of chess, as I have told the sergeant."

"On numerous occasions," MacKim agreed solemnly.

Chisholm became serious again. "By that time, the French will have their siege guns in position. They will bombard our walls, as we did to them last year. Their objective is to make a sizeable breach, destroy our defending artillery and cause havoc with any of our defending forces foolish enough to man the walls. Of course, if we don't man the walls, de Levis might launch a surprise attack." Chisholm shook his head. "I don't think that will happen. He seems to be a methodical man who follows the rules of warfare. It will be a routine siege to grind us down."

Ramsay pulled a face.

"The next stage should be to open the trenches," Chisholm said, "but de Levis has already started that. Sometimes, the besieger will open a trench parallel to the defences – the first parallel – at around six hundred yards away, the maximum cannon range. At other times, they'll just dig a zig-zag trench towards the walls, with a fire step for defence, and a guard of grenadiers with fascines to protect them from our fire."

"We can blast them with cannon," Ramsay said.

"That's what Murray will do," Chisholm agreed. "Once they are within about four hundred yards, the French will open the second parallel, then creep forward slowly and methodically to the third. Once they get there, it's only a matter of time before they launch an assault. They'll either dig a mine under our walls, or try a sudden attack with scaling ladders."

"Which will de Levis use?" Ramsay asked.

"Scaling ladders and an attack on the walls," Chisholm said.

"He knows that our Navy will sail upriver as soon as it's practicable. Time is his enemy as much as it's our friend. The longer we delay him, the more chance our Navy has of relieving us. It all depends on time."

MacKim looked out of the window at the sky. Dawn was approaching, and the French were drawing ever closer. He could hear the steady chink of their pick-axes on the hard ground.

"It's all a matter of time," MacKim said, holding his beadwork. He could see Tayanita standing beside the fire, frowning. *I'm coming, Tayanita. I'll kill Lucas de Langdon, and then I'll join you.*

Tayanita's frown did not ease.

What more do you want from me?

24

The Chevalier de Levis had hurried his progress, missing the first few stages of a formal siege to open his trenches the night of the battle. The generals were also aware of the importance of time and the frost, with de Levis hoping to capture Quebec before the Royal Navy arrived with British reinforcements and Murray trying to delay him.

On 1st May, with the French siege lines taking shape, Murray sent HMS *Racehorse* to Halifax with a message for help and a request for General Amherst to push up to Montreal to distract de Levis. In the meantime, Quebec's artillery pounded the French siege works, hammering at the men hacking out trenches, knocking down the embrasures and sending fascines flying into the air.

"Right, boys, we're off again," Kennedy said. "No fighting; we're just gathering intelligence. The general wants to know what progress the French are making." He glanced over his men. "MacKim, I'll take you, Parnell and Waite, with Chisholm as well, as he is our expert in sieges."

With the French siege lines only eight hundred yards from Quebec's walls, Kennedy could not penetrate close to the enemy headquarters. Instead, he led his men to a slight rise from where he could observe the French through a telescope.

"MacKim, you, Waite and Parnell are on picket duty; Chisholm, you're my advisor."

The French had mounted regular patrols to guard their trenches while men were digging busily, deepening and extending the lines.

"These French lads are working like Trojans," Parnell said. "If they keep that speed, they'll have the first parallel completed in two days."

"Let's hope the Navy arrives soon," MacKim said.

"The French navy is there now," Kennedy said. "I can see their topmasts clear as anything, and there are convoys of men and carts carrying cannon and mortars and stores. The Chevalier de Levis is not wasting time."

"And the Frenchies don't like us being here, either," MacKim said. "There's a mixed Canadian and Indian patrol heading in this direction." He readied his musket.

"We've seen enough," Kennedy said. "Back we go, boys, and don't wait for anything."

They returned at speed, having been in no-man's-land for less than an hour. When Kennedy reported his findings to General Murray, an officious colonel recruited the Rangers to help strengthen the defences.

"We've done our bit," Butler complained. "I thought we were soldiers, not labourers."

"Soldiers obey orders without question," MacKim snarled. "So get to work!"

Along with the other regiments, the Rangers dragged cannon from the riverside walls to that facing the Plains of Abraham. They ensured the cannon were in the bastions and mounted on the curtain walls between each bastion, so that any French attack would meet with a hot reception. For the first time in MacKim's experience, even officers helped with the physical work, as so many of the garrison were weak with scurvy.

"The Frenchies won't have things all their own way," Ramsay said with satisfaction, as the row of cannon pointed their muzzles toward the siege lines.

"No, they won't," MacKim said. He looked over the parapet, where the French worked incessantly to strengthen their lines and push forward saps toward Quebec's walls. He considered the French numbers compared to the British and the garrison's weak state of health. If the French managed to get inside the walls, the odds were in their favour. MacKim knew the British would put up a stubborn resistance, and Murray would not surrender, but in the end, de Levis's numbers and his army's superior health would tell.

Come on then, de Levis. Bring Lucas de Langdon with you. MacKim gripped his musket and stared over the battlements.

When Murray was satisfied that he could do no more within the walls, he sent out a working party to strengthen the remaining outworks, hoping that any delay might give the Royal Navy time to push upriver.

"We have over a hundred and thirty pieces of artillery mounted on the walls," Kennedy told the Rangers. "Because of our actions and their carelessness on the ice, the French don't have nearly that many." He gave his characteristic grin. "Time is on our side, boys. Every day we delay the French gives our Navy more chance to bring reinforcements."

The French crept closer, opening a second parallel and positioning their cannon ready to fire. In retaliation, Murray sent out strong sallies, and no-man's-land became the scene of savage little skirmishes where Rangers, light infantry and King's Americans sparred with Canadians and Indians. Because of his shortage of men, Murray kept the raids to a minimum, and the French forces usually repelled the British with little damage to the besiegers' lines.

When the British were not raiding, the garrison's artillery maintained a regular fire, hammering at the advancing French trenches. When they scored a direct hit and sent men, pieces of men and fascines into the air, the watching infantry cheered. Despite the damage and losses, the French persevered, pushing their trenches ever closer to the walls.

"It all depends on the Navy now," Chisholm said, chewing on his pipe.

MacKim fingered his beadwork, nodded, and said nothing. Tayanita stood in the corner of the room, tossing her hair from side to side.

"A sail!" Ensign Ward of Braggs stood on the battlements with his telescope pointed downriver. "I see a sail in the river!"

It was the 9th May, with the French trenches only six hundred yards from the walls, and the British artillery firing almost continuously to slow de Levis's advance.

"Whose sail? British or French?" A group of officers ran to the battlements and redoubts.

"She'll be in plain sight in twenty minutes," Ensign Ward said. "We'll know then."

"If she's French, come from Old France," Chisholm spoke around the stem of his pipe, "then de Levis has a second queen on the board."

"Is that allowed?" Ramsay asked.

"All's fair in war," Chisholm said.

The Rangers ran to the parapet at the Royal Battery, which afforded the best view of the river.

"Here she comes," Chisholm said. "I'm damned if I know what she is."

MacKim stared towards the ship, which was tacking between Point Levis and the shore opposite. "She looks British to me," he said, "but I can't be sure."

General Murray arrived at the wall, red-faced with anger or anxiety, MacKim was unsure which. The General produced a telescope and examined the ship without making any comments.

"Her master doesn't know who holds the city," MacKim observed. "That's why he's remaining in the deep water channel, out of range of the city's cannon."

General Murray had the same idea.

"Well, French or British," he said, snapping shut his telescope, "we'll let them know who holds this city. Hoist the colours above the citadel and be quick about it!"

"Yes, sir," a young captain aide-de-camp said.

MacKim hid his amusement as the captain and a gunner struggled with the halliards.

"The devil a bit of the halliards can go free," the captain shouted in frustration. "Can anybody get this damned flag up the pole?"

"Here, you!" MacKim hailed a sailor, who was grinning from ear to ear as he watched the artillerymen.

"Yes, Commodore?" The sailor was a bronzed, wiry man with an ugly pug face.

"Can you scale that flagpole and put the flag in place?"

The sailor screwed his face in a smile. "In a jiffy, Commodore," he said. "Just watch me."

Flag in hand, the sailor climbed the flagstaff as if it were a flight of stairs and in three minutes, the Union flag flapped above the citadel, announcing to friend and foe who commanded in Quebec.

"Now we'll know," Chisholm said, squinting at the warship. "If she shows British colours, we have hope. If she hoists the French ensign, we're in deep trouble."

MacKim saw the ensign rise on the mizzen of the warship and heard a collective yell of delight as the officers with telescopes shouted: "British colours! She's ours!"

Nobody objected as news spread around the garrison, and men broke into wild cheers. They knew that one ship was not sufficient to relieve them, but she was the harbinger of hope.

"She's coming in," Chisholm said.

"*Lowestoft.*" The sailor had joined them on the battlements as if climbing a swaying flagpole and nailing up colours was all in a day's work for him. "That's her name, HMS *Lowestoft.*"

News of the warship's arrival spread around the city, and officers and men ran to the ramparts and mounted the parapets to cheer. Men threw their hats in the air, more from relief than elation, MacKim thought, and he even saw an officer toss his wig.

Lowestoft eased towards Quebec until her master thought the harbour beside the Royal Battery was too small for his vessel and dropped anchor in deep water off the city. Within five minutes, the master boarded his gig and steered for the harbour.

"The French have seen her, too," Kennedy reported.

The British artillerymen had stopped firing to cheer, and in the reprieve, French infantrymen, Canadians and Indians had left their trenches to stare at Quebec's walls.

"They're wondering what's happening," Chisholm said.

"Fire at them," Murray ordered.

"Some of the guns aren't properly secured yet, sir," an artillery officer protested.

"We may never have another opportunity like this," Murray countered. "Fire."

The gunners responded by firing a rolling volley that echoed around the town and battered the French positions, with dozens of men hit and others leaping for shelter in their trenches.

"That's the way, gunners!" Chisholm exulted.

"Aye, but they can't fire another." MacKim pointed to the cannon. As the artillery officer had warned, many guns had not been adequately secured and now lay in heaps of metal, shorn of their carriages. One had burst its barrel, and more were similarly disabled.

"There are plenty more guns," Chisholm said. "Did you see these Frenchies jump?"

"I did," MacKim nodded. "Now de Levis will have to withdraw, or attack us before any more Royal Naval vessels appear. The next day or two could either secure Canada for Britain or France."

Chisholm nodded. "Checkmate," he said quietly. Planting his pipe firmly within his teeth, he puffed smoke from the corners of his mouth. "If the Navy appears in force, de Levis will never take Quebec. If he captures the city before the Navy arrives, he can hold out here until winter forces the Navy away."

"The next few days will decide the fate of Canada," MacKim said.

ON THE 11TH OF MAY, THE FRENCH OPENED FIRE ON QUEBEC.

"And now we start again," Chisholm said. "Saint Barbara gives tongue, and we all suffer the wrath of her words,"

"You're a strange one," Butler said.

"Thank you," Chisholm agreed.

The French had three batteries of cannon and a single mortar-battery, that hurtled its missiles above the walls to explode in Quebec itself.

"Thirteen cannon, I make it." Chisholm did not flinch as the French opened fire. "And two mortars, I think."

"Mostly light guns," MacKim said. "Maybe one twenty-four pounder and an eighteen- pounder? The rest are all twelve-pounders or less." He grinned. "Thank God we destroyed some of their siege artillery."

"I wonder what they're firing at," Chisholm said. "If they concentrated at one section of the wall, they could batter a breach within a day, but they're firing everywhere."

As Chisholm spoke, two French cannonballs crashed between the Glaciere Bastion and the Half Bastion at the eastern side of the wall.

"That's better, de Levis," Chisholm said. "Now you've discovered the weakest part of our defences."

Ranald MacDonald involuntarily flinched. "Last year, we wondered how the poor citizens of Quebec felt when we bombarded them. Now we know."

General Murray hurried to the ramparts and viewed the French lines through his telescope.

"Return fire," he ordered quietly. "Silence these batteries."

The British artillery had been firing at the trenches, and now they concentrated on the opposing gun batteries. Still smarting from the loss of their guns in the battle men were calling St Foy, the gunners were determined to make amends by destroying their opponents at every opportunity.

"We have more guns than the French," MacKim said.

Chisholm nodded. He had his tobacco pouch in his left hand and his pipe in his right and was carefully filling the bowl. The French shell landed twenty yards away, with splinters spreading across the area. One piece whined between MacKim and Chisholm, breaking the stem of Chisholm's pipe clean in two, then rang against the wall at his side.

"You dirty blaggards!" Chisholm said and added a string of Gaelic epithets that had MacKim laughing. When MacKim recognised the hysteria in his voice, he closed his mouth.

"It's not bloody funny, MacKim," Chisholm said, holding his broken pipe in his hand.

"Here." MacKim fished his pipe from inside his tunic and passed it over. "Use mine. I gave up tobacco months ago."

Chisholm held the pipe for a moment. "Thank you, Hugh."

The cannon duel continued all that day, with the more numerous British artillery gradually wearing down the French.

"They don't like it when we respond," Chisholm said.

"I doubt they have sufficient gunpowder to maintain a bombardment," MacKim said.

For every gun the French fired, the British fired two, and by the end of that day, a quarter of the French guns were dismantled, slackening their fire. The duel continued all night, with the flashes lighting the dark and the gunners' hoarse orders a backdrop as the men not on duty tried to sleep.

"All winter," Butler said as he rolled onto his cot, "I've prayed for spring, but now that the warmer weather's brought the French, I long for the frost to return."

"The artillery will keep them at bay," MacKim said, with false confidence. He flinched as a French shell exploded not far from the entrance to the Rangers' barracks, and pieces of masonry and shell casings hammered against the walls. "The poor people of Quebec," he said. "No sooner do they rebuild their houses after one siege than another starts. They must despise us now."

However, MacKim was proved correct. The preponderance of British artillery overcame that first French attack. By the afternoon of the 12th May, the French artillery fire had slackened to a few shots an hour, and the British guns continued to pound the French siege lines.

"We're driving them back!" Chisholm said, chewing on MacKim's short pipe. "The Chevalier de Levis will have to concentrate all his guns at one point, or try an assault with scaling ladders without making a breach in our walls. If he accepts the initial casualties, his numbers will overwhelm us."

That day, news came that another British frigate had been seen further down the river.

"The Navy's coming!" The news spread through the garrison, bringing hope to men wearied by a long and hungry winter.

"Now de Levis is in a quandary," Chisholm puffed. "He will know that the Navy is coming, and that might alter the siege completely. It's like the queen on a chessboard. The Navy is our queen, the most powerful piece we possess, as the French army is their queen."

"Our army is powerful, too," Ramsay complained.

"Is it?" Chisholm indicated a platoon of redcoats that filed past. Half the men were staggering as they marched, riddled with scurvy and weak with starvation. He shook his head. "I don't believe so."

The French artillery was quiet the following day, only firing half a dozen rounds. Their solid shot hammered against the walls, while two shells fizzed in the air and exploded inside the city without causing any casualties.

"They're bombarding their own people," MacRae said. "Don't the French have any humanity?"

"No more than we have," Chisholm said. "De Levis will know we've evacuated the civilians."

All except Claudette and Hugo. I hope they are all right. I'll look for them the next time I am off-duty.

Ramsay watched as another shell arced overhead. "Maybe the French will give up, now HMS *Lowestoft's* arrived."

"Only one vessel?" MacKim said. "No, one vessel won't scare the French. They can hold it off easily enough. One vessel might just encourage de Levis to attack all the sooner."

By the 14th of May, the French had advanced their siege lines to within three hundred yards of the walls.

The British made their final preparations for defence. Again, officers helped haul the artillery into position and sick men staggered to the walls, leaning against the stonework for the support their legs could no longer provide. Murray began to transport some of his stores into his small sloops in Quebec's harbour, determined to leave as little as possible for the French when they captured the town.

"The French will come tomorrow," Chisholm said. "De Levis knows the Navy is coming, and how weak we are." He thrust his pipe into his mouth. "Tomorrow is the day, boys, and Canada is the prize."

MacKim looked over the battlements, seeing the French lines. Somewhere out there, amidst the regulars and Canadians, Lucas de Langdon was waiting, with Tayanita's scalp at his belt and murder in his heart.

Tomorrow, MacKim promised. *Tomorrow I will kill you, de Langdon, or you will kill me.*

25

"Rangers," Kennedy could hardly hide his smile as he entered the barrack-room, "the Navy is on its way. The general wants us to watch the river to ensure they arrive and report back to him."

"We can see the river from the battlements, sir," MacKim pointed out.

"I want a small team to check on the French ships, and then journey downriver," Kennedy said.

"Yes, sir. How many men?"

"Six," Kennedy said. "Sufficient to take care of ourselves, but not too many to alert the French. You, me and four volunteers, Chisholm, MacRae, Parnell and Dickert."

"Do the volunteers know yet, sir?" MacKim asked.

"You can tell them as soon as you like," Kennedy said generously.

"Thank you, sir. When do we leave?"

"At nightfall." Kennedy was still smiling. "I hope you had no plans with that French woman I know nothing about."

"No, sir," MacKim said.

Kennedy nodded and slipped away.

❧

"That canoe! Stop!" The officer of the watch on HMS *Lowestoft* was alert.

"Friends!" Kennedy called up to him.

"Who the devil are you?"

"Lieutenant Kennedy of the Rangers," Kennedy replied softly.

"Rangers?" Although the naval officer was invisible in the dark, there was no mistaking the respect in his voice. "Off on some mad escapade, are you?"

"That's what we do," Kennedy replied and paddled on.

MacKim concentrated on his canoe-training from eighteen months previously and followed Kennedy out of the harbour into the dark waters of the St Lawrence. The current was more powerful than he had expected, forcing him to dig deep as he paddled upstream, where the French navy waited out of range of Quebec's artillery.

Kennedy pushed the canoe beside the shore, with the water, still with traces of ice, translucent underneath. MacKim followed, already thankful for a rest. His paddling skills had deteriorated from lack of use.

They stopped where a fallen tree offered a modicum of shelter, and while MacKim positioned the men to watch for the enemy, Kennedy extended his telescope. "Nothing changed here." He sounded disappointed. "The French have two frigates, two armed ships and a host of smaller craft in the river, but no floating gun batteries." He smiled.

MacKim nodded. "Aye, and a dozen of them would make all the difference; they're devilishly hard to sink."

"Murray can thank the Rangers for that," Kennedy said. "Now, we'll look for our Navy. Keep close. Just guide the canoe; let the current do the work."

They headed downstream, with the city lights glinting over the Basin of Quebec and an occasional cannon firing from the

French camp. The L'Île d'Orleans was dark and mysterious to their left, with faint glints of light from the settlements on the river's south bank.

There was something vaguely unsettling about gliding downstream on the St Lawrence as if they were deserting their comrades in besieged Quebec. MacKim glanced over his shoulder as the British cannon unleashed a volley, with the muzzle-flares orange against the night, momentarily highlighting the shape of the walls. The darkness was all the more intense when it returned, and MacKim cursed and looked forward.

"Look there." Chisholm tapped MacKim on the shoulder. "I think the Navy has arrived."

"Either ours or a French patrol," MacKim said.

The ships were ghosting upriver, with a leadsman in the chains chanting the river depth and only topsails set. The nearest was huge, a two-decker with rows of gunports closed and no visible flag. The second was two cable-lengths astern, barely seen except for the gleam of her sails.

"If they're French, then Quebec will fall," Chisholm said.

"Only one way to find out," Kennedy said, "be prepared to paddle for your lives, boys." He raised his voice in a roar. "Ship ahoy! Who are you?"

"His Majesty's Ship *Vanguard*, Commodore Swanton," the reply came, in a reassuringly English West Country voice, "and His Majesty's Frigate *Diana*, Captain Schomberg. Who are you?"

"Lieutenant Kennedy of the Rangers," Kennedy shouted, as a mixture of pleasure and relief swept across the Rangers. "Welcome to Quebec, sir!"

In the evening of the 15th May, Commodore Swanton in HMS *Vanguard* of seventy guns, with Captain Schomberg in HM Frigate *Diana,* with thirty-two guns, joined Captain Deane in HMS *Lowestoft* off Port Levis. As soon as the ships arrived, General Murray sent a message requesting the Navy to remove the two French frigates and smaller vessels that were aiding the siege of Quebec.

MacKim and Kennedy watched as *Diana* and *Lowestoft* slipped their cables on the morning of the 16th, with a hazy mist rising from the waters of the St Lawrence. The seamen worked with a quiet discipline that impressed MacKim, and the ships were soon moving upstream, with the water hissing under their counters and the blue-uniformed officers on the quarterdeck.

"I've never seen a naval battle," MacKim said.

As the Royal Navy moved off, MacKim saw the gun ports open like a score of staring eyes and heard a sinister rumble as the broadside cannon rolled out. The sight was chilling, and MacKim wondered what it must be like to watch a line-of-battle ship surging closer, with thirty cannon or more waiting to fire and nowhere to run or hide.

The French vessels did not remain to fight. With the two Royal Navy ships bearing down upon them, they cut their anchor chains and tried to flee upstream.

The French retreated at speed, with the more powerful Royal Navy vessels following relentlessly. *Lowestoft's* guns drove one of the French frigates, *Pomona,* on shore just above Cape Diamond, with the French crew tumbling from the vessel in near panic.

"That's one French ship less," Chisholm said.

"Still one frigate left," MacKim pointed out.

The second French frigate, *Atalanta,* did not last much longer. MacKim could not see the action but saw a column of smoke and heard the news from the returning Royal Navy.

"We got her," a grinning seaman on *Diana* responded to Chisholm's enquiry. "We ran her ashore at Pointe-aux-Trembles and set fire to her."

"Three cheers for the Navy!" Ramsay shouted, and other regiments joined the Rangers' hurrahs, with even the most straight-faced officers allowing some leeway.

The shore between Quebec and Point au Tremble was littered with minor French vessels and pieces of French equipment. The Royal Navy simply drove the smaller enemy vessels ashore and left them there, blasting holes in their hulls to ensure the French could not quickly refloat them.

"The French have no answer to the Navy," MacKim said with satisfaction.

The news came downstream later that the Navy did not have things all their own way, as *Lowestoft* ran onto a hidden rock. She was lost, although there were no casualties.

Chisholm puffed at his pipe. "And that was that," he said. "We have brought our queen into play and removed the French knights. Now de Levis has to counter. If he attacks quickly and captures Quebec, he can still win this game. Wooden-walled ships won't defeat the stone walls of a city, and we don't have sufficient men here to mount a siege."

"Listen, boys." Kennedy appeared at the door of the barracks. "General Murray intends to make a sortie tomorrow."

The Rangers gave a small, ironic cheer. "Better than sitting behind stone walls waiting for them to come to us," Parnell said. "Are we involved?"

"We're going in front to reconnoitre," Kennedy said, "with a Lieutenant McAlpin." Kennedy gave a small smile that might have meant anything. "General Murray has ordered McAlpin, and I quote, to 'amuse the enemy with small sallies', so that seems to give us free rein to do as we wish."

"Small sallies, sir?" Parnell repeated the phrase. "Small sallies against twelve thousand Frenchmen?" He shook his head. "That will send de Levis running back to Montreal."

"Your sarcasm is noted, Parnell," Kennedy said. "We'll get out there and amuse them as best we can, and, more importantly, we'll gather intelligence and see if they're massing for an assault."

Lieutenant McAlpin was a slim young man with an eager smile despite the deep lines of hardship etched on his face. He led a mixed force of lights and Royal Americans, who nodded to the Rangers as both units slipped out of Quebec.

"Here we go, men." McAlpin twitched nervously as a cannon

barked from Quebec. "Let's hope the gunners don't think we're French, eh?"

MacKim felt the atmosphere alter as soon as he stepped into no-man's-land beyond the wall. He curled a hand around the stock of his musket, drawing strength from the smooth wood.

"Come on, lads, and keep your heads down." He knew that Murray intended these raids to slow the French advance and lower their morale, but he also knew they could have the opposite effect if they failed. A constant trickle of casualties on an already weak garrison would not help the defender's cause.

"I'll take the French left flank if you take the right, Kennedy," McAlpin said and led his men away.

Kennedy kept his head down as his Rangers followed, each man silent, knowing the Indians and Canadians could be hunting for them in the dark. MacKim was unsure if moving in the open spaces was preferable to operating in the forests. He was used to the confinement of the trees now and felt more exposed in this bleaker environment.

With only a few hundred yards to cover before they reached the French third parallel, the Rangers moved cautiously, then dropped to a crawl. MacKim listened, expecting to hear the murmur of sentries talking to each other, a subdued cough, or the rattle of a musket on the parapet.

There was nothing. There was not a whisper of sound in the still air.

Kennedy looked sideways to catch MacKim's eye and shook his head. MacKim nodded and crawled forward, inching over the still-frost-hard ground. Somewhere a bird called, the sound lonely in the night. Keeping his head down, MacKim slid onward, holding his musket so the metal barrel did not clatter against a stone.

There was still no sound. Taking a deep breath and prepared for a sudden eruption of Indians or Canadians, MacKim moved again, very slowly, feeling the tension knot his stomach. His harsh breathing seemed to echo in the dark, announcing his presence like the Brigade of Guard's band.

A voice floated from behind them as a nervous sentry on Quebec's walls shouted a challenge: "Pikestaff!"

MacKim froze, hoping the sound did not alert the French. He lay still, hugging the ground, trying to appear part of the night. The sentry called again and fired his musket, the single report shattering the night.

A sergeant growled a reprimand, and then silence returned, pressing on the Rangers as they lay only yards outside the French trenches.

MacKim slid forward another few inches, stifled a curse as a fickle wind shifted the clouds and allowed starlight to illuminate the Heights. Taking a chance, MacKim looked up; he could not see any sentries. He would expect to see the gleam of a white French uniform caught in the starlight, the reflection of a musket barrel or even a white face as a wary sentry peered towards the British positions.

There was nothing except the shape of heaped earth and the serrated edge of a fascine.

Taking a final deep breath, MacKim crawled the last few feet to the lip of the French trench and peered inside. He looked right and left, seeing a litter of equipment, a scaling ladder, fixed fascines but no sentries.

Kennedy joined him, his face puzzled. On Kennedy's nod, MacKim dropped inside the trench with his musket held ready for an ambush. The ground was hard underfoot, with the trench beautifully squared off but empty of people.

"This is strange." Kennedy mouthed the words and pointed left. MacKim moved that way, with his musket pointing ahead of him. He heard the soft slither of bodies behind him and knew the other Rangers were following. At least he was not alone in this hostile trench.

"God be with me," Ramsay muttered and added, "there's nobody here. The French have abandoned the attack."

"Quiet, Ramsay!" MacKim rebuked in a savage whisper. "They might be waiting for us." He remembered the ambush when Lindsay's Rangers lost half their men.

The third parallel was deserted. The Rangers traversed it from end to end, checking the saps for ambushes; there was nobody here.

"Move on," Kennedy whispered and entered a sap that led to the second parallel.

MacKim located another sap, forty yards away and probed in, very wary of an ambush, his heart pounding as he moved forward, expecting a Canadian to lunge from the dark.

The second parallel was as empty as the first, and MacKim and Kennedy exchanged stares with Lieutenant McAlpin and the Royal Americans.

"Is this a gigantic trap?" Kennedy asked. "Where the devil are they?"

"Listen," MacKim said. "Can you hear that?"

The tapping of the drum was faint, yet the more MacKim listened, the more he heard. The regular tramp of marching feet, the rumble of wheels and even a single barked order.

"The French are withdrawing," Kennedy said in astonishment. "They've lifted the siege."

26

Exploring the French lines had taken longer than MacKim thought, so the night was already fading when the Rangers merged with McAlpin's men and hurried back to Quebec.

"Who goes?" The Rangers expected the challenge.

"Friend!" Kennedy shouted.

"Aye, right. What's the parole?" The voice was distinctly Highland as it demanded the password.

"Pikestaff!" Kennedy shouted.

"Wolfe!" The sentry gave the countersign. "Pass, friend," and the gate opened a moment later.

When the Rangers scrambled through the gate, they found that General Murray had assembled most of the garrison. Amherst's, Lascelles, Townshend's and Anstruther's regiments, together with the Highlanders, the grenadiers and the light infantry, all stood ready to file out and attack the French.

"Sir!" Lieutenants McAlpin and Kennedy approached Murray.

"You look pleased with yourselves." Murray adjusted his wig. "Yet I did not hear any firing."

"No, sir," McAlpin said. "There was nobody to fire at. The French have abandoned their trenches, sir."

"They're pulling out, sir," Kennedy added. "We heard them marching in the distance."

Murray snapped his fingers. "They've pulled out, by God! Then we have them!" He raised his voice to carry past the knot of officers that surrounded him to the mustered regiments. "I intended a sally to disrupt their attack, but now we can inflict such a defeat on them that we'll forget our reverse of the 28th April. With these brave men, we'll give the French a bloody nose and a kick up the breeches!"

MacKim knew that Murray intended his words to put fighting spirit into the men, yet they seemed appropriate. Despite their lingering sickness, the redcoats looked eager to get at the French.

With General Murray at the head, the British force marched out of Quebec, a long, tattered, scarlet column with muskets on their shoulders, drums tapping and the colours brave in the clear spring light.

"Rangers, get in front," Murray ordered. "Lights, guard the flanks."

The column pushed on, crossing the Plains with Kennedy's Rangers trotting in front, hoping to catch the French rearguard.

"The French have moved at some speed," MacKim said.

"They can usually outmarch us," Chisholm said. "Especially when they're marching in the opposite direction to the guns."

"They left behind all their baggage and even their artillery," Kennedy pointed out. "They are marching fast because they're marching light."

MacKim smiled. It was far better to be in the van of an advancing army than to be cowering behind stone walls or creeping through the forest. For the first time since Tayanita's death, he felt like himself again.

The musketry broke MacKim's mood, and he threw himself down, rolled into some dead ground and searched for the source.

A small group of French regulars stood beside the trail, rapidly loading after firing a volley.

MacKim fired and rose, shouting to his men. "Take them in flank, boys." He knew the French would need between fifteen and twenty seconds to reload, so he calculated that length of time and shouted, "Tree all" – the Rangers' instruction to find cover. The French fired by instinct, without a single shot hitting a Ranger, and then MacKim was amongst them, firing and charging with his men.

"*Nous nous rendons*!" ("We surrender!") The French were young, thin and looked terrified as the Rangers surrounded them. "*Ne nous scalpez pas*." ("Don't scalp us!")

"*Personne ne vous scalpera*." MacKim said, assuring them that nobody would scalp them. He knew that Kennedy was not the only Ranger who occasionally scalped the enemy.

The French looked at MacKim as if at a saviour.

"Are you men the rearguard?" MacKim asked.

"No." The speaker was about twenty years old and still trembled with fear. "We could not keep up."

MacKim nodded as Kennedy appeared. "Two dead French and four prisoners, sir. They're stragglers, and the poor devils are terrified." Again, MacKim realised that the French might be as afraid of the Rangers as the British were of the Indians.

"Chisholm!" Kennedy shouted. "Take these prisoners to the General. He will want to interrogate them."

When the French saw Chisholm's ravaged face, they recoiled and followed him meekly to the main column.

"Back on the road, boys," Kennedy said. "The General wants to catch the French before they reach the River Caprouge."

"We destroyed the bridge there," Ramsay reminded. "That should slow the Frenchies down."

However, the French engineers had erected a temporary bridge, and the infantry marched across the Caprouge before the British reached their rearguard. They destroyed the temporary bridge and left a small number of men at the river crossing, greeting the approaching Rangers with a warning volley.

"That's our Canadian friends again," Parnell said.

Kennedy extended his telescope and studied the French rear-guard. "You're right, Parnell. They're waiting to pick us off when we're in the river."

Out of rifle range, Lucas de Langdon stepped out from behind a tree and strode to the river's edge. With his musket cradled in his left arm, he faced the Rangers, silent as any Indian, his presence an evident challenge.

When MacKim stepped to the bank opposite the Canadian, the two men stood in direct opposition. When he was sure he had de Langdon's attention, MacKim removed his bonnet and pointed to the bald patch on his head and then to the Canadian.

"I'll let him know who I am," MacKim said.

Lucas de Langdon watched, unresponsive, as he stood erect.

MacKim raised his musket and pointed it at the Canadian. Both men knew the range was too long, but the intent was clear. Lucas de Langdon did not move as MacKim held the musket in place for ten seconds and lowered it again. Finally, he removed Tayanita's beadwork from beneath his tunic and folded it over his belt.

"Let them go, Sergeant." General Murray appeared beside MacKim, with his wig awry and a pistol thrust through his belt. "We won't catch them on that side of the river. Do you know that man?"

"His men and the Rangers have had a few encounters, sir," Kennedy spoke for MacKim.

"Well, you might have a few more," Murray said, "but not today. We'll consolidate, and then I want your Rangers to remain on the Plains of Abraham as a flying patrol in case de Levis sends his Canadians to raid."

"Yes, sir," Kennedy said.

The British enjoyed picking over the abandoned French encampment. In their haste to escape, the French had left many munitions that Murray claimed as spoils of war. As well as the stores and ammunition, there were thirty-four battering cannon, ten pieces of field artillery, six mortars and scores of scaling ladders.

Chisholm looked at the latter. "I thought de Levis was preparing an assault," he said. "That would have been ugly; the French would have lost hundreds of men as they crossed the open ground, and once they gained a foothold, they'd have gone crazy. Fighting in a town is the bloodiest kind, with no quarter given or asked."

MacKim lifted one of the hundreds of entrenching tools. "I hope de Levis keeps running now," he said. "I would not like to have to fight him every mile to Montreal. The French are a stubborn breed, as we know."

Chisholm brought out a box from under his tunic. "This is French rations."

"We were ordered to hand in everything," MacKim said.

"Yes, Sergeant," Chisholm said meekly. "And now I am handing it to my superior." He gave MacKim the box.

"And I accept this gift with gratitude," MacKim said and broke it open with anticipation. "Dried fish," he said. "I had hoped for something a little more interesting. Still, any food is good when one is starving."

NEWS FROM THE PRISONERS SOON SPREAD AROUND THE ARMY. They heard that the French had not retreated all the way to Montreal, but only as far as Jacques Cartier, where they would lick their wounds while de Levis decided what to do next.

"I heard that most of the Canadians have deserted the French," MacRae said. "Or so the stories go."

"I heard the same," MacKim agreed. "I also heard the Frenchies are short of food and ammunition."

"Not all the Canadians have deserted," Chisholm murmured.

"No." MacKim thought of de Langdon. "Not all."

"Our spies have reported the French as having so many desertions, they've only five thousand men left," Chisholm said. "And General Murray is waiting for reinforcements before he pursues them to Montreal."

Claudette was sitting on MacKim's bed in the Rangers' barracks. "So the French have gone," she said.

"The French have gone," MacKim agreed.

Claudette turned away to look out the window at her shattered city. "The French have abandoned Canada," she said. "They might try to bargain for us back at the end of the war, but we will not forget."

"We?" MacKim said. "Are you not French?"

Claudette sighed. "I do not know what I am now. I may be French, yet I have never been there. How can I belong to a country I have never seen and which fails to protect us from our enemies?"

"Perhaps you can be Canadian," MacKim said, "whichever king lays claim to the land."

"Perhaps that is best," Claudette agreed. "It is hard not to belong."

"I know," MacKim said. "But you belong here, whichever flag flies over the city. You are a Quebecer."

Claudette stood up. "This war has taken my husband and destroyed my city. Now it may remove my nationality. I feel as if the world has turned upside down."

"We are all playthings of kings and politicians," MacKim said. "Pawns on the bitter board of life."

"You will be marching away with your army," Claudette said. "Will you return to Quebec?"

"I do not know. The Army decides my future," MacKim said.

Claudette brushed a hand across her hair. "If the Army decides you should return here, Sergeant MacKim, look for me. Hugo will be pleased to see you." She walked to the door and turned around. “Stay alive, Sergeant, and be careful of Lucas. He is a dangerous man.”

“Thank you,” MacKim said. For one moment, he thought that Tayanita stood at Claudette’s side, and then the image disappeared.

27

"They call this the Quebec Army." Chisholm eyed the men who waited to board the transports that would carry them upriver to Montreal, the final French bastion in Canada.

"We have under two and a half thousand men," MacKim said. "It's hardly an army."

"During the Fontenoy campaign, such numbers would scarcely be a brigade," Chisholm said. "But I hear another thousand men are coming up from Louisbourg."

MacKim looked over Quebec. Since the French retreat, Murray had allowed the civilians back, and the city was beginning to assume some normality. "The war in Canada will be over soon," he said. *And both Lucas de Langdon and the renegade are still alive. I have let Tayanita down.*

"Let's hope so, Hugh." Chisholm glanced at the sky. "It's the 15th of July," he said, "high summer and what a beautiful day to start a new campaign."

MacKim touched the lock of his musket. "Let's hope it's the final campaign in New France."

The Army of Quebec filed on board the thirty-two vessels and several floating batteries with twenty-four and thirty-two-pounder cannon. Kennedy's Rangers filed into small boats that sailed and rowed in advance, the eyes of Murray's army, the point of the sword that King George thrust into the vitals of King Louis of France.

"Let's hope for a quiet cruise upriver." Parnell checked the lock of his rifle.

Kennedy looked ahead. "I have a score to even yet," he said. "After that, they can do what they like with Canada because I'm off to London."

MacRae nodded, eyeing the banks of the river. "It's beautiful here," he said. "Until Man taints it with war."

As soon as the Royal Navy relieved Quebec, de Levis had withdrawn to Montreal with the bulk of his army, but leaving a strong holding force at Jacques Cartier.

"They will try to delay us," Kennedy said, "and they will fail. As a Frenchman, de Levis thinks in terms of land strategy, while the British are men of the water."

MacKim watched as the fleet approached the French positions at Jacques Cartier. Rather than try to fight, Murray sailed wide, using the full width of the St Lawrence.

"If the French had any floating batteries," Kennedy said, "they could have delayed us here."

MacKim watched the shore slide past and remembered how they had to toil through the snowy forests when last he travelled this way. "I wonder if the army will show its gratitude to us."

Kennedy smiled. "You've been in uniform long enough to know that won't happen unless you're the son of an earl, or the nation's darling."

With Murray's force upstream of Trois Rivières, Dumas's French garrison was cut off from de Levis's army in Montreal and effectively out of the war. Any British reinforcements coming upriver could eradicate them. However, rather than wait to be captured, Dumas marched his men out, following the British fleet.

After the Army of Quebec passed Trois Rivières, their

progress slowed as the local Canadians, the *habitants,* appeared by the hundred, selling farm produce or swearing allegiance to King George.

"All our good Canadian friends," Chisholm said. "Until de Levis returns, and they'll renounce their oath and be loyal Frenchmen again."

MacKim chewed on a Canadian apple. "They're confused," he said. "I think we're witnessing the end of an empire."

"And the beginning of one," Chisholm said. "Imagine: Great Britain controls all the land between the Gulf of St Lawrence and Spanish Florida."

"We've got to capture Montreal yet," MacKim said.

"With three armies and a Royal Naval flotilla converging on Montreal, even de Levis won't be able to hold out," Chisholm said. "I doubt we'll see any resistance now."

For once, Chisholm was wrong.

"We're only fifty miles from Montreal," Kennedy said. "After the travails of the winter, we have the French in a pincer movement, yet they're still fighting. You have to admire their spirit."

"They've spent centuries carving Canada out of the wilderness," MacKim said. "They won't want to give it up without a fight." He jerked a thumb towards the shore. "These lads don't want to give up, anyway."

The Rangers peered at the land, where the French commanders, Bourlamaque and Dumas, marched their men along the riverbank, keeping pace with the British fleet. The white uniforms of the regulars were stained and battered, but their muskets were clean, and the men had a determined spring in their steps.

"They've lost their queen, both their knights and one castle," Chisholm continued his chess analogy, "but they're still game."

"We'll see how game they are when it comes to musketry." MacKim tossed his apple core into the river, where it bobbed downstream. "It's easy to look tough when you can't smell the powder smoke."

"True." Ramsay glared at the French on shore. "We'll see you later, Frenchies."

Murray had already issued a proclamation ordering the Canadians to remain at home, saying, "I shall treat severely Canadians taken with arms in their hands, and I shall burn all villages that I find abandoned."

The general had a chance to prove his threats when the Canadians ambushed a small party of British soldiers near the village of Sorel.

"Come on, boys," Kennedy said. "Bring your tinderboxes."

MacKim did not enjoy burning villages, but when he heard that de Langdon had led the Canadians, he set fire to the buildings with as much enthusiasm as any of the Rangers.

After the burning, the army of Quebec sailed and marched on, with no more resistance. MacKim scanned both shores, searching for Lucas de Langdon and the renegade, muttering to himself that he must avenge Tayanita as the fleet crept closer to Montreal.

If the French don't fight, I might never see de Langdon and the renegade again. But I must. If I don't find them in Montreal, I will scour Canada for them. I must avenge Tayanita.

But Tayanita was standing in the prow of the boat, watching him with that small frown of disapproval pursing her lips.

I won't give up, Tayanita, I'll keep hunting. Why are you shaking your head? I can't do any more.

"Hugh?" Chisholm touched MacKim's shoulder. "Are you all right?"

"I'm fine." MacKim shook him away.

"You don't look fine. You were talking to yourself."

"Was I?" MacKim asked. *I am going mad. I'll have to kill these men to return to sanity; otherwise I'll finish my life in Bedlam.*

Murray's Quebec Army reached the outskirts of Montreal before the other two British armies and with no French army waiting for them.

"The French won't fight, boys," Kennedy said. "De Levis's

army is disintegrating, with the Indians returning to their villages, the Canadians surrendering and swearing allegiance to King George and even the regulars, victors of St Foy, deserting to us by the score."

They must fight! I need to see Lucas de Langdon. I can't allow him to escape. MacKim gripped his musket ever tighter as he glared around him.

"It's sad in a way," Chisholm said, "the death of an empire and the end of all the French dreams."

MacKim fingered Tayanita's beadwork. "No," he said. "It's not sad. It's justice after the way they fought. It's justice that the murdering, scalping, torturing savages should lose everything." He realised he was shouting and closed his mouth, with Chisholm putting a hand on his arm.

"Easy, Hugh. The war is nearly over."

"No," MacKim shook his head. "It's not over; it's not over until they're dead."

"Until who's dead, Hugh?" Chisholm asked. "All the French? All the Canadians and Indians? Or only the men who killed Tayanita?" He pressed his face closer to MacKim. "Don't let it consume you, Hugh."

"You don't understand," MacKim said and lurched away. "None of you understand."

Except for Tayanita. She understands what I must do.

MacKim smiled to Tayanita, who stood seven paces distant, unsmiling, with her braided hair reaching to her waist.

❦

ON THE 8TH SEPTEMBER, 1760, GENERAL DE VAUDREUIL signed the terms of capitulation. The war in Canada was over.

MacKim found a bottle of raw brandy, finished it inside an hour and remained stone-cold sober.

28

"Considering all the fighting, the French surrendered rather tamely," Chisholm said, puffing at his pipe. "I had anticipated a last battle in Montreal, with the Frenchies defending the walls and us charging the breach with bloody bayonets. Thank God for small mercies."

MacKim forced a smile. "Thank God," he said.

When the three British armies marched into Montreal, the citizens experienced the skirl of the Highland bagpipes for the first time. When MacKim heard the pipes, he exchanged glances with MacRae and Chisholm. "The lads have arrived," he said.

"Let's say hello." Chisholm pulled his bonnet further over his forehead, stamped his feet and headed in the direction of the pipes. MacRae and Ranald MacDonald followed, with MacKim jogging behind them.

"Listen!" A second skirl of pipes came from the left, and then a third from the right. "What the devil is this?" MacKim asked. "Has every piper in Canada come to Montreal?"

The pipes had attracted Highlanders like iron filings to a magnet, and only then did MacKim realise that men from all three Highland regiments were in Montreal. Soldiers from Fraser's 78th, Montgomerie's 77th Highlanders and the 42nd

Royal Highlanders, the Black Watch, gathered around the pipers.

"It's a gathering of the clans," Chisholm said, as the men of different regiments greeted each other with raucous cries and Gaelic insults. "The Gaeltacht has taken over Canada."

For a moment, MacKim remembered the clans at Culloden, when Prince Charles Stuart had led them onto the massed musketry and batteries of artillery of that bloody moor. He thought of his teenage brother, murdered by the redcoats, and pushed the memory away.

As the Highlanders bickered happily together and boasted of their respective regiment's parts in the successful war, MacKim's scalped head began to ache.

"Tayanita," he said, as she appeared among the Highlanders, easing towards him with that small frown on her face. MacKim backed away, leaving the Highlanders to their union, and returned to the Rangers. Tayanita walked at his side, swinging her hips as her shining hair hung over her left shoulder.

I'll get him, Tayanita, I will kill him.

MacKim looked over the city of Montreal. "Well," he said. "We've done it."

"We have." Chisholm puffed at his pipe. "Who'd have believed that when we looked at the defences of Louisbourg at the beginning of this campaign? We've conquered French Canada."

Kennedy took a deep breath. "Thank God," he said. "Now New Hampshire can prosper. We can sleep at night without one hand on our muskets, waiting for the next war when the French send their Indians to murder and scalp our women."

Unlike Quebec, Montreal was intact when the British marched in. "This is a pretty city," Chisholm approved. "It's as nice as any I saw in Europe."

Montreal sat on an island in the St Lawrence River, with broad streets and solid, well-built houses.

"Thank God we didn't have to fight our way in." MacKim nodded to the eight-foot deep ditch in front of the formidable wall. "Eleven redoubts on the wall! We'd have to batter it into submission with naval cannon and then head for a breach. There would be slaughter."

Chisholm grunted, puffing at his pipe. "If de Levis had held out in that," he thrust the stem of his pipe towards the citadel, "he could have cut us to pieces even if we had breached the walls."

MacKim tried to count the guns of the citadel, which dominated the streets of the city. "We would have taken the place, but the cost would have been enormous. I think the French morale cracked after General Murray held out in Quebec."

"Do you know what I think?" Chisholm said. "I think de Levis was a European-style soldier. He knew the British outnumbered and outgunned him, so he could not win. Rather than kill hundreds of men needlessly, he surrendered."

"Thank God for a decent man," MacKim said. "I'll drink a toast to de Levis whenever I have the opportunity."

"Let's hope our generals treat him with the same respect," Chisholm said. "He played a losing game with great skill."

However, the British refused to offer de Levis the honours of war. In the eighteenth century, a magnanimous victor allowed an honourable enemy to march out of a conquered city with dignity. The defeated regiments retained their colours and the men their weapons. Mindful of the atrocities the Indians and Canadians inflicted on civilians and prisoners-of-war, the British refused these honours to the French.

Rather than have the French colours captured and displayed as trophies of war, de Levis piled them up, one on top of another, and set fire to them. As the regimental flags burned, de Levis took his sword from his scabbard and snapped it across his knee.

Chisholm gave his opinion. "He was a good man in an impossible situation."

MacKim held Tayanita's beadwork. "Here's the lieutenant coming now," he said. "He looks grim."

Kennedy mounted a flight of stairs so everybody could see and hear him. "Rangers!" He called his men. "The French have surrendered," he said, "and that seems to be the end of the war in New France."

The Rangers nodded hopefully.

"However, the war continues elsewhere. The Cherokees are causing trouble, and we have to quell the French and Spanish in the Caribbean."

The Rangers elation ended abruptly. Nobody wanted to be sent to the West Indies, where the black vomit carried off men by the thousand.

"You may have heard that General Amherst has sent Major Rogers and his Rangers to the west to inform the distant French garrisons that their war is over."

The men nodded. Some had met their brother Rangers, and two of Kennedy's men had joined Rogers' force.

Kennedy nodded. "There is also a small matter here to resolve, and I am seeking volunteers. Those men who do not wish to accompany me will return to their parent regiment or another company of Rangers."

The Rangers waited, murmuring and glancing at each other. Nobody was happy when a military unit disbanded, but Kennedy had made sensible dispositions. Chisholm thrust his stubby pipe in his mouth and winked at MacKim, who fingered Tayanita's beadwork.

"As you know, we have been fighting a company of Canadians and Indians ever since we captured Quebec."

MacKim felt his interest grow.

"Lucas de Langdon and his men have not surrendered. They ambushed a picket yesterday and mutilated the dead." Kennedy let his words sink in. "General Murray wishes me to lead a force of Rangers to hunt and destroy these men."

The Rangers fell silent. Each man had been hoping for a reprieve from fighting and death; a few weeks or months free of the constant fear of Indians creeping through the forest, or French regulars attacking with musket and bayonet. Lieutenant Kennedy's words propelled them back to a life of fear and unimaginable agony.

"Volunteers only," Kennedy said.

"I'll come," MacKim said immediately, hiding his satisfaction.

The Rangers looked at him, some curious, a few admiring. Chisholm frowned.

"You'd be better returning to Fraser's," Chisholm said.

"I have nothing to return for," MacKim felt constrained to explain. "You have Harriette waiting for you, James." He did not mention his real reason; he remembered the musket ball shattering Tayanita's skull, and now she stood seven paces away, frowning her disapproval at his failure to avenge her.

Chisholm studied MacKim. "I don't want to desert you."

"Get back to Harriette," MacKim said. "That's an order, Private!"

"Listen to the sergeant!" Kennedy advised. "I don't know how long this search will take or where it will lead, so single men only."

"Bugger," Butler said. "I was hoping for a longer break from my wife."

Some of the married Rangers laughed, while the single men looked confused.

"I'll come," Parnell raised his voice.

"And me." Dickert looked at MacRae, who lifted a finger in acknowledgement.

"Me too, sir."

Ramsay followed with a hesitant hand.

"That will be sufficient," Kennedy said. "Me, Sergeant MacKim, Parnell, Dickert, MacRae and Ramsay. Six of us. The rest of the Rangers will join Captain Huzzen's Rangers, and the others can either return to their regiments or request a permanent transfer."

MacKim looked across at Chisholm, very aware that they may never meet again. Chisholm had been part of his life since he joined the 78th, and he would miss him. MacKim held out his hand. "Good luck, James, and give my best to Harriette,"

Chisholm's grip was like iron. "I will."

They said no more as Chisholm stepped back. Their eyes held for a moment, silently acknowledging the sentiments that neither could voice and then MacKim looked away.

One by one, the six volunteers shook the hands of the other Rangers, equally aware that this might be their final parting. MacKim watched as Kennedy's Rangers split up, thought of Tayanita and again saw her fall with her head exploding.

"When are we leaving, sir?"

Kennedy tapped his musket. "As soon as we are ready, MacKim, as soon as we are ready."

With all the resources of Montreal and three British armies to call upon, Kennedy equipped his small party for the expedition ahead. His first priority was ordering the armourer to cut down the musket barrels, making them easier to wield in the forest.

"They are more like carbines," Kennedy said, lifting the new, shorter Brown Bess.

"That will help," MacKim approved, testing his musket for balance. "I've often swung my musket only to have it snag on a branch or a bush."

"We all have," Kennedy said. "You three riflemen – Parnell, MacRae and Dickert – you can carry a carbine, which is easier, or keep your rifle."

"I'll keep the rifle, sir," Dickert said.

"So will I," MacRae agreed. "One of us has to shoot straight."

"As you wish. You are our marksmen. Parnell?"

"I'll have the carbine, sir," Parnell said.

With lighter packs and equipment than before, the Rangers could march faster and travel longer distances.

"We're travelling by canoe," Kennedy said. "And following the trail de Langdon's men have left."

MacKim touched the lock of his carbine. "Do we know roughly where they are?"

"We have a guide," Kennedy said. "We'll meet him above the Sault Saint Louis Rapids." He gave his quick smile. "Not even the Rangers can negotiate the rapids."

The Sault Saint Louis Rapids extended for three miles, with the Rangers carrying their canoes along the bank of the river. It was fortunate that native canoes were light to carry, easy to manoeuvre and fast. Built from a single sheet of birch bark, with the smooth inner side of the bark inside and the rougher exterior outside, the canoes were waiting for the Rangers.

"If I'd known I'd be a porter, I wouldn't have volunteered," Dickert said.

MacRae grinned. "You just don't want a real marksman to show you up."

"Real marksman?" Dickert said. "You couldn't hit a bull's arse with a fiddle on a Sunday afternoon!"

"Here's our man," Kennedy said. "Rangers, meet Obomsawin, our guide."

The Abenaki was tall, broad and unsmiling, with intelligent eyes. He joined the Rangers as they stood at the side of the river, looked over them and grunted something.

"He says we'll need more men," Kennedy said. "He says there are rumours of tribal wars in the west."

"We won't need more men." MacKim shook his head.

"Off we go, boys." Kennedy stepped into the first canoe, with Obomsawin a second behind him.

MacKim boarded the second, laid down his carbine and lifted his paddle. Tayanita was beside him, kneeling in the canoe, saying nothing as she stared ahead with her braided hair bouncing the length of her spine.

They pushed off in the grey light of dawn, with bird-song sweetening the air and the sentinels watching them curiously. MacKim dipped his paddle in the water, wondering if he would ever see Montreal again, yet determined to end his quest. Live or die; he would hunt Lucas de Langdon and the squat renegade.

With Kennedy, Obomsawin, MacRae and Ramsay in the first canoe, MacKim had Dickert and Parnell with him and paddled slowly into Lake St Louis. Away from the main army, MacKim felt a mixture of emotions. Part of him missed the security of a structured life with every decision made for him and the company of men from his own culture, language and background. However another, growing part welcomed the freedom from restrictions and the excitement of the vast spaces of this continent. The forest, which had repelled and even scared him on his first acquaintance, was now a friend.

The further MacKim paddled from Montreal, the more he felt the shackles of army life ease. He had already attempted to desert once, and now the temptation increased. Out here, the bonds that had tied him all his life seemed fragile, even unimportant. The influence of a clan chief, who ordered his men to a war that did not concern them, and the manipulations of a government thousands of miles away, seemed remote in this vast land. Did it matter which European potentate claimed ownership?

Kennedy lifted a hand to signal to MacKim, then headed for the north shore, with MacKim paddling in his wake.

"We have a long trip ahead of us," Kennedy called.

"Does Obomsawin know where he's going?" MacKim did not fully trust the Abenaki, or any man who could fight for the French one day and guide the British the next.

"I hope so," Kennedy replied.

They headed west and north into a land where people were scarce but wildlife abounded, where rivers ran southward and forests crammed against the edges of lakes. White-tailed deer appeared to watch the Rangers pass, and once MacKim saw a bear, while the calls of loons sounded eerily to torment them.

"Why would de Langdon come here?" Ramsay asked.

"Since the fighting," Obomsawin said, with Kennedy translating, "many people have escaped here, refugees, broken families, groups seeking to escape the British or French."

MacKim nodded. "It's a sanctuary," he said.

"Yes, and de Langdon will spoil that." Kennedy sounded grim. "Although Obomsawin says that some tribes are already fighting here."

They moved deeper into the wilderness, travelling by canoe when they could and carrying the canoe around stretches of white water to find pristine lakes amid ranges of low, forested hills.

"God made this land when heaven grew stale." MacRae looked around him. "A man could live here happily."

"The Indian is taking us to his village," Kennedy shouted, three days later. "He's finding out about de Langdon."

"Is he indeed?" MacKim checked his musket, ensuring his flint was dry.

Obomsawin guided them to a narrow river entrance and paddled upstream. MacKim watched the surrounding forest as the river meandered through dense trees for a few miles before they came to yet another lake.

MacKim looked all around, checking for an ambush as the Indian guided them to a small village by the shore, with the pleasant scent of wood smoke. Children played by the water's edge, and women walked gracefully on different errands. One woman looked so like Tayanita that MacKim felt a pang. He looked away quickly, reminding himself why he was here.

The villagers looked up at these strangers in their midst, with two or three of the younger men stepping forward as if to challenge them.

Kennedy said something to their guide, who snapped an order, and the young men withdrew. MacKim surreptitiously eased back the hammer of his musket, ready for a quick shot as more men gathered at the fringes of the village.

"It's all right, Sergeant," Kennedy said softly. "This is a friendly village now that the French have made peace."

"If you say so, sir." MacKim loosened the hatchet in his belt. After years of treating the native peoples as the most deadly enemy, he was disinclined to accept them as friends. He looked around, seeing the scattering of longhouses and birch bark wigwams, with a simple palisade for defence.

Now armed, the young men formed a circle around Kennedy and his men, occasionally shouting a challenge or making warlike gestures, until the guide spoke to an elderly man.

"That's the sachem, the chief," Kennedy said, trying to look unconcerned, while one hand hovered over the long pistol in his belt. "It all depends on him, although if he's unsure, he'll call a conference of all the adults."

"Form a circle, boys," MacKim said, "facing outwards, and be prepared to fight our way back to the canoes."

The sachem raised his hands and spoke, with even the most vociferous of the warriors listening to him.

"He's telling his people that we are friends now," Kennedy translated.

"But will they listen?" MacKim rested his hand on the hammer of his musket.

When the sachem finished, the tribe remained standing, staring at Kennedy and his Rangers for a full minute before, one by one, they began to drift away.

"Wait!" MacKim took a step forward, frowning. He pointed at a warrior. "That man there!"

Kennedy stared at him. "Sergeant! What are you doing?"

"That man!" MacKim jabbed his finger as the warrior half turned away. "I want to speak to him."

Kennedy shook his head and lowered his voice, speaking urgently. "Whatever it is, MacKim, let it go! These people fought for the French only a few days ago. Don't antagonise them."

"I need to speak to him." Uncaring of the number of Abenaki, MacKim pushed forward. He grabbed the Indian by the shoulder and spun him around. The man stared at him through his single eye, one hand on the long knife at his belt.

"I thought so," MacKim said. "We've met before, my Abenaki friend."

With one eye missing where MacKim had gouged it out and his nose twisted where MacKim had broken it, the Abenaki was unmistakable. He drew his knife in an instant, but MacKim had expected the move and blocked his arm.

"Lieutenant!" MacKim shouted. "Tell this fellow that I don't wish to harm him, only to ask him a question."

Kennedy spoke urgently as a circle of warriors closed around the Rangers. The sachem interceded, speaking quickly.

"Drop your arm," Kennedy said. "For God's sake, MacKim, release that man."

MacKim did so, trusting in Kennedy's word, while still expecting the Abenaki to attack. The man stood still, holding his knife and glaring at MacKim through his single eye.

"This man was with the party that murdered Tayanita." MacKim held his musket ready to fire. *The Indians may kill me, but this warrior will die first*. "He might know where de Langdon is."

Kennedy spoke rapidly to the sachem, who thought for a moment before he replied, and the one-eyed man approached him.

Unable to understand the conversation, MacKim could only watch and try to order his thoughts and emotions. While part of him longed to kill the one-eyed warrior, he knew that would end all his hopes of finding de Langdon. MacKim struggled to force away the red rage that threatened to engulf him. This Abenaki had not murdered Tayanita and had not scalped him. This warrior had been an enemy and was now a wary neutral.

"I need this man's help." MacKim interrupted the conversation.

When Kennedy translated MacKim's words, the tension eased a little. An elderly man stepped beside the chief, his eyes old but bright, his scrawny figure draped in deerskin.

"What do you want?" the sachem asked as the elderly man scrutinised MacKim.

"We are searching for two men," MacKim said and allowed Kennedy to take over once more.

The one-eyed Indian listened, with one hand on the hilt of his knife. Only when Kennedy finished did he release his grip and speak. His voice was deep, and his words rapid, so Kennedy had trouble keeping up as he translated.

"When I fought with the French," the Indian said, "they were our friends. Now the British have shown us how weak the French are. The French have left us; they are not our friends."

MacKim wondered how the Indian felt, talking to the Highlander who had mutilated him. He might also dream of revenge.

"Will you help us find the Canadian and his English companion?"

One-eye touched the hilt of his knife again. "The Frenchman used us to fight his war. When the British defeated the French, the Canadian ran away, leaving us to the mercy of King George."

Kennedy glanced at MacKim. "Let's hope the British keep their word to the Nations, or we'll have an Indian war up here as well as with the Cherokees."

MacKim said nothing. He had as little faith in British government promises as he had in the prospect of lasting peace.

"The Canadian and the renegade headed west," Kennedy translated the Indian's words. "West and north."

"What's up there?" MacKim asked.

"More of what's here," Kennedy translated again. "Forests and lakes and wild animals. If a man wants to lose himself, that's the best place to be."

"Then that's where we're going," MacKim said. "When did they leave?"

"They have a two-day lead," Kennedy replied, after a pause. "We'll follow as soon as we purchase some food."

As Kennedy and the sachem spoke, a group of women gathered behind the warriors, all staring at the Rangers. On a word from the sachem, two of them walked away, presumably to fetch supplies for Kennedy.

MacKim started as he saw Tayanita again, walking side-by-side with one of the women. It was undoubtedly Tayanita, with the same distinctive roll of her hips that always enticed him and the same flick of her long black hair as she looked over her shoulder at him. He was about to shout out when he saw the elder looking at him.

"What did you see?" the old man asked, with Kennedy again translating. "Was it one of your spirit ancestors?"

"This gentleman is a medeoulin," Kennedy said quietly, "a shaman priest. Be careful, MacKim."

Tayanita turned around with an expression of disapproval on her face.

"I know," MacKim said softly, knowing Tayanita would hear him. "I've let you down. You want me to kill de Langdon."

The medeoulin touched MacKim's shoulder, with a benign smile beneath eyes that were suddenly sad, as though he tapped into MacKim's emotions. "What you see might not be the message you think."

"What I see?" MacKim repeated. Tayanita was gone, leaving only her memory. He reached out his hand, trying to bring her back, and withdrew it, mouthing her name.

"Tayanita."

MacKim knew he had momentarily crossed the line into madness again. He knew he could not see Tayanita; she was dead and gone. He must try to remain within the borders of reason, or one day, he knew, he would not return from the other side.

The medeoulin was shaking his head until MacRae spoke to

him in Gaelic. The two conversed, each in their native tongue, as MacKim searched for Tayanita.

"Sergeant?" Kennedy held his shoulders. "Are you with us?"

"I'm with you," MacKim said, not sure if he wished to be back in this world or walking free with Tayanita. The elder was watching him, understanding in his eyes. "Let's find de Langdon."

The evening was approaching when they returned to their canoes and pushed into the lake, heading west into the reddening sky and leaving Obomsawin behind. The surroundings were beautiful, with the trees above the water and below the orange-ochre sky, but MacKim did not notice. The only thing that mattered was vengeance for Tayanita. Until he obtained that, there was no peace, only the disapproval of her frown.

29

The Rangers sat in the dark with the wind ruffling the surface of the lake and little wavelets breaking silver on the shore.

"They could be anywhere out there," Parnell said. "The wilderness extends forever. Nobody has reached its limit; nobody knows where it ends."

"It goes on to the end of the world," MacRae said. "Forest and lakes until you reach the edge of nothing."

MacKim pulled on his pipe, contemplating the vastness of this continent. "A man could lose himself out here, and nobody would find him. De Langdon and the renegade know what they're doing."

Kennedy nodded, staring into the fire. "You told me that de Langdon is a Meti, a half-Indian, who'll want the company of his own kind. He won't wander through the forest for long, not with the cold weather coming. As soon as he finds a snug village, he'll settle for the winter."

"One-eye told us there are about twenty men in the Canadian's party," MacKim said. "They'll need a decent-sized village to feed that number."

"They'll also leave a trail that a smaller number would not,"

Kennedy pointed out. He stirred the fire with a stick, sending a column of sparks into the air. "One day, MacKim, when we're in Covent Garden, we'll look back at these days, laugh, and wonder how we ever lived in the wilderness."

"Aye," MacKim said. "Maybe we will." He could not see an end. When he lifted his eyes from the fire, the smoke assumed the form of Tayanita. She stood at the periphery of his vision, waiting in the shadow of the trees, frowning.

I won't let you down, he promised. *I'll get revenge on Lucas de Langdon and the renegade.*

The Rangers started well before dawn, paddling slowly the length of the lake, investigating every creek and inlet, asking the occasional fisherman and finding nothing. MacKim's hopes faded by the hour, although he retained his fierce determination to seek out de Langdon. The Rangers hunted white-tailed deer and caught fish to supplement their food, and once a party of Ottowas greeted them with suspicious waves. Kennedy questioned the Ottowas from a distance, but they had not seen the Canadian.

"They said they heard of a band of Frenchmen who had run from Montreal," Kennedy reported, "and they thought we were French."

"They don't know where de Langdon is, then," MacKim said.

"They don't know," Kenny agreed.

On the third day from the Abenaki village, the Rangers reached the head of the lake. Leaving the canoes in the care of the others, MacKim and Kennedy scouted ahead, pushing up a small ridge where insects pestered them, and birds shrieked from the trees.

"Sir," MacKim said. "Over here."

Something had flattened the grass in a wide, irregular space, and the remains of a fire stood within a circle of soot-blackened stones.

"Somebody was here recently." Kennedy knelt to examine the fire. "Cold," he said, "more than two days old."

"Over here, sir," MacKim pointed to a cleared patch of ground. "Footprints, sir. Boots and moccasins."

"That's our men, then," Kennedy said. "The trail is the same age as the fire; two days. They're not gaining distance on us."

"Nor us on them," MacKim said. "But now we know we're on the right track, we can move faster."

The trail led over a steep portage to another lake that stretched in an irregular body of grey-blue water into the hazy distance. Kennedy crouched below the skyline, produced his telescope and studied the shore of the lake.

"I'm looking for smoke," he said, "or any other trace of human occupation. Something that might attract de Langdon."

"Can you see anything?"

"I think I see a haze." Kennedy passed over the telescope. "Over on the western shore."

MacKim focussed. "I see it, drifting over the trees. It might be smoke, and it might be mist."

"It could be either," Kennedy agreed. "We'll approach cautiously, whatever it is. Six men can't defeat twenty in an open battle, not even Rangers."

Returning to their camp, Kennedy and MacKim urged the men onwards. Carrying the canoes, they struggled over the portage, slipped over the ridge with their heads down in case the fugitives were watching and eased down the other side.

"Thank God these canoes are light," Parnell said.

Dickert smiled. "I'd hate to carry a whaleboat through this forest."

"I wonder if we're the first British to come here?" MacRae said.

Kennedy smiled. "Maybe we are," he said and shoved the canoe into the lake.

Half the day had passed, and long afternoon shadows dappled the water, mingled with the reflections of the trees, so MacKim fancied he was paddling through the forest. He had developed a rhythm now, kneeling in the canoe, paddling left then right with a mechanical stroke that pushed the vessel into the clear water. At times, he felt as if he had paddled since time began. Life was nothing except movement in this exquisite landscape, watching for signs of life, careful of an ambush as the Rangers remained close to the shore, ready to land or flee. At all times, they searched for signs of their quarry, moving slowly while Kennedy scanned the shore with his telescope.

"We're getting close to the smoke now, lads," Kennedy warned, adjusting his telescope. "It may be our quarry or only an Indian village."

"Sir!" Parnell hissed the warning. "Look behind us!"

There were six canoes in the flotilla, brightly coloured vessels with four warriors in each.

"Run," Kennedy said, after a single glance. "I don't know who they are, but they don't look friendly."

The Rangers powered on, increasing their speed as they dipped and thrust with their paddles, so the cool water bubbled behind them. MacKim looked over his shoulder to see the pursuing canoes spread out across the lake.

"They are Ottowas," Kennedy peered through his telescope. "This is Abenaki territory; what the devil are they doing here?"

"Chasing us!" MacKim replied.

"Dickert," Kennedy shouted. "Is your rifle loaded?"

"Yes, sir," Dickert said.

"Then take a shot to ward them off. We know you're the best shot in Canada."

Dickert threw MacRae a look of triumph as he took his rifle, checked the priming was dry and aimed it towards the canoes.

"Are you going to let him off with that, MacRae?" MacKim asked. "Show the lieutenant who's the better marksman."

Shooting at speeding canoes on a choppy lake would test any rifleman's skill, but MacKim was happy to set MacRae against Dickert. After a few moments, Dickert fired, with MacRae a few seconds later, both canoes jerking with the rifle's recoil. The double report rang across the lake, and MacKim strained to see the result.

He did not mark the fall of either shot.

"Short," MacRae said. "Well short, I think."

"You were short," Dickert shouted. "My ball grazed the leading canoe!"

Both marksmen loaded and prepared to fire again as the pursuing canoes came perceptibly closer. MacKim fancied he could hear the laboured grunts of the paddlers as they strained to close the distance.

The fleet of canoes had not faltered. If anything, MacKim thought, they had increased their speed, possibly to come within musket range. He could make out the features of the paddlers in the leading vessel and saw the second man put his paddle aside and lift a musket.

"They're well out of range," MacRae commented, as other paddlers followed the example of their colleague and exchanged their paddles for muskets.

"The more that stop paddling, the better," Kennedy said, as the pursuing canoes began to fall back.

A few seconds later, the warriors fired an irregular volley that kicked up small fountains of water a good hundred and fifty yards short of the Rangers' canoes.

"The range is far too long," Dickert said calmly. "They may as well throw stones. All they're doing is slowing themselves down."

MacKim agreed. "Get back to paddling, then, Dickert. If you think the enemy is within range, fire away."

"Yes, Sergeant." Dickert laid his rifle down, covering the lock and muzzle with a piece of tarred cloth as protection against the water that lapped inboard. He lifted his paddle and dug in deeply, pushing the canoe at speed.

After five minutes of firing without a shot coming close, the pursuers gave up. The musketeers laid aside the muskets and grabbed paddles.

"Now they'll get closer," Kennedy shouted across from his canoe.

"We'll fire if they get within a couple of hundred yards," MacKim replied. He saw MacRae patting his rifle and nodded to Dickert. "MacRae thinks he's a better shot than you."

Dickert gave a little chuckle. "He's not," he said. "I've been firing rifles since before I could walk. I even make the damned things."

With all their warriors paddling, the Indian canoes made faster progress, inching closer until MacKim nodded to Dickert, who lifted his rifle once more.

"Wait until you can't miss," MacKim said. "We've limited ammunition."

The pursuing canoes altered their formation to an arrow shape, with the largest vessel in front.

"That must be a chief or a war captain," MacKim said. "See if you can hit him."

"Yes, Sergeant." Dickert leaned the barrel of his rifle on the side of the canoe. "I've never fired from a moving canoe before."

"Look ahead!" Kennedy shouted, gesticulating in front.

A second flotilla of canoes had put out from the shore and approached from the front. A dozen strong, the new fleet extended across the Rangers' path.

"We're trapped, by God!" Parnell roared.

30

For the first time since he had known him, MacKim saw Kennedy panic. The lieutenant looked around him wildly before pointing to his right. "Head for the shore!" he shouted, as the two Indian flotillas extended, blocking the Rangers from advancing or retreating.

"We can fight our way through!" MacKim roared.

"The shore!" Kennedy repeated, gesturing with his dripping paddle. "Head for the shore!"

As Kennedy's canoe veered violently towards land, MacKim followed as the two Indian fleets merged with loud cries.

"They're ignoring us!" Dickert replaced his rifle without firing a shot. "They're fighting each other."

Rather than combine to capture the Rangers, the two fleets were firing at one another. The crackle of musketry broke the peace of the lake, and warriors shouted hoarse challenges.

"Obomsawin told us there was trouble here," MacKim said.

"Dear God in heaven," Kennedy said. "Keep moving, Rangers, get on land!"

Steering away from a sizeable Indian village, the Rangers pushed the canoes onto a muddy shore.

"Carry the canoes!" MacKim ordered, leading by example. It

was fortunate that birch bark canoes were light, for the men were shaken by the encounter. They pushed on, passed an area of neat fields and returned into the trees. The men stumbled over the uneven ground and glanced over their shoulders in case of pursuit.

"Don't stop!" MacKim acted as rearguard, looking behind him and leaving the others to carry the canoes. "Keep moving." He saw a woman and a group of small children watching, dismissed them as no threat and pushed on. The Rangers climbed a steep slope with a tumbling stream on their right and open woodland all around.

After an hour, with the Rangers panting for breath and the ground becoming more broken by the yard, Kennedy called a halt. The Rangers stopped at once, trying to recover shredded nerves and checking the woodland for pursuing warriors.

"Nobody is following us, sir," MacKim reported.

The Rangers drew breath, checked their carbines with sweating hands and congratulated each other in escaping.

"They were never interested in us," Dickert said. "The two villages must have some dispute, and we wandered in by accident."

"Thank God for small mercies," Kennedy said, breathing deeply. "We'll have a rest here for an hour or so." He forced a grin. "Grab some food, boys, and get your breath back; that was some climb."

❧

WITH HIS BACK TO A TREE AND THE SWEAT DRYING ON HIM, MacKim looked over an ocean of treetops. "This is a beautiful country," he said. "As MacRae already said, it's a pity Man has to spoil it with warfare."

Kennedy pushed tobacco into the bowl of his pipe with shaking fingers. "Warfare seems endemic to human culture." He waved the stem of his pipe towards the forest. "I've seen enough wilderness to last me forever. As soon as this war is over, I'm going to London."

MacKim nodded. "You've said that before."

"It's what I dream of," Kennedy said. "I want to get away from the wilderness for a while. I want to sleep safe in my bed in the most civilised city in the world." He leaned back. "I want to see the palaces and the great streets, the parks and commons, the River Thames and the theatres." He lit his pipe and drew smoke into his lungs. "Most of all, I want to go to the theatre in Covent Garden."

MacKim smiled. "What's so special about Covent Garden?"

"Charlotte always wanted to go there," Kennedy said with a smile. "My wife. I promised her that I'd take her someday, always someday, next year, or the next, but that day never came." His voice dipped, and MacKim knew he was close to breaking down.

"It's a pilgrimage, then," MacKim said. "A pilgrimage to the memory of Charlotte."

"That's right," Kennedy agreed. "It's a pilgrimage. Will you come with me?"

"I will," MacKim said. "We'll remember Charlotte together in Covent Garden." He knew his words sealed not only the bargain but also their friendship.

❧

"I CAN SMELL SMOKE," MACRAE SAID QUIETLY.

"So can I," Dickert agreed.

They were plodding on, carrying the canoes and stumbling on the rough ground.

"We'll avoid it," Kennedy decided, then quickly changed his mind. "No, no, I'm wrong. It might help us find de Langdon. I'll investigate. MacKim, you take over here."

"Yes, sir."

Kennedy returned within the hour, with his face set and

shadows in his eyes. "They've been here," he said. "And it's a massacre."

"We've seen massacres before." MacKim checked his flint and stood up. "Come on, Rangers."

The small village was a charred ruin, with bodies lying in the grotesque attitudes of death. Some of the corpses belonged to old men, although most were women and children. The majority of the women were spread-eagled on the ground as if they had been violated.

"It might not have been de Langdon's party," Parnell said.

"Count the heads," Kennedy snarled.

There were none. The attackers had decapitated every corpse.

MacKim sighed. "At least we know we're on the right track."

"It's reassuring," Parnell said calmly. "If de Langdon knew that Kennedy's Rangers were hunting him, he'd be more careful."

Kennedy nodded. "His carelessness will cost him his life. Keep going," he ordered, yet although he sounded as determined as ever, some of the spring had gone from his step. He looked like an old man.

MacKim put a hand on Kennedy's shoulder. "Are you all right, sir?"

"Bitter memories," Kennedy said.

"Charlotte?"

"Charlotte."

They moved on, following the trail through open woodland, always wary of an ambush.

"Leave the canoes," Kennedy ordered. "We're getting close."

MacRae nodded. "I can smell death," he said.

The Rangers upended the canoes and slid them beneath the trees, placing a pile of branches on top as camouflage.

"I hope we can find them on our return," Ramsay said.

"See these trees?" MacKim indicated an unusual trio of twisted trees ten yards to the left. "That's our marker."

"Do you get the nightmares?" Kennedy asked, as they toiled up another steep slope. "The nightmares?" MacKim repeated the phrase, to allow him a few moments to think. He did not like to reveal his weaknesses and counted the nightmares in that category.

"I do," Kennedy said. "I dream most nights. I see Charlotte as she died and hear the children screaming for my help, yet I can do nothing but watch." He paused. "It was like that last village."

MacKim was silent for a long time before he replied. "That must be terrible," he said. "How do you cope?"

"I hope every night that there will be no more bad dreams," Kennedy said. "And every morning, I hope that was the last one."

MacKim nodded and touched Kennedy's arm. "They will end when we avenge their deaths," he said.

I hope.

MacKim walked on, stopping at the crest of a ridge to view the landscape, a never-ending vista of forest and lakes beneath a sky of low grey clouds.

"Yes," he said at last, dragging the words from a reluctant conscience. "Yes, I get the nightmares."

"What are yours?"

Again, MacKim was quiet as he pondered his answer, and again he told the truth. "I have three," he said. "One is of my brother as the redcoats burned him alive on Culloden Moor. The second is when de Langdon or the renegade murdered Tayanita."

They walked on, ducking under low branches and leaping across a fast-flowing stream.

"You said you had three," Kennedy prompted.

"Three?"

"Three nightmares," Kennedy reminded.

"Yes. The third is of every man I have killed. I see their faces and their accusing eyes as they point their fingers at me."

Kennedy nodded. "Ah," he said. "That one." He stopped and held a hand in the air. "I heard something there."

"It was musketry, sir," Ramsay said. "I heard it as well."

"More murders," Kennedy said. "Come on, boys." He led them at a smart trot, each man covering his immediate colleague and watching the surroundings.

"It's stopped," Parnell said. "I can't hear anything."

MacKim agreed. The silence was as significant as the gunfire had been. The Rangers waited for a minute, then five, looking around, aware of the dangers that silence might signify. MacKim felt palpable relief when the bird-song began again.

"That's better," Kennedy said. "Move on, lads, but slowly."

The buzzing of a myriad flies alerted them to the body. It lay under a rough screen of branches with one arm outstretched and a bullet wound in its chest.

"Is that another victim?"

MacKim knelt to investigate. "It's an Indian," he said. "A warrior."

"An Abenaki, and he's been shot," Kennedy said. "I wonder what happened here."

"There was a fight." Parnell indicated powder burns on two adjacent trees and torn cartridges on the grass. "Two groups fired at each other." He pointed to bloodstains on the ground and a scar across the bark of a third tree. "I think a knife or a bayonet make this mark."

Kennedy nodded. "There are more cartridge papers here," he lifted one, "French, not British. That would be the firing we heard yesterday."

"There was one company, and they argued and split." Parnell interpreted the signs.

Kennedy scanned the ground. "You're correct, Parnell. One party, the larger, moved that way, northward, and the other, much smaller, headed west." He looked up, met MacKim's eyes for a moment and looked away. "They must have disagreed about something, perhaps even the direction of travel."

"Which trail do we follow?" MacKim asked.

"The larger," Kennedy said at once. "I'd guess that one or two of the Abenaki decided to return to their homes, and de Langdon objected. He wanted to keep his little army together."

"Here's another body." Parnell uncovered the corpse of a French regular, curled into a foetal ball beside a tree. "And I think another three wounded, judging by the blood. These men had quite a disagreement."

"All the better," MacKim said. "The more they kill each other, the fewer to oppose us."

"Take the van, Parnell," Kennedy ordered, "and we'll follow the larger group."

They moved on until night found them at a patch of swampy ground at the foot of a gentle slope.

"I've lost the trail," Parnell reported, swatting at the flying insects that clouded around his head.

"Yes," Kennedy said. "We won't stay here. Move higher up the slope, away from the flies and the marsh. I like to see my surroundings. We'll cast around for the trail in the morning."

"Have we lost them, sir?" Ramsay asked.

"Only temporarily," Kennedy assured him. "We've not travelled all this way to give up at a Canadian swamp."

The flies followed them for a hundred yards, but a slight breeze protected the Rangers as they camped in the more open woodland.

"No fire tonight," Kennedy ordered. "I don't think de Langdon is far away."

MacRae lifted his head. "They're close, sir. I can smell the evil."

MacKim nodded; he could sense them as well, somewhere close in the night. He looked around for Tayanita, but she seemed to have deserted him.

"Have you left me, Tayanita?" he whispered into the dark. "I am getting used to your presence."

"Who are you talking to, Sergeant?" Dickert asked.

"He's praying, Dicky; leave him alone!" Ramsay said.

MacRae put a hand on the nearest tree. "No," he said, so

softly that only his immediate neighbours could hear. "The sergeant was talking to the dead."

"MacKim, you're on watch," Kennedy said. "The rest of you get some sleep. I fear tomorrow might be a bloody day."

MacKim nodded; he knew he would not sleep that night. The wind in the trees sounded like the moans of the dead, and Tayanita was out there, somewhere, watching him.

The noises wakened the Rangers shortly after midnight. It was a cacophony of screams and yells, with bursts of deep laughter and the occasional crack of a firearm.

"It's been building for a while," MacKim said.

"Gather round," Kennedy ordered, and the Rangers came closer. "I'll wager that's our men attacking some Indian village."

MacKim touched the lock of his musket. "Are we going to stop them, sir?"

Kennedy did not answer directly. "Head for the noise," he said. "By the volume, the enemy will be too preoccupied to hear us." His teeth gleamed white as he grinned. "At least we won't have to scout for their tracks."

The noises came from the Rangers' left, on the fringes of the marshland, and effectively masked the Rangers' approach. They moved at some speed, occasionally stumbling over the rough ground, cursing as they struggled to overcome their weariness. A sudden flare made them all stop and crouch until Kennedy waved them on.

"That's a fire," Kennedy said. "The enemy has lit a fire to guide us."

"That's kind of them," MacKim said.

The noise increased as the Rangers closed, with individual voices rising high. One woman screamed, again and again, the sound painful to MacKim's ears.

"De Langdon is having his fun." Ramsay tried to sound callous.

"As long as he's concentrating on the villagers, he won't think of us," Dickert said.

"Maybe." Kennedy was more cautious. "Parnell, move ahead and check for sentinels. De Langdon has been clever so far; it would be unlike him to drop his guard."

Parnell jogged ahead, weaving from side to side and moving from cover to cover.

"Spread out, boys," Kennedy ordered, as they approached the fire. "We don't want to give the enemy a good target."

Parnell arrived ten minutes later. "No sentries, sir," he said. "De Langdon's men are having fun in the village."

"I know exactly what sort of fun they are having," Kennedy said softly.

When they stopped on the hillside, a hundred yards above the village, the scene was like something from MacKim's perception of hell. The Indian village sat at the edge of another lake, with the marsh on one side and a cleared area of cultivated fields on the other. A single, simple palisade surrounded a dozen longhouses, two of which were burning. In the light of the flames, MacKim could see figures moving around.

"De Langdon has arrived," Kennedy said. He swore softly as the woman screamed again, long and loud.

"Are we moving in, sir?" MacKim half-cocked his musket and checked the flint for the third time since they left their camp.

"Not yet," Kennedy's voice was strained. "Wait."

MacKim felt the Rangers shift restlessly behind him. "People are suffering down there, sir."

"Wait, Sergeant. That's an order."

MacKim swore under his breath as he saw a broad-chested Canadian chase a woman around the burning building. For a second, MacKim imagined Tayanita in the woman's place. He began to rise, but Kennedy roughly pushed him back down.

"Not yet," Kennedy snarled. He was shaking, and MacKim wondered what mental agony he was enduring, reliving the death of his family in similar circumstances.

"People are dying there."

Kennedy flicked MacKim's bonnet off his head. "People? How is your scalp, Sergeant?"

Madness. MacKim saw the madness in Kennedy's eyes and realised that he was not alone in balancing on the edge of reason. *Perhaps every soldier has to embrace insanity to survive the horror of war. Maybe Chisholm is wrong; war is not chess, but a much deeper, darker game the devil plays with men's minds as well as their bodies.*

MacKim pushed away the thoughts; he needed to reason if he was to live through these days. He needed to use all his faculties.

"I told you what the Indians and Canadians did to my family, MacKim." Little specks of froth appeared at the corners of Kennedy's mouth as he spoke. "Do you think I care what happens in this Indian village?"

MacKim shook his head. "No, sir." He understood. He could see Tayanita standing in front of him, shaking her head.

What are you trying to tell me, Tayanita? What message are you sending me? Is that really you standing there, or is my mind creating you to guide me?

"Wait." Kennedy repeated his earlier order.

The noise increased to a crescendo and then gradually decreased.

Kennedy hugged his musket closer to his body, caressing it like a woman. Only MacKim saw the bright sparkle of tears in the man's eyes.

"Now," Kennedy said softly. Standing up, he walked slowly forward, with the Rangers following.

"We'll go straight through the gate," Kennedy ordered. "And shoot any Canadian, French or Indian warrior you see, except de Langdon. Leave him to me."

Or for me, MacKim said to himself. *If I see that man first, I'll finish him.* His hands tightened their grip on his musket at the thought.

Working in pairs, the Rangers walked through the village, killing without mercy. Even after years on campaign, MacKim had never seen anything like the scenes in the village as the drunken, violent invaders ran riot. After only a couple of minutes, MacKim lost any sympathy for the men the Rangers shot like rats in the bottom of a barrel. Rape, pillage, casual brutality and murder seemed the order of the day, with the Rangers a cleansing agent.

The irregular crackle of musketry sounded through the screams and yells as Kennedy's Rangers scoured the village.

"I'm looking for a tall Canadian with a tattooed face," MacKim said in French to the terrified women, then he repeated the words in Abenaki. The women stared at him in incomprehension.

"Has anybody seen a tattooed Canadian?" MacKim asked the same question.

Two of the invaders lurched from a house beside MacKim. He glanced over them. One wore the uniform of a French regular, now battered and stained, while the other was an Indian, although of what tribe, MacKim did not know.

"I'm looking for a Canadian with a tattooed face," MacKim said. "I'm looking for Lucas de Langdon."

As the regular immediately ran away, the Indian drew a knife and jumped at MacKim, who levelled his musket and shot him without compulsion. When the Indian staggered back, MacKim crashed the musket-butt onto the man's face. He did not see what happened to the Frenchman but reloaded without haste. There was always plenty of time to kill.

Only when he reached the final house did MacKim find somebody that he recognised.

The renegade emerged from the door, squat, bare-chested and bald. Firelight reflected from the hatchet at his belt, while he held a bayonetted musket in his hands.

"Who the hell are you?" the renegade snarled in his flat English accent.

"Do you recognise me?" MacKim stopped in front of him,

preventing any of the other Rangers from approaching. He eyed the row of scalps at the renegade's belt.

"No." The renegade held his bayonet, ready to thrust. "I don't."

"Maybe now?" MacKim removed his bonnet to reveal his scalped head.

"No." The renegade gave a sour grin. Broad-shouldered and muscular, he looked a dangerous man. The brand on his chest, the letter D, told the world that he was a recaptured deserter, a man who had run from the army at least twice.

"You helped scalp me." MacKim allowed the red rage to overcome him. "You were one of the men who murdered my woman."

The renegade's grin widened. "Plenty more women in the world," he said. "You can have the two in here once I'm finished with them."

The callousness of the renegade's statement only heightened MacKim's anger. He saw Tayanita standing in the doorway, frowning.

"I'm going to kill you," MacKim said.

The renegade lunged without warning, nearly catching MacKim off guard. He parried in time, with the renegade's bayonet clashing against the barrel of his musket.

"Sergeant!" MacKim heard Dickert's voice from behind him and realised the Rangers had formed a circle around them, with a sprinkling of the village women also watching.

"Why?" MacKim asked, as he warily circled the renegade. "Why did you join the French? Does your oath of allegiance mean nothing to you?"

"My what?" The renegade spat on the ground. "*That* for king and country."

"Deserting's one thing, but joining the enemy's another." MacKim feinted to the man's throat, withdrew and tried for his chest. The renegade parried both attempts.

"I was pressed into the army, Sawney," the renegade said.

MacKim nodded. He knew of the system where the army could forcibly conscript any unemployed and notoriously idle character. The unwilling recruit would have to serve for five years or until the end of the war, whichever was the longer.

"You were not a volunteer then." MacKim was less surprised that the renegade had joined the French. With neither patriotism nor pride in his regiment, the pressed men were usually bad characters and seldom made good soldiers. They were one reason the army needed such ferocious discipline.

As MacKim spoke, the renegade lunged forward, feinting left and thrusting for MacKim's belly. MacKim doubled up as the blade ripped through his tunic, nicking the skin and drawing blood.

"Next time, Sawney," the renegade said. He was fast and robust, with his eyes devoid of any emotion. At the periphery of his vision, MacKim saw MacRae level his rifle as if about to shoot the renegade.

"No!" MacKim said. He straightened up, feeling the blood seeping from the fresh wound in his stomach.

"Come on then, Sawney," the renegade challenged and feinted again. This time, MacKim expected the move and subsequent lunge; he ignored the feint, parried the lunge, and thrust forward, low down. His bayonet caught the renegade in the groin, opening a deep wound from which dark blood flowed.

As the renegade winced, MacKim recovered his bayonet, stabbed the man in the hand to make him drop his musket, and delivered a killing blow to the throat. The renegade sunk to his knees, choking.

Tayanita was back, as solid as she had been in life, watching the renegade writhe on the ground.

"I didn't even know his name," MacKim said as the renegade died.

31

"De Langdon is not here." Kennedy had watched the duel in silence. "De Langdon is not in the village." He held his shoulder, where blood soaked through his tunic.

"We can ask one of the prisoners where he is," MacKim said.

"We took no prisoners," Kennedy said flatly. "We killed them all."

Kennedy was correct. When MacKim looked around the village, only women and children stood among the Rangers.

"You're wounded, sir," MacKim said.

"Only slightly." Kennedy removed his hand, allowing the bloodstain to spread.

"If you're sure, sir."

"Now we'll have to find de Langdon," Kennedy said.

"If you recall," MacKim said as he cleaned his bayonet, "the trail split a few miles back. I'll wager de Langdon took the other track."

"Then we'll follow him," Kennedy said. "We'll find what food we can in the village, backtrack to where the trail split, find de Langdon and kill him." He staggered as his wound weakened him, then recovered and lifted his musket. "Come on, Rangers."

Leaving the village, Kennedy led the Rangers back to the split in the track. With every step, MacKim felt Tayanita's presence at his side. He could hear the soft slap of her moccasins on the ground, see the gentle roll of her shoulders and hips, and smell her natural perfume. Yet he knew Tayanita was dead and gone; he had finally crossed the barrier into insanity.

Humming a Gaelic tune, MacKim eased along the faint tracks the Canadian had left. He knew the other Rangers were watching him, discussing his behaviour, but he did not care. Tayanita was with him, walking at his side, guiding his footsteps.

"This way," MacKim said, as the Canadian's tracks were as plain to him as a coach on the King's Highway. He could see the imprint of every footstep on the ground and knew by instinct or unconscious reasoning which direction the Canadian had taken.

"He stopped here," MacKim said, as a single broken twig told him the story as plainly as the printed words in a book. "And he met somebody over there."

Aware of Parnell and Kennedy watching him askance, MacKim crouched on the ground, tracing the near-invisible marks of feet as Tayanita guided his fingers. "Look – one pair of man's moccasins and one pair of woman's. De Langdon met a woman here. She came from that direction."

With no doubt in his head, MacKim traced the Canadian's route between the trees, smiling at the places the couple stopped and singing his Gaelic song. Tayanita was at his side, walking soundlessly as she guided him along the path of insanity.

"Here." MacKim pointed to a broken blade of grass. "They altered direction here and headed south-west."

The Rangers followed MacKim without question, accepting his judgement as they recognised that something was guiding him that day.

"Stop." MacKim raised his hand. "Here, sir. De Langdon is down there."

They crouched on the western slope of a long ridge, with insects buzzing around their heads and the dying rays of the sun warming their faces. At the foot of the hill, another small village crouched beneath the shoulder of the slope.

"Are you sure de Langdon's there?" Kennedy asked.

"Yes, sir." MacKim saw Tayanita give a slow nod.

"You've guided us here," Kennedy said grimly. "Now it's up to me."

MacKim glanced at Tayanita, who stood devoid of any expression. "Is that all right?" he asked her.

The Rangers stepped back, unsure to whom he was talking, now wary of their sergeant.

"Come on, Rangers," Kennedy said. "Let's finish this and get back home."

A barking dog broke the silence of the sultry evening as the Rangers strode down the slope. MacKim saw a woman emerge from a house, carrying a baby while a small child walked at her side. A young man followed, laughing with the woman.

"It looks very peaceful," Kennedy said. "Are you certain our man's in there?" He paused before entering the village.

Again, MacKim looked to Tayanita, but she was gone. "Yes," he said.

"Sergeant, take the rear. The rest, follow me." Kennedy squared his shoulders and marched to the gate in the weak palisade.

The woman with the children screamed when she saw the Rangers stride into her small settlement. Her man stepped to protect her but, without a weapon, he was powerless. Parnell felled him with the butt of his musket, leaving the woman screaming as she crouched over her man's unconscious body.

Lucas de Langdon emerged from one of the other three houses, wearing soft Indian clothes and with his hair tied back in a neat queue.

"*Mon Dieu*!" He looked at the grim-faced Rangers and altered his language to English. "What the devil are you doing here? The war in Canada is over."

"I am Lieutenant Adam Kennedy, at your service, sir." Kennedy gave a mocking bow. "Do you remember me?"

The Canadian remained as he was, standing in the doorway of the house. "I do," he said. "We've been fighting each other for the last year." As he spoke, a scared-looking woman appeared behind him.

De Langdon pushed her gently back.

"I've come to kill you," Kennedy said.

"The war is over," The Canadian said. "You won, we lost. Hasn't there been sufficient killing?"

"There has been too much killing," Kennedy said. "My wife, my children, my sister and my mother, all killed at the hands of you and your men."

De Langdon visibly flinched. "War is cruel," he agreed, "and the innocent suffer along with the guilty." Reaching behind him, he produced a musket and bayonet. "Come then, Lieutenant Kennedy."

"Sergeant." Parnell's voice sounded behind MacKim.

"Not now, Parnell." MacKim pushed him away.

"Sergeant!" Parnell tried again, with urgency in his voice.

"Keep quiet, Private," MacKim snapped. "That's an order."

De Langdon stepped clear of the doorway. "If we fight, and you prevail," he said, "will you allow the people in this village to live?"

Kennedy glanced at MacKim before he replied. "My war will end when I kill you."

"Do you give me your word that you won't hurt the people or my woman?"

Tayanita was back, standing beside de Langdon. "She is my wife," de Langdon said. "She had no part in the war."

"Neither had mine," Kennedy said.

Tayanita held a hand out towards MacKim, pleading for something.

What do you want, Tayanita? What must I do?

"We give our word," MacKim said. "Your wife is safe, whatever happens."

"Then we fight." De Langdon stepped into the sunlight, with the tattoos prominent on his face and the musket in his hand.

"Sergeant," Parnell said again.

"Tell me later," MacKim snarled.

Kennedy stepped forward, staggered and collapsed.

De Langdon lowered his musket. "See to your officer," he said.

"He's lost a lot of blood." MacKim knelt beside the lieutenant. "Take care of him. Bandage his wound."

"I've been trying to tell you, sir," Parnell said.

As the Rangers carried Kennedy to the shelter of one of the houses, MacKim faced de Langdon. "I'll take over here." He hefted his musket. "You killed my woman, de Langdon."

De Langdon nodded. "There is no need for this." He sounded tired.

When MacKim advanced, he felt his stomach wound open up. *I'll have to finish this duel quickly, or I'll collapse as Kennedy did.*

De Langdon was taller than the renegade had been but measurably slower, as if he had experienced his fill of fighting. His first thrust missed MacKim by three inches, and MacKim tripped the Canadian and knocked him to the ground. De Langdon lay still without even reaching for his weapon.

"End it, Sergeant."

When MacKim poised his bayonet above De Langdon's chest, Tayanita stood beside his woman, so alike they could almost be sisters.

MacKim felt his grief return, overwhelming even his anger.

"Why?" MacKim asked. He looked down at de Langdon, with his bayonet raised to plunge into the man's breast. "Why did you kill Tayanita? Why did you decapitate so many British soldiers?"

De Langdon looked up with resignation in his eyes. "British colonials killed my wife," he said simply. "They burned our village with my family inside, and when my wife escaped, a British cannonball cut her head clean off."

MacKim paused. He imagined the hurt of this man, losing his wife and family in one horrific day. He imagined how that must have felt and lowered his bayonet. War damaged both sides and made monsters out of decent men.

"And this woman? You said she was your wife."

"She is," the Canadian said. "A man marries quickly on the frontier."

"That is true." MacKim looked at this man who was so much like himself. After following him halfway across Canada, now they were face to face.

Killing this man has become the mainspring of my life, yet now I have him, the desire has gone. I feel no hatred. My obsession has given me a purpose in life, when otherwise, I would have given way to despair and suicide. In some ways, this man saved my life, as much as he has attempted to kill me.

"Get up." MacKim reached out his hand. "Get up."

De Langdon took MacKim's hand.

"You have a sister in Quebec," MacKim said and turned away. "You are not entirely alone."

He could sense Tayanita watching him, and she was smiling. He had failed in his quest for vengeance, but a weight had lifted from him. As he walked, he fingered the square of beadwork within his tunic.

Tayanita held out one hand, and only then MacKim understood. All this time, he had believed that Tayanita had been encouraging him to hunt down de Langdon. He had been wrong; her frown had indicated her disapproval of his actions, not his failure to kill.

As Tayanita faded away, MacKim wondered if he had ever really seen her, or if she had been a manifestation of his conscience.

Am I insane?

"De Langdon!" Kennedy sat up with his tunic soaked in blood. "Where are you?"

"Here, Lieutenant Kennedy." De Langdon stepped forward.

"You murdering bastard!" Kennedy lifted MacKim's musket, aimed and fired.

The ball took the Canadian high in the chest, knocking him backwards. His wife screamed once and covered her mouth.

"He's dead," Parnell said laconically.

MacKim looked down at de Lucas, wondering at the pointlessness of war. He lifted his musket. "Ramsay, MacRae, help the lieutenant. Parnell, you take the van. Dickert, you're the rearguard. Let's go home, boys."

He looked ahead of him, but Tayanita was not there. He knew he would never see her again; her soul was at peace and he was firmly on the correct side of reason.

APPENDIX

GENERAL MURRAY'S LETTER TO THE BRITISH GOVERNMENT

On the morning of 27th June 1760, Major Maitland and Captain Schomberg arrived in Whitehall with the following letter from the Honourable James Murray, Governor of Quebec, to the Right Hon Mr Secretary Pitt.

Quebec May 25 1760

Sir,

Having acquainted General Amherst, three weeks ago, that Quebec was besieged by an army of 15,000 men, I think it necessary of doing myself the honour of addressing directly to you the agreeable news of the siege being raised ... by your receiving the former intelligence before the latter, some inconveniences might arise to His Majesty's Service.

By the journal of my proceedings since I have had the command here, which I have the Honor to transmit to you, you will perceive the Superiority we have maintained over the Enemy during the Winter, and that all Lower Canada from the Point Au Tremble was reduced and had taken the Oath of

Fidelity to the King. You will no doubt be pleased to observe, that the Enemy's Attempts upon our Posts, and ours upon theirs, all tended to the Honor of His Majesty's Arms, as they were always baffled and we were constantly lucky.

I wish I could say as much within the Walls; the excessive Coldness of the Climate, and constant living upon Salt Provisions, without any Vegetables, introduced the Scurvy among the Troops, which getting the better of every Precaution of the Officer, and every remedy of the Surgeon, became as universal as it was inveterate, in so much that Before the end of April 1000 were dead and above 2000 of what remained totally unfit to any Service.

In this situation, I received certain Intelligence that Chevalier de Lewis was assembling his Army, which had been cantoned in the neighbourhood of Montreal, that he had completed his 8 battalions and 40 Companies of the Troopes de Colonie, from the choice of the Montrealists; had formed these 40 companies into four battalions; and was determined to besiege us, the moment the St Laurence was open, of which he was entirely Master, by means of 4 King's Frigates and other craft, proper for this extraordinary river.

As I had the Honor to acquaint you formerly, that Quebec could be looked upon in no other Light, than that of a strong Cantonment, and that any Works that I should add to it ... My Plan of Defence was, to take the earliest Opportunity of entrenching upon the Heights of Abraham, which entirely commands the Ramparts of the place ... and might have been defended by our numbers against a large Army. But the Chevelier de Lewis did not give me Time to take the Advantage of the Situation; the 23rd, 24th and 25th of April I attempted to execute the projected lines... but found it impossible as the Earth was still covered with Snow in many places and everywhere impregnably bound up by Frost.

The night of the 26th, I was informed, the enemy had landed at Pointe-aux-Trembles, 10,000 men and 500 Barbarians. The post, we had taken at the Embenchure of the River Caprouge. (The most convenient place for disembarking their artillery ... and of securing their retreat) obliged them to land where they did, 20 miles higher up.

The 27th, having broke down all the bridges over the Caprouge and secured the Landing places at the Sillery and the Boulon, I marched with the Grenadiers, Piquets, Amherst's Regiment and two Field Pieces and took Post so advantageous as to frustrate the scheme, they had said, to cut off our Posts. They had begun to form for the Defile they were obliged to pass but thought proper to retreat, on reconnoitring our position; and about four this afternoon, we marched back to Town. Having withdrawn all our Posts, with the Loss of two men only, though they did every Thing in their power to harass the Rear.

The Enemy was greatly superior in Numbers, it is true, but when I considered that our little Army was in the Habit of beating that Enemy, and had a very fine Train of Artillery, that shutting ourselves up at once within the Walls, was putting all upon the single chance of holding out a considerable time a wretched Fortification; a Chance which any action in the Field could barely alter; at the same time that it gave an additional one, perhaps a better. I resolved to give them Battle and, if the event was not prosperous, to hold out to the last Extremity, and then to retreat to the Isle of Orleans or Cenaries, with what was left of the Garrison to wait for reinforcements.

This Night the necessary Orders were given and half an hour after six next Morning, we marched with all the Force I could muster, Viz, three thousand men and Formed the Army on the Heights in the following Order: Amherst's, Anstruther's, 2nd battalion Royal Americans, and Webb's completed the Right Brigade commanded by Colonel Burton; Kennedy's, Lascelles; Highlanders and Townsend's the Left Brigade commanded by Colonel Fraser. Otway's and the third battalion of Royal Americans were the Corpe de Reserve. Major Dallings Corps of Light Infantry covered the Right Flank and Captain Hazzen's

Company of Rangers with 100 Volunteers under the Command of Captain Donald MacDonald, a brave and experienced officer, covered the left. The Battalions each had two field pieces.

While the Line was forming, I reconnoitred the enemy, and perceived their Van had taken Possession of the Rising ground three Quarters of a Mile in front, but that their Army was upon the March, in one Column as far as I could see. I thought this the lucky moment, and moved with the utmost Order to attack them before they had formed. We soon beat them from the Heights they had possessed, though they were well positioned? And Major Dallings Who cannot be too much commended for his behaviour this Day and his services during the Winter, forced their Corps of Grenadiers from a House and Windmill they had taken hold of to cover their left Flank; here he and several of his officers were wounded, his men however, pushed the Fugitives to the Corps which was now formed to sustain them. They halted and dispersed along the Front of the Right, which prevented that Wing from taking Advantage of the first Impression they had made on the Enemy's Left. They had immediately Orders given them to regain the Flank, but in attempting this, they were charged, thrown into Disorder, retired to the Rear, and from the Number of Officers killed and wounded, could never again be Brought up during the Action.

Otways was instantly ordered to advance, and sat in the Right Wing, which the enemy in vain made two Attempts to penetrate. On these occasions, Captain Ince with the Grenadiers of Otways were distinguished. While this passed there, the Left was not idle; they had Dispossessed the Enemy of two redoubts and sustained with unparalleled firmness the bold united Efforts of the Enemy's Regulars, Indians and Canadians till, at last, fairly fought down and reduced to a Handful, though sustained by the 3rd Battalion Royal Americans, from the reserve and Kennedy's from the center, where we had nothing to fear, they were obliged to yield to superior Numbers and a fresh column of Rosillon, which penetrated.

The Disorder of the Left was soon communicated to the Right; but the whole retired in such a way that the Enemy did not venture upon a brisk pursuit. We left most of our cannon, as the Roughness of the Ground, and the Wreaths of Snow, made it impossible to bring them off; what could not be brought off were nailed up.

Our killed and wounded amounted to one third of those in the field; that of the Enemy, by their own Confession, exceeds 2,500 Men, which may be Readily conceived as the Action lasted an hour and three Quarters.

Here I think it my Duty to express my Gratitude to my officers in general, and the Satisfaction I had in the bravery of all the Troops.

On the Night of the 28th, the Enemy opened Trenches against the Town, and at the same Time we set to work within to fortify it, which we never had in our power to attempt sooner from the Severity of this Climate during the Winter, and the absolute Necessity of executing works of more immediate importance last Autumn, before the Frost set in. I wanted the assistance of Major Mackellar, the Chief Engineer, dangerously wounded in the Action, his zeal for and knowledge in the Service is well known but the Alacrity of the Garrison made up for every Defect.

My Journal of the Siege, which accompanies this, sets forth, in full, what was done; and I flatter myself, the extraordinary performances of the Handful of brave Men I had left, will please his Majesty as much as they surprised us, who were Eye-Witnesses to them.

Great Praise is due to Commodore Swanton, and the Captains Schomberg and Dean; I have not words to express the readiness, Vivacity, and Valour they shewed in attacking and destroying the enemy's squadron. Captain Deane has lost his Ship, but it was in a good Cause, and he has done Honour to his Country.

The morning of the 17th May, I had intended a strong Sortie, to have penetrated into the Enemy's Camp, where, from the information of the prisoners I had taken, and the concurrent accounts of Deserters, I conceived to be very practicable.

For this Purpose, I had ordered the Regiments of Amherst, Townshend, Lascelles, Anstruther and Highlanders, with the Grenadiers, and Light Infantry, under arms, but was informed by Lieutenant McAlpin of my battalion, (whom I sent out to amuse the enemy with small sallies) that their trenches were abandoned.

I instantly pushed out at the Head of these Corps, not doubting but we must have overtaken and forced their Rear, and had ample revenge for the 28th April; but I was disappointed for they had crossed the River Caprouge before we could come up with them. However, we took several prisoners and much Baggage, which would otherwise have escaped. They left their Camp standing; all their Baggage, Stores, Magazines of Provisions and Ammunition, 34 pieces of Battering Cannon, four of which are brass 12-pounders, ten field-pieces, six mortars, four petarts, a large quantity of Scaling-ladders, and entrenching tools beyond number: and have retired to their former asylum, Jacques Cartier.

From the information of prisoners, Deserters, and Spies, provisions are very scarce, Ammunition does not abound, and greatest part of the Canadians have deserted them.

At present they do not exceed five thousand Men. The minute I am joined by that part of my Garrison which was sent from hence last Autumn, I shall endeavour to co-operate with Mr Amherst, towards compleating the Reduction of this Country though if rightly informed he can hardly act by the Lakes before the month of July, of which I am the more convinced, because of the Intelligence forwarded to him last February, of the Enemy's Designs by Lieutenant Montrefour, he would certainly have been up on them before now, had it been at all practicable.

Major Maitland, the Bearer of these Despatches, who has acted as Adjutant-General this last Winter, is well acquainted with all our Transactions here; he has a thorough Knowledge of the Country and can give you the best Lights with Regard to measures further to be taken, relative to his Majesty's views in Canada.

I cannot finish this long Letter, without observing how much I think myself obliged to the Lieutenant-Colonel Colonel Burton, his Activity and Zeal were conspicuous during the whole Course of this severe Winter's Campaign, and I flatter myself, sir, you will be pleased to Lay his services before his Majesty.

P.S. Since I have wrote this letter, a Nation of Indians has surrendered, and entered into an Alliance with us.

I have the Honour to be, with Great Regard

Sir

J. A. Murray.

HISTORICAL NOTES

Wolfe's victory at the Plains of Abraham in 1759 is often seen as the decisive battle of the British conquest of Canada. Little attention is paid to the subsequent campaign, where the British endured a Canadian winter without adequate provisions, followed by battle and siege.

Although the exploits of Rogers Rangers are well-known, they tend to detract from the other actions of this unit, who acted as scouts, messengers and skirmishers for the British.

THE RANGERS

Contemporary newspapers carried small pieces which mention the Rangers, such as this mention in the *Dublin Courier* of 10th Oct 1760:

> *An express of rangers had arrived from General Amherst who were 20 days from Crown Point but in crossing the river St Francis on a raft, they were carried down the Falls, by which they lost their packet and all their arms; for that, Gen Murray could receive but little information from them.*

Or this mention from Manchester:

Plantation news

New York March 10 1760

Monday last arrived here by land from Quebec, in Canada with verbal dispatches from Brigadier General Murray, Lt John Montrefor of the 48th regiment, and one of His Majesty's established engineers, he set out, January 20th escorted by one officer, two serjeants and ten rangers and proceeded through the woods by the way of the south branch of the River Chaudiere and was 26 days on his march from Quebec to his arrival at the frontier settlements of New England. On their march they were reduced to the greatest Extremities for want of Provisions, owing to the Distance, severity of the weather, being obliged to Eat their Makasoons and Leather Belts; they were 13 days without bread, and 11 without any other Meat than four small Birds they killed. Two of the Rangers were left behind, much froze. Only two of the party, besides Lieut Montrefor, were able to reach this place, the Remainder were left at Topsham, unable to proceed any further.

FRASER'S HIGHLANDERS

Raised for the Seven Years War, the 78th Fraser's Highlanders were disbanded in December 1763. More than two hundred officers and men decided to remain in Canada, and received grants of land. Many married French-speaking Canadian women and their descendants still live in the area.

THE END OF THE WAR

At the Treaty of Paris in 1763, France surrendered the sovereignty of Canada to Great Britain. By doing so, the threat of French-controlled Indian attacks on the original British colonies was reduced, and the seeds of the future American War of Independence were sown.

Dear reader,

We hope you enjoyed reading *Edge Of Reason*. Please take a moment to leave a review in Amazon, even if it's a short one. Your opinion is important to us.
Discover more books by Malcolm Archibald at https://www.nextchapter.pub/authors/malcolm-archibald
Want to know when one of our books is free or discounted for Kindle? Join the newsletter at http://eepurl.com/bqqB3H

Best regards,
Malcolm Archibald and the Next Chapter Team

Printed in Great Britain
by Amazon